Emma Hannigan is the author of six bestselling novels, including *Keeping Mum* and *Driving Home for Christmas*, and a bestselling memoir *Talk to the Headscarf* which charts her journey through cancer. Emma lives in Bray, Co. Wicklow, with her husband and two children.

For more about Emma,
visit her website www.emmahannigan.com,
find her on Facebook at AuthorEmmaHannigan,
or follow her on Twitter @MsEmmaHannigan.

By Emma Hannigan

Perfect Wives
Driving Home for Christmas
Keeping Mum
The Pink Ladies Club
Miss Conceived
Designer Genes

Talk to the Headscarf

Emma Hannigan
Perfect Wives

HACHETTE
BOOKS
IRELAND

First published in 2013 by HACHETTE BOOKS IRELAND

This edition published in 2014 by HACHETTE BOOKS IRELAND

Cataloguing in Publication Data is available from the British Library

ISBN 978 1 4447 2621 3

Typeset by Palimpsest Book Production Ltd, Falkirk, Stirlingshire
Printed and bound in Great Britain by Clays Ltd, Elcograf S.p.A

Hachette Books Ireland's policy is to use papers that are natural, renewable and
recyclable products and made from wood grown in sustainable forests. The
logging and manufacturing processes are expected to conform to the
environmental regulations of the country of origin.

Hachette Books Ireland
8 Castlecourt Centre
Castleknock
Dublin 15

www.hachette.ie

A division of Hachette UK Ltd.
338 Euston Road
London NW1 3BH

For my perfect husband, Cian.
With love from
your perfect wife!

Acknowledgements

As always I have so many wonderful people to thank. This book wouldn't exist without the wonderful team at Hachette Books Ireland. Sweeping bowing gestures to my fabulous editor Ciara Doorley. Your encouragement is awesome! It's such a pleasure to work with you. Special thanks also to Hazel Orme for her careful and fastidious copy-editing skills. To Breda, Jim, Ruth, Joanna, Bernard, Siobhan and all the Hachette team, I am waving blowing kisses and saluting you. Thank you all.

Huge thanks to my agent Sheila Crowley of Curtis Brown UK. As always you are my cheerleader. I am so grateful.

No words would be written without my parents. Quite apart from the fact that I literally wouldn't exist without them, they keep me bolstered and buoyed, and are always on my side. My love and respect for you both is indescribable.

Thanks to my perfect husband Cian, my perfect son Sacha and my perfect daughter Kim. Together we make up the most wonderful content and flawless family. We never raise our voices, slam doors, argue in the car first thing in the morning. No one in our house ever lies about who ate the goodies or attempts to blame it on the cat.

I'm delighted with our version of perfect! The three of you

are my sun, moon and stars. Also I'd like to take this opportunity to let you all know that it's not illegal to empty the dishwasher or pick up dirty clothes off your own floor.

Thanks to my extended family and amazing friends. I am blessed to have so much love and support in my world.

Outside writing I enjoy my little dabbles on TV and radio. It gets me away from my desk and uses up some of my talking quota for the day! Special appreciation to Elaine Crowley, Declan Meehan, Ryan Tubridy, Mark Cagney and Sinead Desmond for having me on your shows and letting me babble, giggle and generally enjoy myself.

I'm thankfully clear of cancer as I write this message. The people responsible for making me well are angels on earth. I know I am lucky to be alive. I cannot express how kind and wonderful the staff of Blackrock Clinic in Dublin are to me. I owe my life to Dr David Fennelly and his team, Dr Illeus, Sinead, Aoibheann and all the staff in the oncology day unit. Thanks to Liz for always chatting and making me laugh. Thanks to the ladies at the front desk for helping with my constantly lost car park tickets!

Finally, I would like to give all my darling readers a massive cyber hug. I will never tire of the warm and fuzzy feeling that washes over me when I get a lovely letter, email, tweet or Facebook message from one of you. Each one lifts my spirits.

I hope you all enjoy *Perfect Wives*. I have chosen this title as it makes me smile. We all know perfection doesn't exist, right? *Perfect Wives* tells the tale of two unlikely friends who discover that being true to oneself is what really counts. But as many of us come to realise at one point or another, all that matters in life is happiness. I hope you love the characters as much as I do. I actually miss them now the book is finished! I wonder how they're getting on … I hope they're having a good day … Okay, I'll stop now. The men in white coats will take me away.

If you'd like to get in touch, I always love hearing from readers. You'll find me at:

www.emmahannigan.com

@MsEmmaHannigan on Twitter

Author Emma Hannigan on Facebook.

Have a great day!

Love

Emma x

April 2013

Chapter 1

As she walked through the gate of Bakers Valley village school, trying to keep up with Saul, Jodi was overcome with fear. She'd been dreading his first day at the kindergarten. She kept her eyes down and her stride strong, praying that nobody would stop her and try to strike up a conversation. The small primary-coloured rucksack she'd slung over one shoulder seemed to weigh a ton. She'd tucked her wavy dark hair into a baseball cap and purposely dressed down, but a trickle of sweat was dampening her back.

'Hello! I'm Mr Matthews, and I'm teaching the kindergarten this year!' He was a young man who wouldn't have looked out of place on a One Direction poster. 'So who do we have here, then?'

Jodi was knocked off guard. She'd assumed the teacher would be a tiny shrew-like woman with a country accent and ruddy cheeks. The fresh-faced fellow with the lopsided grin who was welcoming her son was about as far away from the schoolmarm stereotype as it was possible to get.

Before she had a chance to answer, Saul stepped forward and held his tiny right hand aloft. 'I'm Saul Drew,' he said, placing his left behind his back.

The teacher bent down and shook his hand solemnly, then raised the other into the air for a high five. 'Nice to meet you, buddy,' he said, winking.

'Are you from London, like me?' Saul said. 'You don't talk like the ladies in the village.'

'You're dead right, Saul. I am from London. I only got this job a couple of weeks back. Miss Myrtle, the previous teacher, decided to retire.'

'Mum and I only just moved here too. Maybe we can settle in together.'

'That sounds like a plan!' Mr Matthews agreed, and smiled up at Jodi.

'Hi,' Jodi said.

'Hi, Mrs Drew,' he said. 'Looks like Saul and I are going to be helping each other out.'

'Well, you'll be in good hands, Mr Matthews. Saul and I have been really excited about today, haven't we?' she said, wrinkling her nose and smiling down at her son.

'Why don't you put your coat and bag over on the rack, Saul?' Mr Matthews said, pointing to the wall. 'Your name is on one of the hooks.'

'He's certainly enthusiastic.' Mr Matthews grinned, as Saul rushed to find his hook. 'If all the little ones are as happy and bouncy as he is, I'll be made up!'

As he spoke, they both heard the sound of terrified sobs filtering into the room.

'Excuse me,' Mr Matthews said. 'Looks like first-day fears are making themselves known.'

'Aw, bless,' Jodi said. 'Nice to meet you anyway.'

Saul was already busy chatting to another little boy at the coat rack, so Jodi stood over to the side of the room and peeped out from under her cap. It was obvious that many of the mothers and fathers knew each other and she figured they'd probably grown up together or had older children in the school. As she cast an eye over the room she noted that most of the children had both parents there to see them off. She hoped that wouldn't upset Saul.

'Mum, can you come and take a photo of my coat hook to text to Dad?' Saul called.

Jodi went over to him, fishing her phone out of a pocket, and dropped to her knees. 'You know Daddy would be here with you too if he wasn't stuck on set, don't you?' she whispered.

'Yes, Mum,' he said. 'I'll call him later and tell him all about it. We need to send the photo now, though. We promised.'

'Sure did. Let's be having you, then.'

'Make sure you get my rucksack and my coat in the shot,' he said, as he put on his best smile.

Jodi took the picture and texted it directly to her husband, Darius. 'Okay, shall we find you somewhere to sit?' She took her son's hand.

'Look! All the chairs have names on the back of them just like the coat hooks!' he said, pointing. 'Here's mine!'

'Good spotting,' Jodi said, as she pulled out the chair for him to sit down. Each large square table had four chairs. Saul was opposite a little blonde girl with wispy pigtails and pale blue eyes the size of saucers.

'Hello, I'm Saul. What's your name?' he asked.

'Lily,' she said, in a small voice.

'I'm excited! Are you?' Saul asked, scrunching his shoulders and grinning.

'My big sister already went here but she had Miss-a-Myrtle. She was the bestest teacher in the world,' Lily said seriously. 'But she got tired.'

'Well, we have Mr Matthews instead, and that's good, isn't it?' Saul said.

'I suppose so. My mum was here but she had to go and put my sister in her class. She said she can't split herself in two.'

'That'd be too messy,' Saul said solemnly. 'There'd be blood on the carpet.'

Lily giggled. Jodi sent up a silent prayer of thanks that her son was so at home in his surroundings.

As Jodi listened to Saul and Lily, Mr Matthews flew around the room introducing himself and welcoming the rest of the children. Jodi wanted to avoid the other parents. She knew she'd have to get to know them at some point, but the longer she could leave it, the better.

'Okay, parents,' Mr Matthews announced cheerfully. 'It's time to say goodbye to your children. Boys and girls, it's only for a little while, remember. Give Mum and Dad a big hug and tell them you'll have lots of news for them when they come to collect you.'

'Are you okay if I go now, Saul?' Jodi asked.

'Yes,' he said. 'Lily knows where the playground is and she's going to show me at break time.'

'Thanks, Lily.' Jodi smiled at her. 'So, Saul, will you tell me the names of the others at your table when I come to pick you up?' she asked.

'You bet!'

'I love you,' she said, as she nuzzled his mop of dark curls. He'd inherited her emerald green eyes, but the rest of his features were his father's. The paparazzi were already after him for photos, but Jodi and Darius had held firm. Their son was out of bounds when it came to publicity. She'd agreed to a single shoot just after he was born, and after that she'd shielded him from the public eye, like a tigress guarding her cub.

4

'His parents are high-profile actors but that doesn't mean he is too,' she'd told her agent, Noelle. 'When he's old enough he can decide if he wants to be splashed across the press, but for now he's ours and he's not for sharing.'

That had been a major factor in their decision for Jodi to return to Ireland when Saul started school. She'd come across Bakers Valley, just thirty miles from Dublin, and fallen in love with the place. They wanted him to make his own way without the pressure of being the son of Jodi Ludlum and Darius Drew.

'Have fun, darling, and I'll be back to collect you before you know it,' she said, tearing herself reluctantly from his side.

'Bye, Mum, I love you too,' he said, waving.

There were still quite a few people huddled at the coat rack so Jodi seized the moment and walked purposefully out of the classroom before she was sucked into a conversation.

The distance from the main door of the school to the gate couldn't have been more than a hundred metres so she knew she could make a quick exit. She pulled out her phone and dialled Darius's number.

'Hey, darling,' he said, sounding sleepy. 'I just got that photo you texted me. He looks so cute! Have you left him yet?'

'I'm on my way across the car park as we speak,' Jodi said. 'He was brilliant, Darius. You'd have been so proud.'

'Great,' he said. 'How were people towards you?'

'Fine. The teacher is seriously cool. He looks just a few years older than the kids,' Jodi joked. 'But he knew exactly how to get them organised into their seats. On first impressions I'd say Saul will love him. I didn't speak to any of the parents, just kept my head down and scarpered straight out of there.'

'That was probably for the best,' Darius said. 'We want Saul to have a chance to mingle without too much staring and pointing. And what about the other kids? Were they friendly to him?'

'Yeah. He had a tiny scrap of a thing called Lily sitting opposite him and the other two hadn't arrived when I left. Hopefully he'll be fine ...' Jodi trailed off.

'Listen, honey, he was so geared up for today. You injected so much positivity into the whole school thing that he was champing at the bit to get in there. Try not to worry, okay? Promise?' he begged.

'I'll try,' she said, smiling through the tears that had sprung to her eyes. 'I just don't want his school experience to be like mine.'

'I know. And I doubt it will be. First, Saul's not the child you were, and second, all he's ever known is love and adoration. He'll rock that class, you wait and see!'

'I hope you're right.'

'When am I ever wrong?' Darius asked, laughing.

'No comment.' She sniffled.

Darius's tone softened. 'It's not good to shut people out. Say hello to a few of the parents later on. Saul won't be able to fit in if you're not friendly. It's a small village and people won't take kindly to the brick-wall approach.'

'I hear ya,' she said. 'Besides, there's a good chance most of them have never even heard of me.'

'Jodi, it's a country village but it's not on Mars,' Darius teased. 'I presume they have a cinema within commuting distance and a DVD shop. They probably even have newspapers and magazines.' He laughed. 'Uh, they know exactly who you are, sweetie!'

'What time are you starting filming?' she asked, changing the subject.

'Not for about five hours.' He yawned. 'Most of the scenes have to be shot in the dark for the next week so I'm a bit topsy-turvy. I'll sleep for another couple of hours, then head in for makeup and all that jazz.'

'All right, darling,' she said. 'Will I have Saul call you when he's finished or will I let you call us later when you're awake?'

'Oh, no! I want a call the second you pick him up!' Darius said. 'I need a full and fresh-off-the-press download of day one!'

'Okay!' Jodi was grinning as she hung up. Darius always made her feel better.

Turning left out of the main school gate Jodi set off towards their cottage, which was less than a fifteen-minute walk. The main hub of local activity was back in the other direction, centred around Bakers Valley.

When she'd decided to move home to Ireland for Saul's education she'd purposely sought a property slightly outside the main village yet within easy reach of the community. She inhaled the clear country air as she meandered along the road, framed on either side by hedges intertwined with brambles and wild honeysuckle. It was a far cry from inner-city Dublin where she had grown up, with its smouldering mattresses, burned-out cars, and gougers loitering on corners – and a million miles from the hotels and movie sets Saul was used to. She hoped he'd settle in here and make lifelong friends.

Darius had been amazingly supportive when she'd tentatively suggested bringing Saul here a few months ago. Their home was in London, but working in film meant they'd travelled extensively with their boy since he was born.

'I know it would mean you mightn't see him as often but I think he'd have a better chance of leading a normal life away from the city,' Jodi said.

'I agree,' Darius said. 'I know I'm being selfish when I say I'd obviously prefer to have you both with me.'

'But you're going to be filming all over the world for this next movie and Lord knows where the next one will be,' she argued.

'I know,' he said softly. 'I can commute and you guys can come to me. It's not going to be that different from the way we've always worked it, I suppose. Just because I'm on location here in the UK at the moment doesn't mean I will be in the future ... But are you sure you want to go back to Ireland of all places?'

'Yes,' she said firmly. 'It may not have been perfect for me as a child but, at the end of the day, it's home.'

As she arrived at the whitewashed cottage and let herself in, Jodi was thrilled she'd gone with her gut instinct and made the move. She'd bought this place a year ago in a derelict state and paid exorbitant amounts of money to have it turned into the beautiful home it had become. It was the original gate lodge to the manor house, which nestled behind the trees and fields she could see from her kitchen window. The old stable-style door let her into the open-plan kitchen-cum-living area.

'If you like we can stick to really stark modern materials, like chrome and slate,' the interior designer had suggested, 'or we can soften it by adding an Aga to the kitchen area, a wood-burning stove to the living room, with under-floor heated flagstones and big colourful rugs.'

'I like the sound of the second option,' Jodi had said immediately. 'I love the idea of a cottage but I don't want it to be dark and depressing. In other words, I want a city person's take on a cottage!' She giggled.

There was nothing gloomy about the finished house. Cornflower blue and white gingham was cleverly mixed with stripes and damasks. The oiled oak table with matching chairs added to the homely warmth that the cream Aga supplied. Squashy sofas with tons of scatter cushions complemented the hand-knotted rugs. It was just as she'd imagined it in her dreams, and, most importantly, Saul loved it too.

'Look, Mum! The shelf spins around so I can choose my cereal for breakfast,' he had yelled, as he'd explored each nook and cranny when they'd arrived a few days before. Jodi had stood with her arms folded and smiled as her precious son ran from room to room, shrieking with glee.

'Look in here.' Jodi unhooked the black latch on a bedroom door to reveal what she hoped would be a little boy's paradise. She'd gone to great pains to appeal to Saul's passion for outer space and was dying to see his reaction.

'Mum my room is the bestest place I've ever seen,' he gasped. The Velux windows looked like a glass roof. 'It feels like I'm in a room with just sky! Mum!' he screeched. 'I have a bunk bed too so my new friends can come for a sleepover!'

'I told the designer you *had* to have a bunk bed and I *needed* a vegetable patch. So you can have friends to stay and I can eat my own lettuce!'

'My deal's better,' he said, throwing himself on to the bottom bunk. 'I don't like lettuce!'

The walls were decorated with stars and spaceships, and a big shiny red rocket adorned the back of the door.

'Happy?' she asked Saul.

'I'm like Buzz Lightyear living in here!'

Jodi hoped Saul would settle at Bakers Valley. She pictured his happy little face when he had waved her off, and she reminded herself that he was in a safe and loving environment.

Jodi hadn't been lying when she'd told Darius why she wanted to move back home to Ireland. She *did* want their son to have a carefree country childhood. But, deep down, there was another reason why she had wanted to return.

She was tired of running from her past mistakes. She wanted true, lasting contentment and for that she had to face her demons and air all the skeletons in her closet.

Lifting the kettle on to the Aga hotplate, she set about making herself a mug of her usual herbal infusion. She remembered what Darius had said about it. 'That stuff tastes so disgusting it must be good for you. Either that or the Chinese-medicine lady just sees you coming!'

'It's got so many cleansing properties,' she reminded him.

'So has bleach and I've no intention of drinking that.'

Deciding to enjoy the peace and tranquillity of her new home, Jodi flopped on to the sofa. The old walls of the cottage seemed to envelop her in their embrace. She felt safe there, away from the bright lights and people vying for her attention. For the first time in her thirty-two years, she had a real home.

Chapter 2

Francine Hennessy was rattled, a feeling she certainly wasn't accustomed to. She'd allowed exactly six minutes per child to settle her three eldest, Cara, Conor and Craig, into their classes. Normally that worked perfectly but this morning she'd been totally thrown by Cameron's behaviour.

'Stop him, Carl!' she'd called frantically to her husband.

Like a little eel, their youngest child had escaped his father's grip and made a mad dash back to their car. 'I'm not going!' he yelled over his shoulder. 'I hate school and I'm not going!'

By the time Francine and Carl had given up on gentle coaxing and resorted to prising each finger away from the headrest in the back seat, the bell had rung in the school, indicating the official start of the day.

'I'm going to die of shame,' Francine said, as cold sweat ran down her back. 'It's day one and Cameron is late.'

'Just keep your cool,' Carl told her. 'I'll carry him and you take his bag. Let's do this together. Team Hennessy will overcome.'

'*Nooooo!*' Cameron yelled. He continued to wrestle and kick in his father's arms as the trio made their way back into the school and towards the kindergarten classroom.

Francine shouldered the door open. She could never be sure that those frequently used handles were clean. 'We're here finally! Hello, everybody, how are you doing?' She plastered a smile on to her face.

A young man came towards her. 'Hello there,' he said warmly. 'We're just getting started.'

'This is Cameron.' Francine gestured at the little boy, who was still doing his best to wriggle out of Carl's arms. 'I'm Francine Hennessy and this is my husband, Carl.'

'Good to meet you. I'm Mr Matthews.'

'So you're Miss Myrtle's replacement.' As Carl led Cameron to the one free chair in the room, Francine lowered her voice conspiratorially. 'You're most welcome to Bakers Valley school. I'm sure you'll enjoy it here. We have a wonderful sense of community. We'll probably get to know one another quite well ...' Francine paused for effect. 'I'm head of the parents' committee, you see.'

'Good for you, Mrs Hennessy,' he said.

'Oh, call me Francine, please!'

The teacher hesitated momentarily, then said, 'Okay, Cameron? You all set, my friend?'

'No! I hate it here and I hate you!' Cameron yelled.

'Cameron!' Francine said, in a high-pitched voice. 'Please have some manners!'

'As you can tell, he's a little bit reluctant to come to school, but he'll be running in the door and loving every second in no time!' Carl said, in an attempt to smooth things over.

Mr Matthews dropped down to Cameron's level. 'It's everyone's first day today, mate, so there's no need to feel upset. We're all going to help each other and find out what's fun about this place.' Cameron pouted and eyeballed the man. 'I have a new house as well as a new school. Maybe you can tell me all about the cool stuff in the village.'

'Okay,' Cameron mumbled.

'I have a desk just for you right over here. It has your name on a sticker. Want to check it out?'

'Okay.'

Mr Matthews took his hand and gave a thumbs-up to Francine and Carl over his shoulder.

'The first week is always the worst, isn't it?' Francine interjected, in a knowing voice. 'Once they all realise this is the plan of action, and everyone has to conform, it's all much simpler. Sit down nicely, Cameron, there's a good lad,' she instructed him, with a fixed smile.

Mr Matthews responded with a silent wave and a wink.

'We should leave him be, love,' Carl said, then turned back to Cameron. 'We're very proud of you, son! See you later on. Cheers, Mr Matthews. Take care! Good luck. Thanks a million. Bye!'

'Catch you later,' Mr Matthews said.

Carl caught his wife by the elbow and led her from the room.

'I'm not sure if I'm happy with that new teacher,' she said, under her breath. 'He's very standoffish with parents, don't you think?'

'Ah, no, love. He's just intent on settling the kids, which is right. Sure he's not there to entertain us. As long as Cameron clicks with him, that's all that matters surely.'

'I suppose,' Francine said uneasily. She'd preferred Miss Myrtle's approach. She was far more traditional and motherly, and had regularly sought Francine's advice. This teacher was of another ilk altogether, with his boyish looks and London accent.

'I'd better head into the office,' Carl said, kissing Francine's cheek. 'Are you going for a coffee with the other mums?'

'Not today. I've things on,' Francine said, a pained look crossing her face. 'I've a lot to organise.'

'I know you do.' Carl paused briefly. 'It'll be fine. Think of all this as a change of direction in life.'

'Of course I will,' she said, and waved to her husband. 'Besides, the parents' committee needs to start up again. We must welcome the new mothers and all of that.'

'I'll leave you to it so,' Carl said.

'Have a good day,' she called, as he disappeared.

They always travelled in separate cars to the school on the first day back so they could shoot off to their jobs afterwards. Francine took a deep breath as she moved towards the small gathering of mothers. 'Good morning, ladies!' she said brightly.

'Hi, Francine,' said Jane. 'You look lovely as usual. You always manage to make me feel like I've just crawled out from under a rock. Look at the state of me, in my jeans and sweatshirt. Your suit is divine.'

'Thanks, sweetie,' Francine replied. 'It's D&G – they know how to cut fabric to set off a woman's body.'

'Well, it helps if your body doesn't have wobbly bits and an unwanted shelving system like mine!' Smacking her own backside, Jane roared laughing.

'Are you flying off to work, Francine?' Sarah asked.

'Where else would I be going?' Francine snapped.

Sarah looked slightly taken back.

'Sorry,' Francine said. 'I'm just a bit anxious. Cameron kicked off earlier on. He wasn't one bit happy about going to school. You'd think he'd be more than ready after years of being brought in and out of here to drop off and collect the older ones.'

'It was probably because you were here,' Jane pointed out. 'When he's with the childminder he's probably an angel.'

'Ah, they save the dreadful behaviour for their mothers, all right,' Sarah agreed.

'Is Annie doing the pick-up today?' Jane asked. 'I can take Cameron, if you like.'

'No, but thank you for the offer,' Francine said tightly. 'Annie is actually having some time off childminding. You know the way I always take August off work to be with the children?' The others nodded. 'Well, I'm extending my annual leave to settle Cameron into school.'

'Fair enough,' Jane said.

'He's my baby. The other three are getting so big now that I'm suddenly realising my time with my youngest is precious.'

'If your job is willing to let you take the time, you're dead right,' Sarah said.

'I've to go in this morning for a quick meeting, but I'll be back in time to collect Cameron.'

Francine excused herself and hurried to her car. Tears were threatening. She knew she'd been a bit snippy with the girls just now, but she wasn't ready to tell them her woes. Not until she'd got her own head around things. She'd even put on her work suit to fool herself into believing things were the same as before.

Chapter 3

Jodi couldn't believe how quickly the morning passed. She'd promised herself she'd unpack all the cases and organise her own room and Saul's by the end of the week. So far, she'd managed to upend two bags, so all she'd done was make a huge mess.

Still, she had oodles of time to get sorted, she mused, as she stepped over a pile of hoodies and sweatpants, grabbing her keys and sunglasses from the kitchen table. Her brand new cream convertible Mini sat like a little enamel and chrome carriage at the front door. She adored it and would never tire of the new-car smell. But while the September sun still shone she was going to make the most of the weather. Patting the car on the way past it, she waltzed off towards the school.

She hoped Saul had enjoyed his first day. If he came out sobbing and begging not to go back, she didn't know what she'd do.

'Things have changed, Jodi,' Darius had reassured her over the phone on the run-up to today. 'When we went, nobody gave a toss if you were traumatised or not. Unless you were bleeding or missing an eye, you just had to get on with it. But kids enjoy school now. I bet he'll love it.'

Now that she'd actually left him there, she was beside herself with worry. She'd been so gung-ho about making sure the renovations were done and that Saul was enrolled at the school, she hadn't had time to properly reflect on any of it. She bit her lip guiltily. What if he was miserable here? She hoped she hadn't acted too rashly in moving them to Ireland when once she'd fled from everything it represented. The misery and hardship had almost destroyed her. Until now Ireland had meant only unhappy memories. She thought back to the last time, fifteen years ago, when she'd been home to the council estate where she'd grown up.

In many ways it seemed like a lifetime ago but Jodi would never forget where she'd come from and how one kind man had changed the course of her life for ever.

He had been none other than the late great Jason Flood, one of the world's greatest talent spotters. He'd come to Jodi's school to audition girls for the role of a Dublin schoolgirl in a film he'd been shooting.

Jodi hadn't even dared to read for him and wouldn't have if he hadn't spotted her sitting alone in a corner of the canteen at lunchtime.

Her teacher, Mr Greg, had approached her and told her the scout wanted to meet her. She was shaking and barely able to stand upright as she entered the hall where the man sat.

'Can you read this page for me?' he asked, leaning forward in his seat.

Once she began to read, Jodi felt herself drifting away from the room and her life. She'd found it easy to be someone else.

'Do you go to acting classes?' the man asked, as she finished.

'No,' Jodi said, barely above a whisper.

'How old are you, love?'

'Seventeen,' Jodi said, as her usual uncertainty took over once again.

Raising his hand, he called Mr Greg over. 'Can you contact this kid's parents and see if they'll pay for drama and elocution lessons?' he asked.

'I don't think that'll be an option,' Mr Greg said, putting his hand on Jodi's shoulder. 'Things at home aren't so easy.'

'Right.' The man put his large hands out and held Jodi's. 'If I pay for them, will you go to some acting classes for me?'

'Oh, yes,' Jodi said, with such conviction that tears filled his eyes.

A couple of days later, she went straight from school to Miss Hazel's school of acting in Dublin and completed an intense four-month acting course. On its completion, she'd gone to London wide-eyed and terrified, with only a few lines to say. She'd almost bottled it but the alternative hadn't been appealing. Jodi shuddered as she thought of the fateful moment when her life had changed for ever. Young as she was, Jodi had understood that the break from the harsh reality that was her life could only be beneficial. The planned two-week stint had stretched to six. Her tiny blink-and-you-miss-it part grew legs. By the time the movie wrapped, she'd been in a total of eight scenes. Jodi knew she had Jason Flood to thank for turning her life around. She never forgot him.

Her cameo performance didn't go unnoticed. Offers began to roll in. Nobody was more bemused by the upturn of events than Jodi herself. She'd been away for several months by the time she finally returned to see her mother. She'd begun filming *Runaways*, which turned out to be her first big feature film.

'Decided to come back, did ya?' her mother Bernadette had sneered, as she'd walked through the door of the shabby council house. 'Thought you'd moved to London and didn't want to know the likes of us no more.'

'This is the first day off I've had, Ma. I've some money for you,' Jodi said, handing her mother the notes.

'About time you gave back. After all the years I've slaved to keep a roof over your head,' Bernadette said, as she flicked through the wad of cash eagerly. Within minutes the front door had slammed and she'd headed for the pub.

Jodi hadn't expected anything else. The real reason she'd come home was to see her six-year-old brother, Tommy, and her nana.

'Nana collects me from school every day now.' Tommy had filled her in on the news. 'Ma is too tired so she lets Nana mind me.' Jodi had felt sick to hear this but relieved her mother was allowing Nana to help out.

Tommy was like Jodi's shadow for the entire time she was at home. She took him to the toy shop and bought him the just-released Sony PlayStation, with a brand new television.

'This is deadly, Jodi. None of the lads has one yet. I'm going to be the coolest in my class now.' He hugged her, his face flushed with pleasure. She bought Nana a pure cashmere coat.

'Jodi, it's the softest thing I've ever touched. I'll sleep in it, I love it so much.' Nana mopped her damp eyes.

Argos was the next stop, where they picked out a leather suite for the sitting room, and a table with four matching chairs for the kitchen. 'Next month, I'll buy new carpets and curtains. By the end of this production, we'll have Ma's place looking like a show house,' Jodi promised them both.

Knowing she had to be back on set by cock-crow on Monday morning, Jodi had a flight booked for the Sunday night. When the doorbell rang she assumed it was the taxi she'd ordered. Instead it was two police officers and a squad car.

'Is this Bernadette Ludlum's home?' the taller man asked.

'Yes.' Jodi wondered what her mother had done now. 'I'm her daughter.' Bernadette hadn't returned since she'd snatched the bundle of notes the day before.

'I regret to inform you we recovered your mother's body from a laneway on the estate early this morning.'

Numb, Jodi agreed to go to the hospital to identify her mother's body. The policemen went outside to wait for her in their squad car, and she called the film's producers to explain that her mother had passed away suddenly. They were full of sympathy and told her to take the week off, adding, 'You must have had a dreadful shock. Please look after yourself.'

'Do you want me to go?' Nana asked, as she wrung a tea towel in her hands.

'No, Nana. You stay here with Tommy.'

'Right, love.' Nana looked relieved.

'Are you all right?' Jodi asked, stroking her beloved grandmother's arm.

'I've been waiting for this moment for as long as I can remember. Your ma was a troubled soul. I lost her long ago. It's just so sad that she threw her life away like that. But now at least I won't be worrying about what's become of her because she's disappeared for days on end.' She sighed. 'I don't know where I went wrong, Jodi love.'

'You didn't do anything wrong. Ma was a sorry mess. None if it was anyone's fault. It was just the way she ended up.'

'You're far too young for such wise words, do you know that?' Nana said.

'I've seen more of life than most girls my age. But now I'm going to use that to go out and get what I want.' Jodi ground her teeth as she fought back tears. The grimy, depressing hole that she'd called home was going to change. Tommy was only little. He had a chance of turning out right, some hope of avoiding a life on street corners sniffing glue and shooting up. If it killed her, Jodi was going to protect her little brother and her nana.

'I'd better go out to the policemen now. Thanks for minding Tommy,' she said, and stroked Nana's cheek.

'You don't have to thank me. I love him,' Nana said shakily.

'I promise you, as God is my witness, I'll come good for you both. I have an opportunity to change our lives now and, believe me, I'm going to succeed if it's the last thing I do.'

'You're destined for stardom, Jodi. You always were. I think you might have had to take a wrong turn when God put you on this earth, but you'll find your right road soon enough, pet.'

Jodi made her way to the waiting car. There was very little talk as they drove to the hospital morgue, and she felt little emotion as they peeled the sheet back to reveal her mother's sunken white face.

'That's her,' she managed.

'We're ever so sorry, love,' one policeman said.

'We interviewed the people she was with shortly before her death and it appears your mother had taken a large quantity of heroin on top of a substantial amount of alcohol,' his partner added.

'That'd be about right,' Jodi said evenly. 'It's probably very weird of me to say this,' she confided, 'but she looks prettier dead, and she can't shout at me.'

Jodi's overwhelming emotion was relief. Her mother couldn't hurt her or Tommy any more.

ɔʒ

Two days later, Nana, Tommy and Jodi were joined by a handful of mourners at the funeral. An enormous wreath arrived from the film's producers, with a note saying how sorry they were for Jodi's loss. It made her cry far more than the knowledge that she'd never see her mother again. She was so relieved they weren't annoyed with her and astonished that they seemed to care so much.

'I'll move into the house and mind little Tommy,' Nana promised. 'You go and follow your calling, pet.'

'I'll send money every week and I'll be home as often as I can,' Jodi had vowed. She'd kept her promise about the funds, which had arrived religiously, but Jodi herself never came. With each week that passed she found it more and more difficult to return home.

'Nana, I'm not going to make it back for the foreseeable future,' she said down the phone. 'It's crazy here and I've gotta roll with the punches.'

'I understand, love,' Nana said kindly.

'I've booked flights for you and Tommy to come over instead.' Jodi was avoiding returning to Ireland, but felt she might ease her own mind if she treated Nana and Tommy to the odd trip instead. She liked to think she'd shielded her brother Tommy from a lot of the misery she'd endured, and was well aware that money couldn't buy happiness, but total lack of it, such as she'd experienced, brought utter desolation too.

Now twenty-one, Tommy lived in Australia with his girlfriend Maisy and Jodi kept in touch with him on Skype every week. When Nana had passed away five years previously, Jodi had flown back for the funeral and begged him then to come to London and live with her.

'I want to teach surfing and that's certainly not going to happen in London,' he had pointed out.

'Then take our place in LA,' she suggested. 'You can surf there to your heart's content. Maybe you'd even continue with your education?' she ventured. 'I know you didn't like school much, but what if you could do a course on a subject that interests you?'

'Sis, I appreciate your thinking of me. Honestly I do, but I just want to get the hell out of here. Surely you can appreciate why.'

'I can, but I wish you'd at least consider my offer.'

'I need to do my own thing. I want to make my own mark on the world.'

'You're so young, Tommy. I can't help feeling I'm not looking after you properly if I let you go,' Jodi mused.

'With all due respect, you can't stop me. I've enough cash to buy a ticket. I'll sort the rest when I get there. I grew up on Dayfield Estate, for crying out loud! So, adding up the less than happy life experiences multiplied by the need to be streetwise by the time I was out of nappies, I reckon I'll survive.'

'Tommy, you might think you know it all, but Australia? It's so far away. I hate the thought of you being so isolated.'

He'd eyeballed her with his hands on his hips. 'Are you telling me you would've listened if Nana had begged you not to go to London years ago?'

'That's different. I had a job. People to look after me.'

'I'll be okay, Jodi. Trust me.'

'Right, we'll have to make a pact. I'll set up an account for you. I'll put money into it each month. If you need anything extra *ever* – you ask. You hear?'

'Thanks, sis.' He hugged her and promised to stay in touch.

Now, as she made her way into the school grounds and towards Saul's classroom, Jodi noticed a group of waiting parents.

Swallowing hard, she urged herself to keep walking. This situation was Jodi's worst nightmare. She could cope with a massive film crew and even a red-carpet event, but none of that required the 'real' Jodi Ludlum. This did.

A slim, perfectly coiffed woman in a tailored suit with smooth chestnut hair, manicured nails and impeccable makeup seemed to be at the centre of the huddle. Jodi yanked at her cap and stuffed her hands into the kangaroo-style pockets of her white hoodie. She stopped a few yards from the others and prayed nobody would approach her. Her heart sank when she saw that the glamorous woman was handing out flyers.

'But it would be super if you could make the time to join us,' the woman was saying loudly. 'We're all under pressure time-wise, but I'd urge you to come along and meet the other parents, even if it's only once. When you're new to the school, this coffee morning is a wonderful way to network.'

The recipients were nodding and making pleased noises. Some were striking up conversations, smiling and looking quite at ease.

Please don't come over to me, Jodi begged silently.

As the other woman approached, she held her breath.

'Hello, I'm Francine Hennessy,' she said. 'You might have missed the beginning of my introductions! I'm head of the parents' committee and we're hosting a meet-and-greet coffee morning on Friday week.'

'Thank you,' Jodi said.

'You're new to the school, aren't you?' Francine asked. Jodi could feel the other woman's eyes boring into her. She tugged the peak of her baseball cap a tiny bit lower and hoped her shades were obscuring her face sufficiently.

'Yes. Thanks for this,' she said, waving the flyer. 'I'll do my best to be there.'

'Come over and meet some of the other mums,' Francine said. Before Jodi could protest, she found herself being led towards them by the elbow, as if she were an unsteady elderly patient. Acting as if she were addressing the United States live from the Oval Office, Francine was off again: 'Our little darlings will emerge shortly, ready to share the excitement of their first morning at school. I'll leave the invitation with you and sincerely hope you can make it on Friday.'

'Great,' said one mother.

'Count me in,' said another.

'Me too,' put in a third.

Jodi was silent, rooted to the spot, her heart thumping. Her mouth felt dry and she wished she could drop the piece of paper and run out of the gate, but she knew she had to say something. 'I'll do my best to make it,' she said.

As soon as she spoke, two of the women's heads shot around. Two more elbowed one another.

The door to the kindergarten class was flung open and the little people poured out noisily.

'Mum!' Saul shouted, flinging himself into her arms.

'Hey, baby!' she said, glad to see his happy face. 'How was it?' Lifting him into her arms, she kissed him and rubbed her nose against his.

'We did painting and drawing and we have goldfish in our class and Mr Matthews said we can help name them tomorrow. So I've to think of names tonight!'

'Wow,' Jodi said. 'We can put our thinking caps on.' She turned towards the other parents. 'Goodbye, everyone! See you tomorrow.' She didn't look back as she headed out of the school gates.

Saul was thrilled with his new school and couldn't get all the news out quickly enough. 'And I have four best friends,' he continued, as she walked towards the gate with him still in her arms.

'Four? Already? That sounds pretty amazing.'

'It is!' he said proudly, as he wriggled to the ground and ran on ahead. She hung his bag over her arm and walked after him.

'Did you like school, Mum?' He stopped, waited for her to catch up and stared intently at her with his hands on his hips.

'Well, school was different back then,' Jodi answered diplomatically. 'I didn't live in a small village like Bakers Valley. I grew up in a large town and my school was huge, with lots and lots of people. It was a little scary at first.'

'Do you wish your mummy could've taken you to live in a cottage like ours so you could go to my school?' Saul asked. He loved to ask Jodi questions about when she was his age. Luckily he was still too small to notice that she didn't enjoy those chats as much as he did.

'You bet, dude. Your school is going to be more fun than you can shake a stick at,' Jodi assured him.

Satisfied for now, Saul ran on ahead again, and she watched him bound along like a puppy. Darius was right: Saul's life was idyllic. Perhaps she had made the right decision in bringing him to Bakers Valley. It wasn't all about facing her past. This was an idyllic setting and he was going to love it here.

The second they got into the cottage Saul flew into action. 'I want to talk to Dad!' he said, grabbing the landline phone and flopping onto the sofa on his tummy. He had only recently learned Jodi's and Darius's numbers and was into dialling them at every opportunity.

'Daddy! I'm back!' he shouted.

Jodi made him a jam sandwich and a mug of hot chocolate. If Darius were here, he'd tell her that wasn't nutritious and she was feeding him junk. He was probably right, she thought, but it was better than nothing. She was determined to learn how to cook, but for the moment she would give Saul food that he'd eat without a fight.

'Mum, Dad wants you,' Saul said, holding the phone out to her as she placed his snack on the table.

'Hi,' she said. 'Seems it was a success.'

'What did I tell you?' Darius said. 'I'm in Makeup so I'd better go. Love you, sweetie-pie, sugar plum and love of my life,' he said, in his most exaggerated saccharine tones.

Smiling, Jodi guessed he was with other people. They always overdid the pet names when a particularly nosy person was listening. '*Ciao*, snot-bag.' She giggled as she hung up.

'That was rude!' Saul reproved her. 'Poor Dad.'

'He knew I was joking.' Jodi ruffled his hair.

Once he'd finished eating, Saul said he wanted to play in his room. As an only child he was used to entertaining himself and enjoyed quiet time doing Lego. Jodi figured the clothes weren't going to put themselves away so she'd go and do some concentrated sorting.

∞

At the school a kerfuffle of a different sort had been going on.

'Am I going totally insane,' Francine asked Jane and Sarah, 'or did that girl look alarmingly like Jodi Ludlum?'

'I thought so too!' Jane said. 'But she was so quiet and shy, there's no way it was her.'

'Let's ask the teacher,' Sarah said.

'God, no! You can't do that, Jane.' Francine was aghast. 'He'll think we're such a bunch of gossips.'

'Speaking of the teacher, I nearly skulled myself on one of those tiny chairs when I walked into the classroom this morning,' Jane said. 'Isn't he the most divine creature you've ever seen?'

'I'm glad you noticed too.' Sarah giggled. 'I thought I was turning into a right lush! I was actually blushing while I was talking to him! He's gorgeous!'

'Girls!' Francine scolded. 'Keep it together, please! Besides, we need to find out about that new woman.'

'Here, I'll ask Mr Marvellous about—' Jane broke off as Francine elbowed her.

'Good afternoon, ladies,' Mr Matthews said, as he approached the group.

'Hi.' Jane recovered quickly. 'I'm Jane, Lily's mum.'

'Everything all right?' he asked.

'Yes, fine. Could I speak to you for a second?'

'Sure.'

'I was just wondering if you could tell me - I just— Well, *we* were wondering if that was Jodi Ludlum who left with that little boy?'

'Mrs Drew?' said the teacher, looking mildly confused.

'Oh, don't worry. My mistake,' Jane said, flushing. 'See you tomorrow, then.'

'Cheers!' Mr Matthews said easily.

'Damn,' Jane said. 'Not only did I make a show of myself in front of Mr Marvellous, behaving like a lovestruck teen, but we're wrong. She's Mrs Drew, apparently.'

'Of course she is!' Sarah hissed. 'She's married to Darius Drew, isn't she? She's known as Jodi Ludlum in the movies but they *are* a family in real life. She probably goes by her married name when she's not acting.'

'Oh, Jesus,' Jane said, nearly falling over. 'It *is* her.'

Francine did her best to assume a nonchalant pose. But she honestly thought she, too, was going to explode with excitement.

'Do you think she'll come to the coffee morning?' Jane was saying.

'She just said she would,' Francine said. 'Well, she said she'd do her best.'

'Wow!' Jane squealed. 'This is just mega! I can't believe we have a real-life Hollywood star living here!'

☙

Jodi was in her bedroom, knee deep in clothes, when Saul ran in holding the phone.

'It's Daddy again,' he said.

'Hey,' she said. 'Did Saul call you? I'll have to explain to him that he can't ring constantly while you're working.'

'No, no, I called you.' He sounded really down.

'What's going on?'

'Jodi, I think I've messed up big time.'

'How so?' She cradled the phone between shoulder and ear.

'It looks like I've a blackmail case on my hands,' he said gravely. 'It's the usual scenario.'

'Okay.' She sighed. 'I'm trying to stay calm here, Darius. What's going on? Have you told Mike and Noelle?'

'Yeah, and they want us to do a shoot for *Celebrity Gossip* magazine, featuring your new Irish pad.'

'Ugh, really?' She groaned. 'This person who wants to blackmail you, are they talking to the press or is it a case of looking for easy cash?'

'It's a blatant gold-digging cash deal. I'll sort it, but just in case, we should do a loving-couple shot. For extra insurance.'

'I hear ya,' Jodi said, feeling somewhat relieved and rubbing her temples. 'I stupidly thought that by moving to a lovely quaint cottage in Ireland I'd escape the venom of Hollywood.' She gave a bitter laugh.

'I'm sorry,' he said quietly.

'I'll get on to Noelle now. When do you think you can do this?'

'That's the snag,' he said. 'It'll have to be Friday week.'

'Ah, Jesus, Darius!'

'I'm sorry, but I'm on location in China after that until October, remember?'

'Okay,' she said. 'It's probably best to get it over and done with as soon as possible.'

'Oh, by the way, they've asked for Saul to be in the photos,' he said, with a sigh.

'I hope you told them where to go,' she said.

'I said, and I quote, "We will happily host a photo shoot in our Irish residence but Saul is never part of the deal." I decided to leave out the piss-off-with-yourselves part,' he said.

'Charming!' she replied. 'Mind you, they've necks like jockeys' arses, that lot. Once you give them an inch they take a mile. Nosy bastards.'

'I love it when you get all sassy and Irish on me.'

'Ah, shut up!' she said, smiling in spite of herself. Jodi knew she had a tendency to fly off the handle but her temper always cooled as quickly as it flared.

'It's a front-cover shoot by the way,' Darius said. 'Ooh-la-la and all of that.'

'Whoop-de-do.' A few years ago she'd have been in a tailspin with excitement at all of this. Now it was nothing more than a drain on her time and a threat to her privacy. Jodi knew Darius was right, though. The public loved nothing more than to feel they were being allowed a glimpse into their private lives. It ensured their continuing support, just in case Darius's current menace decided to try to blight them.

But Jodi was acutely aware that the fans had got her to where she was today. If it would make them happy to see Darius and her looking loved up in a cosy cottage, that was what they'd get.

Fleetingly she remembered the coffee morning at the school and Francine, but decided she could pop her head in for a few moments and get back to the cottage in plenty of time. Those shoots often took for ever to set up, so it'd be fine.

'Daddy's coming on Thursday night next week,' she told Saul, when she'd hung up.

'Yay!' Saul shouted. 'I can show him my bedroom and he can see my best friends!'

'Good plan, buddy!'

'How many sleeps is that?'

'Well, today is Monday so there are a few, but he'll be here before you know it,' she said, delighting him. 'Who are the best friends so far?'

'Well, Lily - you saw her. She's my girlfriend. We might get married,' Saul said.

'Fair enough. She's very pretty.'

'And Max - he's got very, very spiky hair, like a hedgehog,' Saul said seriously. 'And Cameron. He's the funnest.'

'The most fun,' Jodi corrected gently.

'Yep.' Saul nodded. 'Can he come for a sleepover in the bunk beds too?'

'Well, maybe we should have him for the afternoon first and see about a sleepover in a few weeks when we know people a little better.'

'Can we ask Cameron in the morning?' he pushed.

'Sure.' Jodi ignored the sense of misgiving that came over her. She might want to keep herself to herself but she couldn't let that affect Saul's happiness.

Her smartphone pinged to let her know she had an email. Noelle was confirming the photographer's hair and makeup people for the shoot on Friday week. They'd certainly wasted no time. She sighed.

A churning sound from the field behind their cottage propelled Jodi to the window.

'Look, Saul,' she said. 'There's a farmer cutting the corn in the field with a huge machine.'

'Wow!' Saul said, climbing onto the counter so he could see. 'Let's go and watch.' He jumped down and headed out.

Jodi followed, pulling on a cardigan.

Saul ran to the fence, clambered onto the bottom rung and waved to the small dot of a man sitting in the cab of the combine harvester. Much to Jodi's surprise, as it neared them, it chugged to a halt.

'Mum!' Saul yelled, as the man jumped down and started walking towards them. 'The farmer's coming to see us!' He climbed to the top of the fence and waved wildly.

'Hello there,' the man said.

Jodi felt herself blush. Although he was fairly shabbily dressed in washed-out jeans and a woolly sweater that had certainly seen better days, he had a gorgeous face. His blond hair was studded with wisps of straw and he certainly didn't look as if he spent much time preening himself. Still, Jodi mused, beside Darius and the other A-list actors she was used to, he was bound to look a bit rough and ready. She wasn't expecting the shot of excitement that ran through her as his

32

hazel eyes met hers. He drew her in instantly. If he hadn't just got down from a combine harvester she'd have sworn he was wearing false eyelashes, they were so long and sweeping.

'I'm Sebastian, and I live in the manor house beyond,' he explained.

'Oh, hi!' Jodi laughed nervously. She knew she must have sounded like a silly schoolgirl.

'I'd heard there was a new resident.' He hesitated. 'I knew the place was being done up after I sold it but I hadn't noticed anyone living here before now. Anyway, I thought I should introduce myself. I won't bother you,' he added quickly. 'I don't want you to think I'm going to be an awful nosy neighbour.' There was a brief moment of awkwardness as Jodi found herself tongue-tied.

Her son saved her. 'I'm Saul and I'm four and this is my mum, Jodi,' he said, and shook Sebastian's hand. 'I started school today and I have four friends already. And I have a bunk bed.'

'You've been a busy lad, eh?' Sebastian said. 'I'm very pleased to hear you have a bunk bed. That's kind of essential when you're four.'

'Can I have a go in your chopper machine, please?'

'It's called a combine harvester and it's for cutting the crops. Then I'll have straw for the animals' beds in the winter time,' he explained. 'I'm usually finished by now. But it's been such a wet summer, I've been held up considerably. I'd gladly take you out for a spin if you were older, but I'm afraid you're far too young to go near my machine.'

'Never mind,' Saul said, sounding deflated.

'If your mum agrees maybe you could come to the end of the field and see the cows instead. They love having visitors,' he said, raising an eyebrow at Jodi.

'Maybe another day,' Jodi said. Plucking Saul off the fence, she encouraged him to wave to Sebastian. Her eyes met her neighbour's once more. 'Nice to meet you,' she said.

'Yeah, you, too. Sorry, mate,' Sebastian said to Saul.

'Mum, please let me go and see the cows,' Saul begged.

A sixth sense told her Sebastian was all right.

'Maybe I'm being too hasty,' she conceded. 'Go in and grab your coat and you can go for a quick look.' She was so used to shielding Saul from the press that her knee-jerk reaction was to hide him away.

Saul tore off towards the house.

'I'm sorry,' Jodi said, walking back to Sebastian. 'We're obviously new here and we lived in London, among other places, previously. Folk in general aren't kiddie-friendly.'

'I'm used to boys,' Sebastian said, as he dropped his gaze to the ground. 'I used to be one.' He cleared his throat awkwardly. 'My own fella was Saul's age not so long ago.'

'Ah, great.' Jodi brightened. 'Is he around? Saul would love to meet him. It'll be wonderful for him to have a friend living nearby.'

'He doesn't live here any longer I'm afraid,' Sebastian said. 'Ah, here comes Saul now! Good man, let's go.'

Before Jodi could say anything else, Saul had flung himself over the fence and put his hand into Sebastian's.

Jodi perched on the fence and watched them trudge up the field to where a herd of cows stood silently eating grass. As Jodi went back inside and kept an eye on them from the kitchen window, she hoped to God Sebastian wasn't a weirdo.

Twenty minutes later, Sebastian delivered Saul back safely, nodded at Jodi and began to walk back to the combine harvester.

'Thank you!' Saul shouted.

Sebastian turned and winked at him. 'Bye, Saul.'

By the time Jodi had given him some dinner, bathed him and tucked him into bed, Saul was wiped out. 'Good day?' she asked, stroking his hair.

'The bestest.' He yawned.

As she made herself a cup of her Chinese herbal infusion the sun was dipping down behind the half-cut cornfield. Sighing, she wondered if she and Saul would be happy here. Although she knew there would be periods when she'd have to go on location for long spells in the future, she had a nine-month work-free break ahead.

Darius and she had agreed to take things as they came. She'd probably hire a nanny to help out. Saul needed some stability. She wanted him to lay roots here and aimed to avoid taking him away during the school term. But that could all be sorted in good time.

She had no idea what the future held for herself and Darius. She loved him and knew he loved her. But she guessed at some point they'd have to reassess things. As she pictured his beautiful smile and simmering, classic movie-star good looks, she sighed deeply. From the outside he was the perfect husband.

She couldn't wait to show him the cottage. Saul would be on a high after seeing his dad. She'd definitely feel better for his visit too. Not for the first time, Jodi wished their marriage was everything the fans thought it was. Still, she mused, things could be a lot worse.

Chapter 4

The following morning Francine was on schedule with the usual school-time rota. She was determined that yesterday's lateness would not be repeated.

As a working mum for the last twelve years, she had a rock-steady routine to which she stuck religiously. She knew people were awestruck by her capabilities, which pleased her. She baked bread several times a week and made sure that every day Carl and the children left the house with a cooked breakfast inside them and a healthy packed lunch in their bags.

She showered and did her makeup before she woke the children. As far as her family was concerned, she was always a bright-eyed Mary Poppins figure. Annie the childminder arrived each day like clockwork and mothered the little ones until Francine returned from her job at the accountancy firm. She worked strictly from nine thirty to five but, unlike some of her colleagues, she never left a stone unturned. Her clients regularly commented on how efficient she was.

'We knew all about it when you were on maternity leave, Francine. Nobody else operates with such attention to detail,' said Mr Price, from one of her larger accounts.

She prided herself on running a tight ship cheerfully and with apparent ease.

'Up and at 'em, guys,' she shouted up the stairs. 'We can't be late. Hurry up.'

Various shouts came back to her as the children began to thump around and get dressed.

'All okay there, darling?' she asked Carl, as she breezed into the kitchen. 'Don't forget the carrot cake I baked for your colleagues. It's a while since I sent one in. According to my notes, you reported that it went down a storm last time.'

Francine was a firm believer in her boxes of index cards. People were always asking her in astonished tones how she managed to stay on top of things. 'Ah what's that saying?' she'd reply. '"Ask a busy person to do an errand and it'll be done immediately." The more you do, the more you can do!'

She had a small downstairs office in the house with a computer and several shelves of neatly lined-up boxes. Each plastic box was filled with alphabetically arranged index cards, and labelled with a printed sticker on the front. There was a box for Cara's class at school. All the children's names were logged on alphabetical cards, with any relevant information listed below. Francine was never left standing in front of Amy's mother unable to remember that her name was Claire or that she was married to Frank and they had two other children called Mark and Suzanne. Those boxes stretched to dinner parties, the baking she'd sent into Carl's work and many other vital aspects of their lives.

'I'd better get going,' Carl said, finishing his breakfast. 'That was delicious.'

'Darling? The carrot cake?' she reminded him.

'Thanks, love,' Carl said, putting his arms around her and

pulling her close. 'Where would I be without you? All the guys at work envy me so much. I'm the only one with four children and yet I bring in the most home-baked goods, host the best dinners and parties, and I happen to think I'm married to the sexiest woman alive.'

When her accountancy firm had offered her a redundancy package early that summer, she'd laughed. 'Why on earth would I accept that? I'm the backbone of this place and one of the senior employees! Thanks for the offer but I'll stay where I am, thanks.'

Her smile had faded when the MD had held her gaze and told her in no uncertain terms that she should seriously consider the offer. 'The employees who came in after you are being let go with a month's notice and a month's pay. This is the best we can do for you, Francine. The recession's caught up with us.'

Francine had held her head high. She'd thanked them and said she'd need time to think. 'I'll let you know my decision tomorrow,' she'd said.

Carl had been wonderful. He'd immediately said they'd manage. 'That's a decent amount of money they're offering. Something else will turn up. Hey, who knows? Maybe you'll enjoy having a bit more time for a change.'

Francine had agreed and smiled. She'd waited until she was locked into the bathroom with the taps running before she'd broken down and bawled like a baby. She was being tossed aside. No matter what anyone told her, she knew what had happened. She was superfluous to requirements. End of.

'You'll adapt no matter what life throws at you, love,' Carl had said, kissing her. 'Look at how you've coped before, for crying out loud! Motherhood and a full-time job have been a piece of cake.'

'I don't know about that,' she'd said, forcing a smile.

'Well, I do.'

She wasn't about to point out to Carl that her glossy chestnut hair and smooth skin didn't stay that way without a little help. Her beauty regime certainly didn't come free, but that was an advantage of earning her own money.

A chilling thought struck her. How was she going to pay for her regular hairdressing appointments and facials going forward? The mortgage on their gorgeous five-bedroom house in the much sought-after estate of Verbena Drive didn't come cheaply. Thankfully, Carl had been made a partner at his accountancy firm several years before. Despite the recession he had some steady key accounts. He was one of the few people Francine knew of who was still getting bonuses too. All the same, she could do the maths. One wage was not going to allow for too many unnecessary treats.

Carl was the light of her life. They'd been childhood sweethearts so it was no surprise when they had married at the age of twenty-four. They'd both just qualified as accountants and had enough money to buy a starter home. After only two months of trying she had got pregnant. It had been Francine's idea to give the baby a name that began with C.

'I get to be the mother ship in all aspects of the pregnancy and birth, so this way you get a look-in too,' she'd reasoned. 'I love the thought of you and the baby having the same initials.'

Carl hadn't thought of that, but once Francine had suggested it, he instantly warmed to the idea.

Francine had taken to motherhood like a duck to water. Within three weeks their baby daughter Cara was sleeping through the night, and Francine was still baking treats once a week for Carl and his co-workers.

'Jeez, your wife's outdone herself with these miniature lemon meringue pies,' Bob had mumbled, through a delectable mouthful.

'You landed on your feet with her, all right,' Alan agreed. 'My missus was barely able to make it down the stairs for two years after our first came along. Not that I'm giving out, she's a brilliant mum, but Francine certainly puts us all to shame.'

Annie came on board as soon as Francine's maternity leave was up. As a local, she was what Francine called 'traceable to the source and dependable'.

All four children were born exactly two years apart. Cara, Conor, Craig and little Cameron all shared their daddy's initials. Instead of buckling under the mounting pressure of a large family, Francine seemed to thrive even more. Her world was organised and she was as happy as a lark until that dreadful meeting a couple of months back.

The next day she had saved face at the office by exclaiming her redundancy was a godsend: she and Carl were over the moon about it. 'I've been toying with the idea of taking some time off and you've helped me make my mind up,' she fibbed.

Her colleagues had thrown her a lovely lunch. The MD had given her a voucher for the local luxury spa, with a glowing reference, and told her he wished her well. She assured them she was feeling positive about the future.

Thus far, the children hadn't noticed any change. She had always taken August off. But now time had run out for Francine. She was going to have to tell everyone she was unemployed – and she hadn't the faintest idea how she was going to get the words out. All the women at school saw her as Mrs Dynamite. She'd dip into committee meetings, dole out jobs and fly on into work.

Annie was expecting to take up where she'd left off in July. As soon as Francine told her the new situation, it would be all over the village, like a rampant Chinese whisper.

She wasn't ready to face that just yet. If need be, she'd pay Annie to come in for a week or so, until she was able to face the stares and pointing fingers. Looking down at her trouser suit, she felt marginally stupid for dressing in work gear. Sighing, she marched into the hallway.

'This is your final warning,' she called up the stairs.

They all trooped down, except Cameron.

'Where's your little brother?' she asked six-year-old Craig.

'I dunno,' he said sleepily, and tucked into a thick slice of toast.

'Cameron! Are you dressed yet?' she called.

'I'm coming!' he shouted, from the landing. A shoe flew past her ear.

'You're not allowed to throw shoes,' she scolded. 'Now come down and pick that up.'

'Sorry,' he said, arriving down the staircase on his bottom at a hundred miles an hour. 'I'm going to sit with Saul again.'

'Really?' Francine stopped in her tracks. Grabbing the shoe, she sat the little boy on the bottom stair and helped him tie his laces. She didn't molly-coddle her children. All of them were well able to dress themselves and brush their teeth from an early age. Cameron was momentarily surprised that his mother was assisting him now.

'Saul's fun,' Cameron told her.

'Of course he is,' she said, biting her lip. 'What's his second name?'

'I dunno.'

'Okay. Run in and eat your breakfast like a good lad.'

Francine straightened as Cameron ran into the kitchen. Excitement bubbled up in her. Maybe Saul was Jodi Ludlum's boy. Imagine if she could have the superstar as her new friend! Maybe it wasn't a bad thing after all that she had some extra time on her hands.

❀

Francine felt slightly less fractious as she reversed her people-carrier, complete with *Mum Cabs* bumper sticker, out of the drive on schedule.

Ten minutes later the older children kissed and hugged her at the school's main door, then ran off to their respective classes. 'You hold my hand like a good boy,' she said to Cameron. 'I can't believe how big and grown-up you are now.'

He beamed up at her. 'We're allowed give the fishes some names today,' he told her. 'I want to call them John Cena and Randy Orton.'

'Well, you'll have to suggest those names to Mr Matthews,' Francine said. 'He might not want to call them after wrestlers.'

'Why not?' Cameron asked, clearly astonished.

'Let's just keep an open mind,' Francine urged.

'Mummy, look! There's Saul,' he said. 'Can we ask him to come for a play date now?' He ran across to his new friend, Francine following.

When she caught up, she bent down to look at the child. She was certain he was Jodi Ludlum's boy. He had his mother's famous green eyes, but there was no denying he was Darius Drew's son too. He'd the same olive complexion and floppy dark hair.

'I want to have Cameron to my house for a play date too,'

Saul said. 'My mum said I can. She'll talk to you at home time. She's gone now.'

'Oh, of course,' Francine said. 'I'll tell you what,' she ventured, 'if I don't catch her first, would you ask your mum to wait for me and we can arrange it?'

'Sure,' Saul said happily.

Mr Matthews rang his little bell to signal it was time for the parents to leave the room. Francine hugged Cameron, then rushed out, hoping she might catch Jodi leaving. It was a long wait until lunchtime. It would be just perfect if they could accidentally bump into one another and strike up a conversation organically.

Alas, there was no sign of her in the school grounds.

'Francine!' Jane called out. 'A few of us are heading for a coffee in the village. Can you join us for a few minutes? We need to sort out a few details for the welcome coffee morning.'

Looking at her watch and pretending to go through things in her head, Francine scratched her chin. 'I can pop in for a few minutes and then I'll have to fly.'

'I thought you said you were extending your annual leave this year?' Jane said, looking confused.

'Eh, yes, I am. But I need to pop into the office for an hour. I'm always in demand! You know yourself.'

ოჳ

The Coffee Pot was a hive of activity just after school drop-off time. The majority of the mothers congregated there because they offered free top-ups of coffee and there was always someone to chat to. Pushing the door open, Francine received waves from every direction.

'Over here,' Jane called, from a large round table.

'Can I get you a coffee?' Andrea asked, from near the top of the queue.

'An Americano would be lovely, thanks, Andrea,' Francine answered, rooting in her bag for her purse.

'Put your money away. It's on me,' Andrea said.

'Thanks. I'll get you one next time.' As discreetly as she could, Francine searched the room. Jodi wasn't there.

She sat down with Jane, and Andrea soon joined them with a tray of mugs.

'I was in the post office with Mrs Magee a minute ago,' she said, setting the coffees down. 'She had no idea Jodi Ludlum was living in Bakers Valley.'

'Really?' Francine was amazed. Mrs Magee, the postmistress, never missed a trick.

'Gillian in Spar was as much use as a glass cricket bat,' Jane scoffed. 'I went in to see if she'd met Jodi yet and she went off on a mad one, screaming and holding her hands to her face, telling me how much she loves her films.'

'Well, I have to say it's pretty bloody astonishing that Jodi Ludlum has moved in down the road and none of us knows a thing about it,' Andrea mused.

'That's very Hollywood of her, though, if you think about it logically,' Francine said, and sipped her coffee. 'It makes sense, actually. Why on earth would she announce to the world and its mother that she's coming to live here? I mean, she must want some privacy in her life.'

'She's a worldwide star, Francine,' Jane said, pointing out the obvious as usual. 'I doubt she wants to hide away.'

'Well, her son is a gorgeous little boy. Himself and Cameron have hit it off, as it happens,' Francine said smugly. 'I'm organising a play date later. I'll keep you posted on how it goes.'

'Are we pressing ahead with the coffee morning on Friday week?' Jane asked.

'Of course.' Francine pulled a bundle of the flyers she'd made on her computer from her bag. 'I gave out some yesterday, as you know, but we'll need to distribute these later on. We should have a good turnout. There are lots of newbies who'll appreciate the opportunity to network.'

'Not to mention the draw of Jodi!' Jane said.

'It'll be fantastic if she manages to come,' Francine said, with a set smile. 'But obviously we're doing this to welcome each and every parent equally.' She wasn't going to let Jane know she was holding her breath in the hope that Jodi would turn up. She was adamant she was going to play her cards right.

Befriending Jodi would act as a sort of balm for Francine right now. The other women were used to being housewives and hanging around the village, but she'd never seen herself as that sort of person. While she'd nothing against them, she'd enjoyed the buzz of being in a constant hurry all her life. Jodi might unwittingly take the sting out of Francine's having to spend so much time at home. She could just imagine the glossy-magazine headlines …

Jodi Ludlum, with best friend Francine Hennessy, relaxing by the sea on one of their many weekend breaks at the French Riviera.

'Francine and I are soul sisters. I'd be lost without her,' the actress told our reporter.

'Francine! Did you hear me?' Jane was looking puzzled.

'Hm?' Francine said, as she drifted back to reality and the rather burned-tasting coffee she was meant to be drinking.

'I asked if I should bake some cookies for the coffee morning.'

'Let me think,' Francine said. 'That would be great, thanks, Jane. If you do chocolate-chip ones, I'll do scones. Can you manage flapjacks, Andrea?'

'Of course,' Andrea said, looking affronted.

'That's all sorted so,' Francine said. 'Now I have to go. I've so much to do it's unreal,' she said, glancing at her watch. 'See you later, and thanks for the coffee. It's my turn next time,' she reminded them.

She made a mental note to host a coffee-at-home event over the next few weeks. The school ones were marvellous but Francine felt there was nothing quite as lovely as being invited to someone's house. When she'd been working, it had been the only way she could see several mothers at once. Besides, if things worked out the way she was hoping, she and Jodi would be well on the way to being great pals by then. So Jodi would be her guest of honour.

Francine zoomed home and made a few notes in her index cards. With a slightly trembling hand she created the most exciting new card *ever*. As she filed it under 'L' she could barely contain herself. Never in her wildest dreams had she envisaged having Jodi Ludlum's card in her box!

ভ

Francine was astonished by how slowly the morning passed at home. Normally she'd have done a ton of work at the office by now. Dejected, she realised she'd accomplished very little. How on earth was she going to get used to this?

Parking at the school at twelve fifteen, leaving plenty of time for the twelve-thirty pick-up, she pulled down the sun visor so she could check her makeup once more before getting out of the car.

'Cuckoo! Francine, are you coming?' Jane knocked on the car window, nearly giving her a heart attack.

'Jeekers, Jane!' Francine tutted as she opened the door and got out. 'I was miles away there. You gave me such a fright.' She swiftly replaced her frown with a smile.

'I'm dying to see Jodi again. God, I've been wishing the morning away so I can get a good look,' Jane confessed.

'Ah, leave the poor girl alone,' Francine said, pretending to be uninterested. 'Besides, she'll probably send a chauffeur to collect the boy.'

'Do you think so?' Jane looked disappointed.

Before they could speculate any further, Jodi floated through the gate. She was wearing a long, tight jersey dress with a simple wide-brimmed straw hat to shade her eyes from the sun.

'Oh, my God, Francine, there she is! I think I'm going to wee into my wedges,' Jane said, squeezing Francine's arm.

'She really looks like a movie star, doesn't she?' Francine said, losing her nonchalance in the heat of the moment.

'She bloody *is* one, that's why!' Jane giggled.

'Shush, she'll hear us behaving like goons,' Francine hissed. 'Let's go.' As Jodi approached, Francine managed to fall into step with her.

'Hi, there! I'm Francine, we met briefly yesterday,' she said.

'Oh, yeah. Hi.'

'Eh, this is my friend Jane.'

'Hello,' Jodi said, glancing sideways.

'Hi, Jodi,' Jane said, grinning like a drunk chimp. Jodi's eyes shot straight to the ground.

Francine elbowed her friend sharply and motioned at her to shut up.

'What?' Jane mouthed, as Jodi walked ahead. Francine put a finger to her lips.

They trotted after Jodi, jostling to stand closest to her.

'Not much sense of humour, has she?' Jane whispered to Francine, as they stood outside the classroom door.

'She's probably just shy,' Francine said, out of the corner of her mouth. She really wished Jane would go away and stop annoying her. She needed to make sure she nailed this play date.

The children spilled through the door before Francine could strike up a conversation. Much to her delight, Saul and Cameron had one agenda only.

'Cameron, this is my mummy, Jodi,' Saul said. 'Where's your mummy so we can organise our play date?'

'I'm just here,' Francine said, pushing herself forward gleefully.

'Can Cameron come to our house, Mummy? Please? You promised he could, remember?' Saul said.

'Okay,' Jodi said, picking him up and kissing his cheek.

'When?' he pressed.

Francine was secretly thrilled. This was going better than she'd dared hope. If she stood back and bided her time, the boys would arrange everything.

'Can I go tomorrow?' Cameron asked, looking up at Francine.

'Well, that's up to Saul's mum,' she said.

'How about I collect the boys after school and take Cameron to our house? I can drop him home if you tell me where you live,' Jodi offered.

'Oh, now ...' Francine stuttered. 'I hope you don't mind, but Cameron can make strange and I generally don't leave him with people he's not familiar with, seeing as he's only four. Would it be a terrible hassle if I accompany him? Just for the first time? You understand, don't you?' she said.

'Oh,' Jodi said. 'Uh, yes, I suppose so …'

There was an awkward silence as she looked at the ground. Francine was mortified. She didn't know what to do. Clearly this woman didn't want her anywhere near her. Perhaps they weren't going to become bosom buddies after all. Feeling snubbed, she grasped Cameron's hand. 'Maybe we should leave you to settle in here at Bakers Valley a little longer. How about you let me know when might suit better? Come on, Cameron.'

'No, Mummy!' he shouted. 'I want to go to Saul's house tomorrow. You're a fat pig.' As he kicked her in the shins, Francine thought she was going to pass out, both from the pain and the dreadful embarrassment.

'Mum!' Saul said, tugging Jodi's hand. 'You promised!'

'I know I did, dude. Listen, tomorrow's cool by me,' she said. 'Come too, if you like, Francine.'

'Right. Only if you're sure, though,' Francine said, bending down to rub her shin. 'Sorry about this,' she added, pointing at Cameron, who was pouting crossly. 'He's just overexcited.'

'No problem.' Jodi smiled thinly and walked off.

'So I'll see you here at the same time tomorrow and we can go to your house?' Francine said loudly, so all the gawping mothers could hear.

'Fine.' Jodi waved over her shoulder.

Francine told Cameron to fetch his school bag from the classroom as the other mothers surrounded her.

'Is that really her?' one asked.

'She looks so young up close …'

'She's not exactly friendly, is she?' Jane said. 'She doesn't look at you when you speak to her and it didn't seem like she wanted to be here.'

'Girls,' Francine hissed, 'let's not stand around talking about the poor woman. She might hear us. That wouldn't be good. She's just a mum like the rest of us. We don't want her to feel she's on show all the time.'

'Get off the stage, Francine,' Jane scoffed. 'She's certainly not like me! Her clothes aren't washed out, she doesn't need to lose two stone and she hasn't three inches of grey roots on the top of her head. She's a multimillionaire and looks it.'

'Well, in my opinion she'll be happier if some of us can see past all that and accept her as a true friend,' Francine said, with her nose in the air.

'Ah, my arse.' Jane laughed. 'She's a real Hollywood wan. Look at the way she waltzed off barely speaking to us. I'd say she's a real snobby cow. She probably thinks she's too good for the likes of us.'

'She is!' Sarah giggled. 'But the first coffee morning is on Friday week and she might actually come. So we all need to plan what to wear. We can't have her thinking she's landed in a one-horse town with a pack of hicks.'

'Hey, how come you're not working tomorrow, Francine?' Jane asked. The group turned their attention to her.

'I told you. I've extended my usual annual leave. I want to settle this little one and make sure I'm ready for the coffee morning next week,' Francine said.

'Since when have you needed to take time off to get ready for anything?' Jane said, laughing.

'Maybe she needs a breather,' Sarah said, shooting Jane a dirty look.

'Francine and breathers don't go hand in hand,' Jane said, utterly unaware of the anxiety she was causing Francine.

'Back to the coffee-morning outfits,' Sarah said.

This gambit was met with widespread approval as all the

mothers began to discuss what they had in their wardrobes.

'Here I am, Mummy. I got my school bag like you said,' Cameron announced, as he flung it at Francine's feet.

Stooping to pick it up, Francine seized the opportunity to flee and tugged Cameron towards their car. 'You'll be a good boy for me tomorrow, won't you?' she asked her son.

'I'm always a good boy,' Cameron answered.

'That wasn't nice behaviour just now. You shouldn't have kicked me. It hurt and it's very bad manners. I don't like the way you've started throwing things either. It's rude.'

'You didn't want me to play with Saul,' he said.

'Cameron, you're not to kick people, ever. Do you understand me? If you can't behave, you won't be invited to Saul's house again.'

'I'm sorry, Mummy,' he said.

'All right, then,' she conceded. But she was prone to misgivings about Cameron and his behaviour. Only last week they'd been at the removal service for a committee lady's father when Cameron had made her want to crawl into the pine box beside the deceased. Francine had been so deep in prayer that she hadn't noticed her youngest child slipping away.

Cameron had gone behind the altar, removed a white table runner and draped it over his shoulders, mimicking the presiding priest.

The bereaved family had thought he was hilarious. They'd hugged Francine afterwards, saying their father had been a real prankster in his day and would've loved it.

She'd apologised profusely for any offence that might have been caused, adding little phrases like 'the innocence of him', and finished, 'You never know what they'll do next.'

She'd almost needed to be anaesthetised as Carl drove them home.

'He didn't mean any harm. He's only little. None of the grieving family was upset. In fact, I reckon they were delighted with the bit of diversion.' Carl had chuckled. 'We'll have our work cut out with this one all right!'

Francine still didn't see the funny side. She'd frogmarched Cameron to his room and told him he was on time out. 'If you ever show me up in public like that again, there'll be trouble,' she'd said, her hands shaking and her voice cracking. Francine Hennessy did not produce 'problem children'. She wasn't going to stand for it, and if it killed her, she'd stamp out that kind of behaviour before it took hold. She was of the firm belief that any children who were unruly only acted that way if they were allowed to.

Annie had done a great job with the older three, but the more time she spent at home, the more Francine was beginning to believe that the childminder had been spoiling Cameron and letting him get away with murder. If she was going to be with him full time, Francine would end this naughtiness quick smart. Besides, she mused, it wouldn't help her budding friendship with Jodi if her son was behaving like a gurrier.

Francine drove out of the school gate feeling a little lacklustre. Jodi wasn't as friendly as she'd hoped. Maybe the notion of using the A-list star as a new diversion in life wasn't going to work out as she'd imagined.

Chapter 5

The next morning Jodi had to wake Saul. As she opened the curtains in his room and gently shook him, she felt like bursting with joy. Since he had been tiny Saul had always woken around dawn - until today.

'Good morning, beautiful boy,' she whispered, as she kissed his cheek. 'Looks like the Irish air has worked its magic on you!'

'Mummy ...' Saul stretched and rolled over to go back to sleep.

'The bad news is that you have to get up right now for school. But the good news is that you're having your first ever play date later on today,' she reminded him.

That was all it took. It was like he'd been turbo-charged. Seconds later Saul was happily eating his breakfast and choking on a glass of milk.

'Take it easy, dude,' Jodi advised. 'School doesn't even open for another fifteen minutes, and Cameron can't play with you if you've choked to death!'

Saul's milk spewed out of his nose as he burst out laughing. He lay on the floor on his back with his arms glued to his sides, letting his head flop to the side and his tongue hang out.

Jodi giggled and nudged him gently with her foot. 'Off the

floor, little man. Why don't you brush your teeth and I'll get your snack ready to put into your school bag?' she said, swatting him as he skipped past.

The phone rang and Saul gave a shout of delight. He snatched it up. 'Hello, who's speaking, please?' he asked, looking deadly serious. 'Daddy!'

Jodi smiled and leaned against the door as she watched her son have a quick chat with his father.

'I gotta run too, Dad. I'm very busy, you know,' Saul said. 'Here's Mum.'

'Hi, Darius, how are things going on set?' Jodi fixed Saul's school bag on his back.

'It's good to hear a familiar voice. Work is good but the other isn't so great,' he said cagily. 'Did the magazine confirm the photo shoot for Friday week?'

'They sure did. Look, try not to worry and I'll see you next week,' she said.

'I have to go, sweetie,' Darius said. 'I only called to hear your voice for a minute. I'm being called to Makeup. Today's going to be a long one. Give our boy a hug from me. Love you.'

'Love you too and try not to worry about the other thing. Call me if you need me, yeah?' Jodi hung up.

As they walked towards school Saul was quiet. Eventually he asked, 'Who's being mean to Daddy?'

'Nobody. Why?' Jodi kept her voice and face even. Her heart was thumping and she hoped she was hiding her alarm.

'Well, why were you telling him not to worry? Is he ill?'

'Oh, no, darling. He's just sad because we're here and he's on set away from us. That's all,' she lied.

'Poor Daddy. Maybe the director will let him come and stay

with us for a big bit. We could tell him Daddy's on the verge of being burned-out,' Saul mused.

Jodi giggled. 'You, my boy, have spent far too long around sets and melodramatic movie stars. It makes me more certain than ever that we've done the right thing by moving here.'

Just like the previous morning, the school was buzzing with parents and children dodging past one another. The atmosphere was cheerful and Saul clearly couldn't wait to get inside.

'Good morning, Saul,' Mr Matthews said. 'Have you a high five for me?'

'Sure do,' Saul said, jumping to slap hands with the teacher.

'Hey,' Jodi greeted him.

'How's it going? Is Saul settling in okay?'

'He's really happy so far. He couldn't wait to get here today.'

'That's a good sign. It'd be a bad reflection on me if he was clinging to the outside of the gate and yelling obscenities!'

Jodi laughed. 'There's still plenty of time for that, I suppose. Don't count your chickens!'

'Believe me, I won't. I know only too well that I'm in a precarious position here. Not only am I a blow-in British person, but I'm male. I saw more than one second glance yesterday when the parents arrived. I don't exactly look or sound like cuddly Miss Myrtle!'

'Ah, you get used to those double takes,' Jodi said.

Mr Matthews studied her for a second. 'Once the children are happy and they like me, I hope to win the parents over bit by bit.'

'Good luck with that,' Jodi said, before bending down to hug Saul goodbye.

'There you are! Isn't it a glorious morning?'

Jodi stood up to find Francine smiling in front of her.

'Today still okay for you?' Francine went on eagerly.

'Yes, totally. We're really looking forward to our first play date,' Jodi said, with a smile. 'See you here at pick-up time as planned.'

'You're a dote. See you at twelve bells! Better run – I've three others to check on in various classrooms,' Francine said, rolling her eyes. Before she could move, Jodi found herself being grabbed by the shoulders and air-kissed on each side of her face with the speed of a woodpecker.

'Toodle-oo, Cameron!' Francine called, as she fled the scene.

As Mr Matthews began shepherding children to their seats, Jodi dodged past the congregation at the classroom door.

Francine seemed really nice, but Jodi was utterly terrified of her. She'd never been able to deal with seriously outgoing people like that. Up until now it hadn't been an issue. Darius was always happy to be the chatty, sociable one when they were out. Otherwise she could be quiet on set and people respected that. She'd use her scripts as a buffer or say she was keeping her mind on the role. Besides, most people were kind of star-struck when they met her, so she didn't need to make any sort of lasting impression.

When they'd moved here, she'd stupidly assumed the remote setting would afford her anonymity. She was starting to realise the exact opposite was on the cards.

Realising she'd better have some food ready for her guests, Jodi grabbed the key of her Mini as soon as she got back to the cottage and drove to the village.

The last time she'd pootled along the quaint street to view the shabby pre-makeover cottage, it had been like a ghost town. This morning it was a real hive of activity as most of the mothers from a five-mile radius seemed to have descended on the coffee shop and surrounding stores.

The Spar supermarket was one of those massive modern ones, which looked like it would have all the supplies she needed. Finding a space easily, due to the size of the Mini, Jodi sauntered inside and grabbed a trolley. She turned away as she passed the impressive display of papers and magazines. She'd stopped reading them many years previously. Noelle had warned her against leaving herself open to hurtful photos and comments. 'The journalists will stop at nothing when they're looking for a story. If the real version isn't juicy enough they embellish it,' she explained. 'You'll do yourself the best favour of all if you just avoid them.' After she'd sobbed over a pack of lies they'd written about her and Tommy some years back, she'd taken Noelle's advice.

As she made her way up and down the aisles, Jodi was astonished by the variety of products. She'd no idea what she should be serving Francine for lunch so she did her usual and stuck with prepared food. That way there was less chance of her poisoning her first guest. A quiche, some tubs of salad and fresh bread seemed like a good plan. Knowing Saul would stick his tongue out and make vomiting noises at it, she found a pizza for the boys. Unlike herself at the same age, Saul had a highly trained palate. Jodi wasn't often extravagant, but her lack of culinary skills had led her to employ a chef when they weren't on set.

'If you're ever stuck,' he had said, 'buy a frozen pizza and add your own fresh cheese and salami to it.'

Now she added a chunk of Cheddar and a packet of sliced peppery salami to her trolley, and hoped for the best. Then she thought of drinks and dumped a jar of instant coffee and a box of tea bags in too. She reckoned Francine mightn't be on board for drinking her herbal infusion. A chocolate cake in a box near the till looked as if it might be home-made so she took that as well.

If she put it on a plate, maybe Francine would believe she'd baked it in the Aga.

She began to unload her items at the checkout. The dark-haired girl at the till looked as if she was going to lose her mind. 'You're Jodi Ludlum,' she stated.

'Yes,' Jodi said, with a smile.

'I feel like I'm going to vomit,' the girl said.

'Is that a good or bad thing?' Jodi asked. She instantly liked the assistant. Unlike some people she'd encountered, she didn't make her nervous.

'It's all good,' the girl said, still looking green. 'I've never met anyone famous before. You look exactly the same as your pictures in the magazines.'

'Thanks,' Jodi said.

The girl stood motionless and made no attempt to ring in any of the groceries. The items began to pile up in the small area so Jodi had to stop and wait. 'Are you okay?' Jodi ventured.

'No. I feel like I've taken a dodgy acid tab,' the girl said. 'I heard some of the gossipy mothers from the school saying you'd moved in and all that but I never expected you to come in here. Like, I mean, Jodi Ludlum in *Spar*!'

'Mad as it might sound, I eat and drink just like a real doll,' Jodi said, blinking with an exaggerated vacant look on her face.

'Sorry.' The girl grinned. 'I'm Gillian by the way.'

'Good to meet you, Gillian. Have you lived around here for long?' Jodi asked.

'I'm from Dublin originally. It's the usual story. I met a fella who couldn't afford to live near the city so we moved here.'

'How do you find it after living in a city?' Jodi asked, with genuine interest as Gillian finally began to check her stuff through.

'Ah, it can be a bit Valley of the Squinting Windows, you

know. Lots of biddies who have feck all else to do but poke their noses into other people's business.' She snorted. 'But you find that sort everywhere, really, don't you?'

'Certainly do!' Jodi agreed emphatically. 'I have to say I've found people really friendly so far.'

'Of course you bleedin' have.' Gillian laughed. 'You're Jodi Ludlum! What did you think? That people would be horrible to you? I'd say you'll be invited to enough coffee mornings now to keep you going until you're fifty. They'll all want a piece of you!'

Jodi grinned as she shoved her groceries into the plastic bags Gillian handed her.

'I'm meant to charge you for the plastic bags but I won't bother,' she said.

'Thanks,' Jodi said. 'Well, it's great to meet you, Gillian. No doubt we'll be seeing one another a lot more. I've to go and get ready for my son's first play date! He's really excited.'

'Cool! Who's coming to visit?' she asked.

'Francine and Cameron. Do you know them?'

'Know them? Francine is Mrs Bakers Valley. Working mum, millions of kids, perfect house, ideal husband, and does it all with a flawless smile. Think Career Barbie meets Stepford Wife and you've got Francine Hennessy.'

'Oh, right,' Jodi said, feeling sick.

'Ah, she's not a bad auld skin, Francine, but she'll probably run her finger over your sideboard and look for dust. Don't be insulted if she offers to do meals on wheels for you and your son after you serve her shop-bought fare today either.'

'Seriously?' Jodi said biting her lip. 'I'd burn water. I'm such an appalling cook and firmly believe everything tastes better with ketchup.'

'Ah, you're gonzoed so. Enjoy,' Gillian said. 'Do you want a hand out to your car with the bags?'

'I'll be fine, thanks.'

'Can I take a picture of you to put on me Facebook page?' Gillian said. 'Or is that really uncool?'

'Go on, then.' Jodi smiled.

She was still smiling as she let herself back into the cottage. There was very little she could do about her culinary skills between now and lunchtime, so Francine was going to have to take her as she found her.

All the same, she still felt nervous. An image of her mother flashed into her mind. *You're nothing but a useless waste of space, Jodi. My life was fine until you came along.*

Even though it was years since her mother had died, Jodi still carried the scars of her childhood. To the world she was a superstar, but in her own head, just below the carefully guarded surface, she was still 'Gyppo Jodi', the awful name the children at her school had used to taunt her. 'Your ma's an alco and a druggy. You get bottles of beer for your birthday, don't you?'

'Yeah, you go on play dates to the pub!'

'Bernadette Ludlum's poor little sprog.' That was what the men at the bar had called her.

Back then there had been nothing Jodi could say in response. The only person who had shown her love was Nana. Bernadette allowed her mother to take Jodi each Sunday and Jodi lived for those days when she'd have a hot meal and feel secure, even if it only lasted a few hours.

But Jodi Ludlum was different now. Bakers Valley was light years from Dayfield, the drugs-ridden council estate where she'd grown up. Francine might be akin to Nigella Lawson when it came to catering, but Jodi wasn't going to allow herself to slip into that mindset where she felt unworthy.

Francine didn't know her secrets and, as far as Jodi was concerned, she never would. All she had to do was keep herself to herself and things would be just fine.

Back at the cottage, Jodi set the table with the pretty blue and white tableware the interior designer had bought. No wonder the bill for furnishings had been so high. The woman had thought of everything. She took a cake plate from a high cupboard, then looked around her stunning home with pride. She'd come a long way. Nobody ever needed to know she'd clawed her way to the top.

Chapter 6

At home, Francine was pacing the carpet. She didn't know what to make of Jodi Ludlum. She'd stupidly pinned her hopes on finding a new best friend and a fresh source of entertainment rolled into one. This morning she'd done her best to be friendly and upbeat, but the other woman hadn't really reciprocated. In fact, she'd made it pretty clear she was only having Cameron over to appease Saul.

Still, Francine felt it was worth making an effort all the same so she'd headed directly for the hairdresser's in Dublin. She wasn't taking a chance going to Patsy above the chemist in the village. Everyone from here to Pakistan would know where she was going if she did that.

Operation Jodi Ludlum had to be played out to perfection. Francine was feeling enough of a failure at the moment: she couldn't run the risk of all the folk in Bakers Valley knowing she'd been at Jodi's today, only to be shunned tomorrow. Jodi was very guarded and Francine wasn't sure how to take her. Such uncertainty was new to her and she didn't like it. Until this point, Francine had been a team leader who had always been comfortable in her own skin.

With her hair blow-dried to a glossy shine, Francine rushed

to a trendy florist to pick up a stylish arrangement. 'It's for a friend,' Francine said, as she handed the sculpted piece to the girl at the cash desk.

'That's a lovely twist on the usual bouquet, isn't it?' the assistant remarked.

'It's for Jodi Ludlum. I reckon she'll appreciate it,' Francine said.

'Seriously?'

'Yes. We're friends,' Francine added, for good measure.

'That's pretty cool. What's she like?'

'Oh, she's gorgeous when you get to know her,' Francine gushed. 'Very private, though.'

'Right.' The girl looked wildly impressed. 'Well, give her my best. Tell her I love her movies, won't you?'

Francine promised she would and tried not to baulk at the eighty-euro price tag for the flowers. If she hadn't started this show-off conversation she could've said she wouldn't dream of paying that for some skew-ways feathers and a bird-of-paradise shoved into glittery oasis.

'Bye now,' Francine said, and felt some of her confidence seep back.

In Bakers Valley again, she stopped off at home to change her clothes. Her navy D&G cotton skirt, with a striped, nautical-style top and simple espadrilles, seemed an apt choice. Not too fussy, with a nod towards elegant chic. It was a typically Irish September day – the sun had come out and there was barely a cloud in the sky.

Applying a slick of lip gloss, Francine surveyed herself in the full-length mirror in her dressing room. She'd never deviated from a size ten except when she was pregnant. Even then, she'd never allowed herself to put on more than two stone. Within eight weeks of giving birth each time, she was back to her usual weight. 'If I don't walk this flab off immediately it'll settle and stay,' she'd said to Carl.

'Don't be too hard on yourself, love. It'll happen in good time. I know lots of other women who haven't lost the weight after one baby, never mind four,' Carl had said, after Cameron's birth.

'Carl, I'm not *other women*. I don't give two hoots what everyone else deems normal. I'll be back in my usual clothes by the time Cameron is eight weeks.'

And she was.

Her look was timeless rather than up to the minute. She believed in buying quality, not quantity.

'Never buy cheap tailoring or jewellery,' she had told Cara, from the time she was old enough to comprehend. 'The cut of a well-made suit can never be copied. The look of a decent white-gold necklace can never be bettered by a tin counterpart. Buy cheaply and you'll buy twice.'

Today, going to Jodi Ludlum's house, she needed all the confidence she could muster. She prayed Cameron wouldn't behave badly and that it wasn't going to be one of those painful afternoons where she'd have to fill awkward silences with anecdotes neither of them wanted to hear.

Having timed her arrival at the school perfectly, Francine walked calmly to the kindergarten class. She decided to keep her gaze on the closed door. Jodi would spot her and they'd make a connection that way. It would all be very civilised and natural.

What Francine hadn't planned and certainly didn't welcome was the reception she received from Mr Matthews. Just as the other parents were arriving he opened the door and said, 'Mrs Hennessy, may I have a word, please?'

There was more than a slight edge to his voice.

'Of course.' Francine tried to hide her irritation and embarrassment.

'I think it would be better if you came inside.'

Six or seven other mothers were there now, so Francine was less than happy to be singled out.

Before she could close the door to the classroom properly Mr Matthews had turned to her. 'It seems Cameron's having a bit of trouble with his social skills.' He turned to the little boy. 'Isn't that right, dude?' Cameron stared up at him and shrugged his shoulders. 'Why don't you go over and feed the fish for me while I have a quick word with your mum?'

'Okay,' Cameron said. Francine hoped she wasn't going to hear a bad report.

Mr Matthews lowered his voice so Cameron wouldn't hear them. 'As it turns out, he bit Katie and drew blood. I know some little boys can be over-zealous. Hey, I was a bit like that myself once upon at time, but there has to come a point where I draw the line, you know?'

As he carried on talking, Francine felt like she was floating outside her own body. The shock of what she had been told made her break out in a sweat. All she could think of were the dark patches that must be inking their way through the armpits of her blouse. Zoning back to Mr Matthews, she stared in horror as he concluded his hushed rant.

'Do you appreciate where I'm coming from? I want *all* the children to enjoy school. It's not going to happen if Cameron continues to be so rough. We need to get a handle on his bad language too. It's not cool for him to eff and blind at the others ... Don't you agree?'

Francine stared at him.

'Mrs Hennessy, are you listening to me?'

'Yes,' she managed to croak. The voice she heard wasn't her own. The child the teacher had described was the worst version of Cameron she'd ever imagined.

Logically, she shouldn't have been quite so stunned. It wasn't as if she didn't know about his temper. But she'd foolishly assumed he'd never dare lose it with anyone but herself.

She'd believed Carl when he'd said Cameron was pushing the boundaries. That he was simply making himself known in the house. But all the things Mr Matthews had just described – biting, kicking, head-butting and, God forbid, cursing at the other children – weren't part of establishing himself.

'I ... I ... I don't know what to say.' Francine felt as if she was going to be sick. Her prettily made-up eyes blurred and she felt like grinding her fists into the crisp mascara and smudging it violently down her cheeks. Her well-cut skirt felt restricting and tight. 'I'll have a long chat with him and explain that this is not acceptable behaviour,' Francine said, forcing herself to stand up straight and answer the teacher. 'My sincere apologies, Mr Matthews.'

'We'll take it one day at a time,' he said, sounding resigned.

Francine took Cameron's hand and led him out to the corridor, where Jodi was on her hunkers comforting a sobbing Saul. As they approached, Francine heard him say to Jodi, 'Mum, I don't want Cameron to come to our house any more. He's horrible. He scratched my face and poured my juice into the fish tank. When all the fishes swam around in circles being scared, he laughed. That's *soooo* mean!'

Jodi stroked Saul's head and glanced up at Francine.

'But I thought we were doing a play date,' Cameron said. 'The fishes are fine. I just gave them some food, didn't I, Mum?'

Francine patted Cameron's hand and blinked at Jodi numbly.

Jodi scooped Saul up in her arms. 'Just give me a second, please,' she said to Francine.

'I'm so sorry,' Francine said miserably. 'Please, let's leave it for today. Maybe, if Saul likes, we can try again another time.'

At that, Cameron plopped onto the floor, crossed his legs and bawled with his mouth open.

The mothers, who were still at the classroom door, were agog. Jane elbowed Sarah and they stared at Francine.

'I'm sure we can settle this,' Jodi said, surprising everyone. 'Cameron didn't mean to hurt anyone. Let's all go back to our house, as planned. I reckon the chocolate cake I have will fix this problem.'

Immediately Cameron jumped up and wrapped himself around Jodi's leg.

'Thank you.'

'Cameron!' Francine was horrified. 'Let go of Jodi.'

'He's fine. We're friends, and it's good to hug your friends, isn't that so, Cameron?' Jodi held the little boy's eyes.

'Yes.'

'Let's get out of here,' Jodi suggested. 'Why don't you finish your chat with Mr Matthews and I'll meet you outside with the boys?'

'Oh, no need.' Mr Matthews held his hands aloft. 'We're done for today, thanks.'

'Great!' Francine said, in a far too jolly voice.

She followed Jodi to the grass at the side of the school car park. The two boys were happily wrestling on the ground as if nothing untoward had just happened.

'Ready to go?' Jodi asked. 'It's probably just as easy to walk to my place.'

'Absolutely!' Francine said, doing her best not to show how rattled she was. 'Isn't it gorgeous to feel the sun on your face?' she said, as the other mothers passed them, gawping.

'Come on, little dudes, let's go!' Jodi called.

'It's lovely of you to invite us. We're going to have *such* fun this afternoon,' Francine said, loudly enough for the others to hear as they packed their children into cars.

Saul and Cameron ran on ahead, talking excitedly and beating the bushes with a stick Jodi had pulled out of the hedgerow and handed them. 'Little boys and sticks are always a winning combination, don't you think?' Jodi said.

Once they were out of sight of the school Francine put her hand on Jodi's arm, stopping her in her tracks. 'Thank you, Jodi. You were so kind to me just now. I've only just met you and I've no doubt you're already wondering how the hell you're going to get rid of me, but I'll try to make this as painless as possible. We'll let the boys have a quick play and a snack and I'll be out of your hair.'

'Hey! You're fine. Kids have bad days just like us. Don't sweat it. Come on, let's get going.'

After that, Francine couldn't think of a single thing to say. She'd never felt so awkward.

'I'm sure you're well used to the surroundings but I'm still marvelling at the nature and stillness of this place,' Jodi said.

'It's a wonderful place to live, all right,' Francine said. 'I'm so proud to be part of this community.' She was walking beside Jodi like a clockwork doll. She knew she ought to be telling her a little about the history of the village but she was silenced by shame.

Jodi didn't say much either. Francine stole a sideways glance at her. She seemed to be enthralled by the boys, who were charging from one side of the lane to the other, making aeroplane noises with their arms outstretched.

By the time they reached the cottage door Francine felt like she was going to pass out with stress.

'Welcome! You're the first visitors Saul and I have had, so come on in!'

'Oh, it's gorgeous!' Francine gasped, as she walked into the living area.

Normally, a small cottage with stone floors would've been Francine's idea of hell, but somehow, probably because it belonged to Jodi Ludlum, it was cool. Francine and Carl had worked their way up the housing ladder until three years ago they'd managed to buy their five-bed house in Verbena Drive. Their house was all she'd ever dreamed of owning. The garden was sizeable without being a chore, the neighbours were sociable yet not intrusive and, most of all, she knew many other villagers envied her. With a sinking feeling, Francine knew she was going to be the envy of nobody by Christmas. She was jobless with a hooligan of a child.

'I love it here.' Jodi sighed happily. 'It's the gate lodge for the old manor house, but I guess you already know that. I had the entire place redone from the floor to the roof. The first time I saw this place I knew it had to be mine.'

Francine recognised top-notch workmanship when she saw it. There was no doubt that Jodi had put the best of everything into the place. Yet it was still a tiny cottage, no matter how it was decorated.

'Come and see my room!' Saul said, dragging Cameron by the arm. Francine wasn't going to miss out on the opportunity to have a quick nose around, so she hotfooted it after the boys.

'And look!' Saul pulled his curtains and blinds shut so the stars that were dotted around his skylight could shine. 'Want to see Mum's room?' he asked.

'No,' Cameron said, making for a huge bucket of Lego.

'I do,' Francine said, rather too quickly and loudly. She blushed and berated herself. She had to stop behaving like an inquisitive old bat.

'Oh, please go ahead. I hate going into a new house and not being able to have a good old gawk!' Jodi added from behind them.

'You must think I'm dreadful.' Francine giggled nervously.

'Not in the slightest.' Jodi led the way to her modest room, made rustic with waxed floorboards and a white-painted iron bed, finished with blue and white French damask.

Francine tried not to stare at the antique bust, which stood in the corner with rows of pearls and beads strewn across it.

'I loved that bust. It's from a movie set and they were going to chuck it in a skip! Can you believe that?' Jodi asked.

'No,' Francine breathed.

'And I'm a bit of a magpie when it comes to little boxes. I know they're totally useless and most of them are empty, but I love them,' Jodi said, almost reading Francine's thoughts as she peeped at the dressing-table. 'Darius bought me this one when we first met.' She held up a round mother-of-pearl box, its lid studded with crystals and seed pearls. 'I'd never been given anything like it before so he kicked off a bit of an obsession, as you can see!'

'I'm sure you had at least a dozen sparkly boxes as a child, but none as beautiful as this,' Francine said, picking it up for a closer look. As she'd suspected, it had the famous Fabergé stamp on the bottom.

Jodi opened her mouth to say something, then faltered.

Clearly she'd had second thoughts. 'Tea? Or would you prefer coffee with your lunch?' she asked.

'Coffee, please. I'm a terror for it,' Francine joked.

'Coffee it is. I've a chocolate cake for afters, but I'd like Saul to eat some real food first,' Jodi said.

'Oh, I'm right there with you,' Francine agreed. 'I've no problem with treats so long as they have something vaguely healthy first.'

When Francine saw Jodi boiling the cream enamel kettle on the Aga she thought she'd expire with lust. This was so perfect. From Hollywood to a divine country-chic pad, this girl had it all.

The image was somewhat tarnished when Francine saw the food.

She'd been expecting a delicious stew or roast chicken to come out of the top oven of the Aga. Instead Jodi produced what she suspected might've been pizza at some point in its life. Now it was a dried-out, blackened Frisbee. The quiche was equally unappetising.

Francine tried not to squeak in horror as Jodi dumped the shop-bought aluminium tray on her beautiful wooden kitchen table. 'Oh, I wonder if you should put a cloth or something between that and the table?' Francine couldn't help herself. 'That table must've cost you a small fortune and the hot container might end up burning it.'

'Do you think?' Jodi asked, looking a bit hassled. 'I'm not exactly good in the kitchen, as you can see. Could you put this tea towel under it for me, if you don't mind? Boys! Lunch!' she called.

As Jodi put plastic containers of salad in the middle of the table she said, 'I'm sure I'm doing all sorts of awful things here - please forgive me. This is all very new to me.'

'We're here now!' Saul hopped up on to a chair.

'Grab a plate and help yourselves,' Jodi said distractedly. 'I forgot to make your coffee, Francine. I'll get it now.'

Francine tried to coax Cameron into eating something.

'It's yuck!' he moaned.

'Don't be rude,' Francine hissed.

'Would you like something else instead?' Jodi asked.

'Could I have toast?'

'Is it really awful?' she asked, as the two boys grimaced at each other.

Saul grinned but said nothing.

'You see, Saul and I have been living in either hotels or on-set trailers so I need a bit of practice with cooking,' Jodi said.

'Not to worry. You can't be good at everything,' Francine said, with a bright smile. She couldn't imagine how any woman managed to survive without basic domestic skills.

The toast wasn't much better than the rest of the food. Jodi had never used the device that Aga had provided for making it. The long-handled cage-like implement was meant to hold the bread in place while facilitating even toasting. Jodi burned it. 'Cake?' she offered, with a grimace.

An almost silent yelp escaped Francine as Jodi slid the chocolate cake from the box. This was no melt-in-the-mouth home-baked delight but a dry carpet-like imposter with an endless shelf life. Jodi proceeded to hack it into enormous wedges. When she put a two-litre container of milk and a kilo bag of sugar on the table, Francine could feel herself flushing.

'Help yourselves,' Jodi encouraged. 'None of you have eaten a thing! Ease my guilt and have something to keep you going.'

Francine watched Jodi make a cup of dark, murky liquid that smelt putrid.

'What's that?' she asked.

'It's a purifying herbal infusion. It originates from China or some such place,' Jodi said. 'Most of LA swears by it. It's supposed to cleanse your blood, make you look younger and God knows what else. Tastes and smells like the devil's pee to me, but I drink it anyway!' she said, opening her eyes wide and making the boys giggle.

'Let's go and play in my room,' Saul said to Cameron, and they scampered off.

'I'm sorry you can't eat any of the food I bought,' Jodi said.

'Um, well … Gosh, this is very awkward … I … Uh … Oh, Jodi, I'm sorry to sound rude, but I can't drink instant coffee and I hate shop-bought cake.' Francine pulled a face and blushed again.

'Seriously?' Jodi looked amused. 'Will I be a total social outcast around here if I can't be a domestic goddess?'

'Well, if you don't mind me being frank – village life requires a certain amount of social networking.' Francine was on familiar territory now. 'There's no better way of doing that than attending or hosting a coffee morning.' She nodded sagely.

'Wow, I wonder if I should just move out now?' Jodi said. 'What's the story with this coffee morning at the school? Do I have to bring cake or something?' She looked fearful.

'Not at all. Myself and the committee ladies will do all that. You just need to turn up. The other mothers will be thrilled to meet you. I mean, it's not every day we find ourselves rubbing shoulders with movie stars!'

'Even ones that can't cook?' Jodi teased.

'As you said yourself, you've never had the opportunity to learn. If I had staff to make all my meals I'd be more than happy,' Francine quipped.

'Don't get me wrong, acting is my life and I'm so lucky to be where I am, but it's not all glamour and glitz. I often long for a life that's less fraught. I didn't want Saul to grow up thinking the whole world consists of lights and cameras. That's why I came home.'

'I see.' Francine was delighted that Jodi was suddenly talking to her with such ease. 'Where did you live as a child?'

'In Dublin,' Jodi said. 'But I moved away at a very young age. How about you?' She had changed the subject quickly. 'Are you from around here?'

'Born and bred,' Francine said. 'I work full time as well as taking care of my four children. Carl is a great help too, bless him. He's my husband. Obviously.' She laughed.

'Obviously,' Jodi repeated. 'Where do you work?'

Francine stared at her for a moment. 'Eh, well … I'm an accountant … Does your husband come home often?' she asked.

'Nope,' Jodi said. 'In fact, he's about to go off on a shoot so it'll be just me and Saul for the next while.'

'Don't you get lonely?'

'You ask a lot of questions, don't you?'

'Sorry,' Francine said. 'I was just trying to be friendly.' There was a brief silence. She felt she had to fill it. 'You could come over to my house some time, and I'll teach you how to cook,' she offered. 'Only if you're interested, that is. I mean, you might be heading off and leaving Saul with a nanny at the end of the week—'

'Oh, no,' Jodi interrupted. 'I'm here for the next nine months. I've scripts to learn and there'll be the odd job along the way, but this is Saul's and my base camp for the foreseeable future. I'll probably miss the last few weeks of the summer term, but I'm here for the long haul. I'd love to learn how to cook, thank you.'

Just as Francine was beginning to relax she and Jodi were jolted by the sound of smashing glass and screams.

'Saul?' Jodi sprang to her feet.

'Cameron?' Francine followed.

'My star mirror's broken!' Saul cried.

Cameron raced past the two mothers and straight out of the front door. Without missing a beat, Jodi tucked her skirt into her knickers and tore after him. The little boy was fast, but he was no match for her.

Francine was rooted to the spot: her son had trashed Jodi Ludlum's house and was currently being chased up the road by the movie star with her underwear on show. Still, this was a woman who'd done sex scenes with umpteen men in front of hordes of cameramen and God knows who else.

As Francine watched with horror, Jodi caught up with him and Cameron began to flail about like a wild animal.

'Hey, dude,' Francine heard her say, 'I'm not going to hurt you. Let's just go back to your mum, yeah? It's okay about the mirror. We can get it fixed. Come back and see your mum, okay?'

As Jodi stepped towards him, he spat at her, narrowly missing her foot. 'Fuck you!' he yelled, and bolted towards the school.

Francine witnessed the entire scene in slow motion, then ran towards them. 'I'm so desperately sorry. I'll see you tomorrow,' she called over her shoulder as she hurried after Cameron, leaving a stunned Jodi in her wake. When Tommy Hilfiger had designed her espadrilles he clearly hadn't taken into account crazy chases down country roads.

She found Cameron in the school grounds perched on a dangerously high branch of a horse chestnut tree, shouting angry taunts at a small group of older children who'd gathered at the foot.

'Cameron.' Francine heaved, she was so out of breath. 'Get back … down here this minute.'

'*No!*' he yelled rudely.

The sky began to spin as Francine squinted up at him. As she leaned against the tree, gasping for breath, she wondered how on earth her entire life had swung so quickly from such a high to this desperate low.

Chapter 7

Saul was devastated. When Jodi got back to the cottage, he was curled in a ball on the sofa, sobbing. 'Cameron hates me, doesn't he?'

'No, sweetheart, he's just having a bad day. I think he was embarrassed about breaking the mirror so he got angry and upset,' Jodi explained.

'Will he still be angry tomorrow?' Saul looked nervous. 'He bit Katie this morning and I don't know why.'

'Well,' Jodi said, 'sometimes children lash out when they're feeling bad. I'm sure he feels awful after he's been mean.'

'I think I'll play with Peter and Rebecca tomorrow. They don't bite or kick ever,' Saul decided.

'Okay, sweetheart,' Jodi said. She wanted Saul to enjoy school but her heart broke for poor Cameron. It was only the first week and he seemed to be leaving a trail of destruction in his wake. Jodi knew all too well what it was like being a marked child.

As Jodi gazed at Saul, worrying about whether or not Cameron would be his friend the following day, she was overcome with a wave of protective love.

'Saul,' she clasped his little hands in her own, 'no matter what happens, you're going to have lots of friends in school. Today's play date wasn't brilliant but the next one will be better, I promise.'

ᚼ

The next morning Mr Matthews greeted them cheerfully. 'Would you like to go over to the easel and do a painting, Saul?' he asked.

'Can I bring my picture home to Mum later?'

'Of course you can. Let's get started.'

Jodi watched for a moment, wanting to make sure Saul was happy.

'Everything all right?' Mr Matthews asked.

'Yes and no,' Jodi found herself admitting in a whisper. 'We had a play date yesterday. Saul's first ever. It was an unmitigated disaster and I'm a bit anxious he's going to struggle here today.'

'He's a good kid. I wouldn't worry about him. He's really outgoing and well able to hold his own.'

'Good,' Jodi said.

'I'll keep an eye on him for you and let you know how he got on at home time.'

'I'd appreciate that,' Jodi sighed. 'I expect I'm worrying needlessly. It's probably me rather than him having trouble settling in here.'

'I know the feeling,' said Mr Matthews. 'I felt like a real fish out of water when I arrived a few weeks ago. I didn't even leave my apartment for the first six days!' He grinned. 'But I ventured to the pub one evening and was astonished by how friendly the locals are. Give it a chance and I'd say you'll love it around here too.'

'Thanks,' Jodi said.

Mr Matthews smiled and Jodi felt her cheeks heating.

In the corridor, she sidestepped the women gathered there and hurried out of the building. She wasn't sure if Francine had been waiting in the bushes or simply skulking out of sight of the other parents, but the woman pounced as she neared the front gate.

'Francine, what on earth are you doing?'

'I need a word. Can you come and sit in my car for a minute, please?'

'Sure. What's up?'

'I have to chat to you about yesterday.' Francine was looking ten years older. 'I can't begin to tell you how dreadful I feel about the whole drama.'

'Don't worry, Francine. Kids will be kids,' Jodi said calmly. 'Starting school is a massive step for them and I'm sure Cameron'll settle down soon.'

'I wish it was just that, but I'm terrified it's more,' Francine said. 'All I've done over the last twelve hours is cry. Carl tried to tell me I'm over-analysing the whole thing and it'll all blow over but I'm not so sure.'

'I see,' Jodi said, although she didn't really.

'The signs have been there, but I've chosen not to take any heed,' she continued. 'I've been hoping against hope that it's a phase or even that he was coming down with chickenpox or a virus ...'

'Maybe he is,' Jodi ventured.

'Honestly, I don't think so.' Fresh tears threatened, and Francine ducked to root in her bag for a tissue.

'Do you want to come to my house and have a coffee?' Jodi offered. 'I'm probably not the best agony aunt you'll ever meet, but I can listen if that's any good.'

'If it's all the same to you, can we go to mine?'

'Was my coffee that bad?' Jodi smiled.

'Worse.' Francine managed a watery smile.

'At least you're honest.'

'Eh, Jodi ...' Francine took a deep breath.

'Yes?'

'Please may I ask you to keep all this conversation under your hat?'

'I'm the queen of keeping secrets,' Jodi assured her. 'I wouldn't dream of discussing your private business with anyone else. Besides, I don't really know anyone else around here.'

'Thank you.' Francine heaved a deep sigh of relief.

They drove through the village and out the other side, then turned into a small cul-de-sac with a stone plinth marked 'Verbena Drive'.

'This is lovely,' Jodi said politely. Twenty years ago this would've been all her dreams incarnate: a small, intimate, community-based development with large but not imposing houses. But years of living out of a suitcase with nowhere to call home had left Jodi longing for a house like no other, in an area where hustle and bustle took a back seat.

'Welcome, and please come in,' Francine said proudly.

'How long have you lived here?' Jodi peered inside tentatively.

'Just over four years.' Francine led the way to the kitchen.

The house was large, with higher than average ceilings, marble flooring, chandeliers and sweeping curtains held back by thick silk ropes with tassels.

The kitchen was spotless.

'Did you actually feed four kids and two adults in here less than an hour ago?' Jodi asked, astonished. 'Saul poured Coco Pops all over my kitchen earlier and I made a cup of my brew and the place is like a war zone!'

'We had pancakes this morning,' Francine said. 'I'm a firm believer in cleaning up as I go along. I run a tight ship, as Carl says.' She smiled. 'It was essential. I've had to juggle my time for many years.'

Jodi perched on a shiny high stool and within moments Francine had produced freshly brewed coffee complete with frothy milk and a home-baked cake. The pale fudge-coloured icing looked achingly sweet yet delicious.

As Jodi took a mouthful, her eyes rolled in delight. 'OMG! This is to die for! Please tell me you had it delivered or catered!'

'Not on your life. I pride myself on my baking. And that Aga you have in your house is crying out to be used to its full potential,' Francine told her.

'And the coffee is yum. I never normally drink it because it's bad for my skin and all that yadda-yadda – but this is worth the wrinkles.'

Francine beamed, feeling vaguely absolved of Cameron's appalling behaviour. 'About Cameron yesterday ... None of my other children ever acted like that,' she began, as she sat on a stool opposite Jodi. 'He's a law unto himself. It's like he goes into a place where I can't reach him. I'm terrified he's going to become a serious problem.'

'How long has it been happening?' Jodi said, trying not to stuff cake into her mouth. 'Sorry, but this is so delicious I can't get enough of it!'

'I'm ashamed to say it's probably been going on a long time,' Francine said. 'I rang Annie last night. She's our childminder.' Jodi nodded again. 'It turns out she's been having a total nightmare with Cameron for ages.'

'Why didn't she tell you?' Jodi asked.

Francine dropped her head into her hands and began to sob.

'She said she'd tried to but I wouldn't listen. I feel so ashamed. I was so caught up in my job, the house, the cooking, Carl, the other children ...' She looked utterly miserable as she gazed at Jodi. 'I was busy being perfect and didn't notice my son was running wild.'

'Don't be too hard on yourself. Stuff like this happens. You're aware of it now so you can deal with it, right?'

'I suppose,' Francine said.

'I'm sure his antics are normal for a small kid, no?'

'No.' Francine's voice was barely above a whisper. 'I think it's more than that. His anger and frustration aren't normal. He becomes violent at the flick of a switch and flies off the handle. He's very sorry and totally wrung out at the end of it, but it's just not good enough.'

Jodi saw real pain in Francine's face.

'I'm terrified he's not going to behave at school and we'll be asked to take him out. He's been there just two days and he's already causing havoc.'

'Can't you take him to a child psychologist or something?' Jodi asked.

'I know all you movie stars think shrinks are the norm, but here in Bakers Valley that sort of thing is still taboo. I wouldn't even know where to start looking for one.'

'I'm sure the school would be able to advise you better than I can,' Jodi said. 'It might be that he needs some help with social skills or something quite simple.'

'Oh, good Lord, no! I wouldn't *ever* tell the school how I feel. Imagine if it got out to the other committee members that I have a child who requires medical intervention!' Francine looked stricken.

'But surely it's more important that Cameron gets the attention he needs.' Jodi was perplexed.

'Jodi, I pride myself on being an upstanding pillar of the village community. Being looked up to and admired is what makes me tick,' Francine said, dropping her eyes. 'If my friends thought I was falling apart at the seams I'd die of shame.'

'But if they're really your friends, surely they'll understand and want to support you,' Jodi said gently.

'Yes ...' Francine hesitated, '... there is that, but there's always a boundary within friendships. We all need to keep up our guard to some extent. That's the unwritten law of dynamics, isn't it?'

Jodi had always assumed that falseness only existed in her work circle. Actors were renowned for being fickle and cut-throat. That was a given. But part of the reason Jodi had moved herself and Saul to Bakers Valley was to escape that world of pretence. She'd been desperate to raise her son in a more 'real' environment in which people still lived by old-fashioned values, accepted and supported one another. Surely the whole world wasn't playing make-believe.

Jodi spent the entire morning in Francine's kitchen. For the first time in her life, another woman was taking her into her confidence.

Francine talked about her love for Carl and how she'd been so mindful in planning each step of their lives. 'Now I can't help feeling I've failed,' she concluded. 'Look at me! I'm a sobbing mess.'

'You haven't failed, Francine,' Jodi said. 'The only fault I can find in all of this is that you're too hard on yourself. You're a good person and a great mother. I'm sure everything will work out for the best.' She glanced at her watch. 'Look at the time! We'd better get back to collect the boys.'

'I feel like I just wore the ear off you and moaned. Next time I'll try to be a little less suicidal!'

'I really enjoyed the chat. It's lovely to spend a morning talking about real stuff. In my job it's either filming or interviews, which may sound very glam but it's actually exhausting. I'm delighted you felt you could talk to me.'

CB

At the school a short time later, Francine got out of her car and waved at the group of mothers. Her confidence had returned. She turned to Jodi and asked her again not to tell anyone about their conversation.

'Mum's the word.' Jodi smiled.

Francine linked her arm and walked her to the school door.

'Hello, you two,' Jane said, as they approached, unable to hide her envy that Francine had obviously spent the morning with Jodi Ludlum.

'Hi, everyone. How was your morning? Jodi and I were so naughty – we had all sorts to do and ended up in my kitchen gossiping, didn't we?' Francine said.

'Yeah,' Jodi said. She had no problem with Francine wanting to keep their conversation under wraps, but the pretence was a little too Hollywood for her comfort.

'No doubt I'll spend the rest of the day chasing my tail but sometimes we all need a good old natter!' Francine flicked her hair, took a deep breath and strutted towards the classroom door to collect her son.

Jodi had to admit she was stumped. Francine was wasted in Bakers Valley. She should be phoning Noelle on the spot and telling her there was an actress of epic talent just waiting to be discovered.

'*Muuuum!*' Saul shouted, charging over to her.

'Hey, monster, how was school?'

'*Sooo* fun!' Saul said, hugging her. 'Me and Max made a T. Rex from Play-Doh. He has big teeth and everything!'

'Cool!'

'Can Max come tomorrow for a play date? His mum is over there in the red jacket,' Saul begged. 'He's really gentle and I know he won't smash my stuff. Please, Mum? *Pleeease.*'

Jodi glanced around her, hoping Francine hadn't heard what Saul had said.

'Give me a minute.' She steeled herself to approach the tall blonde who was talking to another glamorous woman. Jodi was astounded by the mothers' style. From perfect hair and makeup to up-to-the-minute fashions, the school car park posed as much pressure for her as a red carpet. Her idea of spending her time in Ireland free of makeup and dressed in tracksuits was fading fast. Being a full-time mother wasn't as relaxed as she'd thought. It went far beyond raising a child: it was a whole new world she knew nothing about. As she came up to the small huddle of chatting mothers, she inhaled the waft of delicate fragrance and took in their beautifully manicured hands.

'Sorry to interrupt, ladies, but is one of you Max's mum?' she enquired politely.

'I am. Beatrice Williams, pleased to meet you, Jodi Ludlum.' She smiled. 'I'm a huge fan and beyond delighted you've joined the school. Nothing like a movie star to shake us all up – in a good way!' she joked.

'Thank you.' Jodi blushed.

'I hope Max isn't causing your little fella any grief?'

'No, the opposite. Saul would love Max to come and play, if you were open to that?'

'I'm sure he'd love to. The only snag is that I'm back to work tomorrow. I can only afford to take the first few days of term off. Once I know he and his older sister are settled, the childminder takes over and it's business as usual,' Beatrice explained. 'I run the pharmacy in the town and I have to ask an agency guy to come in and cover for me, which is a bit of a juggle.'

'I can pick up Max and bring him home, if you like?'

'That'd be super. Thank you,' said Beatrice.

As Jodi and Saul walked home and Saul chattered about the friends he was making, she knew with certainty that she'd made the right decision, despite the misgivings she'd had. Ireland was her original home, after all. And Saul was thriving in Bakers Valley.

When Jodi opened the front door, a trickle of sudsy water crept towards her feet. 'Oh, cripes! Where's that coming from?' Jodi screeched, as the landline began to ring.

Saul ran to answer it. 'Daddy! ... I found another friend today and he's called Max. He doesn't bite or anything!'

As Saul talked to Darius, Jodi ran into the kitchen. The water seemed to be coming from the big corrugated pipe at the rear of the washing machine. Puzzled, she went outside to the small boiler house. From the corner of her eye, she saw Sebastian's combine harvester making its way down the field. As he drew closer, Jodi ran to the fence and waved her arms to attract his attention. Thankfully, he pulled up and jumped down.

'Sebastian!' she said. 'I've a bit of a disaster on my hands. There seems to be a leak but I can't figure out where it's coming from.'

Sebastian went inside the boiler house to investigate. 'So you're not from around here then?' he said, as he pulled at tubes and pipes.

'Well, I was born in Dublin.'

'You don't sound like a Dub.'

'I left Ireland in my teens,' she replied, suddenly conscious of her accent, which she hadn't been for a very long time. Not since the day she'd realised her strong Dublin brogue was hindering her career.

'I used to talk like *dat*,' Jodi said now, flicking into the accent she'd been taught not to use.

Sebastian grinned. 'Why did you change?'

'I wanted to become an actor and there weren't many roles for people like me. So I became someone else.'

Sebastian looked at her intently. 'I'll tighten that joint in the pipe,' he said, changing the subject abruptly, 'but you may need to get a proper plumber in to look at it.'

'Thanks,' said Jodi. 'Would you like tea or coffee?'

'I've got my flask, thanks. As I mentioned to you before, I'm already behind schedule with the harvest this year. I need to get the rest of the corn cut, so I'll be making a bit of noise up the back fields over the next while,' he explained.

'Do you run the farm on your own?' Jodi asked.

'Pretty much. The same group of lads come and help during the busy times, but the rest of the year it's just myself and two others.'

'You said your son doesn't live with you any longer. Do you live in the big house on your own?' Jodi wondered.

'You ask a lot of questions.' Sebastian wasn't smiling but he didn't appear to be annoyed.

'Sorry.' She shrugged. 'I'm trying to get used to village life and I'm finding it totally different from what I'd envisaged,' she said honestly.

'How so?'

'Well, the full-time-mother thing is a lot trickier than I'd imagined. Have you seen the mums at the school?' She whistled. 'I'm going to have to spruce myself up if I'm to make my son proud. And I'll have to pay more attention to my catering skills.'

'I wouldn't stress too much. I used to worry what other people thought once upon a time,' Sebastian said, 'but then I realised that being yourself is more important.' He closed his eyes briefly, as if he was blocking something out. 'Anyway, that pipe looks like it should hold for now,' he said.

'Thank you so much. What do I owe you?' Jodi said, ready to run for her purse.

'Ah, go on out of that,' Sebastian said. He smiled and his voice was softer now. 'Keep your front door shut if you're bothered by mice. The combine harvester tends to uproot them and they go running for shelter.'

'Seriously? Give me a spider the size of your head but I can't cope with rodents of any shape or size,' she said, biting her lip. 'Ugh, their little scratchy paws and long wiry tails give me the heebie-jeebies.' She shuddered.

'Good luck with that, living at the edge of a cornfield,' he deadpanned. Then he walked back to the combine harvester, climbed into the cab and started the engine.

∞

Unsure of what to do with herself, Jodi walked back into the cosiness of the cottage. Saul was on the rug in the sitting room making sound effects as he played with a car. Jodi made straight for the kitchen area and mopped up the wet mess from before. When she'd finished, she went to sit on the sofa. 'Come here,' she said.

'What's wrong, Mum?' he asked, climbing onto her lap.

'Not a thing,' she crooned, as she hugged him close. 'You are the most wonderful child in the world. Do you know that?' she asked.

'You're the bestest mummy ever,' he said, grabbing her ears and kissing her face.

As they rolled back on the sofa and she tickled him, Jodi thanked her lucky stars that she'd managed to dig herself out of the life Destiny had originally dealt her. Perhaps she'd been sent a special sat nav system by a guardian angel, or maybe she'd just been in the right place at the right time when the talent spotter had walked into her school all those years ago. She knew, though, that she'd never take her new life and career for granted.

She was about to look for a DVD to watch when her mobile phone rang.

'Hello,' she said happily.

'Babes! Long time no speak!'

Jodi froze. 'How did you get this number?' Glancing at Saul, she was relieved to see he was clicking a car track together, oblivious to her. She went quickly to her bedroom and shut the door. 'I told you to keep away from me. The game is over, Mac. Leave me alone.'

'Ah, don't be like that, Jodi. I'm your Mac, remember? I love you to the moon and back.'

With shaking hands, Jodi turned off the phone and threw it on to the bed. Wrapping her arms around herself, she was suddenly cold and scared.

Chapter 8

Francine was baking as if her life depended on it. It was Thursday of the following week and she'd already enough cakes, scones and cookies to feed the country, let alone the mothers of the school. As her second child-free week had loomed, she'd filled her time by clearing out all the rooms in the house. The bedclothes had been changed and everything she could lay her hands on was ironed. The garden looked manicured and the weekly shop was done. Last weekend had been fine: she and the children had welcomed the extra hour in bed and less frenzied weekend routine.

But this Saturday was going to be interesting, she mused. Normally she spent the morning ferrying the children from one activity to another, cooked lunch, compiled her list for the supermarket and went to buy what they needed. If she didn't do it then, the rest of the week would be mayhem.

But she'd been at a loose end so she'd done it today. She'd even written the menus for next week, updated all her index cards and tidied her already tidy desk drawers.

Francine knew time was running out. She was going to have to tell the girls that she was no longer working. She thought of different ways of putting it.

'I've chosen to take a career break ...' Nobody would believe that. 'Carl doesn't want me to work outside the home any more.' Farcical. 'The economic downturn has knocked me off my perch but I'll find work again soon.' As she spoke those truthful words aloud to the coffee plunger, she felt like sobbing.

Sighing, she weighed the flour for an orange cake. It was one she could freeze, so it wouldn't go to waste if it wasn't eaten. Raising the sieve high in the air, she tried to enjoy watching the cascading white flour hit the creamy butter, sugar and egg mixture.

The fiasco with Saul at Jodi's house had rattled her badly. Jodi had been so lovely when they'd had the big chat, but Francine had woken sweating in the middle of the night afterwards. She couldn't *ever* be friends with Jodi now. There was no way she could find an equal footing with her. Who was she kidding? She was a deranged housewife with a thug of a child, and Jodi was an international superstar with an angelic little boy and a pin-up for a husband.

Francine laughed bitterly to herself as she dolloped cake mixture into the tin. She'd have to avoid Jodi and most of Bakers Valley until things calmed down.

To add insult to injury, Cameron had cried and kicked up so badly this morning when she'd tried to say goodbye to him that one of the teachers from another class had been called to help restrain him as she was instructed to leave.

'We'll call you if he doesn't settle shortly,' Mr Matthews had shouted, over the screams. The shame of it all. Just as she was putting the cake into the oven, her landline rang, making her jump and burn her hand on the stove.

'Hello?' she answered, wincing and licking her hand.

'Mrs Hennessy, this is Mr Matthews, Cameron's teacher.'

The voice wasn't over-friendly. The statement wasn't followed by anything reassuring like 'It's nothing serious,' or 'Don't worry, but ...'

'Hello there. Is everything okay now?'

'I've had a bit of an incident with Cameron – again. I let it go the last time, but I'm afraid he's bitten another child.'

'Oh dear.' Francine felt sick.

'I put the first time down to beginning-of-term behaviour,' Mr Matthews continued. 'But a short while ago he deliberately took another child's hand in his own, raised it to his mouth and bit until he drew blood.'

'Oh, dear Lord,' Francine whispered.

'Mrs Hennessy, I'm concerned because there was no provocation for the attack. In fact, Cameron wasn't even interacting with the other child prior to the incident.'

'I'm so sorry,' Francine said. She honestly thought she was going to pass out.

'I've spoken to the principal and we feel Cameron might need help with social skills.'

'Isn't this a bit rushed? Surely he's entitled to make a couple of mistakes without being branded,' Francine said, in terror. 'I mean, he's only been there five minutes. Perhaps if we allow him to settle in he'll calm down. How about myself and Carl have a serious word with him this evening and get back to you tomorrow?'

Mr Matthews didn't respond.

'I promise Carl and I will have a long chat with Cameron. I'll be up at the school in the morning for the welcome coffee morning and I'll pop in to see you afterwards,' Francine said. 'I really appreciate you bringing this to my attention so swiftly and I give you my word I'll get to the bottom of it. Do you need me to call the mother of the little boy Cameron bit?'

'I just spoke with Saul's mother and she said she didn't need to take the matter any further for the moment,' Mr Matthews told her. 'She was very nice about it, actually, so it might be best to leave it.'

Francine put the phone down and burst out crying. Why was Cameron behaving in this way?

Her conversation with Annie niggled at her. She'd apparently been having trouble with Cameron for a while, but Francine figured it couldn't have been as bad as this or the other woman would've cracked up.

Francine marched into her office. On the shelf, above the index-card boxes, were four leather-bound volumes. One for each of their children. Selecting Cameron's, she flicked through the pages.

She'd carefully documented each pregnancy, then each stage of each child's life. She was planning to keep the books and present them on their twenty-first birthdays.

Cameron's book contained everything from a diary entry on the day she'd had her pregnancy confirmed by the doctor, to his scan photographs, right down to the tiny hospital bracelets he'd worn on his ankle and wrist. As she speed-read through, nothing jumped out at her. She hadn't had any unusual illnesses during her pregnancy, no raised blood pressure or other cause for concern. There seemed no logical explanation for Cameron's behaviour.

She pulled the volumes down one by one. At age two – or even three, in Cara's case – they'd all had their fair share of tantrums. One little story she'd written in Cara's book documented a down-on-the-floor-kicking incident in the toyshop: *Cara wanted the pink My Little Pony so badly she hooked her arm around the leg of the metal shelving unit at Toy City and sobbed her heart out!!*

Francine had thought little stories like that one would make them all smile in years to come. They were the details that were forgotten as the children grew up. It was for good-natured reminiscing, though, rather than a medical-based logging of any behaviour pattern.

Cameron's book told similar stories, although as she thumbed through the pages she realised there were far more of them.

> *Today Cameron made his mark on the world. During his first ever visit to the supermarket he screamed so loudly for so long that the manager came and helped me lift my groceries into the car! He must've been pretty bad if a man in a suit noticed!*

Now the story wasn't quite so cute. Maybe the signs had been there from day one. Moving on a few pages, Francine felt her heart stop as she read an entry from a year and half previously:

> *Cameron seems to have realised he can use his teeth for more than eating. He bit a little girl at the park today. At first I was horrified, but once we all calmed down, myself and the little girl's mother managed to get the toddlers to hug. Ah, his first hug – aged 2½. Lock up your daughters, mummies!*

Francine slid all the books back on to the shelf and went into the kitchen. She sat at the table and stared into space. Then she picked up her mobile and dialled Carl's direct number at work. She breathed a sigh of relief when he answered.

'Carl Hennessy speaking.'

'Carl, it's me.' Francine knew she sounded like a woman possessed but she couldn't help it. 'I've had Mr Matthews on the phone. It seems the school are convinced Cameron has behavioural difficulties.'

'What?'

'You heard.'

'Francine, I'm about to go into a meeting. What's going on, honey?'

'He bit Jodi Ludlum's son and made him bleed. He's been lashing out at the other kids all week. What are we going to do?'

'I have to go, honey. We'll talk to him later on. Kids bite. They kick and fight and say nasty stuff. That's what they do,' Carl said. 'Don't beat yourself up over it. I'll talk to him later on – have a man-to-man chat. How's that?' There was a little chuckle in his voice.

'Okay then,' Francine said. 'Bye.'

There was nothing Carl could do from his office. She really needed to think of a solution to this herself. First she should have a very frank question-and-answer session with Annie.

'Hello, Annie,' she said, when the other woman answered her phone.

'Francine!'

'You sound happy!'

'I'm having a lovely time. I'm with my sister in the shopping centre. We're having a bit of a boozy lunch.'

Francine glanced at her watch. 'It's only eleven thirty in the morning, Annie.' She couldn't hide her shock and disgust.

'We hadn't intended on doing this but we're at the champagne bar in the food hall!' Annie giggled.

'Well, I won't keep you,' Francine said tightly. 'Maybe you'd give me a call over the next few days?'

'Sure talk to me now. What's up?'

'Ah, no, I won't spoil your day.'

'Francine. You can't do that to me. Spit it out, woman.'

'Well, it's a little delicate and I'm not sure I want your sister listening in ...'

'I tell her everything so you might as well say it,' Annie said bluntly.

Gosh, thought Francine. Annie's not that nice when she's drinking. A sudden thought hit her. Was the woman an alcoholic? Was she drinking all the time when she was minding Cameron? That might explain things. Panic washed through her.

'Annie, I need you to answer me honestly. Did you drink during the day when you were minding my children?'

'I beg your pardon?' Annie said, bursting into giggles. When Francine didn't respond she stopped abruptly. 'Jesus, you're serious, aren't you?'

'It's a simple question and I'd like an answer.'

'Francine, you've known me for twelve years. When have I *ever* appeared drunk or incapable?' Annie's voice was rising by the second.

'Annie, please. Don't get so antsy. I was only asking—'

'How dare you, Francine? I'm so hurt you could ask me that. If you must know, my sister insisted I come out with her for the day so I could relax and unwind a little.' Annie paused. 'To be honest, I was at the end of my tether with my job. Much as I love those children of yours, it had got to the point with Cameron where I couldn't have coped any longer. If you hadn't ended our arrangement, *I* would have.'

'Oh ...' Francine's voice was barely above a whisper. 'I see ...'

'I'm sorry, Francine. This is all coming out wrong. It's not the way I wanted things to end after so long. But now that I've said it, I'm afraid I'm going to have to stand by it ...' Annie trailed off. Then she went on, 'Cameron is extremely difficult to manage. His behaviour causes untold problems. It's affecting your other children and, by God, it was beginning to seriously affect me. I did try to tell you …'

'Annie, I'm so sorry I didn't listen to you before now. I'm sorry I haven't been in contact with you since terminating our arrangement. I'm sorry I've caused you so much anxiety. I'm sorry—'

'Francine?' Annie interrupted. 'Take it easy, pet. You're starting to really worry me.'

'Oh, please, Annie, don't you go worrying yourself,' she said, injecting brightness into her tone. 'I shouldn't have bothered you. Go and have your lunch with your sister. I'll talk to you again, but for now, please accept my sincere apologies.' Francine pressed the red button on the phone and cradled it to her chest. Tears coursed down her cheeks. She had always believed the Lord worked in mysterious ways. Her mother, God rest her, had been a very religious woman and had drummed into her that everything happens for a reason. Cameron needed her to be here. Maybe it was only for a while, until he calmed down, but her youngest child had a problem and she needed to fix it.

All too soon it was time to collect Cameron and she'd have to face Jodi too. This wasn't the way she had planned it. She was Francine Hennessy. Her children weren't guttersnipes or bullies. That sort of child only came from a broken home or an underprivileged background, didn't it?

Suddenly Francine wasn't so sure any more. For the first time since her children had started school, she didn't want to show her face there.

☙

As she approached the school gates that lunchtime Francine's heartbeat quickened. The upset she'd experienced that morning had left her feeling so vulnerable and shaken, she was afraid the other mothers would be able to see the hellish emotions she was desperate to hide. More than that, she was terrified word had spread about what Cameron had done that morning.

'Ah, here she is now. The woman of the moment,' Jane said, doing a mock bow as Francine approached the classroom door.

'Sorry?' Francine said, horrified. 'How can you make a joke of it? It's a very serious matter. I'm actually in an awful state ...'

'Hey, I was only kidding,' Jane said, clearly shocked. 'I'm only having a bit of fun with you, Francine, love. We were just talking about tomorrow and how you've managed to muster up great interest during the last two weeks among the mothers as usual ...'

'Well, I'm glad you all think it's a laugh because I certainly don't,' Francine snapped.

'I think you're getting the wrong end of the stick,' Andrea ventured, in an attempt to stick up for poor Jane, who looked as if she was about to burst into tears.

'Yes, of course!' Francine said, back-tracking. 'I'm suffering with one of my migraines today, girls. Don't mind me. I'm on another planet. Apologies. I just had a painkiller so I'm sure I'll feel better shortly.'

'I didn't know you got migraine,' Jane said suspiciously. 'Is everything all right?'

'Of course it is.' She forced a winning smile. 'I'll be fine once the tablets kick in.'

'Here are the children now,' Andrea said, slightly too cheerfully.

'Catch you all in the morning,' Francine said. 'I just need to have a quiet little word with Mr Matthews.'

'I'll be you do!' Jane said, with a snigger.

'What's that supposed to mean?' Francine's head jerked up.

'Ah, come off it, Francine,' Jane said, elbowing her. 'Migraine or not, you've still got eyes. He's a fine thing. Don't tell me you haven't noticed that every mother in the school has attended to their grey roots and started wearing plunging necklines.'

'He's like Bakers Valley's answer to Harry Styles,' Andrea said.

'Yeah, our own little poster boy. He's hardly going to look twice at any of us but it's lovely to window-shop all the same,' Sarah said, giggling.

'Speak for yourself, I'm single,' one of the mothers piped up.

'I'm waiting to speak to Mr Matthews for personal reasons,' Francine said, snappy again.

'I'm telling Carl!' Jane teased.

At least the women were so busy being smutty they hadn't noticed her anxiety, Francine thought.

She waited for the children to pour out before she went into the classroom, looking extremely sheepish. 'How has Cameron been since your call?' she asked Mr Matthews, almost afraid to hear the answer.

'Very quiet,' he said, 'which one might think is a good thing, but to be honest with you, he's either manic or silent. I really feel he's struggling and needs help.'

Mr Matthews seemed about to say more but Francine cut him off quickly.

'Okay, that's fine. I'll chat to you tomorrow,' she said. Now she'd established Cameron hadn't done anything else, she wanted to get him out of there immediately. 'Say goodbye to Mr

Matthews,' she instructed Cameron, as she grabbed his hand.

Mr Matthews held his hand up and Cameron gave him a high five.

'See you tomorrow, buddy. Let's hope it's a better day for you, yeah?'

Cameron ran out to join the other children, who were playing on the grass while the mothers chatted.

Francine was glad they didn't all stop talking as she approached.

'Sure I've already pulled out half my wardrobe and tried it on. None of it seems right when I picture myself standing beside Jodi Ludlum,' one woman said.

'I know what you mean,' Andrea agreed. 'It's not easy to get it right. Especially when most of us have worn our entire repertoire for Mr Matthews already!'

They all cackled.

'Seriously, we don't want to turn up in ballgowns but at the same time she might think we're a right pack of skangers if we pitch up in tracksuits and flip-flops. Do you reckon it might be a bit much to ask her to pose for a photo? I'd love a picture of her and me as the wallpaper on my iPhone.'

'Ladies, please!' Francine exclaimed. 'For a start, Andrea, when have you ever come to one of our coffee mornings in sports wear? And we can't all act like the paparazzi. Seriously!'

'I reckon if you stand beside her, Andrea, I can get a few sneaky pics with my phone from the other side of the room where she won't spot me,' Jane said. 'If you make sure you're close enough it'll be fine. Lean in to whisper something funny and I'll grab the moment.'

'What'll I say?' Andrea was gobsmacked.

'I don't know, do I?' Jane said. 'Say something like "I'd bet this is a far cry from Los Angeles," or "Did you ever see yourself standing in a school hall drinking tea from a metal urn rather than on location in Zimbabwe?"'

'Why would she be in Zimbabwe?' Andrea wondered.

'Well, wasn't one of her movies set there?' Jane said.

'No, that was New Zealand.'

'Ah, you know what I mean,' Jane said, irritated. 'I wish I could fit into skinny jeans. I'd wear dark denim ones with high-heeled boots and a trendy tweed jacket. Not a Farmer Brown-style one, a cool nipped-in-at-the-waist one. That'd give the right tailored-and-suave impression without making me look like a dog's dinner.'

'Go and get a pair of jeggings, why don't you?' Andrea suggested.

'And have my mutton-chop thighs on show? God, no, we're trying to befriend Jodi, not offend her with my cellulite.' Jane groaned.

'We could go back to the slimming club again this year. Aren't they offering free joining this month?' Andrea said.

'Yeah, but there's no point,' Sarah put in. 'We just go along, get the folder of stuff, drink their herbal tea to the point of drowning for two days, buy a load of their snacks and never go back.'

'I suppose. I think I'm the only person who goes to those things and puts on weight,' Jane agreed. 'I buy the bars and shakes, eat and drink them for a day or so and get so ravenously hungry I end up guzzling twice the amount I normally do.'

'Any time I take exercise I put on weight,' Andrea admitted. 'I walk for twenty minutes and stop off to buy the papers, head into the coffee shop and eat a doorstep of chocolate cake with a bucket of cappuccino because I've burned so many calories I deserve it.'

'We could always take a photo of Mr Marvellous and stick it on our fridges. Every time you feel like stuffing your face you'll remember you have to see him. That might work,' Jane said.

'You might be on to something.' Sarah giggled. 'Especially if we ask him to pose in those ripped jeans he wears *without* the T-shirt.'

'None of you is going to morph into someone else by tomorrow morning, and I think it's highly inappropriate to speak about our children's teacher like that. Here's Jodi now, too. Have a bit of cop on, girls, and stop talking like a group of mindless gossips, please. I'll see you all in the morning, shall I?' Francine said.

'See you, Francine.' Jane was looking at her intently.

As she got into the car Francine saw Jane, Andrea and Sarah huddled together. They were probably commenting on how narky she'd been, she thought miserably.

Mr Matthews was very good-looking and he seemed to have a great way with the children, but she simply wasn't in the mood for ogling anyone. Francine also knew she was going to have to come clean about her stay-at-home status.

In the back seat Cameron was humming to himself, seemingly oblivious to all the commotion he'd caused that morning.

'What happened with Saul today?' she said, as they drove out of the gate.

'He was doing a jigsaw and sitting beside Max,' he said.

'And why did you decide to bite him?'

'I only wanted him to be *my* friend. Now he's cross with me.'

'You can't expect him to want to be your buddy if you're mean to him,' Francine said.

'"Three blind mice. See how they run. They all ran after—"'

'Cameron!' Francine said. 'Did you hear what I said?'

'"Three blind mice. See how—"'

'Stop it!' she shrilled. Her stress level was rising like the evening tide.

෮ଓ

Cameron adored the PlayStation and most of the time Francine was *über*-strict about how long he spent in front of it each day but today she was grateful for the distraction.

'You can play for a while if you promise to turn it off when I say,' she warned him.

Francine knew she must talk to Carl properly when he got home but that wouldn't be for hours yet. To keep busy, she sat in her office and did a bit of swotting with her index cards. Once, this had brought her immense pleasure, as she sifted through the various classes and reminded herself of little idiosyncrasies connected with the various mothers.

Joan Byrne

Mother to Niamh (born 2000) in Cara's class

Married to Fred

Lives in Downs Avenue

Has prize-winning cocker spaniel called Lady (black and white), which she seems to prefer to her daughter – if there's a lull in conversation mention the dog and her mood lifts.

Francine took out the card and jotted in the new information.

Youngest child Mark (born 2009) in Cameron's class. The dog is still favoured although she seems to tolerate a noticeable amount of backchat from Mark.

Happy that she'd reminded herself of the dog's name, she shoved the card back in the correct place. She really ought to do some more of this, but her heart wasn't in it.

☙

That night when Carl returned home he was exhausted. 'It's been a long day. I've had so many meetings I'm hoarse,' he said. 'Would you mind if we discuss the issue with Cameron at the weekend?'

'Of course, love,' she said. She didn't want to become one of those wives who nagged her husband constantly.

By the time everyone else in the house was asleep Francine was lying awake in the stillness feeling very alone, fearing the following day. She'd have to make certain she was extremely busy when Jodi arrived. That way she wouldn't have to face any questions from her.

Chapter 9

It was almost ten o'clock in the evening by the time Darius's taxi pulled up outside the cottage.

'Hi,' Jodi said, as they hugged.

'I'm sorry I'm so late. We were grounded at Heathrow for nearly three hours,' he said. 'Luckily my driver waited so I could leave the airport by the side entrance.' Darius waved at the limousine that had delivered him, then shut the cottage door.

'Wow, babe, this is divine,' he said. 'I love what you've done with the décor.'

'Well, it wasn't me personally.' She grinned.

'Fair enough, but it's gorgeous!'

'Thanks, hon. Were there many photographers waiting for you at the airport?' she asked.

'There were a few, but I think the wait put them off,' he said, yawning. 'I presume Monster Man's asleep?'

'Yeah, but I promised you'd go in and give him a hug the second you arrived,' she said. 'Come on. I'll show you his room. You'll see it better in the morning but it's so cute!'

'Daddy!' Saul croaked sleepily, as Darius bent to kiss him.

'Hey, Monster Man!' Darius said, hugging him tightly and burying his face in his son's hair. 'Oh, my goodness, you're twice the size you were the last time I saw you!'

'No, I'm not. It's only three weeks, you silly!' Saul said. But it was obvious he liked the idea that he'd grown so quickly.

'You go back to sleep and I'll see you in the morning for breakfast, okay?' he said, stroking his son's cheek.

'Night-night, Daddy.' Cuddling down into his duvet, Saul promptly fell back to sleep.

'What have you done with him? Normally he'd be bouncing off the walls if he was woken up,' Darius said, as he shut Saul's bedroom door and followed Jodi back to the living room.

'He's wiped out every night now. I think it's the combination of school and the Irish air. Last Saturday he slept until nine thirty in the morning he was so exhausted.'

'So he's settled in school with no issues then?'

'Yeah, bar the fact that one of the kids practically tried to do a Hannibal Lecter on him.'

'What?'

'Yeah, this kid, Cameron, is going through a stage of biting and hitting, that sort of thing.'

'That doesn't sound good.'

'No, it's not, I suppose. But Mr Matthews has a handle on it all. He's an amazing teacher, Darius. He called me immediately after the incident and he was so reassuring.'

'Was he now?' Darius raised an eyebrow.

'He just *gets* the kids, you know? And he has this knack of putting people at ease.'

'Oh, I can imagine,' Darius said, with a wry smile.

'What?' Jodi said. 'But the situation with Cameron is really tricky, Darius. It's awful for his mother. I know she's totally mortified by it all. She's a really efficient and organised sort. One of the committee heads.'

'A bossy-boots, you mean?' Darius grinned.

'Yes and no,' Jodi said. 'I went to her house for coffee a few days ago and she was so nice to me. She made an effort to make me feel welcome and I liked being included.'

'Fair enough. She sounds like a bit of a pain in the ass to me,' Darius said doubtfully. 'What did her kid do to Saul?'

'Oh, it was all a bit cringy. He lashed out at Saul and when he and his mum came here for a play date he went off on a bit of a mad one.' Jodi grinned. 'And he bit Saul at school. He's only a little boy, though. Mr Matthews said that things like that happen. I'd hate to be too hard on him, Darius. I spent my childhood being judged by my mother's actions. I wouldn't want to judge another kid.'

'Being all Christian and forgiving is a beautiful thing,' Darius teased her. 'And I'm sure that what Mr Matthews says is gospel, except when it comes to our boy. Then all gloves are off and anyone who messes with him is fair game for the slaughter! Just keep Saul away from the little tyke. Or even better, tell your Mr Matthews to do it for you. That's what he's being paid for, isn't it?'

'Oh, stop it! He's not *my* Mr Matthews and you're making too much of this altercation. They're just kids. I shouldn't have told you! I'm sure they'll get along just fine in the end. Do you want food?' she asked.

'Uh, no, I had lots of starchy, sugary, awful stuff earlier on. I just want to go to bed. Where are we sleeping?'

'In here,' Jodi said proudly, and led him into their bedroom.

'I packed light. The people from *Celebrity Gossip* are doing all the clothes. I think they've got D&G to cover the shoot,' he said, as he carried his bag into the bedroom.

'So you brought enough stuff to do you for a month instead of two?' Jodi teased.

Any time they went on location or on holiday with Saul, it was Darius's bags that cost extra money because they were over the prescribed weight allowance. Jodi could manage with two outfits and a toothbrush at a push.

'This place is really sweet, Jodi. Oh, my stars!' he said. 'A boudoir fit for a princess!'

'Isn't it perfect?' She beamed.

'It's a lovely place for Saul to call home, honey. Good on you,' he said, hugging her.

'The bathroom's over there,' she said. 'That other door is my closet so don't pee on my shoes,' she joked.

'I'll be right with you,' he said, heading into the bathroom.

As he emerged in his usual night attire, which consisted of a pair of boxer shorts and nothing else, Jodi admired him. 'Looking good, cowboy!' she said. 'You're really fit for this movie, aren't you? God, you're gorgeous!' She whistled.

'Don't! You'll make my head swell.' He laughed. 'Actually, keep it up. I love to be admired. This movie is fairly physical so it's doing me the world of good. Now give me a hug,' he said, as he climbed into bed beside her.

'It's such a shame our marriage is a sham,' she said, for the umpteenth time since they'd met. 'Especially when you're looking as good as you are right now. Not that I'm fickle.' She giggled.

'We probably have a much more compatible marriage than ninety per cent of other couples,' Darius shot back.

'Probably,' Jodi agreed. 'When we first met, did you think we'd still be so close at this stage?' she asked, as she sat up and stared at him.

'Not on your life!' He sighed. 'We're wonderful together, babe,' he said, stroking her cheek. 'But it's going to have to end at some point, isn't it?'

'I know,' she said, as she snuggled into him.

Their marriage was one of Hollywood's most elaborate publicity stunts.

Noelle and Mike, their agents, had cooked it up several years previously.

Both their careers had been going in the right direction, they were building a healthy fan base and the public couldn't get enough of them. Women loved Darius and wanted to be Jodi.

But they had both harboured closely guarded secrets.

'When the fans adore you it's wonderful. But the flip side of the coin can mean you're treading on dangerous ground,' Jodi's agent Noelle had warned her, years before. 'You can end up being despised overnight. We need to keep this publicity machine rocking in the right direction. Once you have a more established loyal base you're less likely to be damaged, should any of the demons rear their ugly heads.'

Jodi could walk the walk and talk the talk when it came to acting but, deep down, she was still the same terrified little girl who'd clawed her way out of the life she'd been born into.

Just as Jodi was nominated for an Oscar for her most challenging role, Noelle had been tipped off that one of the tabloid papers had got hold of a story that might threaten her popularity. 'I honestly think this could ruin you if it comes out now,' she'd said gravely. 'Jodi, your past is one thing. People like a poor-girl-makes-good story but this ... this could be trouble. Why didn't you tell me about it before?'

'I couldn't,' Jodi said miserably. 'I didn't want you to think badly of me, Noelle.'

'Jodi, you have to learn to trust me. I'm your friend for a start, but I'm paid to make sure you shine like the star you are. I can't do that with deep, dark secrets lurking in the closet. I need you to open the door and let me in. Otherwise we could both be out of a job.'

'What can we do to stop the story ruining us?' Jodi asked, doe-eyed with fright.

'I have a very close alliance with Darius Drew's agent, Mike,' Noelle began.

'Right,' Jodi said, wondering where this was going.

'He's doing all he can to keep Darius out of the wrong type of limelight but the walls are closing in on him as well.'

'Oh dear.'

'Mike and I have a suggestion.'

'Go on,' Jodi said.

'We'd like you to agree to be a couple for a while. The press would love it and the fans would adore the thought of you two as the new A-list golden couple.'

'But what does Darius think of this notion?' Jodi asked. She'd never met him but, like most other women with a pulse, she liked what she saw on screen. He was the most divine-looking man imaginable. Of Greek descent with the body of a god, he appeared to have it all.

'Darius needs this arrangement just as much as you do – if not more. I know he'll be willing to play ball,' Noelle vowed. 'I'll arrange a meeting in a discreet location. Let's see how the two of you get on, yeah? Jodi, we need to paint a very clear picture of you as a girl-next-door homemaker type. The fans don't need to be disillusioned and made to feel cheated. They see you as someone to look up to. A good girl. A nice girl. We've got to lay this on with a trowel for a while. Mac, with his history, can do more damage than you give him credit for. I don't want that little weasel pulling the rug from under you. You've worked too hard to let that happen. Trust me?'

Jodi agreed.

Several days later she found herself in a basement apartment in LA face to face with Darius Drew.

'How's it going?' Jodi asked, as they shook hands. 'Sorry, my palms are sweating – hardly the most attractive quality in your potential future partner,' she added, trying to make light of the moment.

'Hey, no worries, I'm scared shitless myself …You're very pretty up close.' He smiled as, unabashedly, he looked her up and down. 'You're much tinier than you look on screen. How tall are you?' he asked.

'Five foot on the button,' Jodi said. 'European dress size six, shoe size four and currently I weigh just over forty-four kilos.' She raised an eyebrow as he nodded.

'Whatever about the raven tresses, please tell me those emerald eyes are enhanced by contact lenses!' he said, stepping closer to peer into them.

'You have it the wrong way around.' Her throaty laugh filled the air. 'I was born with hair a wonderful shade of mouse-brown-meets-muddy-puddle, which was always knotty and looked like it could've been styled by a stray cat, but the eyes are all mine!' She winked.

'Seriously?' Darius clicked his tongue against the roof of his mouth in awe. 'I can see why you ended up on the big screen, little lady.' At six foot one, he towered over her.

'You're not so bad yourself!' Sure she'd seen his publicity shots, not to mention the billboards and the movies he'd starred in, but he was astonishingly beautiful in the flesh. With his deep-set hazel eyes and smooth, bronzed skin, he might still have been in his teens. 'How old are you?'

'Twenty-nine,' Darius said. 'The big three-oh is looming later this year.'

'Well, you look seventeen!' Jodi shot back.

'Thank you, doll. I get my youthful looks as well as my name from my late father. He was Greek, and although he was only forty when he died, he looked much younger.' Darius sounded sad.

'I'm sorry. I didn't know your father had passed away. My mother died young too.'

'So I heard. That's a tough call. How about your dad?'

'I never knew him.'

At this point, Noelle walked into the room with a man, and interjected: 'So, Jodi, meet Mike.'

'Hi, I'm Darius's agent.' He smiled, revealing teeth that were a shade too white.

The rest of the conversation that day was surreal on so many levels. Both agents had drawn up a fact file on their clients.

'Here's a copy for both of you,' Noelle said, removing two neat folders from her briefcase and handing one each to Darius and Mike.

'Thanks, Noelle, and here's yours.' Mike gave her two similar folders.

'We figured this was the safest way of doing everything,' Noelle explained, to a slightly stunned Jodi and Darius. 'We'll organise plenty more meetings before you make your first public appearance, but it's good to have all the stuff you need to know on paper.'

'This is going to be like learning a new script,' Darius quipped.

'It's more like a TV reality show, if you ask me,' Jodi said, leafing through the pages. She felt hollow inside but figured she'd get used to the arrangement in time.

'We all know the reasons why this needs to happen. Jodi has to avoid certain incidents in her past coming out. Or, more to the point, a certain despicable character by the name of Mac. Darius, you need to steer the path away from your present! So, give it your best shot. Yes?' Noelle stated.

The fans had jumped on board instantly. As soon as they'd made their first public appearance, every glossy magazine from the UK to the USA wanted a piece of them. Over the following days and weeks they made the front cover of every newspaper. *When Irish Eyes Are Truly Smiling*, one magazine headline announced, boasting an 'exclusive at-home photo special inside'.

Destined To Be Together, another revealed. The press adored the fact that Darius had dyed his hair to match hers and that she'd taken to wearing white jeans like his. The world agreed that Jodi and Darius were the golden couple of the moment.

'So what's your reason for this charade?' Jodi asked Darius at one stage.

'Can't you tell? *Girlfriend*,' he said, using his most camp voice.

'You're *gay*?' she gasped. 'Fuck me, I'd never have noticed.'

'Well, I won't be fucking you. But that's the whole idea. Nobody is meant to notice.'

'But why?' Jodi asked, confused. 'Surely it's okay to be gay in this day and age.'

'You'd think so, wouldn't you?' Darius said. 'It seems it's still not quite fitting for heart-throbs like me.'

'That's so unfair. Surely your fans won't mind if they know the truth,' Jodi said, aghast.

'Just like your fans won't judge you because of your estranged man Mac-the-knife, and the dagger he holds over your head,' he said, raising an eyebrow.

'I suppose,' she said, sighing.

'If I *have* to marry someone I'd be proud to be your husband,' Darius said, as he hugged her. 'In fact, if I was ever considering any sort of lady loving you'd be first on my list.'

'Ha!' Jodi laughed. 'I'll take that as a compliment! Well, I'm just sorry you're so dead set on being gay. You're one of the nicest men I've ever met and you're so damn good-looking … It's a crying shame for womankind!' she said. 'Will you help me look for my wedding dress, then?'

'Ooh, I'd love, *love* love to come shopping for it with you! The best part about this relationship is that we get to be honest with each other. I promise I'll never hurt you. I'll mind you and look after you.'

'Right back at you,' Jodi said, as she hugged him. 'I'll be here for you always. Let's do what Noelle and Mike want in public, but nobody will know that we're like *this*,' Jodi said, and held two fingers side by side. 'Pinkie promise we'll take care of each other,' she said.

'Pinkie promise,' he said, linking his little finger with hers.

The arrangement fooled the world. Very soon after their first meeting, they married in a lavishly staged setting, with their nuptials making the front of every glossy magazine worldwide. As time passed, Jodi and Darius became inseparable. It was their own idea to have Saul. Both wanted children and opted for IVF to create their precious son. The decision hadn't been taken lightly. They'd mulled over it for several months before finally deciding to go ahead. They'd also vowed to tell their son the entire story when the time was right. So far they were both still happy to keep their marriage going, and although Jodi's move to

Ireland was going to put some distance between them, they'd decided to see how it all went.

'So what's the latest on your little love rat? Have you managed to put him off the scent?' Jodi asked, as they lay in her iron bed gazing up at the ceiling.

'Yeah, he was turfed out of Glitz nightclub and frisked by the cops the other night,' Darius said, yawning.

'Let me guess – he was in possession of something illegal?' Jodi finished.

'Got it in one,' Darius answered. 'Actually, I almost felt sorry for him. He's a mess.'

'He wasn't that pathetic a few days ago when he was trying to blackmail you by selling his story,' Jodi reminded him.

'I know, but he's just so beautiful, Jodi.' Darius sighed. 'Divine.' He went all misty-eyed.

'You're such a fool when it comes to gorgeous guys,' she said, nudging him.

'Just because I'm in love with being in love – unlike you,' Darius teased. 'No love on the horizon for you, then?' he asked.

'Nope.' Jodi was firm. She wanted to tell him about the phone call the other day, but he was comfortably relaxed and she didn't want to taint the moment. She felt a sudden chill. She hoped against hope that he wouldn't call again. They had an arrangement. Mac knew better now.

'Aren't there any irresistible Irish men knocking around here? It's the back end of nowhere. Surely they'd all be delighted to have a famous girlfriend.'

'I have my two men,' Jodi said. 'Now, do me a favour, shut up and go to sleep or the two of us will look like we've been boxed in this photo shoot tomorrow.'

Jodi fell into a deep sleep. The clear Wicklow air mixed with the comfort of having her husband beside her had knocked her out cold.

Darius wasn't quite so lucky. He stared at Jodi. She was like a little doll. All the gutsy determination that kept her in the limelight faded away when she slept. He knew he was one of the only people in the world who knew the real Jodi Ludlum. He adored her, and their son was the light of his life. Being a father was something he'd never thought could happen. He'd almost had to pinch himself when Jodi had divulged that she was longing to be a mother. 'I know what I'm suggesting might seem crazy, but all children need is love. We have that on offer in bucket loads,' she'd said. 'Besides, we are married after all.'

'It sounds so right when you put it that way,' Darius had agreed, 'and I'd love nothing more than to be a father. But are we honestly thinking of the potential child here? Our marriage isn't what one would call conventional, is it?'

'Maybe not, but when do we ever argue? We adore and respect one another. We have each other's backs 24/7... And as for the baby, I'd never stop thinking about our child, Darius. He or she would be cherished. What's irresponsible about that?'

'Nothing, honey. Nothing.'

Not for the first time, Darius had felt a lurch deep inside. It would be so simple if he weren't gay. But that was a concept he'd struggled with since his early teens.

As his star had risen, his parents had been so proud of his success. For years he had managed to fob them off about girlfriends. 'I live for the moment. I've a different girl in every port – this is Hollywood, Dad!'

His father had chuckled and banged him on the back. He'd raised Darius to be a man's man, but neither of his parents ever stopped asking him when he was going to settle down with a nice girl.

Jodi more than fitted the bill. Their wedding had got his parents off his back and had the knock-on effect of securing a massive deal for a blockbuster movie. He and Jodi were cast as an on-screen husband and wife in a big-budget, award-winning production. Darius played his usual role as the sexy criminal rogue who only showed a softer side when his gutsy petit love interest appeared. Although the Quentin Tarantinoesque hard man was a given for Darius, the role of gangster wife catapulted Jodi into the hearts of many more fans. The world celebrated with them as they both scooped an Oscar for their respective performances. Jodi's second and Darius's first.

Darius had sailed through his thirtieth birthday bash with his stunning co-star wife by his side.

Now they'd been together for six happy years. Jodi was the best friend and companion he'd ever had. Although she was four years his junior, she was wise beyond her years. She was the mother of his son. She was a huge part of his world and always would be. But inside he was desperately lonely. Jodi had told him adamantly that she never wanted to fall in love again after what she'd been through with Mac.

Mac had been around when Jodi's career had first hit the big time. She had been just eighteen and had landed the role in *Runaways*, her second movie which had gone on to smash all previous box-office records. It had also catapulted her into a whole new world. Jodi's performance had won her her first Oscar, for best supporting actress, along with two Golden Globes and a BAFTA. She had gone overnight from being vaguely known for a couple of childhood parts to a major player and superstar. Darius still felt angry when he remembered how Mac had taken advantage of her at that time. He'd been a runner on the set of *Runaways* and struck up a relationship with Jodi. She'd sat and talked to Darius for hours when they'd first met. She'd shared her fears and hopes. But most of all she'd poured her heart out to him. He and Jodi were a winning team, but Darius was pretty sure that, underneath her tough exterior, Jodi must have that same gaping void in her heart that he had today.

Closing his eyes, he tried to force himself to drift off. He loved Jodi more than he'd ever loved another person. But he knew deep down that their arranged marriage would have to end at some point. The love they shared was protective and mutual, of that he had no doubt. But he also knew they both deserved to find partners that would provide the whole package. The thought scared him. He'd become comfortable with Jodi. But sooner or later it would be time to move on. He wondered if he'd ever find inner peace. As sleep finally crept over him, his dreams were troubled.

Chapter 10

When Jodi stirred, she found the bed empty. The sound of laughter drew her to the kitchen, where the smell of toast and bacon made her mouth water.

'Hey, sleepy Mummy!' Saul said, waving. 'Dad and I've made toasties and they're yum. This is my third one.'

'Wowzers! You're going to pop if you don't stop!' Jodi said, kissing the top of her son's head.

'Want one?' Darius asked.

'No, thanks. I'll stick to porridge and my herbal infusion.' Jodi yawned.

'I never eat this kind of thing but I figured I'm on holiday. Well, until tomorrow anyway. I'll beat it off in the gym.'

'What time are the camera crew arriving?' Jodi asked, perching cross-legged on the Aga.

'Soon.' Darius looked at his watch. 'You okay about the publicity? You hate it at the best of times but this is on your home turf. Does it freak you out?'

'Nah. You know me. I can separate the real stuff from what the public sees. It's definitely weird having a crew come and take shots in Ireland, though.'

'This gorgeous place isn't anything like Dayfield Estate, as you described it to me,' Darius pointed out.

'No, it's a million miles away from all of that,' Jodi agreed. 'Thank God.' Hopping down, she hugged him briefly. 'I've to drop Saul to school and make a quick appearance at a coffee morning thing. It's for all the new mums and it'd be really bad form if I don't show up. I don't want the others to think I have a God complex.'

'Good for you,' Darius said. 'I'm glad you're making friends.'

'I'm making millions of friends,' Saul said, climbing into his dad's lap.

'I'd say everyone in the class wants to be your friend,' Darius said. 'Tell them they can audition!'

☙

Before they could leave for school, the first car pulled up outside the cottage and two people knocked at the door. 'Hi, we're part of the crew for the shoot.'

'I'm Jodi,' she said, smiling. 'Come on in.' Of course they already knew who she was, but Jodi always introduced herself. She felt it cut out any awkwardness and let people know how they should address her.

'Hair and Makeup will be here in just over an hour. We're going to do the background styling. If it's okay with you, we'll have a quick look around and start making notes.'

'Go ahead,' Jodi said.

'You get ready and I'll make Saul's mid-morning snack,' Darius called out.

'Thanks, lovie,' she said.

Jodi ran into her bedroom and grabbed the first thing she

found, which happened to be a pair of Abercrombie track pants. They were pale blue and she'd owned them for ever. She put them on, then added a frilly white vest top and a cropped denim jacket. She pulled her long hair into a high ponytail. Cream knitted Ugg boots completed her ensemble. Knowing she'd be scrubbed, backcombed and sprayed to within an inch of her life over the next few hours, she saw little point in dressing up.

When she wasn't on set, Jodi used hardly any makeup. The stuff she wore when she was working was like a mask and her skin always felt so much better bare. She picked up a pale pink tube of lip balm, rubbed a smidgen on to her lips, spritzed herself with eau de cologne and rushed out to the car.

'Ready, dude?' she called to Saul.

'Coming!' He kissed Darius and bounded out of the door after her.

'We'll drive this morning 'cause I'll have to rush back,' Jodi explained.

Moments later, as they passed through the school gate, Jodi had a sudden panic attack. Francine's friends, Sarah and Jane, were walking towards the classroom. Both were dressed like mannequins from Bloomingdales. Before she could turn around to drive back home and change, they spotted her and began to wave furiously.

'Shoot.' Jodi stopped the car and forced herself to get out.

'Hello, Jodi!' Jane called across to her, smiling brightly.

Feeling desperately self-conscious, Jodi waved to the women. There was nothing she could do about her clothes and, besides, she was only popping in to the coffee morning to be polite. By the time the bulk of the yummy mummies arrived she'd be out of there.

'Good morning,' she said, smiling. 'I'll just drop Saul into Mr Matthews and I'll be right there.'

As Jodi set off with Saul to the classroom, he tore ahead of her, running confidently to hang his coat and put away his school bag. 'See you later, Mum!' he called.

'Later!' Jodi blew him a kiss.

Mr Matthews was on the floor making a Lego house with a couple of the children. 'Are you going to the welcome coffee upstairs?' he asked.

'Yeah,' Jodi said, 'though it's not a great morning for it.'

'Carry on with that, guys, and I'll be back in a moment,' Mr Matthews said. Standing up, he walked Jodi to the door.

'I've really messed up,' Jodi admitted. 'I just bumped into a couple of the other mums and they're dressed to kill. I look like I got dressed in the dark. I'm mortified.'

'Just be yourself. Nobody can argue with that.'

'I guess,' Jodi said. Inwardly she baulked. Of all the things she was going to be at the coffee morning, herself was not one of them. She had spent the last few years hiding the true Jodi Ludlum from the world. Now she wasn't even sure who she was any longer.

As she went up the stairs towards the hall, she could hear the murmur of voices. It sounded like there were already quite a few women there. She peered into the room and jumped backwards in fright as Jane appeared from behind the door, like a genie from a lamp. 'Welcome, do come in. I've so many mothers for you to meet,' she said, balancing a massive tin teapot in her hands.

'Thanks,' Jodi said, feeling sick with nerves. She glanced around the room. It looked like a casting for the role of First Lady to the President of the United States. She'd never seen so many strings of pearls, pencil skirts and satin blouses in one place. Francine was in an oatmeal trouser suit with taupe court shoes and more diamonds than a Tiffany window display. Jodi went over to her. 'I'm a bit too scruffy for this,' she began. 'I've a magazine shoot this morning and my hair and makeup team are arriving shortly so I didn't bother to dress up. Maybe I should go.'

'No!' Francine stopped beside her with the enormous urn she was hauling around. 'Please don't. Everyone wants to chat to you.'

Lots of the women turned to look at Jodi. Right at that moment, she felt like she was seven again. She was almost expecting someone to point and sneer – *Look at Gyppo Jodi in her tracksuit. With all her money you'd think she'd manage to look better.*

'Hi, Jodi! Over here!' Andrea called, and pulled at the front of her linen skirt uncomfortably.

'Hi,' Jodi said, wanting to die.

'Hi, Jodi,' Sarah said. 'You look a million dollars. I feel like your granny in my twin set. I thought I was doing the classic look but beside you I'm a total fuddy-duddy.'

'Apologies for turning up looking like a tramp. I'll know better the next time. You girls are setting the stakes seriously high. I'll have to get some clothes sent over from LA to keep up with you.'

The women chuckled good-naturedly and assured Jodi she looked fantastic.

The atmosphere in the room was curious. All the women were air-kissing and most of them seemed to know at least one group. But, just like some Hollywood events, they were chatting amicably while simultaneously scanning the room and taking in exactly what the others were doing.

'This is my first taste of being a school mum,' Jodi said hesitantly. 'I'm sure I've got a lot to learn. I'll have to get with the plot or Saul is going to be mortified by me!'

'I don't think so,' Jane assured her. 'You're the coolest mum here!'

'I'm not so sure,' Jodi said, laughing. Inwardly she thought she was going to pass out. This was as scary as her first audition had been all those years ago. Except today she wasn't looking for a part in a movie. Now she needed to fit in to give Saul the secure home she'd never had.

'I'm trussed up like a pig on a spit, poured into magic knickers, thigh-slimming tights, push-up bra and heels so high I have to lean against the wall or I'll fall over,' Jane was saying, 'and you're as cool as a cucumber and looking stunning.'

'You put me to shame,' Jodi said.

'You look fantastic, Jane,' Andrea said loyally.

'I look like a bleeding drag queen. Your skin is immaculate, Jodi. Do you have Botox and fillers and all that sort of stuff?' Jane asked leaning in.

'Eh, well, no ...' Jodi hadn't been expecting that sort of question.

'Jesus, Jane, don't ask her things like that.' Andrea had turned a deep red.

'You don't have to answer, Jodi. Don't mind her.'

'Yes, Jane is known for being outspoken,' Sarah said, glaring at her friend.

'I'm only saying what you're all thinking,' Jane said, unconcerned. 'And your waist is the same size as the top of one of my arms. Do you eat food?'

'Of course I do! Did you think I was tube fed?' Jodi giggled. She was really starting to enjoy this woman.

'You hear such mad stuff about A-listers and how they live.'

'I drink horrible herbal infusions and have to work out when I'm taking on roles,' Jodi explained. 'But I tend to go around in this sort of gear with no makeup when I'm off. It would be nice to dress up a bit sometimes, when it's not a work thing, and I'll make more effort next time, I promise. You all look like you're really enjoying this. It's very civilised.'

'Do you think?' Jane deadpanned. 'I reckon we've all been bamboozled into conforming because everyone else does it.'

'What do you mean?' Andrea asked.

'Well, seeing Jodi walk in here wearing comfy clothes has made me think,' Jane said, and turned to her. 'I feel like a total twat beside you. Sorry, but I do.'

'Why? You're certainly your own woman,' she said. 'I find your attitude very refreshing!'

'Thanks, but I'm an imposter, really. I'm going home to a bedroom that looks like it was ransacked by looters. I had to get up half an hour earlier to plaster myself in makeup and I spent forty euro having my hair blow-dried and teased to within an inch of its life yesterday. My mother had to come and mind the kids and she let them eat jellies so I scraped their dinner into the bin and ended up screaming like a fish wife.' Jane folded her arms. 'For what? To impress other women or, if I'm totally honest, to compete with them? Just so I don't feel like a sad, ageing *Hausfrau*?'

'You're not sad. It's lovely to go to coffee mornings and relax and chat to other mothers,' Andrea said, without conviction.

'Are you honestly relaxed right now?' Jane asked. ''Cause I'm not. You could sharpen a pencil if you stuck it up my arse because I'm so uptight.'

'Jane!' Andrea looked shocked. 'That's very rude.'

Jodi burst out laughing.

'Yup. It is.' Jane grinned. 'I used to be fun, you know, a hundred years ago when I worked in a chain store and drank what was left of my wages after I'd bought more new clothes.'

'But you were young and foolish then,' Andrea said, blinking in dismay. 'You're a mother and a wife now. Your life has moved on.'

'Has it?' Jane mused. 'Or has it kind of ended in a sad and dull way? Are we just like clones of one another, all shuffling through a mundane existence? Is this it? What are we going to do when the kids have left school? When we have no hall to stand in talking crap? What then?'

'If you feel so strongly about it all, just wear a tracksuit and stop being so negative,' Andrea said. 'Jane, you must be having a midlife crisis. If you're not careful, you may find yourself being left off the list when the next luncheon is organised. Now, excuse me, ladies, but I'd better go and mingle with some of the new mums. Someone needs to make them feel welcome,' she said, shooting Jane a filthy look. 'Excuse me, Jodi.'

'Sure,' Jodi said.

'Looks like I'm in deep shit, doesn't it?' Jane winked.

'You should probably behave yourself or you'll be put in the naughty corner,' Jodi agreed.

'Do you want to come and do a quick meet-and-greet with me, then slip away?' she offered.

'That'd be great,' Jodi agreed. She could see Francine out of the corner of her eye, cutting cakes and milling around, and felt stung that the other woman hadn't greeted her. When she and Jane practically walked into her, Francine stopped to speak.

'All going okay for you?' she asked.

'Yes, thanks. Jane is great fun.'

'Yeah, in small doses.' Francine lowered her voice as Jane was distracted talking to another mother. 'She tends to get hideously drunk at evening events. She's been known to let herself down on more than one occasion.' Francine shook her head. 'She's done it all from the can-can on the dinner table to falling in a heap off her chair and knocking herself out on the leg of the table.'

'Oh, right.' Jodi stifled a giggle.

'Yeah, she's on thin ice with some of the ladies. She's actually in danger of being ostracised by some of the more old-fashioned members of the community.'

Jodi certainly wasn't a fan of drunks. She'd seen enough of what booze could do to last her a lifetime. But she found Jane very funny.

'Are you all right?'Jodi asked Francine, lowering her voice.

'Yes, of course. I'm fine,' Francine replied abruptly. 'Excuse me, Jodi. I'd better go and see to the other new mothers.'

As she walked away, Jodi felt cold inside. She'd thought she and Francine had bonded the other day. Now it appeared she was wrong. Everyone in her life seemed to do this to her, except Darius.

She edged towards the door and had just gone out when Francine was behind her. 'You're not leaving so soon, are you?' she asked, looking nervous.

'I've to head back. I've a photo shoot at the cottage,' Jodi said.

'Listen, I'm sorry if I was off with you. I'd like to make amends about what happened between Cameron and Saul. Would he come and play for a little while this afternoon?'

Jodi knew Darius's views on Saul playing with Cameron. She also thought of how upset her poor little boy had been after all the trouble. Saul wasn't able for Cameron's wild behaviour. 'Thanks for the offer but he wants to be with Darius. He's here for the photos, but it's only a flying visit.'

'But you'll be busy with the pictures,' Francine persisted. 'I'll collect him and you can call me when it's all over and I'll drop him home. Please. It'll make me feel better.'

'As I said, Francine, thank you for the offer but he'd prefer to come home today,' Jodi said firmly.

'I insist.' Francine's smile didn't falter.

Jodi felt quite confused. Was the woman not hearing what she'd said? 'Another day I'll take you up on the offer. But not today.' She tried not to sound snappy.

'Fine. Forget I said it. Sorry to have offended you,' Francine said. 'I only wanted to organise a nice afternoon for Cameron. He's been struggling a lot lately.'

Jodi felt terrible for the poor child. She couldn't help it. She still remembered so clearly how it felt to be the one nobody wanted to play with. She was making such a mess of this. She'd never fit in at Bakers Valley if she didn't start to make some friends.

'Francine,' she said.

'Yes?'

'Thank you for the offer. I have to be honest and tell you Saul is a little nervous of Cameron. He's a very gentle soul. But if you could keep an eye on the horseplay and general behaviour, I'm sure the boys will have a fun time together.'

'Great.'

Fresh guilt washed over Jodi as she pictured Saul's little face. He'd freak if she wasn't there to collect him at home time. Dashing back down the stairs, Jodi tapped on the classroom door. 'Sorry to interrupt, Mr Matthews, but could I just speak to Saul for one second?' she asked.

'Come on in.'

Jodi was delighted to find her little boy painting happily at a miniature easel in a corner. Little voices mixed with busy clattering made for a lovely joyful atmosphere.

'Hi, Mum!' Saul was clearly thrilled to see her. 'I'm painting us in our new house with Dad.'

'That's just the coolest thing ever!' Jodi said. 'Maybe you could let Dad take that back to the movie set with him?'

'So when he misses us he can look at my picture,' Saul agreed.

'Listen, dude, Francine is going to pick you up today and mind you for a little while. Won't that be fun? You'll get to go to Cameron's house!' Jodi tried to look enthusiastic.

'Oh.' Saul looked confused.

'It won't be for long, I promise,' she whispered. 'I know you want to play with Dad, huh?'

'Okay Mum, as long as Cameron promises to be good,' he whispered back.

Jodi felt like crying. 'He will, honey. And it'll only be for a short time. If you want to come home just tell Francine and we'll come and get you, okay?'

'Okay. Bye, Mum.' Saul waved his paintbrush at her.

'You survived the mothers' meeting unscathed, I see,' Mr Matthews commented, as she walked past.

'Just about! Ah, they're a decent bunch. They're very friendly.'

'It can be a bit intimidating when you don't know anyone, though. I felt like a neon sign in the desert when I walked into the village pub the first time.'

'Ha!' Jodi laughed. 'I like your imagery.'

Mr Matthews grinned. 'Well if you ever need to compare "newbie" notes, just let me know.'

'Oh, thanks,' Jodi said distractedly. 'I'd better run. Apologies again for bursting in!'

'No problem at all. Any time.'

ରେ

As she sped home, Jodi felt uneasy. She wasn't comfortable with Francine taking Saul. She shouldn't have agreed to it. Jodi also felt hurt that the woman had been so off with her. Darius was always telling her to make more friends, to try to meet a new man. But how could she? Each time she tried to open up to someone it seemed to go pear-shaped.

She hadn't much time to ponder on it all once she got back to the cottage. The hair and makeup team swarmed around her the second she entered the house. Gorgeous clothes were pulled from clear plastic packaging and held up against her face. 'We need to make sure the look stays very daytime,' the stylist said, dismissing a short black dress.

Darius appeared in jeans and an indigo checked shirt.

'Wow, you look stunning,' Jodi exclaimed. 'That colour is amazing on you, sweetie.'

'You like?' Darius twirled slowly.

'God, I should've married you,' Jodi quipped. 'Oh, hang on a minute – I did!'

The team giggled and lapped up the saccharine banter between the couple. Jodi winked at Darius when she was sure nobody was looking.

'Good one, darling,' Darius whispered in her ear. 'The perfect cement to put the kybosh on any rumours that my latest love rat may decide to send out there.'

'Nobody will believe him,' Jodi whispered back.

Jodi and Darius had a name within the industry for being really down to earth. The public loved them, but so too did the business moguls who came into contact with them. Everyone from runners to producers sang their praises. Neither ever played the diva or behaved disrespectfully.

'They're so cute together too,' the hairdresser's assistant was muttering to her friend on the phone, as the photographers began to snap.

Once things got going the time flew, so Jodi was surprised when her mobile rang flashing up Francine's number.

'Hey, Francine,' Jodi said. 'How's everything?'

The line was very crackly and Jodi had to strain to hear the other woman.

'I'm sorry, Francine, we're outside and my neighbour is cutting corn so the noise and wind aren't helping.'

'Saul is a little tearful so he'd like me to drop him home now,' Francine was saying.

'Oh, no!' Jodi said. 'Will I come over?'

'Not at all. We'll be there shortly.'

'Okay, if you're sure, that'd be great,' Jodi shouted, above the noise. 'We're out the back but I mightn't be able to stop and chat,' she apologised in advance.

'I'll just drop him and fly,' Francine said brusquely.

'Thank you,' Jodi said, but the other woman had already hung up.

'Over this way, please, Jodi!' the photographer called. 'Makeup! Can you dab just to the left of her nose? That shine isn't flattering!'

The combine harvester droned on behind them as the shoot continued.

'We're nearly there. Just a few more shots, please, guys,' the stylist announced.

Moments later, Saul appeared around the back of the house. Jodi and Darius both waved and called to him.

'Stunning shot! Brilliant!' the photographer encouraged.

Saul plopped on to the ground, crossed his legs and rested his sullen face on his hands.

'Hi, Monster Man!' Darius called. 'How you doing?'

'I didn't have a very good time today.'

'Was school not fun?'

'It was the after bit that was yucky.'

'Give us a few more minutes and we'll have a catch-up,' Darius promised. 'I want to hear all about your day.'

Saul's attention was taken by the combine harvester, which was hurtling towards the garden. He jumped up and climbed to the top of the fence. He waved, and was thrilled when Sebastian waved back.

'Sebastian!' Saul shouted.

The machine stopped and Sebastian climbed down.

'Hi, Sebastian,' Jodi called. 'We're nearly finished here. This is my husband, Darius.'

'How's it going?' Darius said, waving at the other man.

'Hello,' Sebastian said evenly. 'Will I take Saul to the farm for a few minutes to keep him out of trouble?'

'What do you think?' Jodi asked.

'Wow!' Saul said, looking much more cheerful.

'Thanks, Sebastian,' Jodi said. 'I owe you one.'

Saul flung himself over the fence and ran to him.

'Come on, and we'll see how the cows are doing. They love having visitors, you know. I'm certain they cheered up after you chatted to them last time,' said Sebastian. Saul giggled.

'He'll be made up,' Jodi said to Darius. 'This is all part of the reason I knew he needed to come here. You'd never have an experience like that in Palm Beach or the middle of London.'

'He certainly seems to be having a ball,' Darius agreed. 'And why wouldn't he?' He lowered his voice. 'Who's Mr Delicious Farmer Man? Where did he spring from?'

'He lives in the manor house,' she said, through her teeth, as she smiled at the camera.

'Dishy *and* the local lord. He's too good to be true,' Darius said. In spite of herself, Jodi burst out laughing. Darius joined in.

'Amazingly natural and so happy, you two,' the photographer said. 'I love it. Keep it going.'

The shoot finished and the crew packed up quickly. Just as Jodi was about to look for Saul, he reappeared with Sebastian.

'I'll get back to my machine,' Sebastian said politely. 'See you soon, Saul.'

'Bye, Sebastian!'

'What do you say to Sebastian?' Jodi prompted.

'Thank you!' Saul shrilled.

'No worries,' Sebastian said, over his shoulder, as he walked back to the combine harvester.

'How was that, then?' Jodi asked.

'Fun!' Saul said. 'Sebastian is so nice. He's my friend. Not like Cameron.' He pouted.

'What happened today, then?' Darius asked.

'He was mean again.'

'Mum'll fix it, won't you?' Darius said. 'It's not a good plan for him to hang out with Cameron if he's going to be awful.'

'I'll sort it,' she said. 'I'll talk to his mum – but for now, Saul, you need to give your dad a big hug. He's going to the airport in a few minutes,' she said, with a glance at her watch.

Jodi made herself scarce as Darius hugged their son and snatched a few more minutes with him.

Having removed her makeup, she heard a car pull up outside.

Guessing it was Darius's taxi, she padded back into the living room where Saul and his father were chatting.

'This is for you to bring on set,' Saul said, handing Darius the painting he'd made in school.

'Monster, this is just the best! All my co-stars are going to know exactly what our new house is like now.'

'When are you coming back?' Saul asked, as he sat on Darius's knee.

'Just as soon as I can.'

'We'll go and visit Dad too,' Jodi said. 'Once he's in a slightly closer location, we'll go for the weekend. You'll have midterm break so we'll make sure to see him then.'

'I'm going far away to China in November but I'll be in London before Hallowe'en,' Darius explained. 'You and Mum are coming to see me then. We're invited to a party and it's going to be amazing.'

Saul threw his arms around his father's neck.

'Darius, your car for the airport is waiting, love,' Jodi said gently.

She and Saul walked outside with him, watched him get in, and stood waving until they couldn't see him any longer.

'I'll miss Daddy,' Saul said sadly.

'Me too. But we'll see him again before you know it, okay?' Jodi promised.

Saul promptly burst out crying.

'Hey! What's all this?' she said, dropping on to her hunkers.

'I had a horrible time at Cameron's house. He's really scary,' Saul sobbed.

Jodi took him inside. She was worried, and wondered what on earth had gone on with Cameron now.

Chapter 11

Francine was at sixes and sevens with herself. She'd just dropped Saul off without even calling in to say hello. She'd never done that before. He was only little and she knew she should have delivered him directly to his mother rather than ushering him from her car in Jodi's direction. She should also have explained what Cameron had done. But she simply couldn't bear the embarrassment of confessing to Cameron's dreadful behaviour yet again. Especially when she'd more or less forced Jodi into allowing her to take Saul in the first place.

After dropping Saul home, she drove back to Verbena Drive on autopilot, hardly able to believe what had just happened. On the first Friday of each month Cara hosted a little book club for some of the girls in her class and they were due that afternoon. When she was working, she had always gone in and finished early on a Friday, which had fitted in nicely with her daughter's schedule.

Ordinarily Francine looked forward to the date just as much as Cara did. She took pride in setting the table with a pretty cloth and matching napkins. She loved preparing tiny sandwiches and displaying them on her three-tiered porcelain cake stand. The sweet treats varied, depending on Francine's mood and the time of year. Today she had baby meringues and mini shortbread biscuits. But her usual humming as she laid the table before the girls arrived had been replaced with stifled sobs and a sick sensation deep in her gut. She could still see the look on Saul's face as he'd begged to go home.

'Cameron got cross with me because I wanted to play Lego,' Saul said. 'He's broken the window.'

Francine had been so stunned by what had happened, she'd ushered the boys into the car without even attempting to clear up the glass.

She intended to make certain that none of the visiting girls or their mothers knew about the carnage that had gone on that afternoon. A short while later, feeling like a madwoman concealing a murder, she answered the door with a practised smile on her lips. Nobody needed to know the window was lying in smithereens all over Cameron's room.

'Come in, girls,' she greeted them. 'Cara's waiting for you in the kitchen. Go on through.' She waved to the mother who had dropped them off and felt grateful that they'd agreed long ago that they would drop and collect without coming in. 'Yes, it's all about the girls so we won't turn it into a mothers' occasion,' Francine had said. 'We should let them have their little session and go straight home afterwards. Otherwise it'll get too late and we'll all feel pressured to stop and chat.'

Cara knew nothing about the smashed glass either and Francine wanted it kept that way. She certainly didn't need anyone gossiping about Cameron in the school car park. If they knew he'd broken a window in a fit of rage people might jump to all kinds of conclusions. Francine would be even more mortified than she was now.

Luckily there'd been no further thumping and shouting from

Cameron. Francine figured he must have worn himself out after the appalling outburst of earlier on. He was happily ensconced in front of a video game with his brothers.

'Today we're going to talk some more about *Little Women*,' Cara announced.

Francine kept her smile in place as she put a china coffee pot filled with hot chocolate on the table. 'Don't mind me, girls. I'll leave you to it. I've a few jobs to do upstairs. Enjoy!'

'Thank you!' the girls chorused.

As she fled the room Francine was totally unaware that the conversation had switched to rapid whispers about Simon Doyle's new haircut and what they were all dressing up as for the school Hallowe'en party.

СУ

Upstairs in Cameron's bedroom Francine, trying to be as quiet as possible, put large shards of broken glass into the bin and swept up the smaller pieces. She stowed the bin out of harm's way in her own bedroom. She'd put it outside after the girls had gone home. Knowing she needed to try and get to grips with why Cameron had reacted so violently, she descended the stairs and walked slowly into the playroom.

'Cameron, I need to have a little chat with you,' Francine began. 'Why did you break the window upstairs, sweetheart?' she asked, in as calm a voice as she could muster. Cameron was curled up on a beanbag with his back to her, facing the wall. 'Cameron, I'm speaking to you. Don't ignore me,' she said.

'Because Saul made me cross.'

'Cameron.' Francine walked over to the sofa and patted the space beside her. 'Come over and sit here with me. We need to have a proper chat quietly so we don't disturb Conor and Craig.' She was expecting him to be remorseful – she thought enough time had elapsed for them to sort out calmly what had happened.

'I hate you and I hate him! He's a big fat poo-face!' he yelled, leaping off his beanbag and bolting behind the television stand.

'Cameron! Come out of there! It's so dangerous with all those wires. You'll be electrocuted!'

'Mum!' Conor shouted. 'Cameron just unplugged the PlayStation! Me and Craig were on level six and he's just ruined it all.'

'I'm sorry, darling,' Francine said, trying to sound as if everything was still hunky-dory. Cameron careered out from behind the television and lashed out at Craig, thumping him soundly on the arm.

'Ow!' Craig yelled, and burst into tears.

'Cameron! Cut it out! There are guests in the kitchen!'

Craig sobbed and held his arm, while Conor chased Cameron, attempting to hit him with the PlayStation remote control. 'I'll kill you! You wrecked our game!' he shouted. 'You wreck everything! Wrecker-fecker, wrecker-fecker!'

'Boys!' Francine hissed. 'Stop it! What are those girls going to think?'

'I don't care,' Cameron said. 'Smelly girls!'

Before she could grab him, Cameron opened the door and shot into the kitchen.

'*Muuuum!*' Cara shouted.

'Coming, lovie,' Francine called, hoping to God she could get hold of her child and drag him out of there before he hit one of the girls.

'Cameron's ruining everything,' Cara wailed. 'He's such a little brat. Look what he's done!'

Cameron had tossed the sandwiches and meringues on to the floor and was stamping on them.

'I'll take him away,' Francine said, voice wobbling. 'I'm so sorry, girls. Cameron is just wild at the moment. Any of you who have brothers will know what tearaways boys can be!'

A chase ensued and Cameron flung himself under the table, making the girls scream.

Eventually Francine managed to grab him and wrestle him down the hall into her office. 'You are not allowed to behave like this, Cameron,' she panted. He wriggled and swiped and tried with all his might to free himself but Francine held him back. Kicking the door shut, she hoped to God the girls had resumed chatting in the kitchen.

'Let me go!' he yelled. 'I hate you, let me go!'

The sound of Francine's palm meeting Cameron's leg startled both of them.

'Ow!'

Francine burst out crying. She'd never hit any of her children before. It was something she abhorred. Both she and Carl had always said they totally disagreed with smacking. But it had been a reflex action born of sheer desperation. 'Cameron, I'm sorry!' she sobbed.

'Bold Mummy,' he said, and began to howl.

'I won't do that again. I didn't mean it,' she pleaded. 'Come and sit with me and we'll do some planning for the Hallowe'en party. Please, sweetheart, come over and let's sit for a while.'

Cameron climbed on to her knee and stuck his thumb into his mouth.

As she held him close and rocked him back and forth their sobs finally subsided.

The girls were sure to tell their parents how vile Cameron

had been, Francine thought. And it was almost impossible to expect Craig and Conor to keep the smashed window a secret. They'd be dying to tell their friends on Monday what their naughty little brother had done.

Glancing up at her neatly aligned boxes of index cards and folders, Francine felt like every bit of order was being torn away from her. Her first thought on waking each morning and her final thought each night as she tried to go to sleep was of her youngest child and his increasingly awful antics.

Mr Matthews was doing his best to be understanding and proactive, but this was only the end of the second week and already Francine was ashamed of her son's behaviour at school. Every time she thought of Annie and the heartache Cameron had caused her, she felt even worse.

Word was going to spread. Cameron was going to be labelled a naughty boy if she didn't do something quickly.

'I need to make my shopping list for the Hallowe'en party in school. I have a big meeting with the mums who are going to help me next week,' she explained. 'So, you be a good lad and sit here and make a picture for Dad while I get on with that. You can use my special coloured pens to draw on this paper.' She handed him an A4 sheet and showed him the little pot of felt-tip pens.

'I hate colouring,' he protested.

'Okay, okay,' she said, terrified he was going to start kicking and screaming again. 'Just sit and cuddle up to me while I look in my folder.' He leaned into her and, sighing with intense relief, she assumed he was too tired to create any further disruption.

She flicked through her Hallowe'en folder just for something to do. Cara's book club would be over and the girls would all be collected in the next twenty minutes. Soon Carl would be home and she wouldn't be on her own, wondering what to do next.

Cameron snatched the red felt-tip pen she was holding, yanked the lid off and stabbed the pen into the page forcing the nib back into the plastic casing.

'Cameron! No! You're spoiling the pen. We don't treat things like that,' she said.

He snatched up a fistful and flung them behind the chair. As he reached for more pens, Francine put her hand on his.

'No, Cameron. Listen to me,' she said, in a very slow and calm, albeit shaky, voice. 'If you want to use my special pens you must be gentle.'

Cameron responded by upending the entire pot and scattering the remaining pens everywhere. Then he ran out of the room and launched himself at the front door. He climbed up the wooden panels and wrestled the lock open, then tore down the driveway towards the communal green area of Verbena Drive.

Francine ran after him.

Once he realised she was giving chase, the little boy speeded up and pelted onwards.

'Cameron, get back here this instant!' Jesus, Francine thought. I'm in my slippers yelling like a banshee and my child looks like he's escaping a murderer.

Cameron might have made it to the other side of the country had he not been intercepted by Mr Brady driving towards his house. The elderly man slammed on his brakes, stopped his car, jumped out and grabbed the little boy.

As Francine caught up with Cameron, her throat hurt and she'd a stitch in her side. With a face the shade of a ripe raspberry she lurched forward and scooped him into her arms. 'Mr Brady,' she was totally out of breath, 'thank you so much for stopping. I'm so sorry if he gave you a fright running on the road like that.'

'Ah, sure that's kids today,' Mr Brady said.

'I ran away from Mum because she beat me,' Cameron said, glowering at Francine.

'Cameron!' Francine said in horror. The old man looked at her in surprise.

'Well, you did!' Cameron said emphatically. 'She said sorry afterwards but she smacked me like this.' Cameron lashed out and hit the old man on the side of the head. 'Ha!' Cameron giggled loudly as Mr Brady's glasses landed on the road.

'Oh, my God, Mr Brady, are you all right?' Francine struggled to hold the squirming child while she bent down to retrieve the glasses.

'I'm not sure I am,' the old man retorted.

'Please forgive him.' Francine's voice cracked and tears of shame rolled down her cheeks. Turning, she staggered back towards the house with Cameron tucked under her arm.

'Little gurrier,' Mr Brady muttered. 'Next time I should just run him over. I'm delighted myself and Mrs Brady only have a docile marmalade cat to contend with,' he called after her.

Inside the house, Francine put Cameron into Craig's room – his own wouldn't be safe for him until the window was mended. She tried to pretend she couldn't hear him throwing shoes and God knows what else at the wall. When the book-club mothers arrived she shooed the girls out speedily.

ॐ

When Carl came in a short while later, for the first time since he'd met Francine, there was no dinner ready. The kitchen was in a terrible state, with food trampled across the floor. Cara, Craig and Conor were on the PlayStation and his wife was nowhere to be seen. 'Where's Mum?' he asked anxiously.

'Upstairs with Cameron. He had a total meltdown and beat up one of the neighbours,' Conor said, without moving his gaze from the flatscreen TV.

'Yeah, Mum says he socked Mr Brady in the head after he'd tried to commit suicide by jumping under Mr Brady's car,' Cara added dramatically.

'And,' Craig added, not wanting to be left out, 'he smashed a window upstairs with his shoe earlier today. He's in *soooo* much trouble.'

'Francine?' Carl ran towards the stairs. There was no answer so he stormed into Cameron's room.

The wind was whipping the curtains through the gaping hole where the window glass used to be.

'Cameron?' Carl walked on to the upstairs landing.

'Hi, Dad!' Cameron said brightly, from his brother's room.

'Cameron, what on earth is going on in here?' Carl stared at the devastation in dismay.

'I'm sorting all Craig's stuff,' the little boy said. He'd emptied every drawer of clothes, pulled all the shoes, toys and entire contents of his brother's room into the middle of the carpet. 'I'm doing a spring clean,' he said.

'Francine?' Carl called, backing out of the room. Following the sound of sobbing, he found his wife face down on their bed.

Chapter 12

The weekend brought some much-needed calm for Jodi and Saul. Although she still woke early, Jodi was relieved to see her son fast asleep when she peeped into his room.

Hoping he'd have a rare lie-on, she moved quietly to the kitchen to make some of her herbal infusion. The sound of her mobile ringing made her curse and dive to answer it. The number was unknown, which she would normally have allowed to go to voicemail, but after that awful phone call the other day, a sixth sense told her to answer.

'Hello?' she said, in hushed tones.

'Babe! It's me, Mac!'

'What do you want?'

'That's not a very nice way to greet me after all this time,' he said. 'We must've been cut off the other day.'

'Eh, yeah,' she hesitated, biding for time. 'I thought we had things sorted between you and I?' Her voice wobbled. She squeezed her eyes tightly shut and willed herself to hold it together. She couldn't let him hear how much he frightened her.

'Mac, what do you want?' she repeated, attempting to inject some conviction into her voice. Jodi tried to remind herself she was a long way from the impressionable eighteen-year-old Mac had first encountered. At the same time, Jodi was well aware he could potentially destroy everything she had worked so hard to achieve.

It had been during the first week of shooting *Runaways*. Jodi had just finished a fifteen-hour day, in which she'd stood from dawn until dusk in the freezing wind on the side of the docks in London. Alone, she had gravitated towards Mac initially because they were both Irish, but his easy-going manner and witty comments had put her at ease. He'd made her giggle and chat like nobody else could.

'Don't know about you, but I'm going straight to the pub,' Mac had said one evening, about three weeks into filming, as he strolled towards Jodi with his hands shoved into the pockets of his baggy jeans.

'I might just hit the sack,' she'd said.

'Ah, come on, all work and no play makes Jodi a sad little loner.' He smiled. 'I don't bite, not unless you want me to, that is.' He raised one razor-sculpted eyebrow. 'So, are you coming for a drink, Cinderella, or do I have to talk to the same lot of gimps down the Horse and Coaches again tonight?'

Filming wasn't starting until seven the next night so, apart from exhaustion, Jodi had no valid reason to say no. Besides, she was lonely and knew she needed to make some friends.

Things got off to a slightly rocky start when she ordered a soda and lime at the bar.

'What's that muck? Have a real drink, for Christ's sake. With your posh accent and your model walk, they'll never believe you're Irish if you don't show them how you can drink,' he jibed.

'I'm under age,' she tried.

'As if anyone in here cares about that,' he scoffed.

'I don't touch the stuff,' Jodi said evenly. 'My mother spent my childhood sozzled and high as a kite. I've spent more time in pubs than playgrounds, and I've seen more drunken fights than episodes of *Sesame Street*. So, if it's all the same to you, I'll stick to this.'

'Woo-hoo, look at the sassy attitude on you. If I wasn't so thick-skinned, I'd be afraid o' me shite o' you!'

'I might sound refined now,' Jodi said, with a grin, 'but I grew up on the Dayfield Estate and, believe me,' she leaned in closer to whisper, in her best Dublin accent, 'I'll deck ya if you're not careful.'

'You could've fooled me,' Mac said in admiration. 'From what I've seen on the news back home, there aren't many from Dayfield like you.'

To Jodi's astonishment, he threw his arm around her waist and pulled her towards him.

Her plan that night had been to stay for half an hour and slip away, but within twenty minutes, a large group of the cast and crew had trickled in and the atmosphere was one of celebration. Jodi found herself swept up in the fun.

The minute she hit the dance floor, her inhibitions melted away. Mac was attentive all night, only leaving her side to go to the bar or chat briefly to one of his numerous buddies.

'How long have you lived here?' Jodi shouted over the music.

'Nearly a year. I love London. There's none of the small-town bullshit you can get in Dublin. So many creeds and cultures are mixed up in the pot here that there's no restrictions.' He winked.

A short while later he was astonished when Jodi told him she was going home. 'What do you mean you'll see me tomorrow?

What's wrong with me? Did someone tell you I've a small dick? Do I smell of BO? Give me a break, Jodi. Didn't I look after you all night?' He seemed slightly vulnerable for a split second.

'You were a total gentleman, and I had a ball. I'm tired and I'm going back to my hotel. I'll see you tomorrow. Thanks for a great night.' She raised an eyebrow as if to ask him what his problem was.

'Hey, baby, if you're just tired, I have plenty of stuff to help with that,' he said. 'Come with me to the back of the room and I'll give you a bit of powder to perk you up. How else do you think the rest of us keep going?' He chucked her under the chin and turned to lead the way.

Placing her hand on his arm, Jodi stopped him. 'I didn't know that your attention and friendship over the last week was meant as a bartering tool,' she said, holding his gaze.

'Pardon?'

'You seem to assume that because we're friends I should gratefully get wasted and fall into bed with you. I wasn't raised, Mac, I was dragged up. In a fug of alcohol and drugs. My mother showed me on a daily basis what could go horribly wrong when those substances are abused. So I don't feel the need to be around all of that now that I have a choice.'

'Hey,' he said, looking concerned, 'I'm sorry.' He held his hands up to signal a truce. 'Come over here and talk to me, Jodi.'

'It's no biggie,' she said.

'You and I both know that's a lie. Trust me, Jodi. Please.'

He was so sweet and convincing that Jodi followed him to the back bar where there were very few revellers.

'Two lemonades, please, mate,' he said to the barman.

'You don't have to pretend to be teetotal just because I'm sitting with you.' Jodi grinned.

'Ah, don't sweat it, darling, I'm buzzing off my face on pills. I could do with a soft drink.' He grinned at her. She knew she should probably walk away. He was openly admitting to taking drugs for fun, a concept she'd never grasped, but she was drawn to him. In spite of herself she wanted to sit with him. Before she knew it she was telling him stuff she'd never told a soul.

'I hate to say it to you, babe, but your mother sounds like a total wipeout. I don't know how you're so sane,' he said.

'I don't feel it a lot of the time,' she admitted.

'Well, take it from me, you are. Everyone on set loves you too. You've got what it takes, Jodi. You're going to be an icon. Have a quick line of magic powder and your woes will disappear.'

'I like you, Mac, and I'd like us to be friends, but I won't ever be a drinking partner or a "buzz buddy" who'll take pills and snort stuff. I had a fun night. Thanks a million for dancing with me. I'll never forget you for listening to me. But right now I'm going to bed. On my own.'

Mac leaned forward and kissed her lightly on the lips. It only lasted seconds, but Jodi had felt it. The electric bolt that a million love songs were written about. 'Good night Mac,' she said, forcing herself to walk away.

She might have looked confident but her heart felt as if it would burst out of her chest, she was so shaken. She had a dreadful sinking feeling deep down that she'd probably just lost the only friend she had in the world.

For the next few weeks, she saw Mac every day on set after their fleeting kiss, and although he wasn't unfriendly, he was certainly a little cooler towards her. He made no attempt to kiss her again or suggest going out. A part of Jodi was relieved and a bigger part was disappointed.

When she'd returned from Dublin after her mother's funeral,

he was there offering a shoulder to cry on and a sympathetic ear. Whether it was a cheeky wink or a soothing hand stroking her back when she needed it, Mac always knew how to make her feel better. By the time they were almost through shooting the movie, Jodi had forgotten his previous treatment of her and was smitten with him. He made her laugh with his dark sense of humour. And he was Jodi's first real friend. To him she wasn't the sprog of a dead addict, who'd been kept alive by the handouts of social workers and the pity of neighbours. He taught her about loving, gently taking her to places she had never known existed between a man and a woman. He whispered sweet nothings into her ear and told her over and over again how much he loved her.

'Look at all the other blokes in here, Jodi,' he'd say, at the side of the set. 'They'd eat their own gonads to get close to you. I know you don't see it, but you're the hottest girl in this city and you're all mine.'

Jodi adored the sense of belonging. She thrived on being someone's other half and, most of all, she felt she was finally accepted.

After *Runaways* was wrapped up, Jodi got offers of more work in London and the obvious next step was to move in with Mac.

'We're a team, you and I,' he persuaded her. 'Things are only beginning. I'll look after you. I love you to the moon and back. I'm your Mac.'

Fateful words, which still haunted her.

Now she clenched her eyes shut. Mac's voice had once been so familiar to her. He'd been loving and trustworthy. Or so she'd foolishly thought.

'So, how have you been?' he asked.

'You didn't tell me last time – who gave you this number?' she repeated coldly.

'Ah, don't be so snappy, darling. It doesn't become you … I have my contacts, believe it or not,' he said, chuckling. 'Anyway, aren't you glad to hear my voice after all this time?'

'Cut to the chase, Mac. What do you want?'

'Ah, Jodi! Why the acid tones, my sweet?' He laughed. 'There's no need for us to be enemies. Haven't you missed me, baby?'

'You have five seconds. Tell me what you want before I hang up.'

'We need to meet up,' he said.

'No,' she said curtly.

'Don't be like that, Jodi,' he said, clearly irritated now.

'Mac — after everything that's happened between us—' Jodi stopped herself. She refused to play into his hands. She took a deep breath. 'I told you the last time that you weren't to contact me again. I meant it.'

'Ah, but things have changed a bit,' he explained. 'There's no work around and I've fallen on hard times. You remember what it's like to be in a tough situation, don't you? Of course you do,' he answered his own question. 'You know all about dark times. But your fans don't know the details, do they?'

'Mac, go and swing.' Jodi swallowed, remembering the words of Duke, her first producer, after her mother's overdose. He and a colleague had taken her aside as soon as she returned to the set.

'We can't begin to imagine how awful the last few days have been for you,' Duke began, 'but we wanted to advise you that stories involving drink and drugs won't do you any favours. It's our strong advice to you that you keep this under wraps.'

Jodi nodded.

'Jodi, we know you're not that way inclined. In fact, we've heard you won't even touch a drink. So we don't have any concerns about your conduct. But it might serve you better if you keep your past under wraps.'

'I'm not proud of where I come from and it's not something I want to announce, believe me,' she said quietly, with her eyes downcast.

After that Jodi kept her cards close to her chest. She never spoke about her mother or the poverty she was so anxious to drag herself away from.

'I don't care any more. I'm happy now and you can't hurt me,' she said to Mac.

'Can't I?' Mac let the question hang there. 'You seem to have forgotten what happened between us, honey, but I haven't. And then there's your gorgeous son Saul – is that his name?' He changed tack abruptly. 'Circumstances beyond my control have left me in a bit of a financial dip. If you could just wire me a bit of money to tide me over we can forget this conversation ever happened.'

Four years ago Jodi had given him a hefty sum and they'd agreed he would stay away. Permanently.

With Darius's love rat lurking in the background and now Mac resurfacing, Jodi felt fear rise in her gullet once more. Surely she had enough public support at this point in her life to ride the storm. Flashes of the past and the secret Mac was holding over her sent a shiver of terror through her. He knew it all. He knew about Bernadette and the overdose. He knew about the hideous life she'd worked so hard to leave behind. But, more than that, he knew about *that day*. The day Jodi would never forget as long as she lived.

'Ring me later. It's a bad time,' she said, knowing she needed space to think.

'That's my girl,' Mac said. 'Chat to you soon.' After he'd

clicked off, she took several deep breaths as she wondered how she was going to get Mac off her back for good.

'Was that Dad on the phone?' Saul said, appearing from his room and rubbing his eyes.

'No, darling,' Jodi said, jumping guiltily. 'It was a work person.'

'Why do you look worried?' he asked, staring at her.

'I'm just a bit tired after the photos yesterday. Hey,' she said, trying to throw him off the scent, 'it's a day off school. Why don't we go for a walk and explore?'

'Can we go up that big lane?' He pointed towards the manor house. 'Sebastian lives in there and he said we can call in any time. He told me when we went to see his cows.'

'Let's see where we end up,' Jodi said, not sure she wanted to land in on a man she didn't even know.

Dressed in warm clothes, Jodi and Saul made their way out to the back. As she gazed at the misty field and breathed in the crisp, clean air, Jodi wished her past would leave her alone.

'Mum!' Saul shouted. 'It's Sebastian! Hi, Sebastian! Mum and I are going for a walk! Want to come?'

'Hi, Saul,' their neighbour said, striding over to them. 'Nice day, isn't it?' he said, nodding at Jodi.

'Gorgeous.' She smiled.

'Are you coming with us?' Saul begged.

'If your mum doesn't mind.' Sebastian looked at her questioningly.

'Sure,' Jodi said. 'Maybe you can show us a good place to go.'

'There are loads of lovely walks around here,' he said, plucking a stick from a nearby tree and handing it to Saul. 'Follow me. There's a great meadow up at the back of this field. It's my land so you guys can go there whenever you wish.'

Saul bounded along like a puppy, using the stick to swipe at the longer pieces of bramble that jutted from the hedgerow. Jodi couldn't help but relax. 'This is why I wanted to live here,' she confided. 'It's a child's paradise, isn't it?'

'Adults too,' Sebastian said. 'I love it. It's so peaceful. There are loads of tourist attractions, like the waterfall and the big wooded area with the playground and nature trail, but this is like my own private piece of heaven.' Then he called to Saul, 'If you run on ahead a couple of yards and fling yourself into the long grass you can jump up and frighten us!'

'He adores you. You're very good with children,' she said.

'I've experience with little fellas,' he said, as his gaze dropped to the ground. 'I had a son.' He fell silent. Then, when Jodi didn't speak, he went on, 'Blake died.' He coughed roughly. 'I'm amazed you haven't been well versed on my life story by the gossips of the village.' There was a slightly bitter edge to his tone, but mostly Jodi felt his deep sadness.

'I don't know what to say, Sebastian. I had no idea.'

'Well, now you know,' he said gruffly. 'That was almost six years ago. My wife and I don't talk about it. In fact, I never discuss Blake at all.'

'I see,' Jodi said, trying to read his thoughts.

'So, if you don't mind, I'd rather you didn't bring it up every time I see you. I don't need or appreciate pity.'

'Sure,' Jodi said, holding her hands up.

'Boo!' Saul said, jumping out of the grass. Sebastian made a song and dance of gasping and clutching his heart, then fell over into the grass too.

'Look at Sebastian, Mummy! I nearly scared him to death!' Saul giggled.

'You sure did,' she said, flinging herself down too. 'You'd

better not do it again or he mightn't survive the walk.'

As they clambered back to their feet and made their way to the meadow, Jodi wondered what kind of woman Sebastian was married to that they never spoke of their dead son.

She shuddered. She couldn't imagine how she would go on should anything happen to Saul. But never to speak of him? Jodi didn't get it.

'There's a lovely mossy spot over here where I love to lie down and cloud spot,' Sebastian said.

'What's cloud spotting?' Saul asked, wrinkling his nose.

'You stretch out like this …' Sebastian showed him. 'Then you gaze up at the sky and wait for clouds in odd shapes to float by.' Jodi lay down next to Saul.

'Look over to the right,' Sebastian instructed them. 'That big fluffy white cloud with the second greyish one looks like an elephant. Can you make it out?'

'Ooh, yeah!' Saul said, loving the game. 'The one beside it looks like a monster. See the one eye winking?'

'Sure can,' Sebastian agreed.

As she lay on her back with her knees bent, Jodi thought of Mac once more. She'd achieved so much and took none of it for granted, yet one phone call from him had stirred a deeply buried feeling in a part of her heart that she wasn't sure would ever heal. For now, she forced herself to push it away.

'Uncle Tommy will be on Skype tonight,' she said to her little boy.

'Cool!' Saul said happily, and rolled onto his tummy. 'He lives in Australia, Sebastian. He's a surfer dude and when he's online he shows me the waves out of his window. He has a real shark's tooth around his neck.'

'He sounds great,' Sebastian said. 'Don't you have any family close by then?' he asked Jodi.

'Nope. My mother is dead and I never knew my father. Tommy is the only remaining member of my clan. Doesn't say much for me if he's chosen to run to the furthest corner of the globe, does it?' She smiled sadly.

'People can be right beside you and yet they're a million miles away in their head. So if you two have a good relationship, even on Skype, I'd take that happily.'

Jodi suddenly wanted to ask him a hundred questions. Where was the wife who didn't discuss their son? Why did he look so guarded all the time, allowing himself to relax only for fleeting moments?

'At least you have your wife,' Jodi ventured. 'My husband is away a lot right now. He's filming for the next few months.'

'Those grey clouds are increasing. I think we should get back. Feels like rain's on the way,' he said, standing up and brushing himself down.

Jodi felt awkward. What had she said that was wrong? She'd thought she was the queen of avoiding personal conversation, but it seemed Sebastian took that notion to a whole different level.

'You don't want to get soaked, little fella,' he said to Saul.

'I don't mind,' he said, slotting his hand into Sebastian's. Jodi was going to tell him not to be so forward, but the instant smile that spread across Sebastian's features told her to let it go.

Saul chattered happily the whole way back. 'Why don't you come in and have some coffee?' he asked Sebastian. 'Or a mug of the smelly stuff Mum drinks. It's totally pooey,' he said, crossing his eyes and pretending to strangle himself.

'It's a herbal infusion. Saul's right. It's utterly vile but you don't have to drink it.'

'If that's a promise, I'll pop in for a few minutes,' he conceded. She unlocked the cottage door and they went inside.

'Wow!' Sebastian was taken aback. 'You've done an amazing job in here, Jodi. I love it,' he said.

'Thanks.' She smiled easily. 'We love it too.'

'I'm very glad you bought it,' Sebastian admitted. 'For so long it was unloved and uncared for. I didn't get rid of it for the money. I simply wanted it to be brought to life again. You've done a wonderful job,' he said, glancing around appreciatively.

'If you only wanted the place to be loved and lived in you should have said. I'd gladly have taken it for free!' she quipped. He rewarded her with a twinkly-eyed grin.

Saul clambered on to the Aga as Jodi made them all a drink. 'I like living here,' he said. 'We never went for walks like that before and there's nothing but cars in towns. I'm staying at Bakers Valley for ever.' He nodded firmly.

'I'm glad you like it so much,' Sebastian said. 'How about you, Jodi? Are you happy to have moved here?'

'You bet,' she said, gripping her mug. As her mobile phone rang, her expression changed. 'Can you excuse me for a moment?' She walked towards her bedroom.

'We'll be here being cosy, isn't that right?' Sebastian said, ruffling Saul's hair.

ᴄꙅ

'Well?' Mac asked icily.

'I told you last time. The gravy train has dried up, Mac. Stay out of my life. I'm not going to allow you to bully me any longer.'

'Bully? That's a little strong, don't you think?' he said, through gritted teeth.

'Leave me alone, Mac.' She sighed.

'How swiftly you forget, Jodi,' he sneered. 'You're just like all the rest of the conceited actor ass-wipes. You crawled out of the filth you grew up in and didn't mind taking a leg up when I offered. Now when I come to you for help you slam the door in my face.'

'That's not true and you know it.'

'Isn't it?' He laughed bitterly. 'Maybe your mother was right all along. Didn't she tell you for years you were a jumped-up little cow? She may have been a drunk and an addict but I'm starting to think she knew you better than you thought.'

'That's enough, Mac. I don't have to listen to this crap.'

'What if I were to have a little chat with Saul? Tell him what kind of a mean, nasty woman his darling mummy really is?'

'Mac, you make me sick. Keep Saul out of this. He has nothing to do with any of your lies.'

'Don't you reckon he deserves to know what you're really like, Jodi?'

'I'm telling you, Mac,' Jodi said very slowly. 'Stay away from my son and keep out of my life. You promised.'

'But you haven't kept your promises, Jodi. You said you'd love me for ever. But you lied. Your little boy deserves to be warned about you. You're not fit to be a mother, or have you forgotten already?'

'I'm hanging up now, Mac,' Jodi said. Her entire body was trembling as she swallowed bile.

'You haven't heard the last of me, Jodi. You don't get to push me aside because I'm not good enough for your A-lister lifestyle. Karma has a habit of biting you on the ass, my girl. Get ready to feel the teeth.'

As he hung up, the tightness in Jodi's chest was almost overwhelming. Would she ever be free of her past? Maybe Mac and her mother were right. Maybe she didn't deserve to be free of the shackles she'd been born with. She'd always thought she could make things better and create a wonderful life for herself.

Her mother's scathing words and curled lip echoed in her mind. *You think you're better than me. I can see it in your eyes. You ruined my life, ya hear? I was fine until you came along and tied me to this dive. If it wasn't for you I could've been someone ... I could've been someone ...*

The sound of Saul's chatter mixed with Sebastian's deep, lilting voice pulled her away from the dull ache that was lurking inside and made her smile. She had a chance to live the life she'd always wanted here at Bakers Valley. She needed to ensure Mac didn't destroy it all. She just wasn't sure how to stop him.

Chapter 13

It was two days before Hallowe'en and the children were working themselves into a frenzy when Francine pitched up outside Cameron's classroom. She was living in a nightmare. She'd kept her contact with the school mothers to a minimum. Her nerves couldn't take the constant barrage of complaints about Cameron. Although everyone had been polite to her so far, she was bracing herself for a massive blow-out from someone soon. She figured it was best to keep a low profile.

She hated herself for it, but she'd been avoiding Jodi Ludlum like the plague. Her initial plan of making friends now seemed like the worst idea ever.

As she waited for Cameron to appear, Jodi arrived behind her. 'Francine!' she said cheerfully. 'Long time no see. How are things? I got the flyer about the Hallowe'en party. Jane and I were just walking in together and she was telling me it's usually a lot of fun.'

'Yes, of course! I do hope I can count on all of you to come along and support it! It's no fun if people stay away.' Francine's eyes were wide and she was speaking too fast. 'Now, there'll be the usual games and delicious food, spooky music, wonderful decorations and Lord only knows what else. You'll be there, won't you?' she asked, focusing on Jodi directly.

'Count Saul and me in,' Jodi said firmly.

'Right, right. Good. Great, in fact. Super,' Francine said, yanking at her clothing and flicking her hair in agitation.

☙

Jodi regarded the other woman. Bloody hell, she thought. Francine had lost weight and was drawn and pale. 'Are you okay? You look a bit frazzled,' she asked quietly, as the other women filtered away.

'Sorry?' Francine's smile didn't falter.

Jodi flushed. 'I didn't mean to insult you. I haven't seen you around and I was just wondering if you're feeling okay. You just seem a little, eh, hassled ...' She put a hand on Francine's arm.

'Oh, I'm fine! Everything's great. Just up to my eyes in arrangements, that's all. First there's this Hallowe'en party, and then we're straight into the whole yuletide thing! We have a Christmas ball at the Beech House Hotel, first Saturday in December. It's our main fundraiser for the year. We donate some money to the local Santa appeal and the rest goes to the school. You'll be there, won't you?'

Francine was talking at a hundred miles an hour. Her head was bobbing up and down so quickly she was making Jodi dizzy and her eyes were so wide she reminded Jodi of the lemur in the movie *Madagascar*.

'I'll have to check my schedule but thanks for letting me know about it.' Jodi thought she'd rather gouge her own eyes out with a fondue fork than go to the ball on her own, but she could deal with that at a later date.

'Fine. See you around,' Francine said, and turned on her heel.

'Catch you soon.' The classroom door opened and the children began to stream out. 'Saul, come on. Let's go home.'

Francine stopped dead and turned back. 'I'm taking Cameron to the café in the village for a hot chocolate. Would you and Saul like to join us?'

'Thanks for asking us, but I think we'll go on home,' Jodi said.

'Oh, do come,' Francine pressed. 'Unless you have a prior engagement? It'll be lovely.'

A brief silence hung in the air.

'Perhaps another day,' Jodi said.

'It'll be really quick and we haven't had a catch-up for so long! Jane, you'll come too, won't you?' Francine turned to Jane, who was attempting to coax Katie into the car beside them.

'Oh, I need to go to the supermarket.'

'That's perfect! The café's on the way!' Francine shrilled. 'I need to speak to you both, as it happens.'

Jodi looked at Jane and shrugged. 'Sure. But I'll literally stay fifteen minutes and then I'll need to get home,' she said.

'Super! Thank you. My treat, so let's go. Boys, come along!' she called out.

Saul ran to Jodi.

'We're just going for a quick hot choccie with Cameron and his mum in the village,' she said, sounding upbeat.

'You come with us and we'll meet Mum there,' Francine said, ushering Saul to her car.

'I'll take the boys down,' Jodi said.

'It's fine. I'm on to it,' Francine called, over her shoulder. 'Katie, you too. In you hop, darling.'

Saul stared miserably at Jodi, who shrugged her shoulders. She tossed his stuff into the back of the Mini and slammed the door, wondering why she was about to drive an empty car to the village and have hot chocolate with Francine when she'd already made sandwiches and soup at home.

By the time Jodi found a parking space in the busy little village street, Francine was already at the top of the queue in the café. Cameron was charging up and down with no regard for the other customers. Katie and Saul were huddled together.

'Come on, darlings, let's stand here and wait for our order,' Francine said chirpily.

Saul ran towards Jodi the minute he saw her. 'I want to go home,' he wailed. 'Cameron was kicking the back of his mum's seat the whole way here. Now he's being really naughty. I don't like it.'

'I know, pet, we'll stay a few minutes and then we'll head back. Deal?'

'Deal,' Saul said quietly.

As Jodi attempted to join the queue, Francine called, over the other people's heads, 'Come up here to me. I've ordered you a herb tea as I know you won't drink coffee unless I make it! Will you have a sambo, or there's spinach and pine nut quiche, which looks tasty? There you are, Jane! I've a latte on the way for you. What would you like to eat?'

Jodi made her way past the other people in the queue. At first they seemed miffed, but their expressions turned to delighted shock as they realised who she was. Neither Jodi nor Francine missed the elbowing and muttering behind hands.

'Herb tea is fine for me, thanks,' Jodi said, just above a whisper.

'Well, if you're sure, *Jodi*,' Francine said, emphasising her name to clear any doubt as to whom she might be.

'I'm not hungry, thanks,' Jane said, as she reached them.

'Fine, fine,' Francine said, dismissing her somewhat. 'You two find a table and I'll be along in a minute!' She was enjoying being in charge.

Saul, Katie and Cameron were over near the far corner, so they gravitated towards them. As the mums approached, Cameron yanked Saul into a headlock and began to pull him dangerously towards a solid wall.

'Hey, Cameron! Take it easy!' Jodi said. 'Shoving heads into walls isn't a good plan.'

'That's too rough. I don't like it when boys do that,' Katie said, looking frightened.

'Good boy, Cameron. Come and sit now,' Francine said, as she balanced the tray. 'Boys will be boys!' she said to Jodi.

Jodi smiled because she felt she ought to, but inside she felt like grabbing Cameron and saying, 'Don't strangle my son, you little shit.' But that wasn't the done thing and the staring villagers mightn't appreciate it.

Jodi was aware that Saul had spent a lot of time on set with herself and Darius. They'd travelled so much that he had never been in constant contact with children his own age. That was one of the reasons she'd moved home to Ireland. But now that she was being forced to tackle rough behaviour and uncomfortable situations with other people's kids, she felt out of her depth.

Saul had his father's sweet nature, although Jodi had noticed he was well able to stand up for himself. He had a confidence in himself that she only felt in front of the cameras.

Cameron finally let go of Saul.

'You hurt me, Cameron!' Saul said. 'If you keep on being mean to me, I won't play with you.'

'You can sit beside me,' Katie said kindly, as Saul rubbed his neck. 'I don't strangle.'

'You shut it!' Cameron yelled at Katie.

'Come and sit with your friends, Cameron,' Francine intervened.

Jane and Jodi exchanged a brief look as Francine chirped away, seemingly oblivious to her son's behaviour.

'Doesn't the hot chocolate look gorgeous?' Francine said, sounding rather like Mary Poppins on speed. 'Yummy! Bet you can't wait to taste it,' she continued. 'I must say, the muffins don't look quite the way mine would turn out, but never mind!' She encouraged Cameron to sit still. 'Good boy. Now, you three children do us all a favour and be the best little dotes you can so Jodi, Jane and I can have a lovely chat.'

Her smile never faltered. Her tone remained upbeat. But her back was ramrod straight and Jodi noticed she was perched on the edge of her seat.

'So!' Francine continued. 'Seeing as we're all here I might as well let you know I've decided to give up work. Take a sabbatical for a while.'

'Really?' Jane said, shocked. 'Why? I thought you loved working.'

'Yes, I do,' Francine said. 'But I was made an offer I can't refuse. I'll take the very large cheque. Once an accountant, always an accountant.' She giggled. 'There are a million and one things I want to do, so now's my time.'

'Good for you,' Jodi said. 'When do you finish up then?'

Cameron leaped from his chair on top of Saul, sending all the hot drinks flying and knocking Saul on to the tiled floor.

'Saul!' Jodi screamed.

The thud, followed by a brief silence, was horrifying. As she pulled him up from the floor, Jodi discovered that her son's nose was pumping blood and the poor little boy was bellowing in shock and pain. Katie burst into uncontrollable sobs too, holding her hands out to Jane. 'Mummy, Saul's bleeding! I want to go home.'

'I want to go home too,' Saul cried.

'Okay, honey. Let's go,' Jodi said, hugging him.

Jane jumped up and shoved a paper napkin at her. 'Pinch the top of the bridge of his nose to stop the bleeding. Poor Saul, you're very brave,' she said.

'Oh dear! He'll be fine in a second. Here, let me take him to the Ladies and I'll have that nose cleaned up in no time,' Francine said, attempting to take Saul from Jodi's arms.

'No, thank you, Francine. We're going home now,' Jodi said curtly.

'Cameron didn't mean it, sure you didn't, Cameron.' Francine stared at her son.

'Can you pass my bag, please?' Jodi asked.

'Don't go - we were having such a lovely time. I'm sure Saul will be ready to play again in a minute if he sits on your lap quietly and finishes his hot chocolate,' Francine begged.

'No, thanks. We're going home now,' Jodi repeated. 'The hot chocolate is all over the floor along with my son's blood so I think we're finished here. Can I have my bag, please, Francine?'

'But it's such a shame to—'

'Please pass my bag!' Jodi said, slightly louder.

Francine did as she was asked, and Jodi threaded her way out of the busy coffee shop with the still-sobbing Saul in her arms.

Katie was clinging to Jane like a baby koala, gulping with shock.

'We're going to call it a day too. Besides, I have shopping to do,' Jane said, not making eye contact with Francine.

'Oh, please don't go. I wanted to go through some of the pointers for the Hallowe'en party!' Francine said desperately.

'I'll phone you later. I'm sorry, Francine, but we're leaving now,' Jane said firmly.

Jodi knew Jane was close behind her but she didn't wait around to have any chats. She just wanted to get the hell out of there and back to the safety of their little cottage.

'I said I didn't want to play with him,' Saul said, as Jodi sat him in the car and dabbed at his nose.

'I know, Saul, but that woman doesn't seem to take no for an answer,' Jodi said.

'What do you mean?' Saul looked confused.

'Oh, nothing. Cameron's mummy just really wanted us to have hot chocolate with them. That's all.'

'Is he okay?' Jane appeared at the side of the car carrying Katie.

'He'll be fine. He's just not used to rough-and-tumble, I guess. I know people expect all boys to adore it but Saul's a gentle soul.'

'If it helps, my son doesn't behave like that *ever*. And, quite frankly, if he did, I wouldn't tolerate it. I'm supposed to be her friend so I think I'm going to have to sit Francine down and have some frank discussions with her,' Jane said.

'These things happen,' Jodi said diplomatically.

'Yes, but it's not acceptable when it's all the time,' Jane said. 'All the boys in the class are obsessed with wrestling at the moment. I've seen Saul playing it too. That's about as far as it should go at this age. Messing about in good spirits is one thing, but these constant attacks that Cameron's carrying out have to stop.'

'I'm certain he didn't mean to hurt Saul,' Jodi said.

'See you at the Hallowe'en party on Friday, if not before. Hope you feel better soon, Saul,' Jane called into the car.

Saul and Katie waved to one another as Jodi jumped into the Mini and drove like a bat out of hell, cursing under her breath.

She was reaching a point of no return with Cameron. He was far too rough for his own good.

Parenting was tricky. But Jodi was starting to wonder if it was the mothers rather than the offspring who were the most difficult. One minute Francine seemed to want to be her friend and the next she was behaving erratically. Jodi knew Darius had had a point when he'd told her she was far too uncommunicative with others. She knew she needed to broaden her horizons, get out and make new friends. But each time she did, she got burned.

As she pulled up outside the cottage, Jodi felt like taking Saul inside, locking the door and never coming out again.

Chapter 14

Francine felt as if she was going to vomit. Her stomach was knotted and she could barely focus on drinking her coffee. She had been traumatised enough by having to tell the ladies she was now unemployed but Cameron had made things so much worse. Her plan had been to tell Jane - after all, telling Jane was like putting an advert in the local paper. Then her new status would filter through the community and she could pretend it had been her own choice. But it had gone horribly wrong.

Now she wanted to drag Cameron out of the café. But the place was packed and there were too many people she knew. One of the mothers from Conor's class had popped over seconds after Jodi had fled and asked if she could join her. Thankfully, she'd missed the awful scene between Cameron and Saul. Francine didn't doubt that some busybody would fill her in at a later stage, but for now the woman was a very welcome distraction.

'It's lovely to see you. How are you?' Francine said, clicking into hostess-with-the-mostest mode.

'Oh, not too bad. I thought I'd treat myself to a cappuccino and a sticky bun before I head up to the school and collect the troops.'

'Yes, you're dead right. Sometimes we mums just need a little treat!' Francine said, with forced cheer.

'I couldn't help but notice Jodi Ludlum getting into her car just now. I believe she has a son in the kindergarten this year. Have you met her at all?'

'As a matter of fact we're becoming firm friends,' Francine said. 'She's such a lovely person. Once you get to know her you forget she's a movie star. She's just a mum, like you and me.'

'Well, hardly,' the woman said. 'She's so pretty, isn't she? Gosh, I couldn't believe it when I heard she was living in Bakers Valley. I'm a massive fan – I don't suppose you'd introduce me to her at the Hallowe'en party, would you? Or would that seem too groupie of me?'

'Of course I will, sweetie. She'd love to meet you. Come and find me on Friday and give me the nod,' Francine promised. 'You know me, I'll be flitting around doing my bits and bobs but if you remind me I'll make sure you meet her properly.'

'Ooh, I'm so excited! Thanks, Francine! I hope you don't think I'm a total muppet asking you!'

'Not at all. Before we were friends I was in awe of Jodi too!' Francine confided. 'Not that I don't still think she's very special – obviously she is – but I guess once you know someone well they're just the same as everyone else.'

To Francine's relief, Cameron was busy playing under the table with a Power Ranger figure he'd found in her bag so she hadn't had to scold him or betray how sick she was feeling after what had just happened. 'Jeepers! Look at the time! We'd better get back up to the school and collect the children,' she said. 'Come along, Cameron, there's a good boy.'

'He's as good as gold, isn't he, bless him?' the other lady said.

'They're lovely at that age. Content to play with a little toy! Gone are the days when my lot would be happy to do the same.'

'Er, yes,' Francine said uneasily. 'He's a great lad.'

'See you at school, no doubt,' the other woman said.

'Bye-bye, take care!' Francine said, waving as sweetly as a 1970s air hostess.

Cameron dashed over to the car as Francine clicked the doors open with the remote control. Clipping himself into his booster seat, he continued to play with his toy and began to kick the back of her seat.

'Stop kicking me, please, Cameron,' she said.

'No,' he answered, and kicked harder.

'I've asked you to stop it!' she almost shouted.

Turning to look between the two front seats, she tried to make eye contact with him. 'Why are you deliberately trying to annoy me?' she asked.

He stuck out his tongue at her and returned to his Power Ranger.

'Why did you knock Saul off his chair earlier?' she asked.

Cameron ignored her.

'Cameron!' she yelled. 'Why did you hurt Saul?'

The small boy continued to make sound effects. He turned the little Power Ranger upside down and made him jump on to the back of the driver's seat.

Francine snatched the toy and threw it on the floor in the front of the car.

'Hey!' Cameron shouted.

'Answer me when I speak to you!' Francine shrieked. 'Why did you hurt Saul?'

'I didn't.' Cameron pouted, folded his arms and glued his eyes shut.

Francine was so incensed she actually thought she was going to have a heart attack. She faced the steering wheel and started the ignition. That was it. The final straw. She couldn't take another incident with Cameron. She was going to talk to Carl that evening and beg him to find help for their son. After the episode with Mr Brady, he had convinced her that little boys often did things like that. 'He's a bit wilder than the others but he's the youngest of four, darling. He sees and hears everything. He's around older kids,' Carl reasoned. 'He's bound to end up a bit more flighty than Cara or Conor.'

Francine had desperately wanted him to be right. But she'd known deep down that there was something different about the way Cameron behaved.

Now things had reached the point at which she couldn't take Cameron anywhere without him causing a scene. The other children were beginning to dread him too. No matter how pushy she was, most of the mothers simply wouldn't let their children go to her house.

Something had to give.

Mr Matthews couldn't be wrong all the time either. He'd suggested to Francine weeks ago that they have Cameron assessed. But that had seemed so over the top at the time.

'He's just the youngest of four and flexing his muscles,' Francine had said, quoting Carl.

She'd thought that if she was cheerful and pleasant all the time, Cameron would follow suit and the other mothers wouldn't glower at him so much. She'd taken to avoiding everyone, including poor Jodi. She felt like a heel for not speaking to her. She was certain Jodi Ludlum thought she was a raving lunatic. One minute Francine had been clamouring to be her best buddy and the next she was diving into bushes to avoid her.

She'd tried everything she could think of to get through to Cameron but nothing had worked. She'd phoned Annie to apologise and asked her how she'd managed to keep him in line.

'I didn't, Francine. That was my point all along. Why do you think I'd phone you in work and ask you to bring home milk? I couldn't face bringing Cameron as far as Spar, let alone to the supermarket.'

Francine felt as if she was in prison.

Shouting at Cameron made no difference.

If she sent him to his bedroom, he trashed it. If she made him sit on time out at the bottom of the stairs, like Supernanny on the television, he'd simply scale the front door and run out on the road.

Things were out of control, and Francine had to admit to herself that she was struggling.

She was desperately sad for Cameron as he was clearly having a difficult time, but his behaviour had to be addressed.

Francine couldn't enjoy village and school life now: people stared at her as if she were a criminal. It was awful to realise her friends were running away from her and Cameron as if they carried a contagious disease.

She went to fetch Cara, Craig and Conor that day without stopping to chat to the other mothers. Instead she kept a firm grip on Cameron's hand and marched him at high speed to the collection area.

'I want to climb the tree! Some of my friends are there,' he protested.

Still smiling, Francine bent down and whispered in his ear, 'Don't think of causing another scene. You're coming home with me straight away. You've been far too naughty already today so don't push me any further.'

The searing pain that shot up her arm from Cameron's savage bite made Francine cry out. The child broke free and scrambled up the tree, stepping on little Max's fingers.

Max burst into tears.

'I'm the king of the castle – *na na na-na na*!' Cameron shouted triumphantly.

Francine fought back tears as she hid her hand, which showed clear toothmarks and was already bruised and throbbing. 'Come down now, boys,' she called. 'It's cold and slippy up there!'

Dee, Max's mother, ran over and took her sobbing child into her arms. 'What happened, darling?'

'Cameron stamped on my hands by purpose and my fingers are all squashed and sore!'

'That wasn't very nice,' Dee said, with a furrowed brow. 'Poor you. Let me have a look.'

Some of the other parents had stopped to see what all the commotion was about.

'Cameron, down you come, there's a good boy,' Francine said sweetly. 'You seem to have hurt Max by mistake. Let's say sorry to him and tell him you didn't mean it.' She kept her voice as even as she could.

'No! I'm staying here.'

'Cameron, please!' Francine's voice cracked. She was beginning to lose it.

'No.'

'Come on, Max, let's get you home,' Dee said.

'Wait a moment! Cameron wants to shake hands and say sorry,' Francine cried.

'No way!' he shouted, from the top of the tree.

'Forget it,' Dee said, without hiding her annoyance – she was usually mild-mannered. 'Some kids need a good telling-off in my opinion.' Flushed and upset, she fled with Max and his older sister.

Francine's head was spinning with embarrassment and humiliation. 'Cameron, I'm going home now. If you don't come down this instant, you'll be left up that tree all by yourself for the night,' she warned.

The threat of spending the night at school was enough to make him clamber down. From a dangerous height, he launched himself towards the grass.

Francine lurched forward to see if he was all right. 'You'll hurt yourself doing that!' He jumped up and scurried towards their car.

Cara, Conor and Craig were already ensconced in it, waiting to go home.

'Did you see me jump?' Cameron said proudly.

'You could've killed yourself,' Francine said, as she started the car. All she wanted was to get the hell out of the school car park. She knew she'd have to call Max's mother later and apologise.

Her panic was all-encompassing. The three older children chattered about their day and Francine nodded numbly.

At home, the older children, used to the after-school routine, found themselves a snack and got started on their homework.

'I've only these five spellings and reading out loud to do,' Craig said. He'd watched his older brother and sister doing homework for years and was delighted he'd had some of his own since September.

'I'll help you now,' Francine promised. She'd spent the few minutes since they'd returned wondering miserably how she could pull herself through the next few years with Cameron.

'Mum?' Craig prompted, when she didn't move.

'Sorry?' She sighed. 'Oh, yes, love. Let's get your learning sorted. Come on, we'll go into my office. Cameron, why don't you look at a picture book while we're doing Craig's reading?' Francine suggested.

'No way. I hate books more than dog poo,' he said loudly.

Unable to come up with an alternative suggestion, Francine broke her no-computer-games-during-the-week rule. 'You can go on the PlayStation for a while,' she said.

Within minutes there was calm and silence. Cameron lost himself in the game, and she watched from the playroom door as he wriggled around on the beanbag to get comfy.

'I thought we weren't allowed PlayStation on school nights,' Conor said, appearing from his room.

'I'm making an exception tonight. You can all have half an hour each as a treat once homework is done,' Francine said, not wanting a fresh row.

'*Cha-ching!*' Conor said, balling his fist and pulling his arm down in triumph.

'Me, too?' Craig asked hopefully.

'Yes, you, too,' Francine said, rubbing her temples. 'Maybe yourself and Conor could play WWE against each other in a while. Let's get this reading and spelling done quickly.'

As Craig read from his English book, Francine's mind was whirring. The child could have been skipping words, mispronouncing others and telling her about a brutal murder and she wouldn't have noticed.

'Was that good, Mum? Mum?' Craig tapped her on the arm.

'Oh, sorry, love. That was brilliant. You're a great reader, do you know that?' She smiled, feeling guilty that she hadn't been paying attention. 'Now, once your spellings are learned, you're all done and dusted!'

Craig scribbled each word down without getting a single one wrong.

'Good lad,' she said, stroking his hair. 'Your teacher will have nothing but great reports for me when the parent-teacher meetings come around.'

'I'll put my things in my bag and see where the wrestling game is!' he said, thrilled with the idea.

'Okay, but leave Cameron a little while longer. He hasn't had his half-hour yet,' she warned.

The second her son left the room Francine fired up her computer and typed 'child assessment' into Google. Half an hour later, having surfed the net, Francine had narrowed the search down to a clinic about twenty minutes away. That would be fine. At that distance she wouldn't bump into anyone she knew.

Her hands shook as she dialled the number.

'Good afternoon, Nuala speaking, how may I help you?' The voice was so warm and friendly.

The anonymity the telephone afforded her allowed Francine to describe honestly the nightmare that had taken over their lives. 'I don't know what to do next ... I need help,' she whispered.

'I understand,' Nuala said calmly. 'I'd like to meet with yourself, your husband and Cameron.'

'When?' Francine's voice wobbled. 'I haven't run this past Carl and we always discuss everything, so I hope he'll agree, but I need your advice.'

'I can hear that. I have an appointment available tomorrow morning. I could put you down for that. If Carl doesn't want to go ahead, you can phone and leave a message this evening. The answer machine will be switched on. How's that?'

Relief flooded Francine. No matter what happened from

here on in, it had to be better than the knife's-edge existence they'd all been experiencing of late.

None of this was part of the plan that she and Carl had worked out so carefully. They'd known exactly how their life would pan out. Or, at least, they'd thought they did.

Francine was certain that all they needed now was to see Nuala and follow some pointers. Then, with a bit of hard work – they weren't shy of that in their house – life could get back to normal. Francine could concentrate on the committee and the lovely parts of school life once more. She'd already decided she was going to look for another job after Christmas. She had a niggling feeling this had escalated because she was hanging around at a loose end.

Meanwhile, nobody need know the details of what was going awry. This time next year she and Carl could share a bottle of red wine while chatting about that little spat with Cameron.

More optimistic than she had been for quite a while, Francine hummed as she made dinner.

There was a bit of a row as Cameron was told to give his brothers a turn on the PlayStation, but she'd allowed him to go into the living room and have control of the big television instead. Until she knew how to deal with Cameron's temper, she needed to keep things calm.

When she heard the front door open and Carl calling that he was home, Francine rushed to greet him. 'Hi, love! Good day?' she asked.

'Not bad. You?'

'Well … mixed. Come into the office for a minute, will you? I want to tell you something,' she said, slightly nervous of his reaction.

She began with the misdemeanours of that day and how awful

it had been both for herself and the children Cameron had hurt. She confessed to Carl that she'd been getting more and more worried about Cameron's behaviour and had finally called Nuala as a last resort.

'You've made an appointment with a child psychologist?' Carl was furious. 'I still think you're overreacting. But, more than that, we should've discussed it.'

'I know you hate rash decisions, Carl. I do too, but I was at breaking point earlier,' Francine said, wringing her hands. 'I didn't know how to fix our son. He was violent and behaving like a thug. ' She shuddered at the memory.

'If you say so,' Carl said.

'You don't believe me, do you?' Francine turned on her husband. 'Carl, why would I lie about such a thing? I can't begin to tell you how awful it's been for me. Nobody wants their children playing with Cameron! I used to have a carload of little ones leaving that kindergarten when our older ones were there. Now people shy away from us as if we're diseased.'

'Ah, steady on, love. I can't imagine they feel that strongly,' Carl said, looking uncomfortable. Francine and he were like-minded in their views on socialising and their reputation within the community. He loved to present his colleagues with cakes and scones on random Fridays. He looked forward to the Hallowe'en party at the school. The Christmas ball was one of the highlights of his year, along with his own work do. He couldn't bear the thought of going to any of those events if people were avoiding them.

'As I just told you, he assaulted Jodi Ludlum's son in the café today in front of half the village. Then he climbed up a tree and trampled on another child's fingers and refused point blank to come down when I asked.' Francine was exhausted. 'I can't take any more, Carl. Please try to see this from my point of view. The bottom has been ripped out of my career. I'm stuck at home trying to pretend to the entire village that I'm on an extended holiday and now this. I've tried to act as if Cameron is behaving normally but it's out of hand now.'

'Okay so.' He sighed deeply as he gazed at his wife. 'I'm on board,' he said. 'But promise me one thing?' He tilted his head to the side and wagged his finger half in jest, half in seriousness. 'Don't make such massive decisions without me again. We're a team, you and I. Team Hennessy, remember?'

'Team Hennessy,' Francine echoed, hugging him. Inside, she'd never felt more like a solo artist in her life.

Chapter 15

Jodi grinned as she flicked through the complimentary glossy magazine she'd just received in that morning's post. She and Darius looked the picture of marital bliss on the front cover. She picked up her phone and rang him, hoping she wasn't waking him.

'Hey, sweetie.' He'd answered immediately. 'Let me guess. You're looking at how gorgeous we are on the front of *Celebrity Lies*?' he joked.

'It's a lovely picture.' She giggled. 'We really are the epitome of a wonderful life. Any more rumblings from your annoying little fella?' she asked.

'Nah, he's gone,' Darius said. 'Thank goodness. I really know how to pick baddies, don't I?'

'Not all the time,' she said. 'You have me!'

'Yeah, and you're the best thing that ever happened to me but I didn't exactly orchestrate us, lest you forget!'

'Whatever,' Jodi said. 'We make it work – better than most couples, if you ask me – so we must be doing something right. How come you're so bright and breezy? I was half expecting to get your voicemail or a groggy-sounding bear?'

'I'm about to begin shooting. I've been here since dawn, darling.'

'I'm turning into a real country bumpkin!' Jodi admitted. 'The thought of having to sit and have my hair and makeup done really doesn't appeal to me at the moment. Saul and I spent half the day wandering fields and staring at clouds this weekend. I'm terrified I'm going to want to jack it all in and get hens and live in worn-out wellingtons with grey hair and no teeth!'

'Sounds so attractive!' He laughed. 'You'll get the bug again as soon as they point a camera at you. The silver screen is your home, Jodi. You'll never leave this nonsense. Any more than I will.'

'You're probably right,' she said. 'Saul can't wait to see you for Hallowe'en.'

'I'm counting the days until you guys get to London,' he said. 'There'll be some seriously cool people here at the party.'

'Great,' she said.

'God, don't make it sound like you're being sentenced to twelve months in jail when it's a weekend in London rubbing shoulders with the stars,' he teased.

'I hate all that shit and you know it. Listen, I've had a call from Mac.'

'*What?* How did he get your number?'

'Ah, what does it matter? You know him. He has his dirty spies.'

'What did he want?'

'Money, of course,' she said. 'I thought he'd leave me alone after the last time. Those guys we used to make the delivery were bloody threatening and he got a serious amount of cash out of me. I can't pay him any more, Darius. I'm thinking of dealing with him myself this time. I'm ready for a face-off. If he goes to the press, I'll have to take the heat. Darius, I'm really scared. He could rip our lives apart. Every time I think

I've dealt with Mac, he comes back. Just as I think I can make it all work he steps out of the shadows. I'm terrified, but I'm starting to think it's D-day. I have to muster up the courage to face him down finally. I need to grow up.'

There was silence.

'Darius?'

'I'm here,' he said sadly. 'I know you're probably right, and even though I'm thirty-six I can't say I love the idea of growing up if it means airing our dirty laundry in public. I don't know that you'll do either of us any favours.'

'I get that,' she said. 'But when are we going to draw the line, Darius? That little skunk you had to pay a few weeks ago wasn't the first and, let's face it, he won't be the last. Mac is a scumbag. He's never going to go away.'

'Probably not. But what about Saul?'

'We talked about this a long time ago,' she reasoned. 'We don't have to announce on the front cover of every newspaper that you're gay, but I can set *my* ghosts free. You can step away once the dust settles and we can do a press release to say we're parting on amicable terms.'

'If you decide to challenge Mac and your secrets come out, that's one thing, but I'm not abandoning you at the same time. I won't do that to you,' he vowed. 'At least if the public can see that you're now happily married to a loving partner, it'll defuse the situation quicker.'

'Wouldn't it just be easier to cut our losses and step away from the web of lies that have lurked in the shadows for so long?'

'Leave it with me,' he said. 'I have to go. They're calling me to set. Don't do anything until we see each other at Hallowe'en.'

'Okay. Love you,' she said automatically.

'Love you, too, sweet-pea,' he said, and hung up.

Jodi wasn't sure if the change of scene had prompted her sudden urge to clear her slate. But she knew she'd hit a point at which she didn't want to run any longer. Her secrets were bound to come out some time. But fresh courage had seeped into her soul. It was probably because Mac, scum that he was, had mentioned Saul. Jodi had vowed she was never going to allow her son to be hurt. If Mac was planning on attempting to drag him into things she had to act decisively. She wasn't going to wait for it all to blow up in her face. She was going to meet it head on. How could she be a good mother to her son if she didn't act with honesty and decency? Her mother had never told the truth in her life. She'd always blamed everyone else for her own mistakes. Jodi wanted to be everything Bernadette hadn't been, which meant being true to herself.

It was time for her to admit the real reason she'd moved Saul to Ireland. She wanted to prove to herself that she was capable of giving her son the childhood she'd lacked. But that was only part of it. She had to face up to the awful event that had rocked her world and left her mentally scarred. It was time to stop running.

CB

Saul came out of school with a handful of paintings. 'I spent fifteen hours doing art today,' he said earnestly.

'So it seems.' She grinned. 'We have enough pictures here to wallpaper the entire cottage!'

As they drove the short distance home Jodi's phone beeped.

'It's a text from Uncle Tommy,' she told Saul. 'That's odd – he wants us to call him.'

Jodi worried endlessly about her younger brother. Until she

heard his voice, she always assumed the worst when he asked her to Skype him. She'd long since given up phoning him.

'It's so expensive and pointless when we can Skype!' he'd insisted. 'I'm making a stand and telling you to stop wasting your millions on phone calls.'

'Okay, okay!' She'd laughed. 'I'll convert to Skype!'

'What did Uncle Tommy say?' Saul wanted to know, as they ran into the house.

'We've to turn on Skype this second,' she said, already clicking on the computer. A minute or two later, Tommy was on the screen.

'G'day, sis!' he greeted her.

'You crack me up! I don't know whether or not you're putting on the Ozzie to entertain me or if you've really lost your Irish accent.'

'Weren't you the one who used to correct me and tell me I wasn't speaking properly?' Tommy was referring to the time before she'd become famous, when she had gone for elocution lessons.

'When I think of it now I still cringe,' Jodi admitted.

'Don't knock it, sis, you were right. Look where it's got you,' Tommy said. 'Where's my nephew? I need to hear all about school.'

Saul jumped up and down as he spoke to his uncle.

'Sit down a sec, mate. You're bopping all over the shop!' Tommy grinned.

'Look at my paintings!' Saul said, holding them up to the camera.

'Wow! You're seriously talented, aren't you?' Tommy said, clapping.

'Yes, I am. And I'm a good boy,' Saul told him. 'There's one bad boy in the class.' He leaned into the camera. 'He hits and bites and I went to his house and he was *so* mean.'

'You tell him your uncle Tommy will get him if he goes near you!' Tommy said, looking fierce.

'Tommy! Not cool!' Jodi shouted, from the background.

'Tell your mummy I don't care – nobody messes with my nephew!'

Saul giggled.

'Well, Maisy and I have some pretty cool news for you, guys,' Tommy said.

'What?' Saul asked, as Jodi shot over and scooped her son on to her lap.

'We're engaged!' he said, with a huge grin.

'Oh, my God, that's amazing, Tommy!' Jodi said, as tears threatened. 'I'm so thrilled for you both.'

'Aw, thanks, sis. We're thinking of having the wedding down here, but not if you can't make it.'

'Of course I can,' Jodi vowed. 'When were you thinking of?'

'Early next year,' he said. 'After the baby's born!'

'*Whaat?*' Jodi screamed. 'That's brilliant! You're going to have a little cousin, Saul.'

'Cool! Is it a boy or a girl cousin?' Saul asked.

'We don't know yet, dude. We're going to wait until it's born to find out.'

'How far along is Maisy?' Jodi asked.

'Six months,' Tommy said ruefully. 'Please don't yell at me, but we wanted to wait a while before telling people. Maisy's been really sick and we were scared something might go wrong.'

Tears slid down Jodi's cheeks. 'I'm just glad they're both all right now.'

'Why are you crying, Mum?' Saul asked, as he swivelled in her lap. 'Is the baby not well? Is Maisy not well?'

'Nothing like that, lovie. They were a bit poorly for a while but they're fine now.'

'So, will you think about making the trip down under to see your niece or nephew and come to our beach wedding?' Tommy asked.

Saul didn't give her a chance to reply. 'Will you have sharks and surfing there?'

'Deffo!'

Saul continued to question Tommy about the waves and how many hours he'd be able to spend on the beach when he came to visit.

'Okay, little man, I'm off to get some stuff done,' Tommy said. 'Catch you in a few days, and you make sure that Cameron guy stays away from you or he'll have me to answer to! Tell him I'll send a shark to bite him on the bum.'

'Do you have a pet shark?' Saul asked hopefully.

'No, dude, but I could possibly arrange to find one if we need it!'

'Tommy, enough already!' Jodi yelled. 'He thinks every syllable you utter is gospel.'

'Okay, okay!' Tommy held up his hand in defeat. 'You know I'm only kidding, right?'

Saul looked mildly disappointed. 'I thought you were going to send a big killer shark to chew Cameron's leg off.'

'Steady on, Saul!' Tommy roared laughing.

As they switched off the computer, Jodi hugged Saul to her. She couldn't have been happier for Tommy that he was going to have a son or daughter. Saul had healed so many wounds for her. Tommy and Maisy had a wonderful relationship, but fatherhood would be the making of him.

Jodi hoped his childhood hadn't been quite as bleak as hers.

After all, he'd been raised mostly by Nana. But she knew there must be a similar hollow feeling in his heart at how their mother had treated them. They'd spoken of Bernadette's death a few times, but Tommy claimed he hadn't much memory of it. He was so easy-going he almost annoyed Jodi.

'If I didn't adore you so much I'd want to grab you and shake you!' she'd said, the last time he and Maisy had visited them in London. 'You just float from one day to the next!'

'Do you want me to behave like a wound-up movie mogul?' He'd begun striding up and down the apartment with his fists balled, muttering to himself.

Jodi had giggled and assured him she loved him just as he was.

The dark clouds outside had been threatening rain all morning, so when hailstones battered the cottage, Jodi lit the pot-bellied stove. 'Let's have a story. We'll cuddle up on the sofa,' she said.

Saul was really enjoying the C.S. Lewis book they'd started a couple of days before.

Jodi wanted to freeze-frame these cosy moment with her son. As he clambered on to the couch and snuggled into her, his face filled with anticipation, indescribable happiness flooded her every fibre. Nobody had ever sat with her and read a story like this. 'Now, where were we?' she asked Saul, as he began to suck his thumb and absentmindedly wag his foot.

As if she were acting a script, Jodi immersed herself in each and every story they read together. Saul listened intently as the tale unfolded in Narnia.

'Would you like to go somewhere out of our wardrobe?' he asked.

'I couldn't think of anything I'd love more,' Jodi said.

'Have you ever tried?'

'No, honey, but it might spoil the story if we did. Just in case our wardrobe isn't a magic one,' Jodi said gently.

'But if we don't look how do we know it isn't magic?' he reasoned. 'It could be waiting for us to come and find it!'

'Well, you can go and check, if you like,' she said, trying to keep a straight face.

'Will you come too?'

'Okay,' she said, putting the book down.

'Let's not,' Saul said. 'It'd be sad if Narnia wasn't there.'

'Sometimes it's more fun to imagine the magic rather than going to look for it,' she explained.

Plugging his thumb into his mouth again, he waited for her to continue reading.

The day melted away as they finished the book and shared frozen pizza from the Aga.

'I think it tastes better because it's been cooked by such a gorgeous oven,' Jodi said.

Later, after she'd tucked him up in bed, Jodi pottered towards the kitchen deciding to take a mug of herbal tea to bed and flick through her copy of *Celebrity Gossip*. She'd long since given up buying or reading most glossies. Some of the stories they printed were so far from the truth they'd upset her. Now she'd come to the conclusion she shouldn't take it all so seriously. Still, one of the items that never ceased to make her cross was the comparison of two celebrities in the same dress. She sat bolt upright in bed when she realised she was one of the celebrities in that issue. She was pictured in a D&G gown at a recent red carpet event, and was pitched against an American starlet. She cringed to see that the readers' poll had chosen herself as the hands-down winner. She called Darius and was glad to hear him answer immediately.

'Hey, babe,' he said.

'Hey,' she answered. 'Did you flick through the rest of that god-awful rag we're on the front cover of?'

'Sort of. Why? Did I miss something?'

'I'm in one of those hideous comparison pieces in that red D&G dress you love.'

'Did you win?' he asked.

'Yes, but that's not the point. That poor girl who lost can't be more than nineteen. She's going to see this and feel about two feet tall. What makes them do this to women?' she raged. 'They don't have men dressed in the same T-shirt and rip one to shreds saying he's got a wobbly belly or a double chin. It's really nasty – such a personal assault. It makes me so angry.'

'I don't know why you're so annoyed,' Darius said. 'They love you. As far as I'm concerned, that's good enough for me.'

'That's not the point, Darius. We're both professional women doing our best. Where's the sense of sisterhood? Why would anyone want to look at this kind of thing? It's so demeaning!'

'Calm down, honey,' Darius soothed. 'I told you ages ago to stop reading those magazines. If it winds you up like that, avoid it.'

'But don't you agree or at least see my point?'

'Yes, I do. But people must derive some sort of pleasure out of criticising celebrities.'

'But we're not robots! We're people with feelings just the same as everyone else,' Jodi ranted.

'I guess that's show business.'

'Well, I'll never diss the trade because it's our bread and butter, but we shouldn't be torn to pieces like this.'

'The flip side is that the press have made us who we are today. Look at the front cover. We rock!'

The sound of voices in the background gave Jodi the hint to get off the line.

'I'm out having a bite to eat before I hit the hay,' Darius said. 'I'll talk to you tomorrow. And put that magazine away. You'll only stay awake all night seething. I know you!'

'You're right. Talk tomorrow.'

Jodi gazed at the picture of love and contentment on the front cover. They looked like the happiest couple alive. She wondered if her private life would ever be as perfect as the one the media thought she led.

Chapter 16

The Hennessy household was up and ready for school with plenty of time to spare.

'Why are both you and Dad taking us today?' Cara asked suspiciously, as Carl and Francine made their way to the people-carrier.

'We have a meeting to go to this morning and we're heading straight there once we've brought you to school,' Francine explained.

Carl made it his business to be at his desk before everyone else each morning so he'd left a message with his senior partner saying he'd be late.

'I'd love to be in a position to be here every day to help the kids start school,' he said to Francine, as they drove through the gates.

'At least I'm lucky enough to be able to do it at the moment,' she mused. 'I'll tell you what, I'll wait in the car this morning and let you do the honours.' She patted his hand.

'Okay, love. See you shortly,' he said, with a smile. 'Come on, you lot, let's be having you.'

'Cameron, do you want to go with Daddy and say goodbye to your brothers and sister?' Francine asked. 'You're not going into school today. You're coming to the meeting with Daddy and me.'

'Really?' he said. 'To work?'

'Sort of,' Francine said.

'Wow! Can I go and tell Mr Matthews I can't come to school today?' he asked.

'That's a good plan,' Francine said, winking at Carl. She was delighted Carl was saving her from having to explain why they were both there. She really wasn't able for people right now.

Francine watched Carl as he greeted each person he passed. He was always the same, she mused. Happy-go-lucky and ready to see the positive side of life. He'd been like that since the day she'd met and fallen in love with him.

None of the other husbands at school were like him. They barely grunted when she addressed them and looked as if it was penance to have to interact with their kids. Carl was a marvel and she adored him. She just hoped he'd cope with the assessment business.

Before long she spotted him emerging from the school, holding Cameron's hand. At the same time Jane pulled up in her car. All the doors opened and she and her children spilled out. Sinking down into the passenger seat, Francine hoped to God Jane wouldn't spot her. Glancing at her watch, she tutted. Jane would be late for her own funeral. She was so disorganised that Francine was amazed she got anything done.

'Hello, Carl,' Jane said, stumbling past him. 'What brings you up here at this time of the day?'

'Francine and I have a few bits to do, so I'm helping her with the drop-off today,' he said. 'I love the bit of banter and to see the kids in their classes,' he added.

'Are you having a day off, Cameron?' she asked.

'I'm going to work with my dad today,' he said proudly.

Francine heaved a sigh of relief at his answer.

'Really?' Jane looked puzzled. 'Well, sorry I can't stop but I'm late as it is. You know yourself!'

Francine willed Carl and Cameron to hurry back to the car so they could get away before anyone else saw them and asked awkward questions.

'Morning, Carl – seems it's the fathers' school-run day,' another man said, raising his eyes to heaven.

'Ah, sure isn't it grand to be here every now and again?' Carl answered cheerfully. As a conversation about the local GAA club ensued, Francine began to panic. *Come on, Carl*, she thought. *Let's go!*

It was Sod's Law that Andrea ambled up to the car. She was standing so close to the driver's door she was almost brushing the wing mirror. Francine realised the other woman was so busy chatting on her phone that she hadn't noticed her. Suddenly Andrea's face froze as she spotted Carl.

'Shit! I wish I could hide,' she said, into the mobile phone. 'I've just spotted Carl Hennessy coming towards me. I can't deal with him at this hour of the morning. I was just about to go back into the school to hand in a letter to a teacher, but I'll wait and do it at collection time. Ugh! He's such an old woman, he'll have me snared now, nattering on about nothing for ten minutes. My John dives into pot plants and contorts himself into tiny spaces to avoid him.'

Francine's blood ran cold as she was forced to hear the damning conversation.

'I know you're right,' Andrea continued. 'He's very nice and all that but, Christ, he can waffle on. He's like Ned Flanders from *The Simpsons*. Imagine being married to him. I'd stab him after a week.' Andrea's shrill laugh made Francine want to thump her.

'Ah, I know you're right, of course. He's not a bad egg, really. In fact, I'm probably just jealous. I'm always wishing my fella would take more of an interest in me and the kids,' Andrea confessed. 'John probably wouldn't be able to pick out our kids in a line-up.' Andrea giggled. 'Ah, well, better the devil you know. I give out about my John at times but I can't say I'd want Mr Happy Clappy waving and being so enthusiastic all the time either. Listen, he's just here now. I'll go. Bye.'

Poor unsuspecting Carl bounded over to Andrea. *Don't even say hello to that bitch*, Francine fumed.

'Morning! You're running late! Chop-chop,' he joked.

'Ha! Right! I was actually just about to drop something in to the teacher. Mine are settled already, if you must know,' Andrea said, with a false laugh.

'Fair enough,' Carl said good-naturedly. 'Sorry to be rude but I can't stop and chat – we're in a bit of a rush this morning. Francine is waiting in the car there, so we'd better press on.'

As Cameron and Carl opened the doors to get in, Andrea stooped to lock eyes with Francine. The colour drained from her cheeks and her hand flew to her mouth.

'Morning, Andrea,' Francine managed. She could have hurled abuse but the look of horror on her supposed friend's face was punishment enough for now. Francine wasn't going to stoop to her level.

'Francine!' Andrea croaked, in a strangled voice. 'I didn't see you there.'

'I thought not,' she answered calmly. 'Let's go, darling,' she said to Carl, as he started the car. He slammed his door and they drove away.

'What happened there?' Carl glanced at her. 'Did you two have a row or something?'

'Nothing like that,' Francine said. 'Andrea has a habit of shooting her mouth off and she's got herself into hot water again.'

'She's her own worst enemy at times but pretty harmless, I reckon,' Carl said.

'I used to think so too, but it seems there's a green-eyed-monster lurking in her head.'

'Really? What makes you say that?' Carl asked.

'Just a hunch.'

Inwardly Francine was stumped. How could Andrea say such nasty things about Carl? At least he chatted and made an effort. Her husband John stood with his hands in his pockets and looked at the floor all the time. When he did speak it was only about soccer, whether you were interested or not.

Francine took a deep, cleansing breath and tried to push Andrea's unkind words from her mind. She loved Carl and wouldn't change a single hair on his head. She'd die if he started behaving like some of the other fathers. Most of them only came to the school if their wives were either in hospital, dead or away on business. Even then they ignored most people.

Nights out were different, of course. The men could have a few beers and congregate in a corner to talk about sport and the recession.

Anyway, Francine had no time to worry about Andrea; she needed to focus on Cameron.

'All good?' Carl asked.

'Of course,' Francine said, slightly too quickly.

'It'll be fine, love,' Carl said. 'I know this is all very emotionally charged and it's more than a little scary, but we'll get through it together, right?'

At that moment, not only did Francine not care what Andrea thought, she pitied her. If she thought Carl's friendly and open nature was something to be ridiculed, so be it. She was entitled to her opinion. But Francine wouldn't swap him for anyone.

'We're going to see a lady called Nuala now, Cameron,' Carl explained.

'Who is she and will she be cross?' Cameron wondered.

'Oh, no,' Carl said. 'She's going to have a little chat with you and me and Mum. She's a special lady who organises meetings where parents and children can have a chat about how they feel.'

'Will I have to do any writing? We've only done a little bit with Mr Matthews. Will I have lots of homework like Cara? Will I be able to get a biscuit? Can I leave if I'm bored?'

Francine answered his questions one by one.

'But I don't want to go,' Cameron said. 'It mightn't be any fun.'

'It'll be just like coming to work with me for the day,' Carl insisted. 'I might even have to bring you for hot chocolate and cake afterwards,' he added. 'You'd like that, wouldn't you?'

'I suppose,' Cameron said, taking the bait. 'Why aren't Craig and Conor and Cara going too?'

'Because it's a special meeting just for us,' Carl said. 'How lucky are you?'

By the time they pulled up at the office building, Francine had butterflies in her tummy.

'Let's go! Here we are,' Carl said cheerfully.

Francine loved him even more. She could always count on him to bolster everyone up. Feck Andrea, she thought viciously.

The woman at the reception desk told them to take the lift to the second floor and Nuala's office was straight ahead.

As they huddled in the small, neat waiting room, Cameron immediately ran towards the selection of toys housed in an old-fashioned trunk in a corner.

Moments later the door opened and a small dumpy woman with round wire glasses and grey curls smiled at them. 'Hello, everybody, I'm Nuala. Would you like to come in?'

'You look very like Mrs Claus except you don't have your red and white outfit on,' Cameron said.

Francine nearly died of mortification. 'Cameron, don't be rude to Nuala.'

'That's not rude at all.' Nuala laughed. 'I'll take that as a compliment. Mrs Claus is one of the most adored people in the world!'

'After her husband, Santa,' Cameron said, as he walked into the larger, brighter room. 'Ooh, you have much more stuff in here,' he said. 'I hate painting, though, so please don't ask me to do that.' He eyeballed the oversized easel in the corner with huge sheets of paper attached.

'Cameron!' Francine and Carl said in unison.

'That's okay,' Nuala said calmly. 'Some children love art so they draw great big pictures when they come here. But you don't have to do that, Cameron, unless you feel like it.'

Cameron ran straight for a box filled with trains and pieces of track. 'May I play with this?' he asked politely.

'Sure.' Nuala smiled at him. 'I'm going to ask my friend Tracey to come in and play with you while Mum, Dad and I go into this room.' Nuala pointed to another door. 'Would that be okay with you?'

'Yup,' Cameron said, as he emptied the box onto the floor.

Tracey turned out to be a younger, wide-eyed girl with bright red skinny jeans and a Hollister hoodie.

'You have blue hair!' Cameron said delightedly.

'Isn't it cool?' Tracey grinned.

'Did God give you that hair or did you colour it with a marker?'

'I used special hair dye. It's a good blue, though, isn't it? Not too like Marge Simpson!'

Cameron giggled. 'You're funny!'

Francine was the last to follow into the conference room. 'Behave like a good boy, won't you?' she warned.

'Bye, Mum,' Cameron said, without looking at her.

Nuala was fantastic. She asked lots of questions, but they were all gently put, not accusing.

'Tell me about an incident where you felt Cameron was out of control,' she said.

'How long have you got?' Francine said. Her eyes filled with tears.

'I can see you're finding this very emotional. That's okay. Take your time. I'm not here to judge you or your son,' Nuala reassured her. 'I only want to try to help.'

Once Francine began to talk she couldn't stop. She told Carl and Nuala numerous stories of Cameron's antics.

'I had no idea he'd got so out of control,' Carl whispered.

'It's been a nightmare,' Francine concluded.

'I have a clear picture of your experience, Francine. Carl, you seem stunned. Does Cameron not behave this way with you?'

'Yes and no,' Carl began. 'Sure I've seen him act up and he's certainly a feisty little fella, but I guess I've been choosing to ignore a lot of it, if I'm honest. I always like to look at the bright side of things.' He chuckled. 'It works with a lot of situations, you know. Positive output equals positive feedback!'

'So you accept that the incidents Francine has described could be happening on a more regular basis than you'd imagined?' Nuala asked.

'Sure,' Carl said, taking Francine's hand. 'This is one of the best women you'll ever have the pleasure of meeting. All our other children are a breeze – not to say they don't have their moments, of course, but all in all they're tickety-boo. Francine is a superb mother and I feel dreadful that things have become so sticky. So I'm all on for fixing it.'

Nuala smiled. Closing her eyes for a moment, she took a deep breath. 'Right so. First, Cameron isn't a broken toy car, so we aren't going to be able to put him up on the table and mend him in the space of an hour,' she said firmly. 'I'd like to have an observational session with him now, if it's all right with both of you?'

'Okay,' Francine said, looking nervous.

'Okily-dokily. That sounds like a good plan,' Carl agreed.

Francine shot him a glance. So that was why Andrea had said he was like Ned Flanders.

As they all filed back into the main room, Cameron was engrossed in setting up knights on a large wooden castle with Tracey.

'Look what we're doing,' he shouted. 'Tracey knows how to do battles – there's horses and the men sit on them and we're going to attack the castle. The soldiers are all hiding in here because the wicked king has kept them in the basement!'

'Wowzers!' Carl said. 'That looks like a seriously brilliant game. Listen, buddy, Mum and I are going for a coffee and you'll stay here and play for another little bit. That okay with you?'

'Are you going too, Mum?' Cameron asked.

'Yes,' Francine said, feeling sad suddenly. She wanted to get to the bottom of the naughty behaviour, but as she gazed at her little boy she felt an urge to scoop him up into her arms and run away. He was so small and innocent as he stared up at her for reassurance.

'You said you wouldn't leave me here,' he stated. 'And, Dad, you promised we could have cake and hot chocolate.'

'Yes, I did, and we will. But first we need you to have a little minute with Nuala,' Carl said.

'I won't break my promise either,' Francine assured him. 'So I'll wait in the corridor just here.'

'Ah, no, it's really fun here with Tracey and the castle. You and Dad can go and have a cappuccino. Ask for lots of chocolate on top. I usually get a teaspoon and gobble it all up!' Cameron said, as he smiled at Nuala.

'I love that bit too!' she said, grinning. 'I promise it won't take too long here and then you can have your treat. Is that a deal?' she asked, with her hand in the air.

'Deal,' Cameron said, instantly jumping up to reward Nuala with a high five. Then he ran to his mother. 'Bye-bye,' he said, hugging her.

'Bye, sweetheart.' She was trying not to look as distressed as she felt.

'I'll look after him,' Nuala whispered, as they retreated.

ᘓ

'Do you think Cameron hates me?' Francine asked, as they walked across the road to a nearby café.

'God, no!' Carl said, looking puzzled. 'Why do you ask that?'

'We promised on the way here that we wouldn't leave him by himself and now we've gone back on our word,' Francine fretted.

'But he was happy to stay, and you explained that we'd be back. You even offered to stay and he was fine,' Carl answered.

'I suppose.' Francine tried to look as if she was comfortable with the set-up. She felt immeasurably ashamed that they'd ended up in a psychologist's office. More than that, she felt so guilty that her little son was such a mess.

As Carl stood in the queue, she found a table and sat down. Taking a deep breath, she forced herself to sit straight without hunching her shoulders. This was surreal. She thought she'd done everything right. She'd put her heart and soul into making sure their house was well run, that the children ate nutritious food and had lots of friends to play with. The list of extracurricular activities they attended was well thought out and she felt they were offered the best opportunities in life.

Cara did ballet, horse riding, drama, hockey, athletics and swimming. The two older boys did athletics and swimming at the same club, with rugby, soccer and golf. Every Thursday evening they all had a piano lesson. On the first Saturday of the month a French student came to speak to them for half an hour. Francine had read all the theories on multilingual skills. If children were immersed in foreign languages from an early age, they would have a natural aptitude for them in later life.

Cara had the book club and all the children had limited access to television and computer games. At least one evening a week she and Carl played a board game, like Scrabble or Monopoly, with them. Every Sunday after mass and before their roast dinner, they'd go for a bracing walk either by the sea or, if it was wet, to the woods.

How had Cameron slipped through her carefully woven net? Francine was certain that was what had happened. She was his mother. She should have realised he was heading in the wrong direction. Her conversation with Annie came back to her. That poor woman had done her best. She'd managed to mind the other three and they were all fine, so there was no way she could even consider laying the blame at Annie's feet. He'd been in school only a wet week, so Mr Matthews wasn't to blame. All this rude and unruly behaviour *had* to be her fault.

'Here we go! I decided to go all out and treated us to a slice of carrot cake and a piece of double chocolate fudge,' Carl said, laughing. 'We can share and compare!'

Francine wished she felt even a shred of the relaxed confidence her husband was displaying. As she saw it, she'd made such a mess of raising Cameron that the last thing Carl needed was to have elevenses with a sourpuss. She forced herself to smile and chat in a bubbly way about the cake. 'While I like the carrot one I think my recipe is moister. It's a lovely treat, though, thank you, darling,' she chirped.

Carl hated tension and unpleasantness. Besides, the more she played down this awful situation, the less likely he would be to point the finger at her.

What if he decided she was a bad mother and a worse wife? She couldn't hold down a paid job and she was clearly dreadful at the unpaid one at home.

Guilt and a looming sense of failure made the cake stick in her throat. As she concentrated on being lovely and keeping her breathing even, Francine prayed silently that Nuala wouldn't pulverise them at the end of Cameron's assessment.

Chapter 17

Francine and Carl were waiting anxiously in the small office when Nuala opened the door. 'Come in and see what we've been doing,' she said. Cameron was sitting on a chair near the desk.

'Hi, honey,' Francine said, rushing to her son's side. 'How did you get on?'

'Good,' Cameron said.

'Did it go okay?' Carl asked Nuala.

'Cameron was a great boy,' she said, motioning towards the back office once more. Tracey appeared again.

'She said if I sat and did the talking part that I could play war again,' Cameron said, and made for his castle.

'It's "Nuala", sweetheart, not "she",' Francine corrected.

Cameron was already engrossed in the battle so Francine decided to leave him be.

'Now I'll prepare a full report, of course,' Nuala began, 'but for now, please sit down and we'll have a brief chat.'

Francine felt sick. To her, this was like sitting in front of a judge and jury. She jumped when Carl took her hand in his. 'It's okay, darling, we'll get through this together. Team Hennessy, remember?' He winked.

'I ran a psycho-educational assessment on Cameron,' Nuala said.

'Good Lord, that sounds serious,' Francine said, her eyes filling with tears once more.

'It's not as dreadful as you may think.' Nuala was calm and sweet. 'It involved asking Cameron to carry out some simple tasks, such as a jigsaw, writing, looking at pictures and finding missing pieces in a puzzle.'

'Did he do as you asked?' Francine wanted to know.

'Yes, although he struggled with some of the requests,' Nuala answered. 'He's very young, of course, and we really can't achieve a full and proper diagnosis until he's a little older, but my initial analysis would suggest there is a high probability that Cameron is dyslexic. However, we can't confirm that until he's older.'

'But would that explain his bad behaviour?' Francine asked.

'I need to spend more time with him on another day,' Nuala continued, 'but he also appears to be suffering with attention-deficit disorder. Have you heard of this condition?'

'Yes.' Francine and Carl were horrified.

'Isn't that more concerning children who run around non-stop, never sit still and can't concentrate on anything at all?' Carl asked.

'Not all the time,' Nuala explained. 'A child with ADD can display some of the symptoms you mentioned but they can also be daydreamers or children who become overlooked.' Nuala was patient and kind as she dispelled some of the common myths on the condition. Cameron did seem to fit the bill when she went through a checklist of behavioural traits. 'Does he tire easily of tasks and often look to move on to something else?'

'Yes,' Francine said instantly.

'Would he become angry and swiftly frustrated while you're playing a board game, for example?'

'Oh, yes,' Carl answered. 'We were playing snakes and ladders only the other day and he upended the board and threw it across the room. It wasn't even his go but it was like a fuse went off in his head and he couldn't control himself.'

'Does he make a continual mess which he never seems to clear up?' Nuala pressed on.

'Yes, and we've had endless arguments over this,' Francine told her. 'The other children often complain that he gets away with not tidying up. But, more often than not, I find it easier to clear away his toys myself rather than have yet another battle with him.'

'Is he a good sleeper?' Nuala asked.

'No!' they answered in unison.

'He's always thumping around the room well into the night, yet he never seems overtired,' Francine explained.

Nuala made lots more notes in her book. 'Okay, well done, both of you. I'm going to take some time to go through my notes from our meeting and also the assessment with Cameron. Would you make an appointment to return and we'll try to work through this?' Nuala stood up and led them back into the main room.

'But he can concentrate and play when he feels like it,' Francine said, confused. 'Surely a child with ADD wouldn't sit and play with an intricate toy like that castle for so long. He can do PlayStation or Nintendo for hours too.'

'That's the often misconceived notion about this disorder,' Nuala explained. 'ADD can also result in a child who is totally removed from his or her peers. One who is quiet and shy, forgetful and reserved. There are many forms and indeed plenty of ways of tackling it. I promise we'll do our best to pull together and work with Cameron.'

'Will he have to go on medication?' Francine asked.

'Not necessarily, Francine. In many cases medication isn't a consideration at all,' Nuala said.

'But don't the media talk about children who are on stuff that turns previously insane personalities into teddy bears?' Carl asked, scratching his chin.

'Our son isn't insane,' Francine snapped.

'Of course he's not, love.' Carl seemed crushed. 'That wasn't what I meant. All I was saying is that I've heard of kids taking the recommended medication and it's changed their lives for the better. That's all. I'm simply trying to think positively.' His brow was furrowed.

'That would be a long way down the road, Carl, so let's not jump the gun,' Nuala said. 'It's best if we take this one step at a time. Before long we'll have worked out a good strategy to help Cameron and your home life. Is that fair enough?'

'Is this the disorder that can be helped with omega-three fish oils?' Francine asked, ignoring Nuala's last statement. 'If I stop in the village and buy some in the chemist, would that be a good start?'

'Well, there has been some data to suggest that fish oils are beneficial to children,' Nuala answered carefully, 'but really this needs to happen one step at a time, as I just said. We take each child individually and work slowly through the steps that may suit the particular situation.'

Francine was totally deflated.

'So there's no quick-fix pill or potion,' Carl stated.

'Precisely,' Nuala agreed. 'The biggest step is recognising there may be a problem, and the earlier the issues are addressed, the better the outcome. So you've done the right thing in coming along today with Cameron. We'll work as a team and between the three of us we'll do our best for him.'

'For sure. We call ourselves Team Hennessy, don't we, Francine?'

'Yes.' Francine looked up at him with her most winning smile.

'All I can say is thank you,' Carl said, pumping Nuala's hand up and down. 'I'm feeling good about this. We'll have this ADD thing by the short 'n' curlies before you can whistle.' Banging his hands together and rubbing them vigorously, Carl raised and relaxed his shoulders, gave his neck a quick click to left and right and took a deep breath. 'This is going to be just fine.' He smiled and made for the door.

Francine wished she shared his faith. She hoped to God he was right. He usually displayed fantastic judgement. He was certainly right about one thing, though. They were a good team. If Nuala joined them as a professional extra, things could only improve, surely.

'One thing before you go,' Nuala said. 'A child with ADD doesn't want to be naughty or disruptive. They love to be good and fit in just the same as any other little person. They don't wake each day and decide to be troublesome. Once we can get some guidelines in place for you all, I'd hope to see a really constructive change. But please keep in mind there's no malice attached to his behaviour.'

Francine took Cameron's hand and led him towards the door.

'I'll wait with him while you make the next appointment,' she suggested to Carl.

'Fine, love,' he said.

As they stood outside, Francine stared down at her son. He didn't seem any different from other children. There was no twitch or obvious impairment.

Was there a possibility Nuala had it wrong? How could she

and Carl have had three perfectly normal children, then a problem like this with number four? It didn't make sense.

They could always get a second opinion. Nuala wasn't an oracle – who was to say she even knew what she was talking about? People printed bogus certificates from the Internet all the time. Maybe she was a fraud.

Moments later, Carl emerged from the building looking rather harassed.

'I need to get into the office pronto,' he said apologetically. 'I'll have to call a taxi for yourself and Cameron. I'm so sorry, darling.'

'Nonsense,' Francine said. 'We'll get the bus. Look, there's a stop. It'll bring us to the village and we can stroll up and collect the car in plenty of time for the school run. Besides, it'll be fun, won't it, Cameron?'

'What about my hot chocolate and cake?' Cameron asked.

'Oh, Cameron, I'm sorry. A man needs me to go to work right this minute. Mum will take you to the café before you go on the bus – won't you?' He looked at Francine pleadingly.

'Of course I will. It'll be our special date, just you and me,' she said.

'Okay, Dad! I really want to go on a bus!'

'See?' Francine said, with delight. 'You fly off to work and we'll see you later on.'

Carl kissed his wife and son, then sped off.

They walked back into the same coffee shop that she and Carl had left a few minutes before. Francine ordered sparkling water for herself, then hot chocolate and a slice of cake for Cameron.

'Can we sit on the high stools over here?' Cameron asked, pointing to the far wall.

'Sure,' Francine said, as she followed him with their tray.

Cameron chatted amicably while swinging his legs and munching.

'What a lovely little fella you have there,' the waitress said, as she took their empty tray. She ruffled his hair and chucked him under the chin.

'Me and my mum are going on a big bus in a minute,' he said.

'Wow, you're a lucky boy, aren't you?' She smiled.

'Yup,' Cameron said, and winked.

Francine was suddenly scared. Had she just opened a can of worms for no reason? Maybe the few isolated tantrums Cameron had experienced were all part of him flexing his muscles. It was probably just the poor little fella's way of adjusting to being with her all the time instead of Annie. What if she'd dragged them all to see Nuala for absolutely no reason?

Confusion flooded her as she wiped the chocolate from her son's face.

'Let's go, Mum. The bus might be waiting for us!' he said, tugging at her hand.

It was much colder outside than Francine had realised. As they stood for what felt like hours waiting for a bus to turn up, she wished she hadn't brought Cameron here after all.

'We won't tell everyone about going to meet Nuala today. It'll be a little family secret for you and Daddy and me,' Francine said gently.

'Why? Do you think Cara and Craig and Conor would be jealous we didn't let them play with the castle?' Cameron asked.

'Um, yes,' Francine said distractedly. She just didn't want the whole of Bakers Valley talking about her son, saying he was a problem child or that he had a 'condition'. She didn't want it for Cameron and she couldn't bear the thought of being the topic of gossip among her peers.

Cameron grew impatient. 'When is the bus coming? I want to sit up high and pretend I'm the driver. Can we go up the stairs?' he asked.

'Yes, love,' she soothed him.

The spattering rain had turned into a full-blown soaking shower. By the time a bus hurtled towards them Francine was chilled, wet and miserable. 'Oh, thank goodness! Let's hop on,' she said, taking Cameron's hand.

'No!' he yelled, stamping his feet. 'It doesn't have an upstairs. I'm not going on that one.'

'Cameron, please!' Francine begged, feeling as if she might cry. 'We're both cold and soaked. Let's just go on this bus and I promise we'll go somewhere on a double-decker another day.'

'No!' he said. The sting as he kicked her in the shins brought tears to her eyes.

'Don't kick your mammy like that,' the bus driver bellowed. 'Get on here and stop that behaviour.'

Cameron was totally taken back by the stranger shouting at him. In terror he bolted on to the bus and down to the back, flinging himself under a seat.

'Sorry about that,' Francine said, as she rooted in her purse for the fare.

'You're not the one who should be apologising, it's that boy of yours. I've three at home and I can tell you now if one of them did that to my missus it would be the first and last time,' he said. 'People go on about smacking kids and spout all this drivel about it being bad for them. I'm not shy about giving them a tap on the arse and it does them no harm. You'd want to get him in check before he gets bigger and more violent.'

'My husband and I don't believe in hitting our children.' Francine was appalled.

'Suit yourself, love.' The driver took their fare and muttered under his breath about spoiled brats and parents who don't know how to control kids.

Ashamed, Francine jerked down the bus as it swerved away from the kerb. 'Come out and sit with me, sweetheart,' she coaxed.

'No! I hate you!' he screamed.

Francine could feel sweat beading on her forehead. Every pair of eyes on the bus was boring into her as she sank into a seat close to where Cameron had lodged himself. He was examining a football card another child had dropped. Thanking God for small mercies, Francine prayed they'd make it to the village without any further incident.

Two older ladies with headscarves knotted under their chins and hard handbags clutched at their breasts were unabashedly staring and commenting to one another.

'The youth of today.'

'No respect.'

'The mother's worse to put up with it.'

'Terrible behaviour.'

'Disgraceful.'

Francine wanted the ground to swallow her. 'Cameron, please get up off the floor, there's a good boy,' she tried.

He blanked her.

As the rain lashed down outside, Francine couldn't have felt more miserable. She should probably have pulled Cameron out from under the seat and made him sit nicely. But she really hadn't the heart. If he started yelling again she'd be even more mortified.

As they approached the village, Francine warned him they were getting out soon.

'I want to stay here,' he whined.

'We have to collect Cara, Conor and Craig soon, so you can't,' she said sharply. 'Now stand up, come to the door and you can wait for it to open.'

Instead of moving to the back door, which was much closer to them, Cameron stomped down the length of the bus with his hands on his hips making as much noise and drawing as much attention as he could.

'Bye-bye,' he called to the driver, who responded by glowering at him.

'He's a mean old toad.' He pointed at the driver as the bus pulled away.

'He's cross because you were yelling,' Francine explained. 'If you try not to shout at people they won't be so annoyed with you.'

'He's a poo-brain and his bus is crap,' Cameron said.

'Cameron!' Francine thought she was going to pass out. 'Where on earth did you hear that sort of language?' There was nothing Francine hated more than hearing children curse.

'I know lots of words like that. I know "shit", "fuck", "bastard",' he said, counting on his fingers.

'Hello, Mrs Hennessy,' Mr Clement, from the optician's, said, as he shuffled past. 'That boy of yours could do with having his mouth washed out with soap.'

'I wasn't even talking to you,' Cameron said. 'I was talking to my mum. So you keep your big fat nose to yourself. You look like the mouldy old tortoise that lived in my nana's garden. Now piss off and mind your own business.'

Francine was utterly paralysed with shame.

'What else do I know?' Cameron wondered. 'Oh, "bitch-cow", that's the one Conor says to Cara when she's annoying. And there's boll—'

'Stop it!' Francine screamed. 'Stop it right now. How dare you say those words? How dare you embarrass me and treat Mr Clement with such disrespect?' Once Francine started yelling it was like a poltergeist had taken over. 'You behaved like something from the zoo on that bus. You acted like a child who was raised in a gutter. You are not like my son. You don't behave like any of the Hennessys. I don't accept that Nuala says you don't mean this. You go out of your way to make my life a misery. For years I've ignored poor Annie when she told me you were awful. I've tried to jolly you along—' Francine was heaving and crying. 'You're naughty and horrible and I'm not putting up with this a second longer.'

'You're a mean old bitch!' Cameron screamed back.

Suddenly Francine was viewing the scene through onlookers' eyes. She and Cameron must look like a pair of drunks hurling abuse at one another in the middle of the sleepy village. 'Look at what you've reduced me to,' she said, as she grabbed Cameron's arm. 'Look at what you've done,' she sobbed, as they stomped towards their quiet cul-de-sac.

Cameron was trying to free his arm. 'Ow - that hurts. Stop it, Mum.'

Thankfully, they didn't meet another soul. Francine's resentment and fear spewed forth. As she slammed the front door, she rounded on Cameron. 'Get up those stairs into your bedroom and change out of your wet clothes. If you so much as make a sound, God help you!'

Instead of cowering, Cameron spiralled out of control. 'You're the most horrible bitch-cow. I hope a dinosaur comes and bites you and hurts you very badly!' he yelled, tears and snot pooling on his cheeks. 'I hate you and I wish you'd go back to work and let Annie mind me. She's better at it anyway. You're the worstest person EVER.'

The little boy bolted up the staircase and went directly to his room all right. What he did when he got there shocked his mother into submission.

He picked up a metal truck, which he used to transport his Dinky cars. It was a sturdy, heavy toy that had survived sandpits through winters and summers alike since Conor had first got it years previously. Now Cameron hurled it with all his might at the mirrored wardrobes on the landing. The safety glass shattered into millions of pieces with a loud bang.

'Cameron?' Francine shot up the stairs. 'Cameron!'

The sobbing from the very darkest corner of his bedroom made her drop to her knees and crawl under the bed. In a swift, swooping movement she plucked him out and pulled him into her arms.

As they huddled together on the floor, rocking and shaking, Francine knew she had to accept that Cameron was not like her other children.

Nuala hadn't been mistaken.

They all needed to try to make life better. For the past three years when Cameron had misbehaved she'd gone out of her way to make the situation better. As she sat on the floor cradling her fraught son, she realised that she'd been doing them both a disservice in hesitating to take steps to change things.

Poor Carl had been more than a little stunned at her revelations earlier on. But the shock had only lasted until he'd had the call from his office. He'd gone off feeling certain that this was merely a hiccup and would be sorted in jig time.

Francine and he *were* Team Hennessy in every way except one. She'd hidden the extent of Cameron's problems from her husband. On the occasions when their youngest had kicked off badly in front of Carl, Francine had always managed to throw him off the scent: 'He's probably coming down with chicken-pox – all the children in the village have it,' or, her favourite, 'He was up half the night and I didn't wake you. He's just exhausted.'

Carl worked such long hours and didn't see the children for many prolonged periods. Family holidays were always a bit of a disaster, but again that, too, could be explained away: 'He's not good in the heat'; 'He doesn't like French/Spanish/Greek food'; 'It's the terrible twos'; 'He's the last of four, he's learned from his siblings and added his own five cents worth.'

It stung Francine to admit that Cameron behaved better with Carl than he did with her. He responded to the rough-and-tumble games Carl played, and saved his worst behaviour for herself and Annie. Carl was a wonderful father. When the children were babies, every night after he got home from work he'd sit on the floor and play. As they grew older, he was the one who taught them to ride a bicycle, go on a scooter, bounce on the trampoline and pretend to be a wrestler. None of those things required manners or calm. Sure Cameron was a disaster when it came to board games. He'd kicked the pieces and emptied the Monopoly box umpteen times. He refused point blank to consider playing Scrabble. Snakes and ladders made him furious on sight.

'He's too young for sitting still. Leave him off,' Carl would say. But at the end of the day Cameron was the baby. He'd been afforded a little more leeway than his siblings because they'd pandered to him.

The real problems had only shown themselves when he'd begun school and the more structured routine had been thrust upon him. Francine couldn't run from this any longer. Cameron needed special assistance. But, more than that, she needed to learn how to deal with him. She feared that the bumpy ride she'd been experiencing lately was nothing to what might happen in the future. The bus driver had been right about one thing: if she didn't get Cameron under control before he was older and bigger than her, she'd have a serious problem on her hands.

Picking herself up off the floor, Francine busied herself with finding fresh clothes for Cameron.

'Go into Mummy and Daddy's room and change into this tracksuit,' she instructed.

Picking up the phone, she called a glazier to come and fix the mirrored wardrobe glass. Then, stepping out of her own soaked clothes, she pulled on a tracksuit. Normally she would never even contemplate going to the school dressed like that, but today was not a normal day.

'We'll leave the alarm turned off until the man comes to fix the wardrobe,' she said to Cameron, as they climbed into the car.

'Will Daddy know the truck jumped into the glass?' Cameron asked.

'Yes, but we'll explain that you'll never do it again,' Francine said numbly. 'We don't need to tell anyone else about it either. Okay?'

'Like who?' Cameron asked.

'Like Mr Matthews or other mummies. They mightn't like it, so we'll just have it fixed and that'll be that. I know you're very sorry so that's all that matters.'

Francine drove like a ninety-year-old, crawling along in second gear. Pulling into the school car park, she tucked the car in beside a van. The other mothers were already congregating near the door. She could see them chatting and laughing without a care in the world.

'Let's go, Mum.' Cameron was getting impatient.

'No,' she said. 'Stay here until we see Cara and the others coming out.'

Francine had never felt less like being at the school. The overheard conversation from this morning suddenly came back to her, and a cold, empty feeling invaded her. She felt alienated and very alone.

Cameron undid his seat belt and tried to get out of the car. 'Open the door, Mum! I want to go and play! There's Martha from my class. I'm going to tell her why I wasn't at school today.'

'It's still too wet on the ground. You've been soaked once already. Wait here until the others come out,' she said.

Cara appeared and looked around in mild confusion. Her mother was never late to pick them up. She was always there, chatting to all and sundry. Francine managed to catch her eye and beckoned her over.

'Here's Cara. We'll just stay in the car. We need to get home for the wardrobe man, remember?' she said.

'Mum, what are you doing over here?' Cara asked. 'Why aren't you in the usual place near to the others?'

'We got caught in the rain earlier on and I'm in my tracksuit. I didn't want to make a show of myself,' Francine said, through the window. 'Throw your bag in the boot and call your brothers.'

She had to speak to a few of the committee members that evening to make final preparations for the Hallowe'en party the next day, but she hoped she could deal with them over the phone from home. She'd avoid speaking to Andrea by asking someone else, like Jane, to pass on the message.

Francine drove away from the school with a full brood and a heavy heart.

Chapter 18

The bleak weather and dark evenings should have made Jodi feel depressed. Instead she was enjoying the cosiness of the cottage while immersing herself in Saul's new world. Over the last while they'd had Max over to play, followed by Steven. Both were sweet and Saul had had a ball.

'I like having friends over all the time,' he said. 'I love Bakers Valley and our cottage.'

'I do too, dude,' Jodi assured him. 'Tomorrow is your last day of school before midterm break. You'll have your first Bakers Valley Hallowe'en party. I think it's going to be fantastic fun!'

'I can't wait,' he said, as his bright eyes shone in the darkness of his bedroom.

'Now, let me tuck you in and you listen to the raindrops tapping on your windows. It's so good to feel safe and warm in here, isn't it?' she said, as she curled up beside him on the bed.

'Did you love listening to the rain when you were a little girl in Ireland?' Saul asked her sleepily.

'I don't remember being able to hear the rain from my bed,' Jodi said. 'I didn't have a lovely cottage like ours.'

'What was your house like?'

'It was small and not so comfy,' she said simply. She decided to omit the fact that the noises she had been most familiar with at his age were police sirens and the sound of her mother's drunken giggling mixed with the animalistic grunts of visiting men. Sometimes she'd taken fright and crawled into the wardrobe in case any of them came looking for her.

She stroked Saul's cheek as she said a silent prayer of thanks that her son knew nothing of the life she'd worked so hard to leave behind.

Once he was asleep she took a book into her own bed, feeling safe and happy.

Until swirling thoughts of Mac threatened to spike her calm. The situation with him was headed for closure. Of that she was certain. She just wasn't sure how much damage he would cause. She took a deep breath and did what she was brilliant at: she blocked it out. It could wait until tomorrow at the least.

The next morning, Saul was awake and bouncing on Jodi's bed before dawn.

'Hey, dude, what's the story?' she asked, pulling the duvet up to her chin.

'It's the Hallowe'en party tonight. Get up quick – we need to get ready,' he said.

'Lie here with me for a minute – the heating hasn't even come on yet and it's freezing,' she croaked. 'Besides, you have school as usual. Then we have the whole afternoon to wait. So crawl in here and give me a hug.'

'If we get dressed and go to school now, that part can be over. Then the dark will come quicker and the party can start.'

Jodi grabbed her son. He was so cute standing there in his Spiderman pyjamas with his hair all fluffy from sleep. If only the world could work the way he wanted, it would all be so easy, she mused.

'What do you think everyone else is going to dress up as?' Saul asked. Jodi hoped if she hugged him close that her warmth might make him drowsy and he'd sleep for a little longer, but he carried on jabbering away.

'Um, I dunno,' Jodi mumbled.

'If there's too many Batmans there could be a massive blow-out. 'Cause Max is being Ben 10 and there's two Spidermans.' He furrowed his brow as he tried to work out what kind of superhero war would take place in school.

Jodi giggled softly. 'At least if there are any bad witches, the heroes can save the innocent people.'

'It's all wrecking my head. Little Bo Peep and Cinderella are coming. Do they like each other?'

'Where did you hear "wrecking my head"?' Jodi laughed.

'You say it when you're talking to Daddy on the phone. It means you don't know how to think right, doesn't it?'

'Sure does, dude!' Jodi said. 'You're not going to go back to sleep, are you?' She sighed.

'No! Am I wrecking your head now?'

'You're a goose!' she said, kissing him all over his face and head.

'Ugh! Yucky kisses, Mum! Stop!'

ఴ

Over at Verbena Drive Francine was having a crisis. She'd been awake for most of the night. Unable to lie in the bed, let alone sleep, she'd gone to the kitchen at four that morning and was still there. Francine usually looked forward to the big parties at the school. Usually she couldn't wait to mingle and chat. But today she was struggling. What if one of the parents took her to task over Cameron's behaviour? Thanking God for the invention of makeup, she trowelled it on and hoped her bright smile would mask her inner anguish.

She had brief respite from her anxieties when Carl came down for breakfast. She enjoyed fussing over him and having some light banter with him.

She was glad to have tonight's party to focus on. It was one reason why she'd been doing so much baking recently. It had thrown Carl off the scent too. She didn't want him to know the extent of her stress and anxiety. Constant obsessive baking for no reason would certainly raise an alarm.

'I can't believe the amount of work you're putting in this year,' Carl had worried yesterday. 'Didn't you delegate anything? Why aren't any of the other committee members doing their share?'

'It's no problem. After the fiasco with the buffet last time I figured it would be best if I did most of it,' she explained.

'Well, I can understand that you were miffed with Jane for buying buns and putting them on plates last time you asked her to bake, but this is verging on ridiculous, love,' Carl said. 'You could open a bakery at this rate!'

'I don't mind and, besides, I've had confirmation that there'll be two full busloads coming from the pensioners' association. Those ladies and gentlemen appreciate a bit of home baking. Sure what else would I be doing, love? I'm not used to having all this time on my hands during the day.'

'You're a good person. Kind and thoughtful. The mould was broken the day you were made,' he said, as he kissed her.

'You're one in a million yourself,' she said.

'See you shortly,' he said, as he made for the front door. 'I have the tubs for the apples and the large box of windfalls from Mr Willis. Call me if you need anything else.'

'Thanks, love, I will,' she said.

'I'll be at the hall by twelve-ish, if that's okay with you, love?'

'Perfect.'

The usual military operation of getting four children up, dressed, fed and out of the door took over.

'Please be careful of the cakes!' she begged, as she got the children to help her stack the boxes in the boot of her car.

'How many did you make?' Cara asked with wide eyes. 'Everyone's going to think you're Super Mum!' she said.

'Ah, thanks, lovie.' Francine glowed. 'I wanted to make sure it's all extra special this year! I've more time, seeing as I'm not working right now. So it's all good. Don't throw your school bags on top of the cakes. Take them into the back of the car with you.'

Mercifully, there was no arguing on the way to school. The anticipation of the party and the midterm break meant they were all in top form.

Cameron ran happily into class and the others raced off to join their friends. Francine strode back to the car, where she found her clipboard and grabbed an armful of boxes.

The other committee members were already there, stringing up pumpkin lights and hanging the orange and black paper chains the children had made during arts and crafts that week. As Francine carried in a high stack of plastic boxes, Andrea came to offer help. 'You must've been up all hours every night this week to bake that lot,' she said.

'Almost,' Francine said, without making eye contact. She could still hear every word of Andrea's spiteful conversation. She had no idea which of the women in this room had been at the other end of the phone, so her paranoia was heightened. The only person who was off the hook was Jane because she'd spoken to Carl in the car park that morning. Any of the other chirpy mothers in this room might be the culprit.

'Francine …' Andrea began.

'Just leave it, please,' she said, holding up her hand. 'I've nothing to say to you right now, Andrea.'

She'd had so many imaginary confrontations with Andrea this week, but now that she was in the same space as her Francine felt numb. She couldn't be bothered to talk to her, let alone consider a confrontation.

It hurt to know that she and Carl were viewed with such pity. She longed for him to arrive and be there with her. Part of her wanted to tell him what Andrea had said. But she knew he'd be crushed to hear how spiteful Andrea had been. The last thing she wanted was to upset him.

Sighing, Francine decided to put her energy into sorting the table. She had a small window of time to get as much done as possible before the children were out at twelve. She could bring them up to the hall to wait while she worked but odds were Cameron would get overexcited and something awful would happen.

Balancing cake-stands, she made her way to the table. 'That's coming along beautifully,' she said, gazing at the collage of bats made by the second form children. 'Betty, I think the pumpkins the kindergarten little ones made would be lovely as a door surround. You know, dot them around the frame of the entrance? Can I leave that in your capable hands?' She handed the woman a pile of painted paper pumpkins and a lump of Blu Tack.

'Sure!' she said.

I wonder was it her on the other end of the phone? Francine mused.

'Where will I hang this, Francine?' Jane asked.

'The piñata needs room to swing, so over near the stage would be safest,' Francine said. 'The sweets and lollipops to fill it are in that yellow bag in the corner,' she reminded her. 'Sandwiches will be brought later on, yes? Margaret and Sarah, are both of you sorted with that?'

'Yes!' Sarah shouted from the back corner, where she was stacking the chairs out of the way.

'Hello, ladies! Where will I set up the amp with the iPod for music?' a young man shouted.

'Derik! Gosh, I wouldn't have recognised you!' Francine rushed over to him. 'How are you getting on in secondary school?'

'Very well, thanks, Mrs Hennessy,' he answered. 'I have some flashing coloured lights to make the place more disco-like.'

'Fantastic,' Francine crooned. 'How's your mum getting on?'

'She's great,' he said.

'Tell her we miss her on the committee,' Francine said. 'She's a huge asset to your secondary school, no doubt.' Derik's mother Pam had been a great woman for organising along with Francine. But Derik was her youngest child and had gone to secondary school that September. Francine missed Pam. They'd had a great connection. She worked at a bank and, like Francine, was always juggling a great number of things.

'She was only saying last night that it's all very different from the atmosphere here at Bakers Valley national school. It's so big and the mums aren't half as friendly as they are here,' he said.

'Ah, she'll never meet folk like us, will she?' Andrea said, as she put her arm around Francine.

'Oh, no, you're unique, all right,' Francine said, and walked away. Then she turned back: she didn't want poor Derik to think she was snubbing him. 'Thanks for coming to do the DJ job, Derik. You're a great lad,' she said, smiling.

Andrea was rooted to the spot. Francine didn't care.

The music came on a short time later, making for a real party atmosphere. The black sacks blocked most of the light from the windows and the glow from the pumpkin lights, mixed with the flashing disco bulbs, caused great excitement.

'Looking good!' Francine said to Derik, giving him a thumbs-up.

'It's time to collect the children,' Jane said. 'There are never enough hours when it comes to putting on these events.'

'The place looks super, though. Well done, one and all.' Francine gazed around proudly.

The whole school was finishing classes at midday to allow everyone to make costumes for the party.

'Are you all dressing up?' Jane asked.

'I have a witch's hat and one of those plastic noses on elastic. I'll draw a black mole on my face and wear a long black dress. That'll do, won't it?' Sarah said. 'I hate dressing up. I always feel like such an idiot.'

'I was going to wear a French maid's outfit I got for a party last year but it's a bit boobs out and too much leg for a family occasion,' Andrea said. 'Although it might cheer up some of the auld fellas from the nursing home.' She giggled naughtily.

'I think you'd suit the look of a tart,' Francine said, without thinking. An awkward silence descended as the mothers all stared.

'Francine!' Jane said. 'It's not like you to be so … cutting.'

'I was only joking! For goodness' sake, lighten up a bit, girls.' She giggled. 'You're all terribly serious today. I'm dressing as Little Red Riding Hood and Carl is coming as the wolf. We know how to let our hair down.'

'I'll come as a skeleton or something,' Andrea mumbled, glancing at Francine again.

The bell sounded then, so Francine fled the room and pounded down the stairs to fetch Cameron.

'Cara! Craig!' she called out to the older ones. 'I'm grabbing Cameron. Pop on upstairs to the hall, will you? Dad will be here in a while. I need you to come and look after Cameron for me until we're finished with the final preparations for the party. I won't keep you too long,' she assured them.

'I'll tell Conor,' Cara said, waving at her mum.

'Good girl.'

The little ones piled out of the door as a smiling Mr Matthews waved them off. 'Have a lovely midterm break,' he called out. 'Enjoy the party tonight. Hope you get lots of treats!'

'Thanks, Mr Matthews,' Francine said. 'Have a good break next week.'

'I certainly will,' he said. Francine couldn't help but notice the young man seemed thrilled to be shot of his charges.

'It's nearly party time,' Cameron said, as he flung himself on to the shiny floor and skidded on his knees.

'Come on up to the hall and be a good fella,' Francine called, beckoning for him to follow.

By the time all the children were rounded up and their mothers had put the finishing touches to the hall, the atmosphere was reaching fever pitch. Francine stacked the last of her plastic cake boxes under the table and ensured that the rest of the room was ready.

She was at the back of the hall when Carl poked his head around the door with the containers and the apples. 'Hello, hello, hello!' he shouted. 'Wowzers! Look at this place! Ladies, it's a credit to you all!'

Francine watched Andrea's reaction. On cue, she raised her eyes to heaven and elbowed Betty. A cold sensation ran down Francine's spine. 'Hi, love,' she said, stepping forward to give Carl a kiss.

'Hi!' he reciprocated. 'This is amazing!'

'We've all worked so hard,' Francine said. 'Let's get the apple bobbing set up and head home.'

'Cool-a-boola!' he said happily. Andrea made a faint snorting noise.

'I wonder if you're coming down with something?' Francine said to her. 'You seem to be having trouble breathing,' she added quietly, as she brushed past.

'Uh … no …' Andrea nearly died. 'I'm fine, thanks.'

'Really?' Francine stood with her hands on her hips and stared at the other woman.

'Okay, girls?' Carl looked a little miffed.

'We're just fine.' Francine smiled and stared at Andrea, who ran to grab her coat.

'I'll see you all later on,' she said, glancing quickly at Francine, who was still staring at her intently.

Mercifully, Cameron was transfixed by the disco lights in the corner and was chattering to Derik, who was showing him how to work the small mixing desk.

Carl finished filling the water containers and threw in the apples. Francine laid towels on the floor to mop up the spills.

'Anything else you need me to do before we go?' Carl asked her.

'No, we can split. The rest of the food is being brought in a while. I'll come home with you, get changed and come back here ahead of the posse. I'll take Cara with me to help, but I might ask you to follow on later with the boys.'

'Whatever you like,' Carl agreed.

As they congregated in their own kitchen at home a few minutes later, Carl leaned against the counter and looked pensive.

'Was there a bit of a vibe between yourself and Andrea just now?' he asked, as soon as the kids had left the room.

'No,' Francine said, in a high-pitched voice.

'Could've fooled me,' Carl said. 'She was looking at you as if she was waiting for you to stab her.'

'So she might.' Francine sighed.

'What happened?'

'Nothing, love. She's just not the person I thought she was.'

Cameron unwittingly put an end to the conversation by dragging his costume into the kitchen. 'Can you help me put this on?' he asked.

'You've plenty of time,' Francine said. 'It's not dark yet.'

'I don't care! I want to put it on now!' He pouted. 'Help!' he shouted.

'All right,' Francine said, unable to bear the thought of a tantrum. As she helped him into his Darth Vader outfit, she prayed he'd make it through the evening without causing a stir.

'What are you two dressing up as?' Cara asked, as she sauntered into the kitchen.

'Little Red Riding Hood and the wolf!' her father announced.

'Ah, *what*? That's, like, *sooo* embarrassing. Why can't you be something cooler? All my friends are going to think you're so lame,' she said.

'Well, your friends can go and swing,' Carl said, grabbing her and blowing a raspberry on the side of her neck.

'Stop it, Dad,' she remonstrated. 'You have to stop treating me like a baby. Please dress up as something cool, like a zombie

– or a ghost would be even better,' she suggested. 'Pull a sheet over your head.'

Carl laughed heartily. 'It looks like the time has come when I've become a complete disaster.'

That should have made Francine smile, but she was too much on edge to relax. Cameron's 'condition' and Andrea's criticism of Carl had made her question her entire family. What had seemed perfect only a few months ago was now in disarray.

Chapter 19

Jodi couldn't help but giggle at Saul. He was in his Batman suit complete with plastic mask by two o'clock. 'There's another four hours to wait, sweetheart,' she said.

'Maybe we could go now and stand in the queue at the door,' he suggested.

'I don't think there's any point,' Jodi said, wishing she'd had the foresight to arrange a play date to kill some time.

'Can I go up to see Sebastian at his house and shout, "Trick or treat?" at him?' Saul begged.

'Aren't you supposed to wait until it's dark?'

'He won't mind.'

Before Jodi knew it, she and Saul were ambling up the tree-lined avenue to the main house.

There was no sign of life and the old jeep wasn't parked at the front.

'I'd say he's out,' Jodi said doubtfully.

'I wonder if he's coming to the party – can we leave a note to tell him he's invited with us?' Saul asked.

'I've no pen or paper with me,' Jodi said.

Saul persuaded her to return to the cottage, write the note and accompany him back to Sebastian's so he could stick it on the front door. 'Now he can come if he feels like it.' Saul beamed. If nothing else, the exercise had taken up some of the afternoon, for which Jodi was grateful. They spent the rest of the time cutting a long dress into ribbons, chopping the fingers out of some woollen gloves and tying a headscarf around her head.

'I'm going to be a fortune teller,' Jodi explained.

Francine had asked her to get involved with the party - the locals would be beside themselves to know she was coming along. 'We have crystal ball readings each year. It's not serious - you just make up a nice little story about what's going to happen, like a good-luck thing. The children adore it. Would you do it?'

'Sure,' Jodi had found herself saying. How ironic, she thought, as she looked at herself in the mirror. Here she was, many years after she'd left school, dressed as a gypsy woman, when as a child she'd hated her nickname, 'Gyppo Jodi', and longed for it to be forgotten. Dipping into her makeup bag, she drew dark eyeliner on her top lids and a large red lipstick bindi on her forehead.

'You look pretty, Mum,' Saul said.

'Thanks, honey.'

A loud knock at the door sent Saul running.

'Sebastian!' he shouted. 'Are you coming to the party with us?'

'I'm afraid not,' he said. 'I just got your note so I called to bring you this.' He handed Saul something crackly.

'Hi, Sebastian,' Jodi said shyly, as she entered the living room.

As he spun around, Jodi clocked him giving her a quick up-and-down glance. 'You look ...' he swallowed '... you look great. Your makeup's amazing.'

'Thanks! I am ze great Zelda! I vill read your fortune, kind sir.'

Sebastian grinned as she swished her ribboned dress and

dramatically reached for his palm. 'I see a long life of love, laughter and lollipops,' she joked.

Before he could answer, she plucked a lollipop from the big jar she intended to bring with her and offered it to him.

'Sounds like a bright future.' He smiled warmly.

'Look, Mum!' Saul said. 'Sebastian gave me this huge stick of rock!'

'That's very kind – did you say thank you?'

'Course I did!'

'I got it for himself thinking he might pay me a visit, but when I found the note and realised I'd missed your call I thought I'd better deliver it instead.'

'Thank you,' she repeated. 'Can't you come to the party?'

'No, I'll leave it, thanks,' he said. 'I just spent the day with my wife and I'm ready to crash and watch a movie.'

'Sure,' Jodi said, blushing. She kept forgetting he was married. Or maybe she was choosing to be remiss … 'Would your wife not go to the party?' she asked.

Sebastian stared at her oddly. 'Pardon?'

'Your wife? Doesn't she like parties?'

'Eh, no.' Sebastian looked at the floor, and Jodi wondered what she'd said wrong this time. She longed to question Francine or one of the other mothers about Sebastian, but a sixth sense had prevented her from doing so. She didn't want him to think she was prying if he heard she'd been asking. Nobody ever talked about him, so she hadn't been able to pick up any information at all.

'I'll leave you to it so,' Sebastian said. 'Have a great time trick or treating,' he told Saul, as he ruffled the little boy's hair. 'Happy fortune-telling,' he said to Jodi. His face softened as she curtsied.

The smell of his musky cologne hung in the air as Jodi shut

the door. Sebastian was a funny fish, there was no doubt about it, but Jodi found him intriguing.

'Sebastian's cool, isn't he?' Saul said, as if reading her mind.

'He's a lovely man all right,' Jodi said, smiling.

'He feels really sad sometimes,' Saul said, looking serious. 'His little boy got dead in a river a long time ago but he still misses him.'

'When did he talk to you about that?' Jodi asked. She wasn't sure she liked Saul having such deep conversations with a man he barely knew.

'When we went to see the cows,' Saul said, shrugging his shoulders. 'I told him I miss my daddy so he said he knows what that feels like 'cause he misses his boy.'

'I see.'

'We said we'd help each other. I can be his pretend boy and he can be my pretend dad. But only pretend ones.'

'That's nice.'

'Yep, and that's why Sebastian brung me this!' he said, waving the stick of rock.

Jodi knew there were evil people around who did awful things to children. She knew there was every reason to worry about whom her son engaged with. But she had no qualms about Sebastian being around Saul.

As she padded back into her bedroom to clear up some of the mess she'd made earlier, she found herself wondering yet again what Sebastian's wife was like. There'd been no sign of her at the house earlier and she'd never seen her drive out of the gate. Jodi wasn't even sure that she lived there. As an incredibly private person herself, she never normally wondered about other people's lives. But there was something about Sebastian that made her want to find out more.

Chapter 20

Before she left the house to head back to the school, Francine said a silent prayer that Cameron would get through the evening without kicking off. 'Are you sure you can manage the boys if Cara and I go on ahead?' she worried to Carl.

'Stop fussing. It's all under control here,' he assured her. 'Sure we'll be along in about half an hour so it's honestly no hassle.'

No hassle, Francine mused. That phrase just didn't fit where Cameron was concerned. She wondered if she'd ever have another hassle-free day. Maybe Nuala would help her adjust their lives so she didn't feel like she was living on a knife edge permanently. Apart from the constant fear that her youngest child might erupt, Francine was totally exhausted by it all.

She enjoyed the short car journey with just Cara for company. 'You look lovely,' she complimented her daughter.

'Thanks.' Cara was touchingly pleased. 'I was going to go as Katy Perry but I decided at the last minute to be a zombie bride.'

'Well, even though you're meant to be dead, you still look very pretty.'

Cara hesitated. Then she said, 'There's a boy I kind of like. He's going tonight. He's in the first year of secondary school.'

Francine knew this was a pivotal moment for Cara. They'd

had many conversations about the birds and the bees but her daughter had never before been forthcoming about crushes. 'What's his name?' she asked, trying to ignore the urge to tell her daughter to find a boy her own age.

'Uh, I'd rather not say.' Cara blushed.

'Right,' Francine said. 'Does he like you too?'

'Well, we've been texting for the last week and he said he'd hook up with me when we go trick or treating. Naomi likes his friend so we're going as a foursome.'

Francine made a mental note to get Carl to keep an eye on them if he could. She'd be stuck in the hall tending the old folk, but Carl would lead a posse.

'Well, I hope he's a nice boy,' Francine said, sounding ancient. 'I'm sure he's very slick,' she amended.

'Slick?' Cara giggled. 'That's such a funny word! I'll tell him you said that.'

As her daughter walked ahead of her, Francine reassessed her outfit. The very short white ra-ra skirt with knee socks and white lacy top over a neon vest was suddenly not quite as sweet as she'd first thought. Francine used all her willpower to keep her mouth shut and resist the impulse to shove her daughter back into the car and drive her home.

'Is my veil on right?' Cara wondered.

'It's perfect,' Francine managed. She'd been so busy focusing on Cameron that she'd almost missed her daughter turning into a stunning young woman before her eyes. 'Mind yourself tonight, won't you?' Francine said suddenly, catching her by the arm. 'I hope you have fun but don't forget boys can break your heart if you let them.'

'I know, Mum.' Cara sighed. 'I had my first broken heart last year. But I'm over it now.' With a toss of her talc-whitened hair she ran towards the school building, leaving her mother astounded.

'All right, Francine?' Barbara, from the committee, asked, bustling up behind her.

'Yes, thank you. Apart from the fact that my daughter is twelve going on thirty-five. Did you know she's already had a broken heart and is going on a double date tonight?'

'That'd be about right,' Barbara said. 'My Harry is nearly fifteen and he's probably almost ready to take on running the country.' She giggled. 'They're streets ahead of us at the same age, aren't they?'

'So it seems,' Francine marvelled.

'I'll catch you later. I need to make sure the punch is mixed properly and keep the teenagers away from it. I laced it with vodka. I reckon we'll all need a stiff drink after traipsing around out there with the children.'

'People would be disappointed if your punch wasn't lethal!' Francine agreed. 'The village is looking very festive. I love all the decorations people have put up. My kids are so excited about going around the houses.'

'It's a bit of gas, isn't it? See you in a while,' Barbara said.

Things were going according to plan in the school hall. Derik had positioned a separate CD player outside the building playing creepy Hallowe'en music. Fake cobwebs were stretched around the doors and people were arriving in droves.

Francine felt her tummy do a flip as Andrea pitched up. Not wanting to be near her, she busied herself with putting the finishing touches to the booth where Jodi was going to sit and do her fortune-telling. She hadn't advertised the fact that Jodi had agreed to take on the role as she was worried the star might pull out if she did.

Francine noticed she hadn't arrived yet. She wouldn't blame her if she didn't show up. The girl walked the most prominent red carpets in the world, so their local village party probably seemed like a joke to her.

Carl arrived with the boys, who split up into their separate gangs. Francine noticed Cameron had nobody to play with. 'Where are your classmates?' she asked him, as she waved at another family arriving.

'Over there.' Cameron pointed.

'Well, go and join in. It'll be trick-or-treat time very soon, so go and see who wants to go with you and Daddy in the first group.'

'I went over and Max told me they don't want to play with me,' Cameron said sadly.

'Here's Jane with Katie,' Francine said, brightening. 'Coo-ee! Jane! Over here,' she called. 'Would you be a love and take Cameron and Katie to the rest of the kindergarten group? Carl will take some of them off to the village fairly soon. They can't understand waiting at that age! So sweet!'

Katie was cowering behind her mum.

'Go on off and play with Cameron,' Jane said.

'No!' Katie hissed.

'Okay, let's go trick or treating!' Carl announced, and rounded up some of the children. 'Katie, you come with me,' he said, taking the little girl's hand.

'Parents are welcome to come too or stay here and have a glass of Barbara's delicious punch,' Francine put in.

Most of the older children's parents opted to stay and chat as Francine and the other committee members passed out canapés.

'Come on, Cameron, let's rock and roll,' Carl encouraged him.

'Why didn't any of the boys from my class want to come?' he asked. Carl had managed to gather just a small group of girls.

Francine bit her lip. 'You go with Daddy and Katie, and I'll be waiting here to see all your treats. And here's Saul! He'll go with you.'

Jodi looked taken aback as Carl scooped up her son and took him across to his group.

'You look fantastic!' Francine gushed. 'I have your fortune-telling booth all organised. People are going to be blown away that you've supported the local community. Thank you so much, Jodi.' She lowered her voice. 'I wasn't sure you'd come.'

'Really?' Jodi looked puzzled.

'Listen, I owe you an apology,' Francine said.

'Do you?'

'I've avoided you for the last while. I'm sorry. After Cameron frightened poor little Saul again, I was so ashamed. I didn't know what to say. I'm so sorry.'

Jodi's expression softened. 'Hey, thanks for saying that. I honestly thought it was something I'd done.'

'Oh, no. You've only been kind and lovely. Please, could we start over after the break? Maybe we could have a chat and a cup of leaves or whatever rocks your boat.'

'I'd love that. Could we have some of your amazing coffee?'

'It's a date,' Francine said.

'Cool.' Jodi smiled. 'I know you're probably going to think I'm being silly, but I'm just a tiny bit concerned about Saul. He's never really done the whole trick-or-treating thing.'

'He'll be just fine, Jodi. Carl!' Francine called. 'Keep a special eye on Saul, won't you? It's his first time so be mindful of the dark and all that.' Carl gave Jodi and Francine a wave to say he understood.

'Sorry, you must think I'm being silly,' Jodi said. 'He's not used to going off without me or Darius. It's not that I don't trust Carl ...'

Francine whisked her around the room, introducing her to people.

'I would especially like you to meet a couple of mums who are massive fans,' Francine said. Jodi played the part perfectly and made each person feel they were the only person she'd come to see. Eventually she said, 'I'll go over and settle myself in my gorgeous booth now.'

'By all means!' Francine felt better than she had in ages. 'Give me the nod when you're ready for your first punter,' she said, as Jodi set off across the room.

'She's so normal, isn't she?' she overheard a woman say.

'Totally! You'd never know she's a huge star,' another agreed.

'Shush, ladies!' Francine hissed. 'She's not deaf. We can't act like we've never seen anyone like her here before. It'll make her uncomfortable.'

'But we haven't,' the second woman said. 'And you'd know from fifty paces she's a star. Look at her skin and the way she can work the crowd with total ease. I'd say she's never looked in the mirror and sighed in dismay at what gazes back.'

'That's for sure,' the other woman agreed.

Francine marched off to make sure all the elderly folk had a drink and some cake. 'There are loads of tasty treats over to here,' she told them. 'Tea and coffee or soft drinks are on offer for those who don't want our alcoholic option,' she added.

'You never cease to amaze me.' Jane had wandered over to her. 'Francine, the food looks fabulous.'

'Thank you, darling. It's fantastic to have Jodi as our fortune-teller, isn't it? Look at the queue.'

'It was a superb idea – and it's a total bargain. One euro to meet Jodi Ludlum!'

'Jodi made me promise not to say this in public, but she's offered to match whatever we raise at this year's party. A lot of the money is going to a fund to buy Christmas gifts for local children in need, the rest to the school.'

Francine surveyed the room and her gaze rested on Andrea, who had her hand over her mouth as she muttered to a woman beside her. Andrea winked at her friend and tapped her nose, as if to say, 'Keep that to yourself.'

Francine's mouth dried.

'Will you have a mug of punch?' Barbara asked, as she passed with a tray.

'I'd love one,' Francine said, still eyeballing the two women. 'I'll take one for Carl too. He'll be back shortly and I'm sure he'll be gasping.'

'No bother, but it's seriously strong,' Barbara said. 'I've only had one glass and I'm feeling kind of merry!'

'That sounds marvellous,' Francine said, as she drank one entire mugful and started on the second.

Chapter 21

Jodi was having a ball. The villagers were so kind and chatty. Every single person who pitched up at her booth was lovely to her.

'It's so great to meet you,' one teenage girl said. 'I've seen all your movies. I started going to my drama classes after I watched you in *Catch a Falling Star*.'

'Really?' Jodi said, delighted. 'Well, I'm so glad you enjoyed the film. Are you still doing your acting classes?'

'Yes, and I dance too,' the girl said.

'I'm sure you're brilliant at both. In fact,' Jodi looked at the crystal ball and squinted into it, 'I can see a very bright future ahead of you, my child,' she said, in a mysterious voice.

'Thanks, Jodi! Could I have your autograph?'

'Sure!' Jodi said, and signed the little book. It still gave her such a glow inside when people asked her to sign things for them.

Jodi was glad that most of the funds raised by the party would go to the local Santa toy appeal. Her chest tightened as she thought back to Christmas when she was Saul's age. The closest thing to magic that she had seen had been the reindeer head with the flashing nose behind the bar in their local pub.

Her mother had had no interest in preparing Christmas for her children. Some of the less pickled alcoholics Bernadette hung out with would try to talk to Jodi. 'What's Santa bringing you this year, Jodi?' Jack, one of the pub's regulars, asked as he stubbed out a cigarette.

'A clip around the ear,' Bernadette had answered, rolling her eyes. 'Every day is bloody Christmas for kids. They've no idea what it takes to make ends meet.'

Jodi had learned at a very early age to stay out of her mother's sight when she started one of her rants. She'd go and sit on one of the low stools at a small table in the lounge area of the bar. Bernadette didn't buy colouring books for her so inevitably she'd take out a schoolbook and work on her sums or comprehension.

'Looks like you've a little mathematician on your hands there, Bernadette,' old Jack commented once, as he drank his pint.

'Don't know where she gets it.' Bernadette guffawed. 'A magician would be more useful to me. If she can start turning water into wine I might love her.'

The following day was Christmas Eve. Bernadette had loved it because the pub was always thronged with people on a high and enjoying a good few drinks.

'I never understand what all the fuss is about when it comes to Christmas Day,' she'd said. 'The pubs are shut and people feel obliged to trot from pillar to post delivering expensive gifts that aren't appreciated.'

'Ah, sure it's a time for families to get together, I suppose,' old Jack had mused. 'I'll head over to my son's house. His wife does a grand dinner and I'll have a few beers and fall asleep. What about yourself, Bernadette? Will the little one have you up at dawn with excitement?'

'She will in her barney,' Bernadette had scoffed. 'If she wakes me early tomorrow I'll string her up. It's my well-earned lie-in,' she'd declared, as if she worked a twelve-hour shift every day.

'But don't you like to watch her little face when she sees all the Santa stuff?' Jack had asked, looking a bit astonished. 'She's only little, isn't she?'

'She's seven and we don't go on with all that crap in our house. Fills their heads with empty hopes and pointless dreams,' Bernadette had answered bitterly. 'There's only one direction she'll go coming from Dayfield Estate and that's directly to the dole office.'

Now Jodi remembered looking up at her mother's downturned mouth as she'd mindlessly written off her daughter's future. She'd felt an odd sensation rip through her. She was only seven and she didn't know what she wanted to become or where her life would lead, but she was certain of one thing: she wasn't going to spend her days sitting in this bar with the overflowing ashtrays and sticky floors.

It was dark, wet and unbearably cold when Bernadette had finally fallen out of the bar that Christmas Eve. It took them almost half an hour to walk home as Bernadette swayed in and out of fences and walls. 'Wait, for Christ's sake. You're like something possessed,' she'd snarled at Jodi.

'I'm freezing and it's lashing rain.' Her teeth were chattering.

'It's not my fault you refuse to wear a coat. Stupid, that's what you are,' Bernadette had yelled. Jodi had known there was no point in telling her mum she didn't have a coat. Instead she'd tried to take her mother's arm in an attempt to steady her and hurry her along.

'Get your hands off me!' Bernadette swiped but missed her head by inches.

The moment they'd got through the front door Bernadette

had conked out on the sofa in the living room. Jodi had run up the stairs and pulled the bedspread from her mother's bed. The room smelt of stale booze. Dirty clothes littered the floor. The once-white Formica bedside locker was dotted with brown burn marks where her mother had stubbed out cigarettes, not bothering with an ashtray.

As she'd dragged the grubby bedspread down the stairs and thrown it over her snoring mother, there was a tap at the front door.

'Who's there?' Jodi called, through the glass.

'It's Helen from Santa's workshop,' said a voice.

Bernadette had told her many times not to open the door, but Jodi couldn't resist. As she undid the latch and peeped out she could see a lady in a brown coat holding a box wrapped in Christmas paper.

'I met Santa just now and he asked me to give you this. Don't open it until the morning. Merry Christmas, love.'

'Thank you! Merry Christmas,' she'd called back, as she cradled the present.

She had kicked the door shut and rushed to her bedroom. Placing the wrapped gift on the floor, she had stared at it for the longest time.

Her mother had convinced her Santa wasn't real. The other kids in school said he was. She was only seven but Jodi had worked out a long time ago that Bernadette was a liar.

As long as she lived, Jodi would never forget the excitement of that night. She'd barely slept. Every time she'd closed her eyes she'd snapped them open again, terrified that she'd imagined the present. Each time she saw it she had to stifle a scream.

The following morning as dawn broke she'd allowed herself to think about opening the present. Picking it up, she'd padded down the stairs to show it to Bernadette.

As she hovered in the living room her mother's snores filled the air with the stench of stale drink. She was never in a good mood when she woke up and Jodi was worried she'd snatch the present and not give it back. She'd returned to her room and sat for as long as she could bear it.

Then she'd pulled apart the paper. Inside she found a small teddy, a pair of red and white pyjamas, matching hairclips and bobbins, and a chocolate selection box. Squealing with glee, she'd put the pyjamas on and tied her hair into two stringy pigtails. She'd climbed on to the sink in the bathroom and gazed at herself in the cracked mirror. She'd felt like a movie star.

By the time Bernadette surfaced, Jodi had cut out the puzzle on the back of the selection box and coloured in the picture.

'Look what Santa brought me last night,' Jodi said shyly, as she twirled to show her mum her new pyjamas. 'I coloured this myself too,' she added proudly.

'Where did you get this stuff?' Bernadette had snatched the picture roughly.

'Last night—'

'Whatever,' Bernadette had snarled, tossing the picture to the floor.

Jodi had gone to Nana's house in her pyjamas. 'Look at me, Nana!'

'Where did those come from?'

'Santa!'

'Well, he must've thought you were a specially good girl because he left you a parcel under my tree too.'

'You shouldn't fill her head with nonsense,' Bernadette spat.

Nana had never answered when Bernadette tried to start a row. She simply walked away.

Each year after that, a kindly stranger had called to the door on Christmas Eve and handed Jodi a parcel wrapped in Christmas paper and a ribbon. She'd treasured whatever she found inside it and convinced herself it had come from a man at the North Pole who cared about her.

So, when Francine had approached her a couple of weeks previously and said they were going to use this year's Hallowe'en party to raise funds for local children, Jodi had forced herself to appear composed. She was the patron of her own charity called Dare to Dream, which worked with underprivileged children, but this would be different. Jodi could help the less well-off children in her own community, the kids on her own doorstep who were living in misery.

'If it's too much trouble, please just say so.' Francine had hesitated.

'I'm thrilled you asked me,' Jodi had assured her. 'Saul and I have never been part of a community like Bakers Valley and I'm honoured you've asked me to help.'

Now that the party was in full swing Jodi was enjoying every second of being a local. The atmosphere in the hall was one of relaxed cheer, elderly ladies and gentlemen chatting to parents as teenagers hung out in huddles.

All conversations came to an abrupt end when Cameron burst through the door. 'NO, I WON'T, AND I HOPE YOU DIE!' he yelled, as he ran towards Francine.

A red-faced Carl arrived after him, panting. 'Okay, girls, in you go,' he said to his little group of trick-or-treaters, trying to sound his usual cheerful self.

'Mummy!' Andrea's daughter, Claire, ran to her and began to sob.

'What happened, sweetheart?'

'Cameron tried to take my trick-or-treat bag and when his daddy told him not to he started hitting and kicking me and Katie.'

Katie was attached to Jane's leg, howling.

'Carl?' Francine was aghast.

'All the excitement just went to Cameron's head. Too much sugar and tearing about. Sorry about the disruption, folks!'

Saul brought up the rear. He wasn't crying but he looked white and shaken. 'Mum!' He ran to her.

'Okay, dude?'

'It was fun until Cameron started to be nasty again,' Saul whispered. 'Can I stay here with you now, please?'

'Of course. You can be my helper and sit on my lap,' Jodi said, as she soothed him.

Carl came up to Jodi. 'Is Saul okay?' he asked. 'I'm sorry he was upset. Cameron's got a terrible temper for such a little fellow. You think once the toddler stage is past they'll calm down, but I guess some kids are just very feisty.'

'I'm sure he didn't mean to hurt the girls,' Jodi said.

'It's the story of his young life so far,' Carl confided. 'Trouble seems to be his constant companion.'

Before Jodi could answer, a frazzled Francine had dragged a struggling Cameron over to them. 'Why didn't you try to stop him?' Francine hissed. 'Now he's just made a complete show of me again. He won't say sorry. Sort him out, Carl.'

'What do you want me to do? Tie his arms and legs together and gag him?' Carl hissed back. 'He was utterly feral out there. He would've injured those little girls if I hadn't stopped him. He was using the light sabre like a lump hammer.'

The light went out in Francine's eyes. 'Cameron,' she said firmly, 'you will stop this appalling behaviour this instant. I'm not having it any more. Come and apologise to Claire and Katie. You are not going to ruin the party.'

Cameron dashed past her at full throttle towards the girls. Francine followed, wearing her most winning smile. By the time she'd caught up with him, she truly wished she hadn't made him apologise.

'You're a bitch and you're a bitch!' he screamed at Katie and Claire. Then he ran into the small booth where Jodi was sitting and dived under the table.

Francine burst into uncontrollable sobs, burying her face in a tea cloth.

Several people rushed to comfort her.

'Well, I've heard it all now!' Andrea said. 'You should take that child home, Francine.'

'Steady on, Andrea,' Jane remonstrated. 'Francine, don't you fret. Our house is like a war zone. Cameron'll get over himself in time. My eldest boy is the same. The other two were angels in comparison.'

'Your eldest causes havoc in the village. Don't try to condone Cameron's violent, foul-mouthed behaviour!' Andrea shouted.

'Pay no attention to her, Francine,' Jane said. 'Some day one of her children will tell her to feck off in front of the mayor or, worse, they'll hit their teens and get addicted to cocaine.'

'My children will not end up like that, thank you very much.' Andrea retorted. 'Just because you two are making a bags of motherhood doesn't mean I have to.'

Jodi began to giggle. 'Wow!' she said, standing up with Saul in her arms. 'I sincerely hope your children all make it to medical school or wherever you think they should go.'

'Sorry?' Andrea reddened.

'You clearly reckon they should all be perfect,' Jodi said. 'I don't know about you, but I'm certainly not perfect.'

Cameron was sitting cross-legged with his arms folded under the table. Carl attempted to drag him out. 'Come out here and don't even think about wrecking the place or making this any worse for Mum and me. If you step out of line once more tonight I won't be held responsible for what I'll do to you.'

'Don't touch me!' Cameron screamed.

'Good Lord!' Carl said to Jodi. 'I've never seen such blatant defiance. I have to admit to being unnerved by this fella.'

'Could you take Saul to get a drink?' Jodi asked Carl. 'Cameron might come out for me. A different face?'

'It's worth a try. Come on, Saul,' Carl said, gazing helplessly at his son.

'Go with Carl, Saul. I'll come over to you in just a second, okay?' Jodi promised.

Cameron was curled into a tight ball, sobbing.

Jodi sat on the floor, cross-legged, under the table holding her arms out. The little boy peeped through his fingers at her, then crawled towards her. 'It's okay. I feel like hiding some days too,' she said soothingly. 'Let's just sit here for a bit and let the others get some food.'

∞

Francine knew she was beyond salvaging the situation. If people wanted to judge her harshly and point the finger at her, she'd have to live with it. She decided she might as well make herself useful so she went to dole out cake with Jane while two other women poured coffee.

'This is delightful, dear,' an elderly lady told Francine. 'You're a wonder, and I hope all the other parents appreciate you.'

'Thank you.' Francine forced a smile.

'Did you make any of these cakes yourself or does someone else do that?'

'I made them all,' Francine said wearily.

'Well, you're ever so talented.'

'It's just a pity I'm not so good as a mother. Perhaps I should open a café and put my children in a crèche,' Francine said sadly.

'Not at all, dear,' the old lady said. She laid a hand on Francine's. 'Children are meant to have spirit. They're like tiny sponges. They soak up the world and try to process it as best they can. My first child was silent. We discovered he was severely autistic. To this day he's totally non-communicative. I've never known what he's thinking or feeling. Embrace your little fella's spark.'

Francine had a lump in her throat. She'd never seen Cameron's behaviour in a positive light. She didn't think she'd ever get used to his violent fluctuations but that wise woman had given her a sharp dose of reality.

Jodi was leading Cameron to the apple bobbing. Before long he was sitting at a low table with Saul and two other children, munching brack and watching the older children dunking their faces in the large vats of water. Jodi was making them giggle as she pulled faces and told them a story.

'Isn't she the most lovely person?' Jane murmured. 'I'd say the only reason she doesn't have tons of children is because of her career. She's an amazing mother.'

'She really is,' Francine agreed listlessly. 'It's astonishing the pre-conceived ideas we can all have. I assumed before I met her that she'd be a total diva with little or no interest in kids. But she's incredibly keen to set down roots for herself and Saul.'

'I guess it's easy to forget she's a regular person when the world thinks we own her through her acting.'

ის

By the time Francine pulled up at the house, the clearing-up complete in the school hall, Carl was carrying Cameron up the stairs.

'He's out cold after all the shenanigans.' Carl shrugged.

She followed them into the bedroom, where Cameron crawled on to his father's lap.

'Sorry, Mummy and Daddy,' he said, peering up at them.

'It's okay, son. These things happen. We'll have to try and work out some sort of system to stop you getting so cross. Nuala says she knows lots of ways of doing that,' Carl explained.

'Okay,' Cameron said, into his daddy's chest.

'Hop under the duvet there and we'll tuck you in,' Francine said gently. 'As Daddy says, we'll go and talk to Nuala a little bit more and see if she can help us with a little plan to keep away the crossness.'

'It just jumps out and does what it likes.' Cameron yawned.

'We'll try and fix it together.' Carl bent to kiss him.

Chapter 22

Early the next morning, Jodi boarded the plane with Saul.

'I can't wait to see Daddy!' he said.

'It's going to be brilliant,' Jodi said, patting his head.

'Hello, Jodi,' the excited stewardess greeted them. 'I'm a massive fan! It's great to meet you.'

'Thank you,' Jodi said, shaking her hand and smiling.

'We're going to see my daddy. He's very famous too,' Saul said.

'Oh, I know.' The stewardess laughed. 'Will you tell him Emily said hello?'

Saul chatted nineteen to the dozen for the entire flight, as Jodi nodded and smiled.

'You've a real little character there,' a nearby passenger said, as they disembarked.

'Don't I know it!' Jodi said cheerfully.

The neatly dressed chauffeur had already found their small bags and was waiting patiently at their usual spot in Arrivals.

'Hello, ma'am, Saul,' he said politely.

'Hey, G!' Saul gave him a high five, complete with a leap in the air.

'Hi, George,' Jodi greeted him.

'How was your flight?'

'Good, thanks,' Jodi said, as they settled into the back of the car. She had used George all the time since her career had taken off. His darkened windows and pleasant, unobtrusive manner made for a combination she appreciated. They always used the same drop-off and collection spots in the airport so she knew he'd be there to whisk her away before a crowd had time to follow.

The traffic was light for central London and they arrived at the apartment quickly. Letting them in with her key, Jodi inhaled the familiar smell of furniture polish mixed with cologne.

The press would've assumed Jodi had been in charge of the décor, but in truth this place was Darius all over. From the pony-skin rug to the accents of acid green and fuchsia pink, the place screamed drama and plush excess. It had made Jodi giggle the first time she'd seen it. 'Jeez, Darius, all that's missing is a flock of flamingos and Barry Manilow crooning "Copacabana" in the corner at a white baby grand piano,' she teased.

'Why a baby grand? What about a full man-sized version with crystal-encrusted legs?' Darius had said, with a cheeky grin.

'I wouldn't put it past you,' Jodi had replied. 'I'm worried that I'll arrive here some day soon and you'll have bought one!' Smiling, she dragged her bag into his room. Thankfully, there was still no piano.

'Can I get a drink, Mum?' Saul called out.

'Sure, lovie. You know where the kitchen is.'

The kitchen was more like a cubbyhole with a couple of expensive accessories. The fridge was gigantic, usually stocked with booze and the odd bottle of sparkling water. It was really only for show. Like Jodi, Darius was never going to win any awards for his culinary skills. 'I wouldn't even consider cooking in here,' he said, waving a hand dismissively. 'Apart from the fact it might make a mess, imagine if my three-thousand-pound rug got to smell of onions!'

The two bedrooms were just as dramatic as the entrance area and living room. Darius's room was dominated by a huge leather-headed bed with enough silk cushions in graduated shades of green and cream to create a seascape for a large movie set. Little seahorses in twinkling palest green adorned everything from the bedside lockers to the curtains.

'What's with the seahorse obsession in here?' Jodi had once asked.

'Male seahorses bear the babies and are in some sense the mothers in their species, so this is my nod to being a nurturer,' Darius explained. 'I told the designer to make this room like a mermaid's palace.'

Jodi found Darius's view of the world extraordinary. He believed that it would be a better place if everyone allowed themselves to dream. In that, he was the exact opposite to her. His bubble would never burst. He would drift through life with hope shining from his soul. 'That's why you and I were destined to be together, darling,' he often said. 'You lean towards tragedy and I believe in fairies!'

'You *are* a fairy!'

Jodi had been born in a popped bubble with the harshest side of life on her doorstep. While Darius had played on beaches and been loved, Jodi had sat in pubs or A&E departments, waiting for her mother either to get drunk or to sober up.

Darius brought an element to Saul's life that she couldn't offer. She simply didn't know how to teach their son about rainbows and stardust and was eternally grateful to Darius for providing that extra bit of magic in their world.

'Hello, hello, hell-ooo?' Darius was home.

'Hi!' Jodi said, dropping the things she'd rooted out of her case and running to hug him.

'Daddy!' Saul shrieked, rushing to his arms.

'Are you two ready to party tonight?' Darius said to Saul. 'Jodi, my darling, how are you?' He carried Saul over to her so they could have a family hug.

'When are we going?' Saul asked.

'Soon!' Darius said. 'You know how much my friend Garrison loves giving parties and this year he's going all out! There'll be loads of other children there. Mummy and I are going to dress up, and you are too!'

'No, I'm not!' Jodi protested.

'Yes, you are!' Saul and Darius shouted in unison.

'I have your costume all ready. You'll be Dorothy, I'm the Lion,' Darius made a pretend paw swipe, 'and Saul is the Tin Man. Everything's organised!'

'Where are the costumes, Dad? Show me!'

'In your room. Come on!'

A moment later, Saul couldn't contain himself. 'Look, Mum! Mine's just like the one in the movie!'

'Super cool! I'm not too sure about mine, though,' she said, picking up the blue and white gingham dress.

'That cost a fortune, I'll have you know,' Darius scolded her.

'It's more the wig with the two wired plaits I'm bothered about.' Jodi grinned.

Saul was thrilled when his parents zipped him into his Tin Man costume. 'It's so comfy,' he said. 'It looks like tin but it feels like my pyjamas.'

Darius covered his own face in an orangey colour. 'Wait until you see my nose and whiskers!' he said.

Jodi stepped into the glittering red shoes Darius had provided. 'I've always wanted to follow the Yellow Brick Road. If only we could walk into the living room and find hundreds of Munchkins!'

'Shoot!' Darius said, clicking his fingers. 'I knew I forgot something.'

The buzzer sent Saul cavorting to the door. 'The car's here!' he shouted.

They piled into the limo for the short ride to the venue.

When they arrived, Jodi peered out of the window. 'The place is thronged with paps.'

'I figured it might be.' Darius looked pleased. 'I can't wait to show them my costume!'

'You'll have to get someone to take Saul around to the back,' Jodi instructed.

'That's all arranged,' Darius assured her. 'Ah, here she is now.' Rolling down the window, Darius asked if she was there to mind Saul.

'Yes, I am. I'll usher him to the back once you two have emerged from the vehicle,' she said. 'Garrison will meet us there.'

'Okay, honey, you know the drill,' Jodi said, and kissed Saul. 'You wait a couple of minutes until Dad and I are out having pictures taken and the lady will take you to meet Uncle Garrison. We'll be in as soon as we can, okay?'

'Okay, Mum.' Saul pulled a fed-up face.

'What's up?'

'I want to be in the magazines too. Why can't I have my picture taken?'

'We've told you before, dude.' Darius took over. 'We think it's wrong for little children to be in pictures like that. When you're older, if you want to be in photos, it'll be up to you.'

''Kay.'

'See you in five, sweetie,' Jodi said, and opened the door to a seizure-inducing array of camera flashes.

'Jodi! Darius!' the photographers called. 'Over here! Gorgeous! Amazing!'

Jodi and Darius came together and performed beautifully for the press, prancing, giggling, stroking each other's faces and hugging. They even kissed quickly.

'Do you think we're in Oz yet?' Jodi said, raising a hand to her mouth and gasping.

'I can feel my courage seeping through my paws so I guess we are, sweetie,' Darius answered loudly.

They stood for a few more minutes to make sure each photographer had at least one shot. They were known in the business for being generous to press and fans alike.

'Great to see you back on British soil, Jodi,' someone called out.

'We've missed Darius but our son is happily settled in school in Ireland,' she said. 'We're thrilled to be reunited for the midterm break while Darius continues with the shooting of his new movie, *The Devil's Children*.'

'We'd better go inside or they'll send out a search party!' Darius said. He waved and led her away. 'Nicely done, darling. We love a good movie plug,' he whispered, as he gave her an oh-so-nonchalant kiss on the cheek and hooked her towards him in a protective arm.

Pausing pointedly, they gazed into each other's eyes, offering the paps a 'wonderful moment' picture before the automatic doors of the hotel swallowed them.

Saul was running up and down with two boys he'd met many times before.

'Okay?' Jodi called to him. He replied with a thumbs-up and an impish grin.

'Oh, me! Oh, my! There's no place like home!' Jodi and Darius heard behind them.

'Garrison, darling!' Darius exclaimed. 'You look utterly obscene! Priscilla, Queen of the Desert, with nothing left to the imagination.'

'I do try. It's not my fault I'm hung like a donkey.'

'Too much information, thank you!' Jodi said, pretending to be disgusted.

The place was decorated to look like a cave, complete with spooky music.

'This is lavish even for you,' Darius teased.

'Old age is making me eccentric,' Garrison said, with a heavy sigh.

'You were born bats, sweetie,' Jodi laughed, 'but you've surpassed yourself here!'

'How are things? Are you loving the country-cottage chic of Ireland?' Garrison asked Jodi. 'It suits you. You look ravishing. If I wasn't gay I'd *want* you.'

'You really know how to compliment a girl,' she said, chucking him under the chin.

For the longest time Jodi had tried to convince Garrison and Darius to fall in love.

'If we could, we would have aeons ago,' Darius had said. 'But the electricity just isn't there.'

'We love each other but it's brotherly rather than va-va-voom!' Garrison sighed.

He was one of the only people in the world who knew about the marriage arrangement. He was Saul's godfather and a fabulous support to both of them. An amazing success in the acting industry, he was always flamboyant and in-your-face gay, but he'd never been any different.

'If only I'd taken a feather from your glittering cap way back when,' Darius had lamented, 'I could be out there as my true self.'

'But you wouldn't have Jodi and, more than that, my godson wouldn't exist.'

'True. I wouldn't swap either of them for all the gay kudos in the galaxy.'

'Besides,' Garrison had flicked his hair, 'this town ain't big enough for two queens.'

The atmosphere was jovial and relaxed as Garrison ensured his guests' glasses were topped up and the canapés plentiful. Face painters and a magic show kept the children occupied while the adults mingled.

'Do you need me to come and sit with you?' Jodi asked Saul. She was so used to using him as a crutch when they attended such events, she found it mildly unnerving to discover he wanted to hang out with the other kids on his own.

'I'm fine, Mum. You go and talk to Daddy and the grown-ups.'

Ever since they'd met, Jodi had loved the way her husband looked after her at social gatherings. Darius could barely contain himself at parties and press events. He lived for the buzz, so all she needed to do was find him, link her arm through his and she'd be safe.

That had been the main reason she'd stayed with Mac for so long. That, and the fact that she'd fallen head over heels in love with him.

'Boo!'

Jodi knew the voice before she turned around.

'Mac,' she said, knowing she must be blushing.

'How's my girl? Love the outfit, by the way!' he said, pulling her into his arms.

Jodi noticed he still wore the same musky scent and still had the impish look that had melted her heart. Panic rose as she tried to remain in control.

'Mac,' Darius said curtly, appearing at Jodi's side like her knight in shining armour.

'Darius, the gorgeous Greek god who stole my one true love!'

'Do you need to split, sweetie?' Darius asked, looking into her eyes.

'I'm fine for a few minutes,' Jodi answered. She squeezed Darius's hand to let him know she was really okay. She'd probably be shaking and crying her eyes out later, but she was sick of running from the hurt Mac had caused her.

You're a married woman with a son. He doesn't know it's all a sham. Stand your ground, Jodi.

'I'll just grab us a drink, then,' Darius said, and bent to kiss her lips.

'I'm fine, thanks,' Mac said cheekily.

'That's a matter of opinion,' Darius answered icily.

'Your husband doesn't like me much, does he?' Mac remarked, with a smirk.

'He has high standards.'

'Ouch. Nasty, nasty, Jodi, darling.'

'How's life with you?' she tried.

'Ah, you know yourself,' Mac leaned against the wall, unabashedly staring at every inch of her, 'never the same since you left me high and dry.'

'Oh, Mac, get over it. Time has well and truly marched on. Things change. We were kids, we had fun ...'

As his eyes narrowed, she felt he could see straight into her soul.

Please, God, make him believe he doesn't affect me. Don't let him break me down.

'We were so good together, Jodi. I've never met another girl like you. You know the reason, don't you?' He chewed the end of a drinking straw. 'I gave you my heart and you never returned it.'

'Mac, please, change the record, yeah?' She didn't trust herself to keep up the farce. After all this time he still made her ache inside. She still loved him. Sad but true.

'But don't you remember …'

She walked away, trying not to run. Seeking Saul and Darius, she panicked and rushed to the Ladies. Slamming herself into the safety of a cubicle, she clunked her forehead against the cold wall.

Yes, Mac, I remember it all. I spend my time trying to forget. I wish I'd never met you. I wish I'd never loved you.

She'd resisted for as long as she could all those years ago. She'd known Mac was trouble. She'd known he would break her heart, but she'd fallen for him hook, line and sinker. 'I have a pressie for you!' Mac had winked and grinned mischievously. He'd dangled a silver key above her head.

She'd looked up and tried to focus on the chain. 'What's that for?' Her heart was beating like a drum.

'It's the keys to our new flat. We're moving out of the kippy area of town, and into Chelsea!' He'd picked her up and swung her around.

'But the place we live now is dear enough. How are we going to afford it? The money from my next movie'll be decent, but I need to look after Nana and Tommy. I can't spend every last penny on rent,' Jodi explained, above the din of the swish nightclub they were in.

'Relax, baby, the world's our oyster. Things are on the up and so are we,' he'd said, kissing her mouth.

Jodi had felt an overwhelming urge to put her hands over her ears and block out the world. It was too much too soon. 'I can't keep up, Mac. I can't keep us all afloat. I'm at the bottom of the hill and we need to stay where we are for the moment, take it slowly,' she pleaded.

'It's all taken care of. Don't you worry your pretty little head about any of it,' Mac said, scooping her up and spinning her around. 'It's on me! I'm hardly going to sign your name on the dotted line and expect you to pay up. It's done, the first six months paid up front! We're on the pig's back, baby!' Dropping her to the floor, he clapped to the rhythm of the music.

Bounding onto the dance floor, he left Jodi standing alone. Usually she'd have been there with him, dancing and laughing, enjoying the feel of his arms around her. But none of this added up.

Mac was a runner on set. He had the lowest-paid job with the least responsibility and would never be guaranteed work from one production to the next. Unless he had an in with the producer, he was no different from a thousand other lads.

How was he signing for new apartments and paying rent up front?

Jodi knew she should have voiced her fears immediately, but she'd learned never to look a gift horse in the mouth. She'd taken him home to meet Nana and Tommy, and both had adored him. That counted for a lot.

'He's a keeper, that lad. You've done well for yourself, Jodi love.' Nana had beamed. 'He's not like them wasters that hang around our estate. All they think about is drinking cans and causing trouble. You'd do a lot worse than staying with Mac.

He's Irish too, which makes a difference. He knows the essence of who you are and understands where you come from. Your roots mightn't be the prettiest but they're what make you yourself. I'm glad he's got your back, love.'

After that everything had happened in jig time. One minute she and Mac were living in a dingy flat with a broken cooker and no proper bathroom, the next they were hosting parties in a swish two-bedroom penthouse with a balcony the size of a small planet.

'Look at those stars, baby,' Mac said, as he held her tightly on the balcony one night. 'You're going to be the brightest one of all. This place is only the beginning. We're going to rise right to the top.'

On so many occasions Jodi had tried to sit him down for a grilling. She'd wanted to know how he'd managed to pay six months' rent up front on a Chelsea address. But each time she'd broached the subject he'd convinced her he had it all under control. One evening as Mac had led yet another procession of party-goers into their apartment, Jodi had had enough.

'Mac, I have to ask you a few questions. None of this shit adds up. Where are you getting the money for this lifestyle?' she'd asked. 'Please tell me you haven't got yourself up to your neck in loans. I'm scared. I don't want us to start off with a brick around our necks.'

'Babe, trust me. It's all taken care of, I told you.' He'd kissed the top of her head and stroked her face. 'I love you so much. You look so sexy when you're worried.'

'Mac, I don't come from this stuff.' She'd waved at the lavish furniture and the people swilling beer and champagne. 'Talk to me, please!'

He had taken her hands and sat her on the coffee table.

Kneeling down, he had looked deep into her eyes. 'I would never do anything to hurt you, Jodi. You're the best thing that ever happened to me. I'll come clean. The money came from my aunt. She died six months ago, just before we started going out. She was a spinster with no kids and I was like her surrogate son. She left me a house in Margate, which I didn't want to take on, so I sold it. Hence the partying of late and the new gaff.' He had stroked her hair lovingly.

'Why didn't you mention her before?' Jodi wasn't convinced.

'I don't talk about my family, and you're hardly a fount of information about yours.' Mac raised an eyebrow. 'I've never pressed you about your mother but, believe me, I get it. You don't want to talk about it. That's fine by me,' he said easily. 'We don't need to go backwards, babe. You're going to be the most famous leading lady ever and I'm going to manage you. I have it all worked out. You and me against the world, what more do we need?' He put his arms around Jodi and held her close.

He had made her feel safe and special. Until the day she died, Jodi would never take that for granted, the sense that she was wanted, that she belonged, was cared for and, most of all, loved.

The house move and Jodi's next film had happened with lightning speed. But she still couldn't look in the mirror and truly like what she saw. Deep down she was still the daughter of a dead addict, still the unloved child waiting without a friend at the back of the school dining hall for a teacher to remember she had no lunch.

But Mac's predictions had come true. All of the things he had promised and more. Jodi had finished one film, and before she could even contemplate what to do next, the phone was ringing.

'Jodi?'

'Speaking,' she'd said fearfully.

'Imelda Stone here. I'm doing the preliminary arrangements for *Into the Sunset.* Can you come down to the temporary site office immediately? We need to speak with you.'

'Yes,' Jodi answered, barely above a whisper.

Imelda hung up and Jodi burst into tears.

'Hey what's up?' Mac asked, full of concern.

'I think they're going to fire me, Mac. I've to go to the site office now. Your woman sounded really snotty.'

'Ah, feck her.' He waved a hand dismissively. 'She's probably being paid five pence to do a shit job and is taking her frustration out on you. Go and see what's up.'

A short while later as she sat outside the Portakabin office, she was riddled with self-doubt and had to force herself not to run away.

The door was flung open. 'Jodi, come in and sit down. I'm Imelda.' She was a scraggy woman with dark, wiry hair and a cigarette hanging from her lips. 'Coffee?'

'Uh, no, thanks.' Her voice cracked. Clearing her throat, she willed herself to stop being such a scaredy-cat.

Imelda sauntered away from her, across the Portakabin, and Jodi turned towards the only desk in the dank room.

She couldn't believe she was face to face with Reggie Wilson, the world's most successful movie producer. He'd logged six box-office smashes in the previous ten years, along with endless awards. Unremarkable to look at, he was squat and plain, with a shaved head, wire glasses and a bulbous nose. In jeans and a white T-shirt with a fitted jacket, he had a commanding presence.

'Mr Wilson, I had no idea I was coming to meet you. I was just …'

Stop stuttering like a deranged primate. Pull it together. This man doesn't know I grew up on an estate where the pizza delivery van wouldn't even go. Hold your head up high and act like your life depends on it.

'Come and sit over here, kid,' he said. 'I don't bite. Not unless you really piss me off!' He guffawed.

Now Jodi spotted his entourage, who were also stuffed into the cramped cabin. One man was pacing up and down, shouting to himself in a rather menacing manner. He swung towards her, and Jodi realised he had one of those headpieces on and was in fact on the phone.

'Pull up a pew, if you can find one.' Reggie exhaled loudly. 'Can someone get me a strong coffee? And a chair for Miss Ludlum!' he yelled. 'Excuse our appearance, sweetheart. This is all a bit disorganised but by the end of the week we won't be sitting in a dive like this and I won't have to yell for coffee!' he said, leaning back in the chair. 'Ya want coffee, darlin'?'

'No thanks, Mr Wilson. I'm fine.' Jodi was terrified of him. 'I don't need a chair either. I can stand.'

'Jeez, baby, stop with the Mr Wilson shit. Call me Reggie. You're givin' me a complex here. I'm trying to hang on to my youth and I don't need you to act like I'm your granddaddy, for cryin' out loud.' He tipped his chair backwards, balancing on the two back legs, pointed at Jodi with his pen and gave a wheezy laugh. Realising she was supposed to join in, she giggled.

'Miss Ludlum,' Imelda said, and plonked a chair so close to the backs of Jodi's legs that she fell into it.

'Thanks,' Jodi said, alarmed.

'Okay.' Reggie's smile faded. 'Here's the deal. I like you. You're fresh, new, and you look great on screen. I just saw the scenes you shot in your last movie. You've got star-quality, kid. I want you to be Carrie. She's not the leading lady, but she's a damn fine supporting role. Can you ride a horse?' He clicked his pen against his teeth.

'I've never tried.' Jodi could barely speak. Reggie Wilson *liked* her! He wanted her to call him by his first name! He thought she could be a star!

'Hey! You! Doll-face! Get this kid on to a horse this afternoon. She only needs to be able to do the close-up stuff – we can get a double to do distance work,' he bellowed at Imelda, who began to punch numbers into a mobile phone. 'Who's your agent, kid?'

'I don't have one properly sorted yet. I was with a local woman in Dublin. She's called Hazel. She got me my first part, but I don't really have anyone here.'

Jodi had expected Reggie to laugh or shout at her. But he had been astonishingly kind. Flicking his mobile phone open, he had made a series of calls.

'Noelle! It's Reggie. I've a kid here who's gonna be the next big thing …' Reggie boomed laughing. 'You got it in one, lady. What I says goes … Yeah, I like that. Okay here's the deal. You get your pretty ass down to me and we work out some figures. She's fresh and impressionable and I don't want some badass shark swallowing her whole. I've had enough of my good actresses end up in rehab. So this one needs to be looked after, ya hear?'

Reggie threw his phone on the desk and stretched his arms high above his head. 'Listen to me, kid. This is a tough business. People tell ya they're your friends – they ain't. Noelle's a smart agent as well as a good person, which is rare in this business. You'll be okay with her. She's coming to meet you in a while. She'll see you don't get shafted. This is your chance to make it big. Don't blow it. I like you,' he repeated loudly. 'You're gonna do good, yeah?'

Jodi sat quivering at the other side of the desk, feeling as if she was in a dream. She was terrified and thrilled in equal measure.

Reggie was imposing and utterly intimidating, but Jodi knew she could trust him. For all his brashness, he'd just gone out of his way to have her looked after.

'Thank you,' she said quietly. 'I promise I won't let you down.'

'Good for you, kid. D'ya know what? I believe you too,' he said, as he flung his chair back and walked out.

The background staff had swooped forward. Less than an hour later, Jodi's entire life had been turned upside down. Scripts had been dumped in front of her. Wardrobe people had measured every inch of her body. Hairdressers had sidled up behind her and lifted her hair, ruffled it and held fake tresses up to her face. They had argued about her. 'I think taking all her hair to a honey blond shade would make her more striking,' a gum-chewing woman said.

'No. The depth is what makes her stand out. Reggie said you can't fuck with her look,' Imelda shouted.

Jodi was too timid to speak. Not that the hairdressers or wardrobe people seemed remotely interested in engaging with her. It was almost as if they were dressing a plastic mannequin rather than a real person.

There was so much note-taking, pencil-chewing, to-ing and fro-ing that Jodi had figured the best policy was to keep schtum. The odd person acknowledged her with a grin or a word about lack of time and changing crews. Only one had divulged that Reggie was a hard taskmaster and they'd all be on the go for the next forty-eight hours without a break.

Otherwise Jodi felt like the queen bee, sitting on the swivel chair with all the drones buzzing around her.

She was so caught up in the craziness, she barely noticed the unassuming woman in the dull brown trouser suit with mousy hair and no makeup who sidled up to her. 'Hello, Jodi,' she said.

'I'm Noelle. Reggie called and asked me to come and talk to you. Would now be a good time for you?'

She was the first person to ask Jodi's opinion or even stop to hear an answer. 'Hello, Noelle,' Jodi said. 'I'd love to talk to you.'

Noelle's handshake was firm and swift as she slipped into the chair that Reggie had occupied earlier.

'Now, Reggie thinks he's decided all our fates. He's certainly very powerful, and if you and I feel we can work together, I reckon we'll make a winning team. This is all a little unusual as time isn't really on our side.' She paused and stared at Jodi, a warm smile curving her lips. 'You seem like a lovely girl. Really you do. I've no qualms about representing you.'

'Thank you,' Jodi said, and her shoulders relaxed. She smiled back.

'I'm sorry we can't do more of the getting-to-know-you stuff, but I'm sure you don't need me to tell you that this is the chance of a lifetime Reggie's offering. So shall we try and do this together?'

'I'd love that,' Jodi said. 'I might be young and green but I have a good feeling about you.'

Noelle stretched across the desk and patted her hand. 'Us girls have to stick together, don't we?'

'Yes!'

'Right. I'll go through the contract and make sure it's all as it should be,' Noelle said calmly. From her briefcase she produced a file. 'Here's some information on me,' she said. 'Although it's already a bit late for that!' She laughed.

Jodi read the blurb Noelle had handed her, which listed some of the people she represented. 'You're Kim Fraser's agent!' she blurted.

'Yes,' Noelle said, without looking up from the contract she was scanning. Kim was one of the most successful actresses of the last ten years. A household name and the face of one of the best-known makeup lines. 'She's a great girl. Works like a slave and never complains. You remind me of her in the early days. I can see the same potential in you,' Noelle said, meeting Jodi's gaze. 'To be a star you've got to be willing to give your all. It seems terribly glamorous to outsiders, but this industry is brutal. Do you think you can handle it?'

'I grew up on an estate that made soup kitchens look like the Ritz. If you've heard of the phrase "the school of hard knocks", well, that was my kindergarten. I graduated from there to hell on earth the day the police called to the door to tell me they'd found my mother dead in a laneway, a victim to her booze and drug habit.'

'I'm sorry. I didn't know.'

'Well, now you do, can you handle working with me?' Jodi had turned the tables on Noelle.

'I'm even more sure that we're going to make a fine team.'

Jodi soon learned that Noelle was as sharp as a razor when it came to deals, but that her biggest asset was her unwavering sense of calm. Over the many years they'd been working together, she'd never lost her temper or let Jodi down.

But while Jodi's life had shot off at a pace she hadn't known existed after that first meeting with Noelle, the same couldn't have been said for Mac.

Part of *Into the Sunset* was to be shot in a seaside town called Cap Ferrat in France. Reggie decided they would go there first, spend four weeks on location, and return to London for the remainder. Mac had applied for a job as a runner but was passed over.

'Hey, it's no biggie,' he said, to a crestfallen Jodi. 'You go and become a star. I'll wait for you here.'

As he looked into her eyes she saw all the love she'd yearned for.

'I'll be here if you still want me,' he said gently. 'But I'll understand if I'm not enough.'

'Oh, Mac, you're more than enough,' she said, choked with emotion. 'You're all I've ever wanted and needed.'

'Ditto,' he said, as he stroked her face. 'We're meant to be together, Jodi. It'll always be you and me against the world.'

'Always.' She sighed happily as she sank against his chest.

Their time apart was bittersweet. Jodi was growing more as an actress with each passing day, but she missed Mac so much that at times it physically hurt. 'When they say love hurts, I never understood that until now,' she crooned down the phone to him one evening. 'I thought it was more to do with people like Ma whacking me for annoying her!'

'Christ, Jodi!' Mac laughed. 'You really were dragged up!'

'Don't you know it. But that's all in the past now.'

'It's you and me against the world now, Jodi,' he repeated.

'Just you and me, Mac.'

She'd been happy in the shabby apartment they'd first called home. So when she returned and joined Mac in their new plush pad, she was worried. 'Mac, the bills for this place are staggering. I don't know how much money you've inherited but even the proceeds of Buckingham Palace couldn't sustain the place indefinitely.'

'It's cool, honey,' Mac said. 'I'll ask you for a dig-out if I need it. You just worry about your own shit and leave the apartment to me. It'll all work out evenly in the end. We make a great team. It'll be you and me all the way, baby!'

'But why don't we move to a less expensive place? At least until I finish this movie,' she suggested. 'I've a few more months of filming here and then I'll know where I stand.'

'It's cool, baby.' Mac fobbed her off.

Mac still went out at least four nights a week. If there wasn't a party it was to a club or a bar but that was the norm in London. Especially in the film business. Any time Jodi had the energy she went with him. Although she'd no interest in getting wasted, she loved the glam, carefree atmosphere.

Now, as she stood in the Ladies, dressed as Dorothy, her resolve was weakening. Mac could still reduce her to a quivering mess.

'I love you to the moon and back, my Mac,' she whispered, and sobbed into a wad of tissues.

'Jodi?' Darius's voice pierced the bubble of sorrow that had engulfed her.

'I'm in here.' She unlocked the door and fell into his arms.

'Get yourself together and we're out of here. That idiot always has the same effect on you,' Darius soothed. 'I'll find Saul and you go out the back to the driver. Let's go home.'

'The first cut is the deepest,' Jodi said, smiling through her tears.

Darius blew her a kiss. 'See you in five.'

'Why do I still love him, Darius?'

'I can't answer that for you, darling, but I can try to help your heart to heal.'

'Thank you for not judging me.'

'You do the same for me, darling girl. We've got each other's backs. That's the way it is,' he said, matter-of-factly.

Saul was clearly loving every second of the party. 'Dad, we're getting animal balloons! Magic Marvin can make anything you want! I got a sword and the guys are all having a fight with me!'

'It looks like a brilliant war,' Darius said, crouching down and holding his arms out. Saul jumped on to him, nearly knocking him flat.

'Wow! You're getting too big and strong to jump on your poor old dad!' Darius hugged him, then whispered in his ear, 'Mummy has a bad tummy ache and she needs to go home now.'

'Can I stay? I could get a taxi home later on.'

Darius roared laughing. 'I expected you to say something like that to me when you're a teenager, not at four!'

'But I'd be fine! Uncle Garrison will call me a cab.'

'I'm sure he would, but I need you to come home and see me,' Darius said, sticking out his bottom lip.

'Okay then.' Saul sighed. 'Let me say goodbye to the guys.' He wriggled free of his dad. Darius watched him high-five the other children and heard him promise to catch up next time he was in town. It was so cute, he didn't know whether to laugh or cry.

Jodi was already in the car by the time they emerged.

'Poor Mum, is your tummy really icky?' Saul asked, as he climbed into the back seat.

Glancing at Darius, she nodded. 'Sorry, pet, but I really need to go home. Did I ruin the fun?'

'I would've come home later in a cab but Dad said I'm a bit young for that.'

The moment they got home Darius shot into the bathroom. 'You go and have a bath. I've put in your favourite Jo Malone bubbles. Saul and I are going to have some boys' time together,' he told Jodi, when he came out.

'Thank you,' she said. 'You're the dearest human being I've ever known.'

'I do my best,' he said, flicking his hair dramatically. 'I can't help being fabulous, can I, Saul?'

Saul giggled and hurled himself at his father. As they wrestled and growled, Jodi slipped away. The citrus-smelling steam and the bubbles lapped around her tense body, making her sigh from the depths of her soul. She closed her eyes and berated herself for allowing Mac to make her cry again. Years had passed and so much had happened since they had parted. She was so successful, but Mac was her Achilles heel.

Darius knocked gently on the door, then let himself in. 'You okay?' he asked, as he perched on the side of the tub.

'Yup. Just feeling a little silly,' she said. 'Saul didn't realise I was upset, did he?'

'He's fine.'

'Good.'

'Jodi,' Darius began, 'you need to put this situation to bed once and for all. It's been too long. We all have skeletons but Mac can't be allowed to control you like this. You've got to stop him.'

She sighed. 'The time has come.'

'I'll be here.'

She smiled sadly and reached for his hand.

'Besides, it probably won't be as bad as you think. Let the story run, the press can go to town on it, and then it'll be over. We're strong, you and I. We'll cope,' he promised. 'Enjoy your bath and I'm going to call our agents and get a meeting set up. It's the end of the line for Mac blackmailing you.'

'Okay.' Jodi waited until he had gone before she allowed herself to cry once more. She knew Darius would do everything in his power to get her through the controversy when Mac spilled the beans, but she wondered if coming clean would ever ease her pain. How harshly would her fans and, more importantly, Bakers Valley judge her? When they knew her secret, how would they think of her?

Chapter 23

Francine gave up after the fourth phone call. No one would have Cameron at their house or send their child to hers.

'Paul would have loved to go and play but we're off to the dentist today,' his mother had said. 'You know how it is during school holidays - these jobs need to be done.'

'We already have plans, Francine, sorry. Thanks for the call,' Jordan's mum said curtly.

'My sister is arriving with her new baby and I'd prefer to keep the house quiet,' said another.

'Well, let me have your Liam here and you can have some quality time with your sister,' Francine offered.

'Liam needs to bond with his little cousin.'

Cara, Craig and Conor were all occupied with friends and Cameron would have to join in with them, Francine decided.

Arguments erupted all day.

'Mum!' Cara yelled. 'Tell Cameron to get out of my room. We're trying to do nail art and he's jumping on my bed.'

'Come down to me, Cameron, and we'll read a story,' Francine said.

'No!' Cameron growled. 'I'm playing with Conor.'

'*Muuuum!*' Conor called. 'He just trashed the Lego fort we've spent hours building.'

'All right, all right, I'm coming,' Francine said, through gritted teeth. 'Cameron, why don't we go into the garden and do some watering? You can do the hose and I'll pull weeds. That'd be fun.'

'I don't want to play with you. Leave me alone.' He burst into Cara's room again.

'*Muuum*, get him out of here, will you?'

'Ah, girls, won't you allow him join in for a few minutes? If he promises to sit quietly?' Francine begged.

'Mum, he kicked Jackie in the head earlier. We're trying to do beauticians here. Being beaten up doesn't go with whale music.'

'Okay,' Francine said. 'We'll do something fun together, darling.' She reached over and scooped Cameron into her arms.

''Snot fair,' he said sulkily, as she carried him down the stairs. 'Nobody wants me.'

'Oh, they do. What about me? I've nobody to play with. Won't you keep me company?'

'Can we play PlayStation?' he asked hopefully.

'Okay. But only for half an hour – deal?'

'Deal. We'll play Grand Prix Drivers! It's my favourite.' He looked so delighted that Francine sighed with relief.

The game was beyond her. She marvelled at how swift he was with the controls and how precise he was at negotiating the car into the sharp bends. 'You're so good at this, Cameron,' Francine said. 'I keep crashing and you're miles away shooting off like a bullet!'

'I'm the fastest!' He giggled.

She groaned in frustration as she ended up mashed into yet another barrier. 'I might just watch you, if that's all right?'

''Kay, Mummy,' he said, hitting the restart button. 'I'll click it on to single player and you'll see how fast I can take the track.'

'Good plan.'

Francine found his accuracy mind-blowing. Yet again she found herself questioning the idea that he had attention deficit disorder. She hadn't a thing wrong with her, yet she couldn't even master driving in a straight line. Cameron was four and he was negotiating the twisting and turning track like a pro.

Once the agreed half-hour was up, the trouble started again.

'You promised it would be half an hour and that'd be it,' she warned. 'It's already forty minutes. As soon as you finish this lap of the track you have to turn it off.'

'No! I'm only getting good now.'

'Cameron!'

He ignored her.

'Cameron, I'm going to get cross,' she said, to deaf ears. 'I'm going to switch it off now.' She stood up to unplug the television.

'Don't! I need to finish the round and save my times,' he begged.

Francine didn't want to be cruel and erase his great work, but at the same time she knew he needed to do as he was told. 'Right. I'm standing here until you finish that round. Then it's going off.'

As he hit the finish line and the cheering on the television erupted, she warned him she was turning it off.

'You're such a meanie,' he shouted, throwing the control pad at her. It hit her leg, and Francine felt anger rising. Stay calm, she reminded herself. He's only small. He can't help it. You're the adult.

'I'm going into the kitchen to make pizza for everyone. You come and help me set the table, please,' she instructed.

He accompanied her to the kitchen, but instead of doing anything constructive, he lay on his back and gave out. 'I hate it here. I'm bored. I don't want pizza. I want to go to the swimming pool. I want to go to the play centre. I want to have an ice cream. I want crisps …'

'Cameron, please!' she said, in exasperation. 'Give it a rest for a few minutes, will you? The others will be down for dinner and you can join in with that. Then we'll go upstairs and you can have a nice deep bath and play with the water toys, okay?'

The arrival of the others seemed to quell Cameron's temper. Food and a drink meant he was much calmer by the time the other children's friends had been collected.

'Let's go up and you can have that bath,' Francine coaxed him. 'I need to put the laundry away so I can keep an eye on you. I'll give you all the pirates and the ship and you can have a nice long bath,' she promised.

By the time she'd finished doing her bits and pieces the bath water was only barely tepid and Cameron was looking cold. 'Right, lovie, out you hop,' she said. 'Come here and I'll wrap you in a big fluffy towel.'

'Leave me alone!' he screamed, trying to bite her.

'You're freezing,' she said, as she struggled to lift his flailing body out of the tub.

'I'm fine!' he said, kicking wildly. 'Leave me alone, bad Mummy!' As he charged off, naked and wet, to his room, Francine plonked herself heavily on the lid of the toilet. She felt as if she'd been beaten up.

By the time Carl arrived home, calm had been restored. Cameron was in his pyjamas with a Puffa coat, hat and scarf on, ready to run into the back garden with his father.

'It's dark and cold so we'll only do a few quick minutes, okay?' Carl warned.

Francine was standing in the kitchen, cradling a mug of tea, when Cara tiptoed in to sit at the table. 'They make so much noise we're going to end up in trouble with the neighbours,' Cara said grumpily.

'I don't think they're doing any harm,' Francine said.

'What is it with boys and football?'

'I don't know, honey, but they seem to love it. I suppose they don't know why you sit and paint tiny flowers on your nails,' she said.

'Sometimes I wish I had a sister,' Cara mused.

'Well, you're my special princess and I love you,' Francine said, and went over to hug her. 'I think our family is quite complete.'

'If you'd had another baby we could've ended up with a second Cameron. That would have been a total disaster,' Cara said.

'Cara! That's not very nice,' Francine scolded.

'Seriously, Mum, he's a demon.'

Just then Francine realised how difficult it must be for her older children when Cameron behaved badly. 'He's okay some of the time, isn't he?'

'If you say so.' Cara was thumbing through a comic.

'You do love him, don't you? He's your little brother after all. He's really cute at times.'

'If you say so,' Cara repeated, not looking up.

'Cara, help me out here. You know we're having problems with him and he's going to this lady,' Francine said, putting her arm around her daughter's shoulders.

'Yes,' Cara said. 'But you've told us not to discuss it and that it's not a big deal.'

'I know, and it's not a big deal ...'

'So why are you looking like it's terrible?' Cara was puzzled.

'I'm not. I suppose I just want to make sure you and the other boys are okay with all of this. I know Cameron can be very disruptive.'

'He's just annoying. But so are the others. That's just brothers, Mum,' Cara said. 'As I said, at times I wish I had a sister, but knowing my luck she'd steal my stuff and annoy my friends and be totally embarrassing.'

Francine smiled. Cara was such an easy-going girl. At least one of her children was stable.

 C3

Francine and Carl had watched a movie, which they'd enjoyed, but now it was late.

'Are you coming to bed?' Carl asked yawning.

'I need to sit for a few minutes longer,' she answered listlessly. 'I'm exhausted but I wouldn't sleep if I go up now.'

'Was your day that bad?' he asked, full of concern.

'No.' What was the point in moaning to Carl all the time? He couldn't change their youngest child. He didn't own a magic wand. She just needed a bit of time on her own and silence. 'I'll be along in a while. I think most of my problem stems from the fact that I'm not at work. I've too much energy for my own good!' she fibbed.

The serenity of the silent house was quite soothing. But the quiet was soon unnerving so Francine padded upstairs to check on the children. Opening Cara's bedroom door softly, she tiptoed in to kiss her daughter. She was growing up so fast it was scary. The smell of nail polish and the mess of glitter on the carpet made Francine smile. She was nearly a teenager, making strides towards true grown-up behaviour. She was yearning to experiment with makeup and big-girl stuff, yet she still enjoyed making pictures and shaking glitter over them. Her pyjamas were still adorned with Hello Kitty, although they were black now rather than cough medicine pink. Cara had never been any trouble. She was sweet-natured without being a pushover and never lacked friends.

In the next room, Craig was sprawled sideways on his bed wearing pyjama bottoms and a soccer shirt. Popcorn lay on the floor at one side of the bed. Francine picked it up, deciding not to mention it. She'd told them all a million times not to bring food upstairs, but every now and again kids needed to get away with a bent rule.

She kissed his flushed cheek and went into Conor's room. He'd been messy from the word go. No matter what the lad did, he seemed to make the place untidy. But the most endearing thing about him was that he was so oblivious to it all. Even in his sleep a smile played on his lips. She rescued his pillow from the floor and placed it near his head, straightened his duvet and scooped up some dirty socks.

Lastly, she made her way into Cameron's room. At first she paused, trying to figure out where he was in the bed. Then she lunged forward and pulled back the duvet. He wasn't there.

'Cameron?' she whispered, not wanting to wake anyone else.

Nothing.

'Cameron?'

A soft groan came from under the bed. She fell to her knees and found him curled in a ball, clutching an armful of teddies.

Gently she dragged him out and laid him on the bed where he instinctively cuddled into his duvet. As she stroked his hair, she felt sad. He was a beautiful little boy. Her baby. As she watched him sleep he looked like any other child, innocent, pure and perfect. The demons that seemed to infest his spirit when he went off at the deep end weren't remotely apparent when he slept.

'What goes on in your little head?' she whispered. 'I wish I knew.'

Other people's opinion of her had always been important to Francine. She longed to be looked up to. She thrived on being in charge. She genuinely enjoyed social occasions and helping others. But lately all of that had come into question. As she looked at her beautiful son, she wondered if keeping up appearances was important at all. More and more she was coming around to the idea that none of it mattered one jot. The most important thing now was helping Cameron.

She changed into her nightdress, cleansed her face and brushed her teeth. Her mind was so addled she knew there was no point in going to bed. She'd only end up tossing and turning, disturbing Carl.

She went downstairs and yawned as she flicked on the kitchen lights. She picked up her favourite recipe book. Oranges were piled in bowls all around the house to fall in with her Hallowe'en colour scheme, so Francine decided she'd put them to good use and make some chocolate orange Victoria Sandwich cakes. The old folks in the home just outside the village were always appreciative of her baking. Carl could take one into work as well. At least she'd maintain some sort of community respect, even if she did feel she was bribing people.

The recipe was just the therapy she needed as it involved lots of different steps, like grating the peel and segmenting the fruit. Francine eventually felt her shoulders leave her ears.

By the time the cakes were cooling on a wire rack, she'd made the butter-cream icing and placed it in the fridge. The large, old-fashioned wall clock read three fifteen. Her eyes burned as she laid a tea cloth over the steaming sponges.

Turning the lights off and rubbing her eyes, she ascended the stairs, hopeful she might manage at least a few hours' oblivion.

Carl stirred as she spooned herself around him in the bed. 'Okay?' he murmured.

'Fine,' she answered, kissing his shoulder. 'Go back to sleep.'

ଔ

Early the next day Jane, Andrea and Sarah met up with a few of the other mothers and children from school at the local indoor play centre.

'I feel really bad for not mentioning this to Francine,' Jane admitted. 'She's so good about having people over. She put such effort into the food and the Hallowe'en party in general.'

'I feel like a right battleaxe too, but every time we include Cameron in play dates like this, all hell breaks loose,' Andrea reasoned.

'Well, I for one wouldn't have come if that child was here,' Sarah said. 'He's hurt my son one time too many. They're all afraid of him. He's a bully, and I know you two are friends with Francine, but she needs to get her finger out and sort that child. He needs to be taught some manners. If he was mine, I'd change his tune, I can tell you.'

'I agree,' said another mother. 'A week in my house and he'd soon stop hitting and kicking people. Some kids just need a firm hand. Francine Hennessy is too busy organising coffee mornings. She needs to take stock and look a little closer to home.'

'I'm sure he'll grow out of it,' Andrea said. 'None of my kids is sporting a halo or a pair of wings, I can tell you. We can't be too harsh. You know what kids are like. One of ours could be the demon of the hour next week. If I've learned anything from motherhood it's that being smug always comes back to bite you on the ass.'

'But seriously,' Susan said, 'Cameron was like a child possessed the other night. I'd have locked myself in the coal shed if one of mine had behaved like that in front of people.'

'Poor Francine was devastated,' Jane said in her defence. 'What could she do? Throw us all out of the school hall, then bind the kid's arms and legs with duct tape and gag him? Once they go off on a mad rant like that it's hard to salvage the situation.'

The fact remained that a large group of people Francine considered long-standing friends were out for the morning with their children and they'd purposely excluded her because of Cameron's behaviour. If she found out, she'd be deeply hurt.

'As long as nobody mentions us all meeting up there'll be no harm done,' Jane said, hoping to leave the matter at that.

CB

In Verbena Drive Francine was waving Conor and Craig off in their friends' car.

'Enjoy the movie, and thanks for taking them!' she called. Cara had gone across the road to her friend Kathy for the day.

'Would you like to go to Silly Sam's play centre?' she asked Cameron.

'On my own?'

'Well, there'll be lots of other children there. It'll be fun!' she said cheerfully. 'Then you and I can get chips for our lunch. We'll just drop the chocolate orange cakes into the old people's home and I'll take you there. How's that?'

''Kay,' Cameron said, staring out of the window. Francine

couldn't bear to do another round of phone calls to people who didn't want to see Cameron. It would be easier to amuse him herself.

The elderly people were thrilled with their visit and Cameron behaved very nicely.

'You were so good in there,' she praised. 'I'm very proud of you.'

Cameron grinned and wagged his foot happily as they pulled up outside the play centre.

As she paid and Cameron took off his shoes to leave in the locker spaces behind the counter, Francine saw Jane, Andrea and at least five other mothers facing her.

'We're just leaving,' Andrea said, red-faced.

'Hello, Jane, ladies,' Francine said curtly. *Don't cry and don't get annoyed. It's quite obvious what's going on here. Just act like a lady. You've done nothing wrong.*

'Francine!' a couple chorused. An awful moment followed in which the women avoided her gaze.

'Why didn't we come before, so I could see my friends?' Cameron rounded on Francine. 'You're so mean! If we didn't go to the smelly house with the old people I could've had fun here!' Cameron smacked Francine's leg, then kicked her shin for good measure. That done, he dashed to the far corner of the centre, curled into a ball and buried his head in his lap.

Quivering with muffled sobs, Francine pushed past the group of women and children and rushed to her little boy.

ひ

'What'll we do now?' Andrea hissed.

'I knew we should've asked her along,' Jane lamented.

'Well, we didn't - and, for crying out loud, he's only here five seconds and the child could be done for GBH on his mother. We'd all be nursing bruised and scared kids if Cameron had been here all along.'

'I'm out of here. I'm not getting involved,' one of the mothers announced.

'Me too,' another said.

Within minutes they'd dispersed, leaving Jane and Andrea to face Francine.

'There's nothing we can say to make this any better. We're going to have to tell her the truth, that people can't stick Cameron's bad behaviour any more,' Andrea said.

'Yup,' Jane said. 'And I'm really up the creek. I lied that I was having lunch with my mother-in-law today. Francine called yesterday to arrange a play date and I panicked and told her a whole pile of spoofs.'

'I thought your mother-in-law was dead,' Andrea said.

'No, that's my father-in-law. Jesus, Andrea, I'm not that bad!'

The two women walked over to where Francine was trying to console Cameron, rocking him on the floor.

'I'm sorry we didn't ask you along,' Andrea began. 'This is really awkward for us.'

'Well, I'm sorry if my being here has made things difficult for you, but it's a public place,' Francine snapped. 'I won't prolong the pain. Goodbye.' She turned back to Cameron.

'Francine!' Jane said, crouching down to touch her arm. 'Let us explain,' she pleaded. 'I can't think how to say this without offending you—'

'Well, let me help you. I'm already offended so just shoot.'

Francine felt as if her heart was going to burst from her chest. She hated confrontation. She went out of her way to include people. If she had a party or coffee morning, she took pains to make sure nobody was left out. How did these people, her 'friends', repay her? They sneaked around behind her back. Francine stood up, her hands on her hips.

'We arranged this at the last minute, but the thing is that some of us are finding Cameron's rough behaviour too much to deal with,' Jane tried.

'Every time he's put in the mix there's trouble and people are sick of it,' Andrea said.

'So neither of you thought that you ought to sit me down and have a chat?' Francine suddenly felt more confident than she'd ever have believed. 'I thought we were friends. I thought friends looked out for one another. Why couldn't either of you have taken me aside or even phoned me and explained that Cameron was out of control?'

'We didn't want to hurt you,' Andrea said quietly.

'So lying to me and excluding me was kinder, was it? Don't you think I've noticed that none of the children wants to play with Cameron? Do you think I'm so blinkered that I can't see people ushering their children into cars so I don't see they're all going for a play date and Cameron's been left out again?'

'I'm sorry.' Jane tried to stroke Francine's arm.

'We didn't know how to approach the matter with you,' Andrea said honestly. 'Your other kids are lovely and there's never been any bother with them, so we weren't sure if you were aware of the difference in Cameron. Francine, we're all so fond of you and Carl. It's not an easy situation for us.'

'God, you make me sick!' Francine exclaimed.

'Pardon?' Andrea looked affronted.

'You're so two-faced it's a joke. I heard you on your phone in the school car park recently, Andrea, remember? You were slating my husband, saying he's like Ned Flanders.'

Andrea blanched. She opened her mouth to speak but nothing came out.

'Don't bother adding to the lies. Jane, I do consider you my friend and I accept your apology for today. Andrea, go swing.' Francine turned on her heel and walked away. Cameron had picked himself up and gone off to play on a slide.

Francine stopped in her tracks as she debated telling the women that Cameron was about to embark on a programme to deal with his behaviour. In fact it would've been like a weight lifting off her shoulders to share the trauma she'd been hiding.

But as she looked at the two people she'd considered close friends, she decided they didn't deserve to know her innermost thoughts. It would only be fodder for the next coffee morning she wasn't invited to. No doubt there'd be a big meeting the following Monday morning in the village café at which the mothers would all express how mortified they'd been when she'd walked in.

Let them gossip, Francine thought.

Cameron was all that mattered to her. Carl would be by her side. Sod the rest of them. She was probably better off knowing where she stood.

Despite that, Francine was desperately hurt. She'd never felt so isolated in her life.

For the first time she wished they lived in a huge soulless city where nobody knew anything about her. The intimate village setting and lovely local school had changed from a warm cocoon to a hostile hell.

Chapter 24

Jodi and Saul always hated saying goodbye to Darius. Now they were about to go home to Ireland without him.

'I'm going far away for filming until Christmas, dude, but the good news is that, before I leave, I'm coming to Ireland for a whole week and we're going to have a whale of a time,' he promised.

'Cool!' Saul said, hugging him. 'I can't wait for you to meet my friends. But after that you'll be gone for months. I'll miss you, Daddy.'

'I'll miss you even more, little dude, but we'll do Skype and I'll call you often. It won't be too many months either, three at the very most,' Darius said. 'You'll have to look after Mummy for me and keep me posted on all the action at school, yes?' He looked heartbroken as he held his son close. 'I love you more than life itself.'

'I love you too, Daddy,' Saul said.

Jodi and Darius hugged for the longest time.

'Mind yourself,' Darius said. 'No more crying over Mac. You're better than that and your heart will heal one day.'

'You keep saying that to me and I want to believe you, but he still gets me here.' Jodi thumped her chest.

'I love you.' Darius stroked her cheek. 'I know that's a poor second but I do.'

'You're not a poor second! I thank God for every day I've known you. I love you too,' she answered.

∽

It was after midnight before they opened the door to the cottage. Saul had been fast asleep in the car so Jodi carried him to his bed. She took off his shoes and coat, then his combats, and tucked him up in his long-sleeved T-shirt. The driver had deposited their bags just inside the hall door. Jodi paid him and said she'd see him again soon.

Then she undressed, brushed her teeth and used a makeup wipe as a nod towards her bedtime skin regime. The delicious silence of the Wicklow countryside worked like a sedative and before long she was deep in sleep.

At nine thirty the next morning her phone, ringing in her handbag, woke her. Slightly disoriented, she managed to grab it before it went to voicemail.

'Hello?' she croaked.

'Jodi, it's Francine. Did I wake you?'

'Sort of, but don't worry. We got home quite late and Saul's still out for the count. How are you?' Jodi yawned, as she curled up in her duvet.

'Not so good,' Francine said flatly.

'Oh dear, I'm sorry to hear that. What's up?' Jodi tried to sound more awake.

'It's kind of a long story. I don't suppose there's any way I could pop by today, is there?' she asked.

'Sure!' Jodi said immediately. 'Bring Cameron too, if you like. I'm sure Saul would be delighted to see him.'

'That's very kind. I baked a lovely double-chocolate fudge gâteau last night,' Francine said, 'so we'd come with a bribe!'

'You don't have to do that, but if it's going begging we won't say no!' Jodi laughed. 'Come whenever you like.'

'We went to mass last evening because Conor and Craig have soccer matches this morning and Cara has athletics training. Cameron and I would love to pop in for an hour. We won't stay any longer as I'll have to grab Cara.'

'Sure,' Jodi said. 'What time suits you?'

'Would ten be too early?'

Jodi peered at her watch. It was already nearly twenty-five to. 'Eh, sure, come on over - you'll have to take us as you find us, though,' she said.

'That'll be lovely,' Francine said, sounding more like her usual self.

Throwing herself out of the bed, Jodi shuffled into her slippers and padded towards Saul's door.

'Mum,' he said, stretching. 'Who were you talking to?'

'Francine. Herself and Cameron are coming now with double-chocolate fudge cake!'

'Ooh, yum! Can I have that for breakfast?'

'Do you know what? You can!' Jodi said. Ah, what the heck, it wouldn't kill him, and, besides, they'd no fresh food. Knowing Francine, it would be divine and probably had more nutritional value than anything she'd pull out of her kitchen cupboard.

A knock on the door made her jump. They weren't here already, surely. She pulled on an oversized grey cable-knit sweater Darius had left behind and went to open the door.

It was Sebastian. 'Hello, sorry to disturb you,' he said awkwardly.

'Sebastian, how are you?' She smiled.

'Would the little lad like to come with me? I'm going off up the back fields to do some pheasant spotting and thought he might enjoy it,' he said, coughing gruffly.

'Sebastian!' Saul said, running to hug him.

'I know he'd love to but he's got a little friend calling in the next few minutes,' Jodi apologised. 'They'll only be here for an hour tops ...'

'Maybe his buddy would come too, if I hang on?' Sebastian suggested.

Jodi hesitated. 'Saul, run and get dressed, like a good boy, and I'll try to arrange something with Sebastian.'

Saul did as he was told.

'I'll have to ask Francine, Sebastian, but a word of warning: Cameron, the other little boy, can be rather difficult.'

'Ah, I'm sure I can handle him. Most boys are as quiet as lambs once they have fresh air and plenty of space to run about!' Sebastian said. 'How was London?'

'Good, thanks,' she said. 'It's always great to see Darius. Can I get you tea or coffee?'

'Nah, thanks all the same. I've to get my things ready. I'll call back down in about fifteen minutes. You'll hear the jeep. If the lads want to come, send them out. If it's not to be, just give me a wave,' Sebastian called over his shoulder, as he went back to the jeep on the other side of the back fence.

Jodi and Saul were ready with seconds to spare when Francine pulled up. As she opened the door to welcome them, Jodi looked down at her own worn-out denims and sloppy sweater. Francine was wearing a pair of smart charcoal slacks with a cashmere twin set. Her pearl necklace matched her earrings and she was perfectly made up.

Jodi's hair was caught up in a wide-toothed comb with some unruly tendrils falling at either side of her bare face. 'Hi! You look gorgeous! As usual I'm like a gypsy with no makeup and the house is a tip,' she said, as she tried to shove the suitcases behind the sofa. 'We haven't even unpacked.'

'Don't worry about that! We're just delighted to come and see you both,' Francine said warmly. 'How was London?'

'Great!' Saul answered for them both. 'My daddy was so much fun and we did lots of stuff together, didn't we, Mum?'

'Sure did, dude.'

'Can Cameron and I go with Sebastian to look at the birds?' Saul asked Francine.

'Oh, my goodness, I'm not sure about that. Who is Sebastian?' Francine looked horrified.

'He's our neighbour and he's really nice,' Saul said. 'He'll take good care of us. He promised, didn't he, Mum?'

'He lives up in the manor house. He's taken Saul before and he honestly seems like a lovely guy,' Jodi vouched for him.

'Yes, of course. I wasn't thinking straight for a minute there. I know him of old,' Francine said. 'His own son died tragically.'

'He told me,' Jodi said. 'I think it means a lot to him to spend time with Saul. If I say they can go for an hour, would you consider it?'

'Well, I'm not sure Cameron would be able to—'

'Please, Mum, please!' he begged. 'I promise I'll be so good. I'll do what the man says.'

'Could I have a word with Sebastian first?' Francine asked.

'Sure. And here he is. Come on out and you can meet him,'

Jodi said, slipping into her wellingtons, which lived on the doorstep. 'Grab your coat and hat, Saul.'

Francine tottered after them, talking in hushed tones to Cameron.

'Hi, Sebastian, meet Francine Hennessy,' Jodi introduced.

'We've met,' he said, without looking up.

'Hello, Sebastian. I'm just a bit concerned that Cameron might be a little excitable. It's in his personality, you see.'

'Once the lad knows I'm in charge, and he's to stay where I can see him, he'll do fine. Do you think you can do that, son?' Sebastian asked Cameron directly.

'Yes!'

'Ready to go, then?' Sebastian asked.

'Yes!' they chorused.

'Right! Come on so.'

'Can you wait for five minutes, please? I need Saul to have a quick drink and a piece of toast,' Jodi asked. 'Anyone else like some?' They all declined.

'I don't need anything either. I'll be fine,' Saul argued. Sebastian gave her a nod and Jodi ran back to the kitchen. Sebastian kept the lads chatting until Jodi returned with a glass of juice and a slice of toast.

'Drink this down, and you can take your toast with you. How's that?'

'Thanks, Mum,' Saul said, and glugged the drink.

Jodi accepted the empty glass and waved them on their way. 'Could you make it just an hour?' she called after them.

'As you wish,' Sebastian said, leading the way.

'He's not over-friendly, is he?' Francine said, as they walked back to the cottage.

'He's always sweet with Saul, and with Darius being away so much, it's great for him to have a man around.'

'Blake, Sebastian's son, was in Cara's class at school. A sweet boy, even if he did take after his mother,' Francine said.

'What do you mean by that?'

Francine turned pale and suddenly couldn't speak.

'Francine? Are you okay?' Jodi took her arm.

'Yes,' she whispered. 'All the parents, myself included, used to talk about how badly behaved Blake was. We judged him and labelled him as naughty. Imagine, he was only four, the same age as our two ... We all thought it was okay to decide he was bold.'

'I'm sure you meant no harm,' Jodi said, as they went into the cottage and sat down.

'No, we didn't, but Blake's mother was in and out of psychiatric institutions and we thought it was fine to put that little boy in the same box.'

'Don't beat yourself up over it, Francine,' Jodi said. 'How is Sebastian's wife now?'

'We don't see or hear of Diane. I think she never got over Blake's death. She was there the day he fell in the river and drowned ... Sebastian cut himself off from all outsiders after that. He's very protective of Diane, and we gave up trying to contact her after a while.'

'Maybe that was how they coped,' Jodi mused. 'Tragedy changes people.'

Tears rolled down Francine's cheeks as she flopped into a chair at the kitchen table.

'Francine?' Jodi rushed to her and put an arm around her back.

'Oh, Jodi, that little boy Blake was ostracised by us, me especially. He was always in trouble at school, he caused a rumpus at every party and he was totally wild.' Francine looked up, with mascara running down her cheeks. 'I was one of the first to say it was his parents' fault and they ought to take a firm hand with him.'

'People say things they don't mean all the time. You weren't to know he was going to die,' Jodi told her.

'No, but I'm so utterly ashamed to say that I almost felt he died as a direct result of his mother not being a proper parent. I almost justified it by thinking she must've been in one of her trances and hadn't been watching him properly,' Francine sobbed. 'She used to do that, you see. We'd all be chatting in the car park or outside the classroom door, and Diane never joined in. She appeared to be elsewhere.'

'Poor woman,' Jodi sympathised.

'Yes. Then it came out she suffered with depression and couldn't help it.'

'That's so sad.'

'It's tragic. Looking back, I think Blake might've had ADD.'

'Really?' Jodi made coffee. 'Look, I have real stuff this time, so you won't be poisoned!'

Smiling wanly, Francine thanked her and stared into space. 'Cameron has ADD too. We've just been to a specialist.'

'Really?' Jodi said, keeping her face as neutral as possible. Thankful for the years of acting, she pulled out a chair and sat next to Francine. 'Tell me all about it,' she said evenly.

Francine stared at Jodi momentarily. 'You don't seem that bothered. Aren't you going to look aghast or treat me like it's my fault?'

'Why would I do that?'

'Because that's what most other people, myself included, would do.'

'Well, I'm not just anybody, now, am I? Don't you know who I am?' Jodi raised one eyebrow and allowed herself to smirk.

'You certainly aren't just anybody, Jodi.'

Over the best part of the next hour Francine poured her heart out, finishing up by telling Jodi about the awful situation the day before.

'You must have felt so hurt,' Jodi said, munching cake. 'This is delicious by the way.'

'I baked it in the middle of the night,' Francine said, sighing. 'I do that all the time now. I can't sleep so I crawl out of bed and create things dressed like a fleece Dalmatian.'

'Well, any time you need to offload your wares, I'm here!' Jodi said.

'Thank you, Jodi.'

'For what? All I've done is eat your cake for breakfast.'

'You haven't dropped your head to the side and told me you knew Cameron was a problem. You haven't judged me or looked at me like I'm a lunatic. You've just listened.'

'Girlfriend, I spent my entire childhood being stared at and made to feel like I didn't belong. For reasons I won't go into right now, I was always an outsider,' Jodi admitted. 'So there's no judge and jury in my house. I'll help you in any way I can.'

The boys arrived back shortly afterwards.

'Where's Sebastian?' Jodi asked.

'He had stuff to do,' Cameron answered.

'I'm starving, Mum,' Saul said, with his tongue hanging out.

'I'm not surprised – you've only had a piece of toast this morning! Sit up at the table and I'll make you boys a drink and you can have some of Francine's cake. It's to die for!'

'How was it, Cameron?' Francine asked.

'We saw some lovely birds. Me and Saul had to sit as quiet as mice with some pretend leaves on us like a disguise so we didn't frighten them away. Sebastian lifted us up into a tree and we could see the whole world.'

'Yes, and we stayed as still as this,' Saul said, pretending to be a statue.

'Well done, boys,' Jodi said. 'Would you go bird watching again?'

'Yes,' Cameron said. 'I wasn't a bit naughty either, Mum. I did ezackly what Sebastian said. He told me if I had a feeling in my tummy or my head that I wanted to shout or jump I was to waggle my leg and he'd let me down and we could bounce up and down like Tigger to get it all out!'

'That was a clever idea,' Francine said, smiling.

'But I didn't need to be Tigger,' Cameron said proudly.

The two women looked at each other and smiled. The boys devoured cake and hot chocolate, swinging their legs happily as they chatted.

'Want to bounce on my bed?' Saul asked. 'That was the best proper breakfast ever,' he said to Francine, as they ran towards the bedroom.

'Five minutes, Cameron,' she called.

'Sebastian sounds like he had it all sussed,' Jodi said.

'God bless him. After the way he handled Cameron today, I'd bet my life on it that Blake had a behavioural disorder too,' Francine said.

'I know all my peers thought I was the spawn of a devil woman and therefore must be bad too. I was never given a chance and I'm sure most of the people in my class think of me with disdain even now that I'm successful. Those who even remember I was there, that is.'

'Why?' Francine asked.

'My mum was an addict and a drunk,' she stated simply.

'But you're happy now, aren't you?' Francine asked.

'Most of the time,' Jodi said honestly. 'But that's for another day!' Smiling, she began to put the plates into the dishwasher, indicating she wasn't prepared to delve any deeper for now.

ᏣᏝ

The Francine who had existed a couple of months ago would've taken that small snippet of Jodi's soul and tried to probe further. Now she could understand that people might want to keep things to themselves. If Jodi wanted to tell her about her past, she would do so in her own good time. Also, Jodi was a movie star, whom Francine had assumed hadn't a problem in the world purely because she was rich and famous. Now she could accept that nobody's life was plain sailing.

Francine was certain of one thing: good friends were hard to come by. Friendship needed to be based on trust. The people she'd thought were her friends had let her down. If she wanted a new friend, she'd prefer to find one she could rely on. Trust was a two-way thing and she wasn't going to betray that with Jodi.

'Thank you for having us over. I appreciate the kind, listening ear this morning,' she said.

'Any time,' Jodi said, hugging her.

'Jodi, you've no idea how much this means to me,' Francine said. 'And it's not because you're famous. For the record, it's because you're one of the most genuinely lovely people I've ever had the privilege of knowing.'

'Wow, thank you,' Jodi said, looking stunned. 'When I first met you, I envied you so much. You represented everything I've never been. You're confident, capable and socially accepted. Most of all, you're a pillar of community life.'

'Ha!' Francine scoffed sadly. 'The tables have turned. I'm

now a social outcast with a child nobody wants to associate with, someone to be avoided and shunned.'

'I think you're being a little harsh on yourself,' Jodi said gently. 'People don't understand what's going on with Cameron. Perhaps if you explain what's happening they might prove their friendship.'

'I don't know …' Francine sighed. 'I'm not sure I want anything to do with people who took against him so quickly. They've never stopped to wonder if there might be a genuine issue.'

'Didn't you say you'd done the same thing with Diane and Blake?' Jodi raised an eyebrow.

'Mmm …' Francine looked at the floor.

'It's not going to be easy working things out for Cameron over the next few years. You shouldn't try and do it alone. If you let people in, you might be surprised at how much support you'd get …'

Francine kissed Jodi's cheek and called her son. If she wanted to give her friends a chance to help her, she'd have to admit that things weren't peachy and perfect in the Hennessy household. The very idea was terrifying – she'd be leaving herself open to even more gossip and criticism. Francine wasn't sure that she was ready to reveal all her cards to the folk of Bakers Valley.

'Cameron, come on, please. Don't make me call you again,' she warned.

'No!' Cameron's face screwed up. 'I'm staying here.'

As Francine felt the familiar panic set in, Jodi stood between her and her son. 'Cameron,' she knelt down in front of him, 'if you go as Mummy is asking, I'll cut you a deal.'

'What?'

'I'll ask Sebastian if you and Saul can go bird watching again.

You can come after school one day next week and I'll have sandwiches and a drink ready. Then you boys can go out with Sebastian. But only if you do what Mum asks now.'

'Deal,' Cameron said slowly.

'High five,' Jodi said, holding her hand up.

Cameron clapped her hand and shot out of the door towards the car, followed by his mother.

'Why does Cameron get so rude like that?' Saul asked his mother.

'He finds it harder than other boys to do what he's told sometimes,' Jodi said simply.

'But if I was like that you or Dad would get cross,' Saul reasoned.

'I know, and, believe me, it's not easy to understand, but Cameron doesn't seem to be able to calm down once he gets angry,' Jodi explained.

'Is that why he hits and bites people a lot?'

'Yes,' Jodi said, 'and he's having a lonely time as a result. The other kids don't like him hurting them so they leave him out.'

'Poor Cameron,' Saul said. 'He didn't bite or kick me today.'

'See? He can be a good boy.'

'I'll try to play with him in school. Maybe when we're outside in the playground we can pretend we're going bird watching. We can stand like statues and see who is the stillest.'

'Good plan,' Jodi said, hugging Saul to her. While the selfish part of her didn't want Saul in the firing line when Cameron blew up next, she could empathise with any child who was treated as an outsider.

Chapter 25

The next day Saul ran happily into school.

'Good morning, folks,' Mr Matthews said, with a wide grin.

'Hi, there!' Jodi answered cheerfully. 'How was your midterm break?'

'Pretty uneventful, really. I was going to go back to London but I decided to wait until Christmas.'

'We were in London with my dad,' Saul chimed in. 'It was so much fun! Maybe you could come the next time. Can he, Mum?'

'I don't think Mr Matthews needs to see us during his time off, dude! He has enough of children at school.'

'It depends on who I'm hooking up with,' Mr Matthews said easily. 'If you were there too I'm sure it'd be fun,' he added, looking at Jodi.

Feeling her cheeks flush, Jodi bent down to hug and kiss Saul goodbye. 'Have a good day,' she said, looking at Mr Matthews.

A little flustered, Jodi left Cameron babbling to Mr Matthews about his midterm break. As she walked home, breathing in the clear air, she pulled the hood of her Puffa coat snugly around her head. It meant everything to her to see her boy so happy. Mr Matthews was a great guy too. So easy-going and down to earth.

Her marriage to Darius was better than either of them had

ever envisaged. The plan initially had been for Jodi to move away from Darius pretty much as soon as Saul had arrived. They had been all set to announce a separation and allow the relationship to fizzle out. But when she'd taken Saul home from the hospital, Darius had been amazing. He'd been just as smitten as Jodi and, more than that, a fantastic help.

Like any other new parents, they'd spent hours staring at their baby. Every facial expression he made was a joy. When he burped after a feed the two of them would clap. Darius loved bathing, changing and playing with Saul. As they walked around Hyde Park in London, they were snapped by paparazzi. Darius always had his arm around Jodi's shoulders and they were seen as Hollywood's most adoring couple.

'On paper we're perfect,' Darius had said, as he flicked through a pile of glossies.

'How does it make you feel?' Jodi asked, searching his eyes. 'Do you want the split to go ahead as planned?'

'No,' he said. 'I love *us*.' He motioned at the cover picture of them sitting on a park bench gazing into Saul's pram.

'I do too, but don't you want a proper relationship?' she asked.

'So I can be used and dumped? I'm still doing that from time to time, as you know, but none of them care about me the way you do. What about you? Are you ready to face the world and find your one true love?'

'You're my one true love. You know me inside out, you're Saul's father and you mind me like nobody I've ever known. It's just such a damn pity you're gay.'

'If I wasn't, would you fancy me? *Do* you fancy me?' Darius turned and posed, pouting.

Giggling, she swatted him with a baby wipe. 'No,' she said.

'Sorry. I love you deeply, but without the messy sex part.'

'Don't you crave a bit of messiness every now and again?' he wondered.

'Not really. I had it with Mac, but the other stuff spoiled it,' Jodi said. 'I'm happier by far to know where I stand and not have that pain in my heart.'

'Some day one of us will find the right person, with the right balance between heart, minding and messiness,' he vowed.

'So, until that time comes, are you happy to keep going the way we are?' she asked.

'I am,' Darius said.

They'd told Noelle and Mike to hold off on orchestrating the split.

'Fantastic,' Noelle had said immediately. 'The world loves you both, so if you're happy to keep it going, great.'

Over the years, Darius had had his little flings with men, each time hoping he'd found *the one*, but Jodi was happy to leave all that to one side. Mac had left scars that she wasn't sure would ever heal.

She'd trusted him at a time when her life was changing fast. She'd leaned on him and thought he was her rock.

Now, as she let herself back into her cottage, the sound of crunching on the gravel at the back of the house made her jump.

'Sorry to startle you,' Sebastian said. 'I was just about to put a note in your letterbox. There's a tree with Dutch elm disease on the avenue and it'll have to come down. The tree surgeon will be here over the next few days. Keep young Saul safe, won't you?'

'Thanks for letting me know,' Jodi said. 'I don't suppose you'd like to join me for a cup of tea?'

He hesitated.

'Only if you have time, no pressure.' Jodi smiled.

'Go on, then,' he said gruffly.

'Don't do me any favours,' Jodi joked.

Sebastian slipped out of his wellingtons and stood into her kitchen.

Jodi took a packet of mini Swiss rolls from the cupboard and threw it onto the table. 'I'm probably supposed to have a pretty tin with home-baked cake to offer you, seeing as I've a state-of-the-art Aga, but I can't boil an egg.' She poured water over a teabag for Sebastian. As she placed the cup in front of him he was miles away. 'Sugar?' she asked.

'No. Thank you,' he said, sounding odd.

'Are you all right?'

'Blake loved those chocolate rolls. The packaging is slightly different but they're the same purple colour. I haven't seen them for a while,' he said. 'Isn't it stupid how a few little cakes can open the floodgate to the memories?'

'I find it scary sometimes how a sound or smell can unlock all sorts of forgotten stuff.'

'When he died, at first I didn't think I'd survive. I never knew pain could cut so deep. You adore Saul – anyone can see that. Can you imagine being without him?'

'No.' Jodi shuddered.

They sat in silence for a while. The rustling of the cake wrapper brought Jodi back to reality.

'They taste the same,' Sebastian said, trying to smile.

'You told me that you and your wife don't ever talk about Blake,' she began. 'May I ask why?'

'Diane isn't able to,' he said, staring ahead.

'That must be really hard for you,' Jodi said.

'You just get on with life as best you can,' Sebastian said. 'After the first anniversary of Blake's death I came to the conclusion that I didn't have the energy to spend every waking moment in regret. I knew I either had to end it all or make up my mind to move on.'

'So did you just block the emotions?'

'Pretty much. But I've also learned what's important in my life. The people who don't really care or only want a bit of gossip aren't worth wasting time over. I do what's important and try to avoid any toxic influences.'

'Did you and Diane ever consider having another child?' Jodi asked.

'That wasn't an option.'

'I'm sorry, I'm being very nosy. It's none of my business.'

'At least you ask me the questions to my face. There's a lot to be said for that,' said Sebastian. 'In your line of work I'm sure you get pretty fed up with people jumping to conclusions and fabricating stories about you to spice up their own lives.'

'I try not to read much of what's written,' she said. 'I decided long ago to accept that the media think they know me. The wonderful thing is that the Jodi Ludlum they've created is nothing like the real me, so I'm actually quite happy to hide behind the façade.'

'That's a good way of looking at it.'

'I've been lucky too. Without the media I wouldn't have made it in my industry, so I feel I owe it to them to allow them their fairy tale,' she admitted. 'The real me involves Saul, drinking horrible herbal infusions and being a total washout when it comes to baking or hosting coffee mornings.'

Sebastian grinned. For a split second his face lit up, and Jodi glimpsed a totally different man. 'Well, your tea is drinkable, just about, and I happen to think you've the best taste in confectionery,' he said.

'I'll be sure to let the ladies of the committee know that you approve of my culinary skills. I'm pretty sure it's the way I open the box, not to mention the presentation.'

Sebastian moved his chair away from the table. 'Thank you for the tea, and especially for the moment of clear memories.' He paused. 'That's what I fear most. Forgetting Blake. I worry that I'll wake up one day and not remember the sound of his voice, so when I get a rush of vivid and vibrant memories, like you sparked just now, it means the world to me.'

Before Jodi could answer he'd gone out, shoved his feet back into his boots and closed the door quietly. Jodi sat in a trance at the kitchen table and allowed her mind to wander. How would she feel if Saul died? How would she ever pick up the pieces of her life and continue? She wondered what kind of woman Diane was. None of the villagers spoke about her but, then, Jodi didn't really talk to them. Francine had mentioned she suffered from depression. But that wasn't surprising. Jodi figured *she*'d be depressed if anything happened to Saul.

She watched Sebastian climb into his jeep and throw it into reverse. He was a bit odd but she really liked him – and Saul loved going on little adventures with him.

A text arrived from Noelle: could Jodi call her at once.

'Hey, Noelle, what's up?' Jodi asked moments later.

'There's trouble stirring. That little weasel Mac is making threats. I've had him on saying he'll speak to *World Wide News* again.'

'Oh, for Christ's sake. What does he want now?' Jodi asked, feeling sick.

'Oddly, he doesn't want money or to be bailed out of trouble this time. He just wants to meet you,' Noelle said. 'It's up to you, Jodi, but I reckon it might be time to call his bluff. He's had his claws embedded in your heart for too long now, honey.'

'As a matter of fact, Darius and I were thinking the time has come,' Jodi said.

'Mac's furious you gave him the slip in London last week.'

Jodi shivered. She'd only been thinking about him as she'd walked home that morning and now here he was again. 'You'll always know when I'm thinking of you, babe,' he'd promised, many years previously. 'I'll send you the vibes!' She'd giggled at the time and swatted him. But now it didn't seem quite so amusing.

Jodi took a deep breath. 'Tell him I'll see him. Please could you book him a return flight from London for this Friday?' She put the phone down and burst into tears. A point Sebastian had made earlier hit home. She should get rid of the toxic influences in her life. Mac was a parasite. She might love him, but the only person he truly cared about was himself. She was finally ready to let go of the past.

Chapter 26

'Who wants to go bowling this afternoon after meeting Nuala?' Carl asked, over breakfast.

Cara brightened. 'Can we bring a friend each?'

'Not today, honey. We're having a family day, remember?' Carl said. 'I rarely get to take a day off, so humour me.' He and Francine had explained to the older children that Nuala had asked to meet them all.

Later that morning, as they all filed in to her office, Nuala explained that Tracey was going to play with Cameron while everyone else chatted in her office.

Then she talked to Cara, Craig and Conor, trying gently to gauge how their little brother's behaviour affected them.

'He can be really embarrassing when we have friends over,' Cara said, looking guilty.

'How so?' Nuala encouraged her.

'He has a terrible temper, and if I'm with my friends and he wants to barge in, he goes insane if I say no.'

'Don't all brothers and sisters do that?' Nuala asked.

'Not like Cameron does. The other two can be annoying as well, but they don't totally lose it if I say I don't want them in the den while we're watching MTV, for example.'

'Yeah, and we don't want to sit with your friends anyhow,' Conor told her.

'Do you prefer to keep away from the girls, then?' Nuala asked, smiling.

'Uh, yeah. They're so annoying, they sit and talk about boys and hair and who has a crush on who.'

'At least we don't spend our time rolling around in mud with a ball, like you and your lame friends,' Cara riposted.

'Hey, guys! Manners!' Carl interjected.

'That's okay,' Nuala said. 'When Cameron kicks off, how is his behaviour different from the normal annoying stuff?'

'He goes loony,' Conor said.

'Yeah, it's like he's totally possessed,' Cara agreed.

'He really hurts when he bites and kicks,' Craig added.

Francine was dizzied by her children's candour.

After a further hour, Nuala said the children could join Cameron and Tracey.

'There's Xbox and art stuff, so you can play for a few minutes while I chat to your mum and dad. We won't be long,' Nuala promised. 'Well done, guys, you were great.'

Francine huddled into Carl as the children left the room. When the door was closed behind them, Nuala said, 'There are more tests I need to carry out. I'll need to see Cameron regularly for a while too, but I have an immediate suggestion to make that I think could benefit the whole family,' Nuala said.

'Shoot!' Carl said enthusiastically.

'How would you feel about getting a puppy?'

'*What?*' Francine looked stricken.

'It's been proven that dogs are incredibly beneficial to children with conditions from autism to visual impairment.'

'I always liked the idea of a dog, but you weren't so keen, love, were you?' Carl said.

'Pets are a lot of work,' Francine said. 'Dogs in particular aren't that easy to mind.'

'You're right to be dubious, Francine,' Nuala agreed. 'Dogs do require care, but the idea would be that Cameron and the other children would take on some of the responsibility.' She handed them a couple of leaflets, which they began to study.

'It says here that pets offer a host of benefits,' Carl said. 'They relieve stress and the children learn how to take care of them. I think that could be really good for Cameron. It'd get him outside playing with purpose rather than just tearing around mindlessly as he tends to do.'

At the end of the meeting Francine promised to consider the idea.

'I reckon we should put it to a vote,' Carl whispered, as they waited for their children to join them.

'I suppose ...' Francine was thinking of all the hair that might stick to the furniture and the smell of wet dog. The thought of muddy paw prints everywhere didn't fill her with joy either.

The idea was met with near hysteria by all four children. Francine and Carl had never seen them so united about anything.

'We'd have to figure out what type of dog would suit,' Francine said, now being swept along in the wave of universal enthusiasm.

'Can we have a Dalmatian?' Cara asked. 'They're so cool. We could get it a red collar and call it Cruella!'

'No, a German Shepherd,' Conor said. 'They're guard dogs so we'd never get broken into.'

'This dog is to be a pet, Conor,' Carl interjected. 'We don't need a guard dog that'd be likely to chew our legs off if we needed a glass of water in the middle of the night.' They all giggled.

'I'd like a noodle,' said Cameron. 'A white curly noodle.'

'Don't you mean a poodle?' Francine said, smiling.

'I don't care what we get, so long as it's a dog,' Craig said easily. 'Imagine being able to bring it for a walk and brush it!'

'Can we get one that likes fetching a ball?' Cara asked.

Francine looked at Carl and knew the decision had been made. Of course, they'd research carefully and decide on the correct breed to suit their needs, but it looked like Team Hennessy was about to welcome a four-legged friend on board.

The trip to the bowling alley that afternoon went surprisingly well. Francine found herself more relaxed than she'd felt for a long time. Carl was fantastic with the children, as usual, and enjoyed the banter with them. Cameron didn't fly off the handle, and the older children were making a marked effort to be nice to him.

'Good job, Cam,' Cara said, offering him her hand for a high five.

'I'm good at bowling, amn't I, Mum?' he said proudly.

'You sure are,' Francine said, pulling him onto her lap.

'I'll be good at being friends with the dog, too, won't I?' he said seriously.

'Of course you will,' she assured him.

'We're all going to be brilliant at minding the dog. I can't wait,' Cara said, so excited that Carl laughed.

When they returned home the boys went out to play football while Cara found her paints and sat at the kitchen table to create a masterpiece.

Francine went to her office and started to research dog breeds. She'd been there just half an hour when Carl burst in. 'I've news!' he announced. 'I've found a breeder who has pups. She's won umpteen awards and provides dogs especially for children with special needs. I just spoke to her and guess what?'

'What?' Francine asked.

'She has one left and it's got our name on it! Don't kill me but I've told her we'll take him.'

'Wow!' Francine felt a bit rushed. 'What breed is he?'

'He's a Golden Retriever and he sounds perfect for us, honey.'

'Carl, this is all very quick,' she said. 'I'm not as impulsive as you are. I think I need a little time to get used to the idea. Could we not think about it for a couple more weeks at least?'

'Well, the lady's going away and she said she could organise for him to be minded, but I thought it might be nice for him to have the weekend to settle in.'

Francine knew the children would be ecstatic. Besides, if it helped Cameron and his behaviour, she'd have welcomed an elephant into the house.

Carl promised he'd sort it out tomorrow. 'I'll buy the bed, food and all the paraphernalia that goes with the new addition. The breeder is emailing me a list so I'll get that done during my lunch hour, then swing by and collect the little fella. He'll be settled and part of the team before you know it!' Carl said, planting a kiss on the top of her head.

'Great!' Francine said, feeling utterly compromised. Still, it was about time she started getting used to all the changes that seemed to be thrusting themselves upon her.

'Oh, by the way,' Carl stuck his head back into her office, 'what do you think of keeping the dog as a surprise for the guys? Let's say nothing and I'll arrive home with him tomorrow night! Sound like a plan?'

'All right, love.' Francine forced a smile. She needed to relax about this – to take a chill-pill, as her daughter would say. Besides, her way of doing things hadn't worked with Cameron so she'd nothing to lose by trying to change her perspective.

All the same, Francine found herself putting the finishing touches to a lemon drizzle cake in the middle the night. At least from now on, she mused, the dog might keep her company in the wee hours.

ᛞ

The next morning Francine bumped into Jodi outside the school and filled her in quietly on the new addition to the Hennessy family.

'Great! I'm sure a dog'll help Cameron no end. Saul and I'll pop over to see him in a couple of days, if we may.'

'I'd love that,' Francine said, feeling more positive about the puppy by the second.

'Talk to you later,' Jodi said, pulling the zip of her coat up to her neck. She seemed distracted.

'Jodi?'

'Yes.'

'Are you okay? You don't seem yourself today.'

'I didn't sleep too well – I'll be fine. But thanks for asking,' Jodi said. For a split second she looked as if she was going to say something else. Instead she said goodbye and rushed away.

On her way out of the school, Francine passed Jane and Andrea, who stopped talking as she approached.

'Hi, Francine. Bit of a cold one, isn't it?' Jane said.

'Yes, but it is November so it's to be expected,' Francine said. She'd sounded rather snippy, she thought.

'We're going to the village for a quick coffee and we'd love you to join us,' Andrea said.

'I don't think so …'

'Please, Francine, we feel terrible about what happened. We'd love to catch up with you,' Jane said. Wanting support, Francine searched the car park for Jodi – maybe she'd come too – and spotted her dashing out of the gate, obviously in a hurry. Put on the spot, she found herself agreeing to join the others.

Moments later, she walked into the coffee shop feeling nervous. She'd always thought of herself as one of the stronger women in the village, but it was clear to her and the others that her position had shifted. Mercifully, there was no queue so she didn't have to wait long to be served. She ordered a mug of black coffee and joined the table of eight mothers. 'How was everyone's midterm break?' she asked.

'Great.'

'Fine.'

'We were so busy,' Jane said.

'Things have been a little manic in my world too,' Francine began. 'In fact there's something I'd like to tell you.' Silence descended. All eyes were on her and, for the first time in her life, she found it stifling. 'The thing is … well …'

'Go on,' Jane said gently, leaning forward.

'Well, as you're all aware, Cameron has a habit of stepping out of line.' Nobody commented. 'I know you think I don't notice, and I've no doubt some of you reckon he's just unruly and needs a good clip around the ear.' Still no comment. Francine took a sip of her coffee, and continued, 'Carl and I have had him assessed. Cameron has ADD. We're working with a professional and we hope to help him deal with his unusual behaviour in time.'

Francine felt as if hands were gripping her throat as she struggled to go on.

'The other thing is that I was made redundant in September. So there you have it, ladies.'

'Francine, we'd no idea,' Jane burst out.

'How awful for all of you,' Andrea added.

'How can we help?' Susan asked.

'Sorry?' Francine said, feeling utterly overwhelmed.

'Tell us how we can try to make things better for you,' Andrea said, putting an arm around Francine's shoulders.

Francine didn't care that tears were dropping in a hot salty stream down her cheeks. She wouldn't try to suppress her feelings any longer: pretending she was Mrs Perfect had gone horribly wrong.

As she poured out her heart to the other women over the next half-hour, Francine felt more in control than she had for months.

That day, instead of hiding at the back of the car park, she stood with the others once again, chatting.

'Francine,' Andrea called, as she was about to get into her car.

'Yes?'

'I'm so very sorry for being catty about Carl. I have an awful habit of gossiping and shooting my mouth off,' she said sheepishly. 'I don't mean any harm and I really hate the thought that you don't want to speak to me any more.'

'You were quite nasty,' Francine said honestly. 'I thought you were my friend. I'd never say such awful things about you.'

'I know you wouldn't. I'm a bitch. I've no excuses, I'm just not a very nice person.'

In spite of herself, Francine burst out laughing. 'What can I say? I can't be angry with you for ever. Besides, it's bloody exhausting trying to ignore or avoid you all the time.'

'I'm like a bad smell,' she said, elbowing Francine. 'If it helps, you can tell everyone what I did so they all know what a bitch I am.'

'Oh, no.' Francine was shocked at the very idea. 'I wouldn't get any pleasure out of that. In fact, it would make me feel even worse.'

'Sorry,' Andrea said, as she lowered her eyes to the floor. 'Of course you wouldn't do that. You've too much class.'

'Give me a hug,' Francine said. 'Water under the bridge?'

'Thank you,' Andrea said humbly. 'I wasn't joking when I said you're a better person than I am.'

'Ah, go on out of that.' Francine laughed. '*Bitch*,' she whispered behind her hand, and winked.

Perhaps her good mood had rubbed off on the children – they weren't fighting that evening. Carl had phoned to let her know he'd collected the puppy and, bursting with excitement, Francine had found it almost impossible not to tell them.

'Hi, everyone, I'm home!' Carl called from the front door, as they milled around in the kitchen getting ready for dinner.

'Hi, Dad,' Cara called back, as she dumped the cutlery on the table.

'Hi,' Conor yelled.

'Oh, Dad!' Cameron shrieked. He'd run into the hallway to greet his father.

They all rushed out to find out what was going on and squealed in unison. Carl placed the puppy on the floor, then stood back to let the children cuddle and make friends with him.

'Oh, Carl, he's a little dote!' Francine exclaimed. The puppy ran up and down, yapping excitedly, skidding into the wall. 'He's a bit like the pup in the toilet-tissue advert!'

Instinctively the children threw themselves on the floor and called out to him. Instead of being nervous of his new surroundings or worried by the strangers, the puppy bounded around giving out delighted licks. Within minutes he'd christened the kitchen floor and followed it up with a little puddle in the dining room.

'We need to show him where the newspaper is,' Carl instructed. 'I've been assured by the breeder that he understands to pee on folded paper. She was so helpful, I must say. He's had his vaccinations, too, which is fantastic. He needs his booster jab next week and then he'll be good to go outside.'

The new red kidney-shaped dog bed with the paw-print-decorated lining took pride of place in a corner of the kitchen as Cara and Cameron worked together to fill the puppy's dishes with food and water.

'Let me give him a drink,' Cameron said.

'Put it down carefully for him,' Carl said. 'Now, we all have to remember he's only a baby and we've to be kind and calm with him.'

'What are we going to call him?' Francine asked.

'Piddles!' Craig giggled.

'Too rude,' Francine pointed out.

'Blondie,' Cara suggested.

'That's too girlie,' said Conor.

'What about Poo? He just did one behind the sofa!' Cameron yelled.

'Oh, Jesus!' Francine said.

'That's a terrible name.' Carl laughed.

The commotion continued all through dinner until the puppy finally fell asleep at just after nine when Francine managed to cajole the children up to bed.

'He's gone to sleep now, so we all need to do the same,' she told them.

'But we can't go to bed until he has a name.' Cameron pouted.

'I'm staying in the kitchen with him. He'll be scared all on his own.'

'He needs to learn to sleep in his bed just the way we sleep in ours,' Carl coaxed.

'He has to have a name!' Cameron shouted.

As if a switch had been flicked, a tantrum kicked off. Cameron lay on the hall floor and screamed.

The puppy woke up and, frightened, began to howl.

'Oh dear!' Francine said. 'Now look what's happened. You'll have to stop yelling, Cameron. You're terrifying that poor pup.'

'Let's call him Howie - that's what he seems to be saying,' Cara suggested, blocking her ears. 'For a small puppy he can make an amazing din.'

Right at that moment Francine would've agreed to call him Satan if that could end the noise.

'Cameron, Howie is his name and it's bedtime!' Carl said.

Cameron quietened and lay still on the hall floor. The puppy ventured over to him and snuffled in his ear.

'His nose is all wet and sniffy,' Cameron said, and smiled. The pup licked his cheek and plopped down on top of him.

'Cameron, he's trying to tell you it's sleep time,' Carl said.

'Howie, we need to go in our beds,' Cameron said. The puppy closed his eyes and stayed where he was on Cameron's chest.

'Leave them for a minute while we get the others settled,' Francine whispered to Carl.

The bedtime routine was shorter without Cameron.

'Night, sweetheart,' Francine said, hugging Cara.

'Night, Mum, and thank you for letting us get Howie. He's the cutest thing I've ever seen. Can we get a pink lead with some diamonds in it for when I'm bringing him around the estate?'

'I don't see why not,' Francine said, stroking her daughter's head.

'Do you think he'll like catching a ball?' Craig asked, his wide eyes twinkling in the darkened room.

'He'll love it, sweetheart,' Francine said. 'Maybe you and I could go to the pet superstore and find a special one for him. You could be in charge of training him to fetch. From my research online, it's important for puppies to have proper training from the start. If we all have a specific job that we do with Howie, I reckon he'll learn very quickly.'

'I think he's very smart,' Craig decided.

'Of course he is. He's ours, a member of Team Hennessy,' Francine said, kissing him.

'Night, Mum.' Craig yawned.

Conor's light was still on and he was looking a little worried. 'Do you think Howie will be all right here with us?' he asked.

'I hope so, pet,' Francine said, sitting on the side of his bed.

'I'm just thinking about how I'd feel if someone took me away from you and Dad. I hope Howie's not homesick.'

'It's so lovely of you to think that, Conor, but I'm sure he knows we're all happy because he's come to be our dog. He might find it a little strange at first, but he'll settle in really quickly.'

'If we all pet him and play with him lots and lots he'll know we care, won't he?' Conor asked.

'Sure he will. Animals are very clever, especially dogs. He'll pick up on our love and I know he'll be the most spoiled little puppy in the world.'

'Should I stay downstairs in the kitchen with him tonight? I don't want him to think he's been left all alone in a strange place,' Conor said.

'No, darling. You're the kindest boy to think of that, but he really will learn very quickly that night-time is for sleeping and that we're all right here in our rooms,' Francine explained.

'Thanks for letting us get a pet, Mum.' Conor was looking less anxious now.

As she descended the stairs Francine stopped in her tracks. Cameron was still sprawled on the floor with the puppy beside him. As he chattered to Howie and stroked his little body, she saw that a new calm had crept over her youngest child.

Francine felt fresh guilt. The children had been asking for a dog for years but she'd always dismissed the idea, thinking only of the dirt it would leave around the house. The thought of excrement in the garden still made her shudder, but there was no denying that Nuala had been spot on to suggest they add a dog to their family.

'Will we go up to bed now?' she asked Cameron, as she stooped down to him.

'Yes, Mum,' Cameron answered, with tired, glassy eyes.

Howie was floppy and relaxed too, so Carl lifted him into his new bed as Francine led Cameron up the stairs and tucked him in.

By midnight, though, Francine and Carl were having second thoughts. Howie was living up to his name. The children were taking it in turns to come into their room worrying and even sobbing about the puppy.

'He sounds so scared and sad,' Conor lamented. 'Please let me go and sleep with him just for tonight.'

'I'll have him in my bed,' Cara begged.

'The breeder and the puppy book I bought agree that we must start as we mean to go on,' Carl said firmly. 'I know it's upsetting, but he's a baby and he'll learn. This time next week he'll be familiar with the routine and he'll love his cosy bed.'

By one o'clock, Francine was ready to sneak down and sit

with the puppy for the rest of the night. She pulled on her dressing-gown and padded into the kitchen to fill a hot-water bottle. According to the book, if pups had a source of heat, they felt as if they were curled up with their mother.

As she wrapped the hot-water bottle in a towel to prevent him chewing it or burning himself, Howie decided he wanted to play.

'Oh, Howie, please settle down. It's late and I can't deal with you,' she said.

He responded by grabbing a corner of the towel and dragging it backwards as he wagged his tail and shook his head, growling.

'Here, Howie! Good boy,' Francine said, trying to catch hold of him and sit him back in his bed. Eventually, she managed to contain him inside the kitchen. She slid out into the hall and tried to calm him by whispering, through the closed door, 'Shush, Howie! Good boy, go to sleep.'

'*How-how-howieeee*,' he yelped.

Opening the door a crack, Francine watched as he scraped like a mad thing.

She bent down, picked him up and carried him into the living room. There she plonked herself on the sofa. Petting his silky head, she felt him relax. She propped the hot-water bottle into the crook of the couch and gently lifted him on to it. He opened his eyes again and looked at her sleepily.

'Good boy, you go to sleep now,' she soothed, stroking him again. His head flopped on to his paws and he sighed deeply. He was ready for a snooze.

Francine was at odds with herself. She scolded the children for putting their shoes near the couch yet she was allowing the dog to sleep there. But, quite frankly, she would've let him lie on her second-generation linen tablecloth dressed in her one and only Chanel suit if it meant he'd stop the racket.

The upside of the situation was that she was so wiped out by the time she slipped into bed that Francine fell into a deep sleep for the first time in months.

⁂

As dawn broke the next morning the Hennessys realised they didn't need an alarm clock any more: Howie's barking and crying had jolted them all awake.

Groaning, Francine squinted at the alarm clock. 'It's not even six yet,' she croaked at Carl.

'He's an enthusiastic little fella, that's for sure,' he said, grinning. 'Anyway, I might as well get up and at it!' Carl had always been a morning person and could go from dead-to-the-world to raring-to-go in ten seconds.

'Hey, boy!' Cameron said, as he plopped down the stairs on his bottom to open the living-room door. The puppy lolloped up to him, delighted to see some form of human life.

Carl stopped dead in his tracks as he came down the stairs after his shower. Bits of fabric he recognised were strewn up the hallway, with yellow stuff mixed in with it. 'Oh, holy God.' Howie had shredded the couch during the night.

'Do you think Howie's in trouble?' Cameron asked, looking a bit worried.

'Bring him into the kitchen and we'll close the living-room door for the moment.'

Not sure how to break the news to his wife, Carl did something he wasn't proud of. He clicked the front door open and slipped out to work.

Chapter 27

That Friday morning, Jodi turned off the alarm clock before it had a chance to activate the radio. She felt like she'd been drinking Red Bull all night. Wired and twitchy, she was glad it was finally time to wake Saul. 'Hey, buddy,' she said, creeping into his room. Curled around his favourite teddy, Saul looked like a little angel. Love surged through her as she perched on the edge of his bed. His eyes fluttered open.

'Mum,' he murmured. 'I'm tired. Can I stay at home today?'

'No can do. School calls,' she murmured. She knew that once he was properly awake he'd be ready to rock and roll. He never slept past nine o'clock, no matter where they were.

'I love you so much,' she said softly.

'I love you too,' he said, stretching and turning on to his back.

Jodi felt sick as she pictured Mac boarding his flight in London. This was it, the day she'd avoided for so long. It was showdown moment, whether she liked it or not. Today, the past would be put to rest. If Mac insisted on playing dirty and going for a kiss-and-tell story, so be it.

Saul was in flying form once he'd woken up properly. Having finished his breakfast he was as giddy as a goat. 'It'll be fun at

Cameron's house today. His mum said she's going to bake yummy chocolate cake for us.'

'Will you keep me a piece?' Jodi said, grabbing him and blowing a raspberry on the side of his neck. Saul squealed and ran around the kitchen table.

Her phone pinged with a new text message. 'Oh, wow! Guess what?' she said to Saul.

'What?'

'Cameron's got a puppy and you're going to be the first of all his friends to meet him later!'

Saul punched the air. 'It's going to be the bestest day ever. Cake *and* a puppy!'

☙

When Jodi got home from dropping Saul at school, she tried to decide what to wear. She didn't want Mac to think she'd gone to much trouble, but part of her wanted him to know he'd cocked up by losing her. Her leather jeans were the right balance of sexy and cool, teamed with a cream silk shirt and a string of Chanel pearls. She finished the look with biker boots.

Jodi, you're a chick with attitude.

It was irrelevant that she felt like puking and bursting into tears.

Her beloved Mini helped quell her nerves as she drove to the plush Dublin hotel to meet him. Pulling up at the door, she handed her keys to the valet.

'Hello, Ms Ludlum,' he said. 'I'd heard you were living back on Irish soil, but I never believe what I read in the papers.'

'You're right not to, but in this case it's all true! I'm living in Wicklow and love it.' She flashed him a warm smile as she read his name badge. 'Thanks for taking care of the car, Josh. I won't be long.'

As it happened, Mac was on the other side of the enormous revolving glass doors and was waving to her. She adopted a relaxed air as she approached him.

'Baby, you look stunning as always.' He pulled her to him, making sure that everyone in the place knew she was there to meet him.

'Calm down, Mac,' Jodi hissed, although the smile never left her lips. 'I've a meeting room booked. Shall we?' Untangling herself very obviously from his grasp, she strode to the reception desk. 'Hi, there. I'm Jodi Ludlum and I have a small conference room booked for a quick meeting,' she said, loudly and clearly.

'Yes, Ms Ludlum,' the receptionist answered, as she tried not to stare at Jodi. 'It's all ready for you, if you'd like to follow me. Would you like refreshments?' She showed them into the room, with a vast table and a PowerPoint presentation area.

'I'll have some sparkling water, please,' Jodi said.

'Can I have a steak sandwich, a portion of chips and a pint of your finest Guinness?' Mac said, without looking the girl in the eye. 'I always have to drink some of the black stuff when I'm here. Ain't that so, babe?' He winked at Jodi.

'If you say so,' Jodi said, as if she were dealing with an errant toddler.

The girl left, promising to return with their order, and Mac sidled over to Jodi. 'Alone at last,' he schmoozed.

'Cut the crap, Mac,' said Jodi. 'What do you want?'

She turned to face him, put her hands on her hips and looked him straight in the eye. Her heart thudded and fear made the hairs stand up on the back of her neck. Yet she forced herself to stay calm.

'Hey! Some courtesy wouldn't go amiss,' he said, holding his hands up.

'I don't have the time or energy for playing games. Noelle tells me you're making threats again.'

'Ah, Jodi, why do you always have to think the worst of me? What happened to *us*, eh? Where did all the love go? I know I acted like a fool but we were young and silly.' He tried to take her hand but she snatched it away and strode across the room to sit at the large table.

'I still love you, Jodi. I never stopped loving you.'

It was ironic. For so many years, those were the words Jodi had longed to hear. Sadly, until very recently, she might even have believed him.

What a fool she'd been.

So blind and unsure. Her broken heart had hampered her for so long, in spite of all she'd achieved. Not any more. This was it.

'Cut to the chase, Mac.'

'The only reason I told the old battleaxe I was going to talk to the press was so I could see you. You disappeared last week and I've been a mess ever since.' Pulling his fingers through his hair, he waited to see if she'd take the bait.

'Mac, this isn't going to work any more,' Jodi stated.

A soft knock at the door broke the tension.

'I'll leave your order here, madam,' the waiter said.

'Thank you so much,' Jodi replied.

Mac paced the room, looking more agitated by the second.

As the door closed, Jodi smiled. 'You really are a pompous little sod, aren't you?' she said.

'What do you mean?' Mac said, taking a deep slug of his pint.

'You never look people in the eye unless you want to manipulate them. You're rude and dismissive of anyone you think won't gain you social standing. The couple of people who've been dealing with us since we got here might as well have been invisible, as far as you're concerned. You haven't spoken to them at all.'

'Yeah, whatever,' Mac said dismissively. 'Listen, it's been six years, babe. We belong together, you and I,' he continued. 'You don't love Darius. He's in love with his own reflection. Any fool can see that.' Mac slid into the chair beside her. 'We're the same, you and me. We fit together like beans and toast, tea and biscuits. We're both Irish.'

'Mac! I loved you – far more than was good for me. But you're toxic. You're like a cancer that's been festering in my heart. You tried to destroy me, Mac, and you're still trying. I've lost enough.'

'Listen! We were young and foolish. We know what matters now. We're good together.'

'No! Mac, we're not good together. You nearly buried me. On every level. I can't and won't forgive you. *I don't love you any more.*' She held up her hands and stared at him.

'I don't believe you, Jodi.'

'Well, you'd better get with the plot because it's all over. Go to the press, if that's what you want. Tell them everything you can think of. If it doesn't seem enough, make some up. Be my guest. But you won't get another cent out of me and, most importantly to me, you aren't going to hurt me any more.'

'You're making a big mistake, my girl,' Mac said, banging his hands on the table. 'You're going to regret this.'

'I won't.' With that, Jodi pushed her chair back and calmly left the room.

଼ଃ

Mac was so stunned that he didn't follow her. He kicked over a chair, grabbed his Guinness and downed it. The bitter aftertaste made him shudder. He was up against it financially. He couldn't get work – well, none that suited him. He'd gone off jobs where he had to be up at all hours of the morning in places that were cold and uncomfortable. He owed rent to his landlord and God knew to how many others. His sideline business was too dodgy. Drugs squads were clamping down on dealers, even small guys like himself.

Being a bit broke had never bothered him before because he'd always known that Jodi would bail him out when he needed her to.

He'd still have been with her if she hadn't freaked out and run for the hills after that fateful episode. But that was Jodi, always looking over her shoulder, always terrified she'd be told she wasn't worthy.

Stupid, really, that the only one who couldn't see she was a star was Jodi. Little did she realise that, no matter what she did, the public would probably still love her. She'd captured the hearts of the world with her shy demeanour. She was like a living doll with a little bit of punch. She was a bloody brilliant actor, too.

He'd been a fool ever to let her go. Of course he knew that now. He'd known it for years. But he'd been so caught up in the whirlwind of their lives at the time that he'd taken his eye off the prize. He'd looked his gift horse in the mouth.

He picked up the steak sandwich and bit into it like a savage.

Fuck her. This was not what he'd planned. He'd have to go to a few of the papers now and feed them a bit of the story. If he wanted to make a decent amount out of it he'd have to dangle the carrot – bounce the papers off one another and try to secure a good price.

But the recession had hit everyone. None of the red-tops had the cash to pay massive amounts for stories these days. He'd have to call the *World News* and spoof his way to a quick payout. He'd tell them one of the others had an offer on the table.

As he strode out of the conference room, he saw Jodi zooming away in her convertible Mini. She looked shattered. She was wearing big bug-like shades but he could tell she was distressed. A brief moment of compassion swept through him. He knew she didn't deserve the filth he was planning to spew about her. She was a hard-working, lovely girl.

'Can I call you a taxi, sir?' the receptionist asked politely, making him jump.

'No,' he answered. 'I'm meeting someone else around the corner.'

'Sure,' she said easily, and turned away.

Mac noticed she was very attractive. He really did need to take more notice of people, like Jodi had said. If he'd flirted with her a bit from the beginning the receptionist might've agreed to go on a date with him that night and he could've stayed in Dublin for a day or two. He could have done with a good shag and she probably had access to the residents' bar. Instead he'd have to get the bus back to the airport and catch his return flight.

By the time he'd paid his bus fare, Mac was stony broke. He hadn't even enough to buy a pint. When he'd got to the airport and gone through security, he shoved his hands into his pockets and skulked towards the airside bar, glancing around for any half-decent-looking women. He'd work his usual charm and scab a few drinks before take-off.

He'd three hours to kill, annoyingly enough. Jodi really had given him short shrift. Anger rose within him. He was going to carry out his threat. He'd call her bluff. He was certain that once a newspaper erupted with the story she'd be back, trying to get him to shut up.

He had to stay positive. This spell of hardship would pass. Soon he'd be on the pig's back again.

⊗

Jodi's hands were still shaking as she pulled up outside the cottage. Mac was such a low-life scumbag. She turned off the car engine, called Darius and slid down in her seat, unable to face walking inside to the emptiness.

'Hey, little lady,' he answered, sounding groggy.

'Sorry – what time is it where you are?'

'Uh … Five or six, I think. How did it go? You talk and I'll grunt.' They'd been texting one another the previous night and Jodi had promised to call him and fill him in.

'It was pretty horrendous. But, on the upside, I'm cured! I've finally had my epiphany! I now see with full clarity what you've tried to tell me for years. What did I see in him, Darius?'

'I'm glad you've seen the light, but sorry you're hurting. I wish I wasn't so far away. You need a hug right now.'

The silence was broken by her soft sobs.

'Oh, sweetie,' Darius said, starting to cry too. 'I hate that asshole for doing this to you. Let it out, though. We'll cry together for the last time over him.'

'Thanks, darling.'

'You're welcome, honey. So what's his beef? Is he still planning on spilling the beans?'

'So he says. But I *am* going to let him, Darius. He can do his worst. Let him talk to everyone he can find. I'm ready to face the music. It'll be a horrible few weeks but then it'll be someone else.'

'You said it. I'll be here in every way I can and I'll do whatever interviews are required. I'll push the perfect marriage and heroic husband who healed your heart.'

'Thanks, Darius,' she said sadly. 'And as usual I'll be the perfect wife.'

'Okay, gorgeous girl. I'm not on set until midday today, which is like, um,' Jodi heard his bedclothes rustle, 'oh, ages. Call me again if you want. I'll be behind you, no matter what comes out.'

Her head hurt as Jodi got out of the car and let herself into the cottage. She knew she'd have to phone Noelle and fill her in. At least Mac didn't know the details of her marriage to Darius, she thought. What he wanted to tell the world was bad enough but Jodi was finally ready to view the skeletons in her closet.

Chapter 28

Francine had to keep reminding herself that Howie was a positive addition to their home. As she knelt to clean yet another patch of pee, she figured she might as well keep her rubber gloves on all day and invest in a carpet spray that clipped on to her belt for easy access. She was John Wayne meets Mr Proper.

The couch was shredded at the corners and she'd lost count of chewed-beyond-salvageable shoes. Her baking had been limited too, not because she was sleeping soundly but because it was a futile exercise. Once Howie knew she was in the kitchen he wanted to be there with her. But no matter how many times she tapped him on the nose or told him *no* in a stern voice, he didn't understand: he clambered on to the chairs and knocked her tins or bowls on to the floor. The cherished pottery mixing bowl that had been her mother's had been the first casualty.

On his third night in their house she'd decided to try a gingerbread recipe. Just as she'd finished grating the ginger, ready to fold into the mixture, Howie had snatched the mini grater, crushed it in his jaws and swiped the mixing bowl on to the floor. The dark molasses-laden batter had oozed over the tiles and he'd licked up quite a lot of it before she could get around the table to stop him.

Utterly demoralised, Francine lowered herself on to the nearest chair and sobbed. Moments later Howie vomited the mixture all over the hem of the curtains and she buried her face in the oven mitts to muffle her screams.

By the time she'd cleaned away the mess, unhooked the heavy kitchen curtains and bagged them for the dry cleaner, she felt beaten. Knowing she wouldn't sleep that night, but past caring, Francine made a pot of fresh coffee. She poured herself a generous mug, then sat and stared into space until she finally heard Carl's footsteps overhead, then coming down the stairs.

'Hey,' he said, leaning over to kiss her. 'You're up early.'

'I thought I'd get the curtains cleaned and start on the pre-Christmas clean-up,' she lied.

'Good plan. Hello, Howie,' he said, patting the puppy's head. 'The little fella seems to have calmed down already. That's great, isn't it?'

Francine hadn't the energy to explain why Howie was acting like he'd been anaesthetised.

'Early meeting and all that, better fly,' Carl said.

'Have a good day,' Francine said, as brightly as she could.

The second the front door banged, Howie's head shot up, which signalled that he'd had enough sleep, and Cameron tore out of his bedroom looking to play.

Somehow she got through breakfast. On auto-pilot she made four packed lunches and ensured everyone had the right coat, hat and scarf.

'I hate that hat, Mum. It makes my head itchy and it's such a vile colour,' Cara said grumpily.

'How about this one, then?' Francine said blandly, rooting in the wicker basket that held all the winter woollies.

'Seriously?' Cara looked at her mother as if she was sick in the head.

'Well, you find one, then,' Francine said, placing the basket back on the shelf in the utility room.

'I don't want to wear a hat,' Cara moaned.

'Don't, then. I'll be in the car. You all have exactly five minutes to follow me with your bags before I turn on the ignition and reverse out of the driveway,' she said quietly. Wearing her Dalmatian dressing-gown, nightie and slippers, her hair matted, she got into the car.

The four children made their way outside, dragging their bags, silenced by her astonishing attire and that she'd pretty much abandoned them.

Francine watched in the rear-view mirror as Conor was left to wrestle with Howie. 'No, Howie, you can't come,' he said. Grabbing a ball from just inside the front door, he tossed it down the hall and the puppy charged after it, allowing Conor to slam the door.

'Nicely done, Conor,' Francine said, smiling at him.

'Thanks, Mum.'

'Are you seriously driving to the school in your dressing-gown?' Cara was clearly unnerved.

'Yup,' Francine said, gripping the steering wheel.

'But what if someone sees you?' Cara asked.

'I won't get out of the car. You can bring Cameron into Mr Matthews and the rest of you can go in on your own for today.'

'But you're meant to come with us,' Craig said.

'Well, you can tell your teacher that I was busy cleaning dog poo all night and I'll make it up to her,' Francine said evenly.

The boys roared laughing and Cara joined in.

'You're funny, Mum!' Cameron said.

A few minutes later she was pulling up in the school car park. 'Bye, guys,' she said. 'Cara, make sure your brothers all end up in the right rooms.'

The boys waved, seeming pleased at the idea of wandering into school unaccompanied. But Cara gazed at her. She was well aware that her mother never went out in her nightwear and had never left them to walk into their classrooms alone.

'See you later, Mum,' she said eventually.

'Bye, love. I'll be fine later. I think poor Howie has a tummy bug,' she said.

'I love you, Mum,' Cara said, and banged the car door shut.

Her daughter's words made Francine's heart leap for joy. Things would work themselves out. They were good kids and this was a little hiccup in life.

Everyone had them and, although she hadn't thought she'd ever be included in that club, like it or lump it, this was hers. She'd go home, clean herself up and snap out of this silly behaviour.

Francine's determined calm didn't last long. By the time she returned from the school run, Howie had passed the remainder of the gingerbread mixture in a runny stinking stream up the stair carpet. The silence meant he was busy. Francine found a basin and the scrubbing brush, then worked her way up the soiled staircase. Her blood ran cold as she spotted the puppy gnawing the heel of a cherished Prada sandal. '*Nooo!*' she wailed, lunging forward to wrest it from him.

He bounded down the stairs with the shoe in his mouth, squatted at the front door and yelped as his bowels opened again.

Francine opened her mouth and cried like a toddler.

Howie cantered back up the stairs, positioned himself beside her, stuck his nose into the air and joined in.

It took her for ever to scrape herself off the floor, make her way to the office and Google the number of a local vet.

'You'd better bring him in to see us. He might become dehydrated, poor fella,' the nurse said, on the phone. 'If you can make it straight away we'll fit you in.'

'He's almost due his booster injection. Would you give him that too?' she asked hopefully.

'I'm afraid he can't have any inoculations while he's ill.'

'I suppose that makes sense,' Francine said, deflated. The sooner she got the puppy sorted, the sooner the children could play with him outdoors.

Francine put on her tracksuit and attempted to tidy her hair. Then she yanked on a warm coat and clipped on Howie's lead. Somehow she levered herself, Howie and the bag of curtains into the car.

An injection, some 'helpful' advice on puppy care and 180 euro later, Francine made her way to the dry cleaner.

'We'll do our best but that's glazed linen and it's a pale colour,' the lady said. 'They're also triple lined. It's going to cost you.'

'Super,' Francine deadpanned. She declined the offer to pay in cash and receive a five per cent discount. 'I've no money with me and the nearest cashpoint is at the other end of town.'

'More money than sense, some people,' the lady muttered.

Francine walked numbly out of the door. Her mobile phone rang.

'Hi, Jodi,' she said.

'Hi, Francine. I know you're meant to have Saul this afternoon, but I've had a bad morning and I was wondering if there's any way you might consider letting me take the boys to my place.'

'Are you okay?' Francine asked.

'I will be. I promise I'll explain it all to you later, but right now I can't go into it. Saul was so excited about seeing the puppy, so I could have him as well, if you like. You probably think I'm crazy but I need the distraction and would really appreciate the loan of your son and puppy!'

'Yes! Actually, I didn't get much sleep last night. Howie, the pup, wasn't well – he's absolutely fine now, though,' Francine said. 'And I'd be more grateful than you'll ever know to have a few hours' peace. The only problem is that he hasn't had his final booster injection so he can't go outside. I'm so exhausted, though …' Francine trailed off.

'I'll drive to the school and meet you there, transfer the boys and the pup into my car and bring him straight to my kitchen. Seeing as we don't have any other animals, I'm sure he'd be safe. What do you think?'

'This could be massively irresponsible of me, Jodi, but I'm going to risk it,' Francine said.

'Brilliant.' Jodi sounded relieved. 'I'll meet you at the school and take the three of them off your hands.'

'You've no idea how good that sounds right now.'

The injection seemed to have done the trick because Howie hadn't soiled the car. Tucking her handbag into the space between the two front seats, Francine set off towards the school. Fleetingly she worried that she'd promised Saul chocolate cake, but she'd make it up to him another day.

As she neared the school Francine heard crunching and looked in her rear-view mirror to see what Howie had found. At the next red light, she stopped and leaned back. At first she thought it was a calculator.

'Where on earth did you find that?' she asked him, then heard a familiar beeping noise. He'd just killed her phone.

She pulled into the school car park, jumped out and opened the back door to prise the phone from Howie's jaws.

Wagging his tail, he cocked his head sideways in confusion, as Francine burst into uncontrollable sobs. Lowering herself back into her seat, she dropped the three pieces of her phone on to her lap. His sharp teeth had punctured the keypad in several places.

⋘

Jodi had spent the morning talking to Noelle, and Mike, Darius's agent. They were all on standby for the possible fallout should Mac spill the story. Now she walked into the car park, spotted Francine's car, waved and walked over. She nearly died when she saw the poor woman's face. The normally polished and perfectly presented Francine was blotchy and red with tears flowing down her puffy face. Jodi wasn't sure if she'd rather be left alone to gather herself but Francine beckoned her over.

'What's happened?' Jodi asked.

'Everything and nothing, I suppose,' Francine said. 'I've been awake all night. As I told you on the phone earlier, Howie was really sick. He ate raw cake mixture. I took him to the vet and he's fine now but he just ate my phone.' She burst into fresh tears and dropped her face on to the steering wheel. 'I think I'm having a nervous breakdown.'

'Oh, Francine, you poor love.' Jodi leaned through the open window and hugged her. 'What can I do for you?'

'You're already doing the kindest thing by taking Cameron and this blasted puppy. I know he's very cute and I'm sure Howie and I will become friends at some point but right now I hate him.'

'Poor you,' was all Jodi could think of saying.

'Would you mind if I just hand him over to you and buzz off out of here? I don't think I could face meeting people in this state.'

'Sure,' Jodi said, feeling she was being completely useless at helping Francine. 'Hello ... Yes, you're beautiful ... Hello, Howie ...' Jodi grabbed his lead, picked him up and brought him out of the car. She cuddled the wriggling pup. 'I'll get him into my car so he won't pick up an infection. Try not to worry and I'll see you later on,' she said, waving.

Howie jumped into the Mini and seemed delighted to have a sniff around. Jodi closed the door gently and locked the car. Slightly early for the boys, she stood outside the classroom door to wait. Saul and a few of the other children caught sight of her and began to wave. Mr Matthews opened the door and called her over. 'We were just having a chat about the different things people do for a living, weren't we, children?' he said to the class.

'Yes, and we all knowed your job because you do it on the television and at the cinema!' one of the girls shouted.

Jodi flushed and felt slightly uncomfortable, until she caught sight of Saul. He was grinning from ear to ear, like a Cheshire cat.

'You have a very proud little man here,' Mr Matthews said. 'I pointed out that his dad is a great actor too, and he made us all laugh by saying his dad isn't quite as pretty as his mum!' Mr Matthews pushed his hair off his face. 'I have to say I agree.'

Jodi became utterly tongue-tied. 'I ... uh ... Oh, thanks!'

Mr Matthews roared laughing. 'I thought a movie star like you would be well used to compliments at this point!'

'Ah, us women never take them for granted. Especially now that I'm hurtling towards middle age!'

'Do you want to go ahead with Saul, seeing as I've mortified you now?' he said, raising an eyebrow.

'I'm actually taking Cameron too,' she said. 'I have your puppy in the car, dude. You're coming to our house for a while. Is that cool?'

'Yes!' Cameron said happily.

'Wow, brave lady,' Mr Matthews said. 'That'll be a big bundle of energy at your place this afternoon.'

'I like a challenge,' she said, grinning.

❧

Once they were inside the cottage and the front door was securely shut, Jodi unclipped Howie's little red lead. 'Make sure you don't let him out of the front door. He's not allowed out yet and, in any case, he's a baby – he might run off and get lost,' Jodi warned.

'Okay,' the boys chorused.

Jodi filled a plastic bowl with water for Howie and put down some newspaper. She made hot chocolate, toasted sandwiches and a large cup of herbal infusion for herself. Lunch was crazy and fun. Howie drank some water, chewed his newspaper and leaped on to the table to finish the crusts of the sandwiches.

Jodi giggled and kissed his head. 'You'd better get down, naughty pup,' she said, lifting him, wriggling, to the floor.

'You're very happy about his badness,' Cameron observed. 'My mum gets cross when Howie climbs on our table at home. He eats lots of clothes and shoes. He doesn't mean to, it just happens. He's a bit like me at times.'

'How?' Saul was confused by this.

'Sometimes I get things wrong too,' Cameron said. 'But

Howie never minds. He's my friend all the time. I can stroke him when I'm cross. I have a thing called ADD.'

'What's that?' Saul's eyes opened wide.

'A condition,' Cameron said proudly. 'It means I do stuff that's not sept-u-bill.'

'What does that mean?'

'When I hit people. It's that,' Cameron explained.

'And now you don't do it any more?' Saul wondered.

'Some days I can't help being cross but I go to a lady called Nuala and she's helping me to stop my temper winning,' he said.

'Cool.'

'Me and my family are all working on dealing with ADD,' he added.

Jodi folded her arms and stood back. She was amazed by how able Cameron was to talk about his ADD. She'd tell Francine how well she and Carl were handling it. Cameron was lucky to have such a wonderful family to help him. She hoped he would improve. She hated to think of any child being shunned or left out. Perhaps because she had been a neglected child, she felt a connection with Cameron and vowed to make her home a place he felt comfortable visiting.

Chapter 29

Francine got home knowing she had just a couple of hours before she had to collect the older children. She went to the bathroom and tried to ignore the fact that her house smelt of dog. The warm water and Jo Malone shower gel did little to enhance her mood. Binding her hair in a towel turban, she phoned Carl from the landline to ask if he could organise a replacement mobile for her.

'Oh, no!' Carl laughed. 'How on earth did he manage to get your phone?'

'He stuck his nose into my handbag while I was driving,' Francine said snappily.

'No need to bite my head off. I'll get you a new one,' Carl said. 'It's not life-threatening, Francine. Don't worry about it.'

'I can't do this any more, Carl,' Francine said suddenly.

'What?'

'I can't pretend everything's hunky-dory any more. It's not. I feel like I've been captured by aliens and thrust into a parallel universe where nothing goes right and everything I used to love has been either pooed on or chewed.'

'The puppy will settle down, darling.'

'It's not just the puppy. It's everything. I haven't slept for months. I miss my job. I miss using my brain for things that don't involve washing, cooking or wiping. Cameron is like a rare zoo exhibit,' she ranted, 'and I never know when he's going to blow his top. I feel like I'm living on a knife's edge. I hate my life, Carl! All I wanted was to be the perfect wife. I'm about as far away from that as a cold-blooded murderer.'

'Stay where you are. I'm coming home.' He hung up.

∞

Carl marched through the open-plan area at his office and called to his boss that there'd been a crisis at home. He'd been as dependable as rain in April ever since he'd started his job so nobody minded him leaving.

Since the day they'd first clapped eyes on one another, his Francine had been in control. She'd been happy and breezy, and he loved her for it. And his love came without conditions, not because she was the perfect wife.

Twenty minutes later he pulled up in the driveway. Francine was sitting at the kitchen table wearing a plain black dress with no makeup and matted hair.

He pulled her into his arms and stroked her back as she sobbed. 'Sweetheart, why didn't you tell me things had got so bad?' he asked, leading her to a chair.

'I didn't want you to think I was the world's worst wife as well as the world's worst mother,' she said miserably.

'You're an amazing wife and mother. Who told you otherwise?' He was aghast.

'Look at the state of Cameron. It's my fault. I should've known he wasn't right. I went to work when he was a baby and left him with a woman who did her best, but she wasn't his mother. I know you're being very kind about it all, but the fact remains that I did this,' she said, shuddering.

'Francine, darling! Cameron has ADD. It's a condition any child has the potential to have. Not only are you being fantastic at helping him but, as far as you can, you're making sure the other kids aren't being affected,' Carl said, holding her hands. 'I might miss some things that go on around here, but I can see what an amazing mother you are.'

'I don't feel it right now,' she said.

'That's okay too, you know.' He smiled. 'No parents want to go through what we're dealing with right now. It's a bloody nightmare. But we'll get through it as best we can. We're a team, love. Always were, always will be.' Carl pulled her into his arms again, rocking her back and forth. 'I know it seems hopeless at the moment but it'll get better. The puppy will stop chewing things and, with Nuala's help, Cameron will find his own path in life,' Carl promised. 'It mightn't be the one we'd assumed he'd travel but there's nothing wrong with that. You can look for a new job and, before you know it, things will be on an even keel again.'

Francine was so grateful to Carl for his optimism. But, more than that, she knew she had a wonderful husband.

'Now you stay here and relax. I'll go and collect the kids and we'll have dinner delivered tonight. You and I are going to have several glasses of wine, followed by a large brandy, and even if the dog chews the leg off the table, you will sleep tonight!' he said, grinning.

Francine felt better already. 'You don't think I'm a desperate wife?'

'You're *my* perfect wife, Francine,' he said, as he kissed her tenderly. 'Raising children certainly isn't easy and you've been very hard on yourself in the past. You need to take our daughter's advice!'

'A chill-pill?' Francine said, with a watery smile.

'Uh, loike, todally!' Carl said, in his best bored-teenager voice.

'Cameron is at Jodi Ludlum's with Howie and she's going to drop them back later, so it's just Cara, Conor and Craig for pick-up,' she told him.

Carl saluted and disappeared to fetch them. With no dinner to prepare, no children shouting and no dog whining, soiling or chewing anything, Francine flicked on the kettle. For a brief moment she considered reaching for a baking book. Stopping herself, she made a cup of tea and did something she hadn't done for at least a decade. She turned on the television and flicked through the channels, looking for a chat show to watch.

Chapter 30

After a couple of hours Jodi could see that Cameron was getting tired. As a result he was becoming increasingly difficult.

'I want to play something else,' he said, kicking over the Lego scene that he and Saul had painstakingly built.

Saul's face fell. 'Why did you spoil our town? I thought we were going to do a rescue where the policeman drove in the car to help the people in the yellow and red house I made?'

'It's stupid,' Cameron said, and his eyes began to flash.

'Will we bring Howie for a walk up and down the hallway?' Jodi suggested. 'You could show us how to hold the lead, Cameron.'

'But, Mum, our game ...'

'I'll play that with you another time, dude,' Jodi said quietly. 'Cameron, do you need to go to the bathroom?'

'Okay,' he said, staring up at Jodi to gauge her mood.

'You do that, and we'll do a little bit of training with Howie before bringing you home, okay?'

As Cameron ran to the toilet Saul flung himself at Jodi. 'It's not fair,' he said, and burst into tears. He wasn't used to anyone kicking his games about the room.

'Honey, I know you find this hard to understand, but Cameron

347

needs to learn over time how to be calm,' she soothed. 'I need you to be a good lad and not make a fuss. It's not nice to kick Lego like that and usually we'd be a bit cross about it. But Cameron doesn't mean to be difficult. He can't help it.'

'If we tell him that's naughty, maybe he won't do it again,' Saul reasoned.

'You're right to think that might work, but when children have ADD, which Cameron has, they get more upset. It won't help him. Will you trust me on this and help me play with Howie? Then we'll see if Cameron feels calmer. He'll be going home really soon. Then I promise we'll come back here and I'll play Lego with you for as long as you like. Deal?'

Saul nodded.

Bless him, Jodi thought.

Cameron ran out of the bathroom and grabbed Howie. 'Come on,' he said, as he buried his face in Howie's furry back. As he cuddled the puppy, Jodi could actually see him settle. Howie responded by spinning around and licking Cameron's hand.

'He kissed me!' Cameron said, as his frown dissolved and a smile spread across his little face.

'He loves you, doesn't he?' Jodi said.

'Yup.' Cameron patted him.

'Come on, Saul, let's get Howie's lead and Cameron can show us how to walk him. It'll be good practice for when he's allowed to go outside.' Jodi winked at him and tweaked his cheek. Saul clutched Jodi's hand. 'Good boy,' she said.

It was soon clear that the space in the hallway wasn't adequate for training Howie. The boys were too boisterous and the puppy was beginning to become agitated.

'Maybe we should let Howie have a little rest for a few

minutes while we go for a quick run up the avenue?' Jodi suggested. 'Then we'll put him in the car and bring you guys home.'

'Okay,' Cameron said politely.

Once they were safely off the road Jodi let the boys run ahead and burn off some steam. She shoved her hands deep into her pockets and closed her eyes for a moment. The November sun was low in the sky, offering little warmth, but she was grateful for the brightness.

'Sebastian, look, it's Cameron. He and his puppy both came for a play date,' Saul shouted to their neighbour, who was brandishing secateurs.

'So I see. Where's your puppy gone?' Sebastian asked, looking around.

'He's too little to go outdoors so he's having a little rest in Jodi's kitchen,' Cameron said knowledgeably.

Piles of clippings littered the pathway from the main house.

'Is that a scissors?' Saul said, wildly impressed.

'It's a special tool for cutting small branches and bushes,' Sebastian explained. 'It's not for messing with – it'd chop your finger clean off your hand.'

'Oooh!' the boys chorused.

'The part you've done looks so much better,' Jodi ventured, as she caught up with the children.

'It's slow work and I should really use the electric clippers, but they tend to take too much of the hedge away,' he said. 'I prefer to leave a bit of growth.'

'It's probably quite satisfying to look back and see the results too,' said Jodi. 'Will I give you a hand? I could pile the clippings into your wheelbarrow if you like?'

'Don't you have enough on your hands with the lads?'

'We'll all help, won't we, boys?' Jodi asked.

The time flew as the four of them cleared up the avenue.

'After all that work I reckon you should be paid in hot drinks and treats,' Sebastian said cheerfully. 'Would you like to come into my house and warm up?'

'What about Howie?' Cameron asked.

'We'd better leave him at the cottage for the moment,' Jodi said. 'We won't stay too long.'

Jodi was secretly thrilled. She'd only ever seen the manor house from the outside. Now the stunning granite double-fronted Georgian residence, with its duck-egg blue front door, beckoned. The place was immaculate. The three stone steps up to the main door were swept while the turning circle was weed free, the gravel raked.

'Come around the back into the kitchen. The main door is almost always locked,' Sebastian said, over his shoulder, as he led the way.

'Your house is big!' Saul said. 'Our entire school could live in here.'

'You could have the biggest sleepover ever!' Cameron put in.

Sebastian laughed, making Jodi jump. She suddenly realised she'd never heard him laugh properly before.

'Come on in, lads and lady,' he said, grinning. Much less shy than usual, Sebastian showed them where to kick their shoes off as he opened the door to the kitchen. It was more modern than Jodi had expected. With a classic cream Aga and floor-to-ceiling cupboards, it also had stainless-steel worktops and contemporary furniture. The pale yellow walls added warmth to the dominant chrome theme.

'What an amazing kitchen,' Jodi exclaimed. 'I love the way you've mixed the modern with the old. I don't think I'd be brave enough to do that in a Georgian house. It's gorgeous.'

'Thanks. I do enjoy this room, I must admit,' Sebastian said. 'The rest of the house is a similar style, but I seem to spend ninety per cent of my time in here.'

He pressed a remote control and the mirror on the main wall turned into a television.

'Wowzers!' Saul yelled.

'Are you magic?' Cameron asked, looking at Sebastian as if he might be related to Harry Potter.

'Not quite!' Sebastian said, laughing again. 'It's pretty nifty, isn't it?'

Sebastian rose even further in the boys' estimation when he produced the most divine hot chocolate they'd ever tasted.

'What's in it?' Jodi asked.

'I don't think you want to know!' Sebastian smiled. 'Put it this way, no slimming club would endorse it.'

The boys curled up on the black leather sofa and watched *Ben 10* on the large screen.

'Is Diane not home, then?' Jodi enquired.

Sebastian's smile faded and was replaced with a tight, uneasy expression.

'No,' he faltered. Lowering his voice so the boys wouldn't hear, he leaned in closer to Jodi. 'She hasn't lived here since Blake died.'

'Sebastian, I'm sorry. I've put my foot in it. I didn't realise you were separated.'

'We're not.' He looked at the table. 'She's in St Jude's psychiatric hospital.'

'I had no idea,' Jodi said, shocked.

'I'm amazed you haven't been filled in on my entire life by the local gossips.' He looked sadly at her.

'I don't go in for gossip. I know what it feels like to have an entire town talking about your every move. I had it as a child and since I've grown up, it happens on an even larger scale.' She shrugged. 'Even if people had told me things about you, I wouldn't have believed them unless you'd told me yourself.'

'Fair enough,' he said. He seemed to relax slightly.

'Do you want to talk about it or would you rather skip that? I'm good at not discussing stuff, if that's what you'd prefer.'

Much to Jodi's surprise, he reached across the table, put his hand on hers and squeezed it. 'Thank you for being so understanding.'

Jodi was so aware of his touch. She felt like a teenager on a first date. The feel of his skin against hers was electrifying. 'Hey,' she said quietly, 'don't sweat it. I've so many skeletons in my closet I could fill a large graveyard. Believe me, your past would have to be pretty sordid to raise my eyebrow.'

Realising his hand was still resting on hers, Sebastian withdrew it and folded his arms across his chest. For such a broad man he looked strangely vulnerable as he began to talk.

'Diane was there when Blake died,' he said softly. He glanced at the boys, but they were totally engrossed in the television.

'They were out walking near the river when the weather turned. Torrents of rain poured from nowhere, making the ground instantly soggy. Blake had been poking at a pile of weeds, hoping to unearth an eel or an otter. When he slid into the river, Diane jumped in after him.' He closed his eyes and sighed. Jodi remained silent. 'The lashing rain had caused the river to swell and speed up. Blake was swept downstream.' He looked into Jodi's eyes. She held his gaze, letting him know it was okay to continue. 'Diane had swallowed and inhaled so much water she lost consciousness. I didn't find her until after dark. By some miracle her coat had hooked on to a branch. Her head and face were clear of the rushing water so she didn't drown.'

Instinctively Jodi rose from her seat opposite Sebastian and rounded the table. As she sat beside him with her arms held out, he pulled her in close.

'Police, firefighters and locals turned out in force. We searched all night and eventually recovered Blake's body at dawn the next morning.'

Tears soaked Jodi's blouse as she tried to stifle her sobs. The two boys were still glued to the television.

'Diane was in hospital for several days. She came home for the funeral and collapsed before we made it to the grave for the burial.' Sebastian hesitated. 'I honestly thought she'd come out of the shock. That she'd somehow find the strength to fight through the trauma and come back to me.'

'Did she?' Jodi managed.

'Never.'

Jodi's heart broke for him.

'The hospital were unable to keep her any longer, so I took her home. She didn't eat and wouldn't even drink water. If I tried to talk to her or encourage her to get out of bed, she'd become violent,' he said. 'I did my best to help her, Jodi. I honestly tried.'

'I'm sure you did,' she soothed.

'After three days, I called the doctor again. I feared she'd starve to death or, worse, that she'd try to take her own life.' His voice cracked as he tried to go on.

Jodi stroked his arm.

'The doctor said she needed to be admitted for psychological help. It was meant to be for a short time,' he said, 'but she didn't respond to any of the programmes or drugs on offer. She seemed to have gone to a place where nothing could reach her. She was on suicide watch for a long time. She harmed herself, once seriously, and now she's heavily sedated all the time. The once-vivacious and beautiful woman I loved is a scraggy shell with haunted eyes, who looks at me with no recognition.'

'Do you visit her?' Jodi asked.

'I used to go every day,' he said. 'I'd sit and talk to her. I'd show her photos of Blake or talk about happier times. But she didn't answer or even acknowledge my presence.'

'So what happens now?'

'I go once a week and she sits and rocks back and forth until I leave. The nurses tell me she shouts a lot, especially at night, but when I'm there she's utterly silent.'

'Oh, Sebastian ...' Jodi hugged him, wishing she could squeeze out the hurt.

'Thank you,' he said, and handed her a tissue.

She dabbed her eyes and blew her nose. 'Whatever for? Being utterly useless and sobbing?'

'You're not useless, Jodi. You're a warm and understanding person. I did to you what all the locals do to me.'

'How do you mean?' she asked.

'I judged you when you first arrived here,' he said. 'I assumed you were some jumped-up Hollywood star who thought the world should be at her feet. I thought you'd be full of crap and constantly want attention.'

'God knows I get enough of that while I'm at work,' she said, smiling. 'Don't get me wrong, I'm so grateful to my fans, but underneath it all, I'm just a girl who makes money by pretending to be other people.'

'I think there's a bit more to you than that. I always hate this phrase but you certainly have the X factor.' He grinned.

'Are you crying, Mum?' Saul had turned and stood on the sofa as the episode of *Ben 10* ended.

'Yes, lovie,' Jodi answered. 'Sebastian told me a sad story and I felt like crying so I did.'

'What sad story?' the boys asked.

Jodi looked at Sebastian.

'I had a little boy a long time ago and he died in a terrible accident,' Sebastian explained. 'I miss him all the time, but it's been wonderful for me having new friends like you two.'

'That's very sad for you,' Saul said, walking towards Sebastian. 'What was his name?'

'Blake.'

'That's a nice name, isn't it, Cameron?' Saul said.

'Yes,' Cameron agreed. 'We can come and play with you any time you like,' he offered. 'I have ADD, which means I can be cross at times,' he said carefully, 'but I promise to do my best to be a good boy when I come here. Lots of people think I'm naughty but I'll be the bestest I can be if you let me come and look at your mirror telly.'

'Thank you, guys,' Sebastian said. 'I don't feel sad when you're around. And for the record, Cameron, I *know* you're not naughty.'

Cameron grinned.

'I love my dad but he's away filming a lot. So it's nice that we can be pretend-family, isn't it? Mr Matthews at school is always saying we should try to think of others and help when we can,' Saul mused. 'We could try it and if you decide I'm not very good at it I won't be sad.'

Sebastian went down on his hunkers and took Saul's hands in his own.

'That's a great idea. I'd love for us to mind each other.'

Saul hugged him, then went back to the sofa. 'I'll be here watching the mirror television,' he said. 'Tell me if you need me.'

Sebastian's grin was infectious.

'I've a lump in my throat the size of China,' Jodi said, as her son sat down.

'He's a ticket!' Sebastian said. 'Yourself and Darius are raising a fantastic little human being there, Jodi.'

'Thank you,' she said. Suddenly she wanted to take Sebastian aside and tell him the truth about herself and Darius. And she wanted to let him know that her heart beat faster each time she looked at him.

A text pinging through on her phone stopped her. 'We'd better get going, boys!' Jodi interjected. 'Your mum's just texted, wondering if she can have you and Howie back home now, Cameron.'

'Aw, no!' the boys chorused.

'You can come again soon,' Sebastian said. 'In fact, you can visit any time you like.'

'Tomorrow before school?' Saul asked hopefully.

'That might be just a bit too soon.' Jodi giggled, wrinkling her nose and winking at Sebastian.

'Maybe after school might work best,' Sebastian suggested.

'Okay. See you then,' Saul said. He hugged Sebastian's legs quickly and ran to grab his shoes and coat. Then they went outside, waved and set off back the way they'd come.

'That was fun, wasn't it, Mum?' Saul gabbled.

'It was lovely,' Jodi agreed.

By the time they'd trudged back to the cottage, collected a delighted Howie, bundled themselves into the car and made their way to Francine's house in Verbena Drive, the boys were exhausted.

'How was Cameron? Did he behave? Was Howie a nightmare?' Francine fired questions at them as she flew out of the front door to greet them.

'Everyone was fantastic, isn't that right, boys?' Jodi said.

'We went to Sebastian's house and watched his mirror,' Cameron announced.

Francine looked understandably confused.

'He has a television that looks like a mirror when it's turned off,' Jodi said.

'Wow! I hope Cameron didn't misbehave while he was there.'

'Sebastian said I'm a good boy,' he said proudly.

'Oh, Cameron, I'm thrilled,' Francine said, eyes shining.

The boys ran upstairs, with Howie in lolloping pursuit.

'Thank you so much for giving me a break from the two of them,' Francine said, as she and Jodi went into the kitchen. 'You must think I'm making it all up when you spend an afternoon with Cameron and he's an angel. Believe me, he's like that here sometimes, just not always.'

'I know he can be difficult. I've witnessed it. You don't need to justify anything to me,' Jodi assured her. 'It just happened that we were outside – we left Howie having a hard-earned nap in my kitchen – and Sebastian was doing a bit of manual work. The boys loved joining in and *Ben 10* was on his cool TV, so it worked really well.'

'Thank you,' Francine said again. 'I'm so relieved he managed to behave for once. We're working really hard on being positive with Cameron and I know he's come on since Nuala's been helping him too.'

'You're doing everything right, Francine – oh, Jeez, I didn't feed the boys any proper dinner!' Jodi thumped her forehead with the heel of her hand. 'I'm a disaster.'

'Not at all. As it happens, we're having a takeaway tonight. I was really upset earlier and I phoned Carl. He came home and took over. I'm banned from cooking! You and Saul must stay and eat with us,' Francine said, brightening. A hint of the woman she'd always been – a person who could help out and be admired – had crept back.

'Well, thank you, I should probably be *über*-polite and say no, but I'm going to take you up on the offer.' Jodi smiled.

'Goodie!' Francine said. 'I'll set a couple of extra places at the table.'

Moments later, Carl appeared, laden with brown paper carrier bags of Chinese food. 'Hi, Jodi, I was hoping I'd catch you. I've enough here to feed the army so you'll stay, won't you?' he said.

'I've already accepted Francine's kind invitation,' she said.

'And the extra places are set,' Francine said, as she began to open the foil containers.

Cara couldn't hide her delight that there was a movie star in their kitchen. Conor and Craig were shy at first but soon opened up when they realised how easy Jodi was to chat to. They'd seen her around the school but hadn't actually spoken to her.

'Do you like being a star?' Conor asked.

'Conor!' Francine flushed.

'Ah, don't worry!' Jodi giggled. 'If a film actress had come to dinner in my house when I was a kid I'd've been dying to ask questions! Yes, it's brilliant being in movies but it's hard work.'

'Can I take a picture of you with my phone?' Cara asked, before anyone could stop her.

'Why don't I sit beside you and your dad can take our photo?' Jodi offered.

'Seriously?'

'Sure! You might have to tell people who I am, though. I

don't really look the same with no makeup and my hair scragged back like this!'

'You still look amazing,' Cara said in awe. 'Is that necklace real Chanel?'

'Cara!' Francine and Carl spoke together.

'Yes! I bought it years ago, and do you know what? I still get a bit of a thrill every time I put it on. Want to try it on?' Jodi was unwinding it from her own neck and placing it on Cara. 'You've got to make sure the two Chanel Cs are visible in the photo. It's no good if all your friends don't know it's genuine Chanel!' Jodi teased. 'Now, Daddy, take our picture, please. Turn your head slightly to the side like this, Cara. Tilt your chin up a tiny bit. Oh, yeah! *Faaa*bulous!' They all wanted a photo then, so Jodi obliged.

Once dinner was over the children dispersed.

'I'm ringing my friends! They're not going to believe I'm in a photo with you, Jodi,' Cara said. 'They've all seen you, like, a tiny bit in school but we've been told not to stare and, like, not to annoy you. So I'm going to be totally cross-examined now that I know you. Oh, can I say I *know* you?' she asked, biting her lip.

'You can say we're friends and I come to your house for dinner. I'll tell you what,' Jodi said, 'why don't you guys come to my house – I can't cook, but you could all come for pizza and ice cream next week. Good plan?'

'Ohmigod! Ohmigod! Seriously?'

'Yes!' Jodi laughed.

'This is epic!' Cara squealed. 'Can I say you gave me posing advice too?' she checked.

'Sure can!' Jodi nodded.

Cara thundered up the stairs, already yelling down the phone to another girl.

'You don't have to do that,' Francine said, looking alarmed.

'Absolutely not,' Carl added. 'Cara shouldn't have been so forward with you. We've told them before that when adults are friendly that's still no reason to become too familiar.'

'Please,' Jodi said quietly. 'I love the way your children chat to me openly. I'm more than delighted to have my picture taken with them and, furthermore, if you can stomach shop-bought pizza I'd be so excited to have you all come over. Without going into too much detail, I never had that sort of opportunity as a child. I value your friendship and how you've welcomed Saul and me into your home.'

'Oh, well, thank you,' Francine said, looking from her husband back to Jodi.

'Yes – thank you, Jodi,' Carl echoed.

They chatted for a further few minutes until a loud slamming noise in the playroom silenced them.

Cameron's yells had Francine darting out of the kitchen. 'Calm down,' she said loudly.

'We were here first,' Cameron shouted. 'He's a horrible shit-bag!'

Carl blanched and followed his wife, Jodi close behind.

Cameron was on top of Craig, pulling his hair and punching him. Carl scooped Cameron into his arms and started up the stairs.

Craig ran to Francine and buried his face in his mother's embrace. 'I only wanted to join in with the driving game on PlayStation,' he sobbed.

'I know, love. Cameron shouldn't have been so rough. We'll calm him down now and have a talk with him.'

'It's not fair! He always ruins everything,' Craig cried.

'Saul,' Jodi whispered to her shell-shocked son, who was

perched uneasily on a beanbag. 'It's home time, sweetie. It's late and we need to get you into bed.'

'Please don't feel you've to run away,' Francine said, sounding panicked.

'It really is home time, and I promise we'll see you all next week for pizza,' Jodi said, laying a hand on Francine's arm.

Cameron's tantrum raged on upstairs as Jodi and Saul said goodbye swiftly.

'Mummy, why does Cameron turn into someone else like that?' Saul asked, as they drove the short distance home.

'He can't help it, love, remember? I think he had so much fun with us today that he didn't want to share you with his brother.'

'I get scared when he's cross like that,' Saul said, as they emerged from the car and went into the house.

'I understand why you do. But I also know that all small children want to have friends,' Jodi said, and gave him a quick kiss. 'Now, hop into your pyjamas, there's a good boy.'

'Max and some of the others at school won't play with Cameron now because they don't like the cross part of him. He's scary.'

'I know, honey, and that's so sad for Cameron. He can't help it. So we're going to try extra hard to be his friends. If he knows we'll be kind and patient with him, that might help,' Jodi said, as she tucked her boy into bed. 'I didn't have a lot of friends when I was your age.'

'Why?' Saul looked astonished.

'I was very shy,' she lied. 'Once I got older I learned how to make friends.'

'And you learned how to be a movie star so now the whole world loves you,' Saul said proudly.

'Thank you, darling,' Jodi said, fighting back tears. 'But I still remember how awful it feels when nobody wants to be your friend. So let's try to make sure that Cameron knows we're his friends. Deal?'

'Deal.' Saul yawned.

'I'm sorry we didn't have time to fix your Lego from earlier. We'll do it tomorrow, okay?'

'Okay, Mum.'

'Sleep tight, little soldier,' she said.

'Night, Mum.'

Jodi pulled a woollen blanket around herself, too tired to light the stove. Cameron and his difficulties had put one thing into perspective for her: no matter what Mac decided to do, who he approached and blabbed to, she'd deal with it.

She was no longer the meek little girl who longed to be loved. She had Darius, her precious Saul and an increasing number of friends.

Her thoughts flicked to Sebastian and how she'd felt as his hand had rested on hers earlier. There were so many real people in her life now. She wasn't prepared to run from the past any longer.

Her mobile phone beeped a message.

Have you reconsidered? Can we work something out? We have something special you and I. Don't let it end this way. Remember you said you loved me to the moon and back? x x Mac

Jodi exhaled. What a sad, deluded and horrible piece of work Mac was.

Do what you like, Mac. The game is up for me. I'm not afraid of you or your threats. If you want to play hardball go ahead. I feel sorry for you.

Jodi hit send. Instead of bursting into tears or feeling an awful rush of fear course through her, she switched her phone off and turned on the television. Then she took a DVD off the shelf beside her and slid *Dirty Dancing* into the player.

As the music kicked off, she smiled to herself as she waited for Patrick Swayze to deliver his famous line – 'Nobody puts baby in the corner.' Well, Jodi Ludlum was coming out of the corner. Mac wasn't going to hold her back any longer.

Chapter 31

Francine always felt calmer when they'd been to see Nuala. Somehow the threat of bad behaviour seemed less scary.

'Cameron's responding well and Howie will make an even bigger impact as the combined training progresses,' Nuala said.

Howie had received his final booster shot and was able to go outside. A specialist trainer was working with the puppy and the little boy. 'You're his master and he needs you to help him.'

Cameron couldn't hide his pride when Howie sat for him or chased a ball. Francine and Carl couldn't believe the positive effect the dog was having on their son. 'When I feel the fire starting in my head, Howie helps me,' Cameron admitted. Stroking the dog quelled his rage and frustration.

Francine was still producing enough cakes to start a teashop but she'd made a pact with herself that midnight was her cut-off point. Come hell or high water, she wasn't allowed to wander down to the kitchen after that time.

'You're like that story of the elves and the shoemaker,' Carl said sadly. 'If I leave a box of eggs, a bag of sugar and another of flour on the kitchen counter, when I wake up you've turned them into a beautiful cake.'

'I'm more like Cinderella now,' she said. 'When the clock strikes midnight I have to be in bed.'

'Why don't we book a holiday, even a weekend, away from the children? It'd make all the difference for us to have a bit of civilised time together.'

'Who would look after them and that mutt?' She sighed. 'I'd love to, but there's no way we can abandon ship now. Besides, we can't leave Cameron at the moment. He needs the continuity and support.'

'Then we'll all go,' he decided. 'Leave it to me. I'll find a dog-friendly hotel – there are plenty in Ireland.'

The following evening as they were eating dinner Carl shoved his chair back. 'I have an announcement to make.' He coughed dramatically. 'Tomorrow you guys are all missing school!'

The children all cheered.

'We're going to a hotel in Kerry for two nights and Howie is coming too.'

They were thrilled. They threw down their cutlery and raced off to start packing.

'I've left two suitcases on the upstairs landing, so put in a pair of pyjamas each, some clean underwear and a change of clothes,' Carl shouted. 'They have a pool so swimming gear is essential.'

'When did you book it?' Francine asked, in mild shock.

'I went online today and found a great deal so I went for it!'

'I see,' she said, sighing.

'It'll be fun, sweetheart, just what we all need. A break from the old routine.'

Carl ran up the stairs, calling to the children that he wanted to see them all packed in jig time.

Francine sat at the kitchen table feeling wrung out. She piled up the dirty plates, scraped the scraps into the bin and began to clear away the rest of the dinner things.

She understood her husband was only trying to help, but all Francine wanted was her *old* routine back. The one that had existed and worked before Howie had come crashing into the house, before Cameron had been diagnosed with ADD, before she'd been made redundant and before she'd felt compelled to fill each second of the day and night to stop her terrified mind wandering out of control.

Twenty minutes later, she gasped when she reached the landing. Pretty much the entire contents of all the children's rooms were strewn from their doorways to two overflowing cases. The TV was blaring downstairs as they all yelled answers at a game show. She pushed open Cara's bedroom door and felt like crying. Her chest of drawers was virtually empty and what looked like an entire library of books was piled on the bed with an iPod and a pencil case.

The boys' rooms were worse.

Lowering herself to the landing floor, she tried to sort the tangle of clothes into piles. Eventually she had packed both cases, putting most of the clothes back in the children's rooms and keeping the things she knew they would actually need. She filled a separate bag with goggles, swimsuits and caps for them all.

'Okay, folks, bedtime!' Carl instructed. 'Brush your teeth and get into your scratchers. We'll leave early in the morning to make the most of the time in the hotel.'

Francine moved into their bedroom, choosing clothes for herself while closing the drawers Carl had pulled open earlier.

'This is going to be amazing, isn't it?' Carl said, as he bounded into the room, like a toddler off to a birthday party.

'Great,' Francine said flatly.

'Team Hennessy is on the move!' Carl clapped his hands and went off to police the brushing of teeth and getting into bed.

Francine sank down on the bed. She was so wrung out that she wasn't in the mood for Team Hennessy right now. Especially when the majority of the team were acting like apes and charging around, making a mess. There was no point in her packing toothbrushes until the morning, but she'd leave a large washbag in the family bathroom ready to be filled.

Peeling herself off the bed, she rubbed her tired eyes and pottered towards the bathroom.

The scene that greeted her made her want to scream. A thick snake of toothpaste had been squirted across the washbasin. The lid of the mouthwash was on the floor. One of the boys had left the toilet seat raised and forgotten to flush. The hand towel was in a ball on the floor. Howie was sneezing out puffs of chewed toilet roll.

Francine sighed.

'Night, Mum!' Craig called from his bed.

'I'm coming now to say good night to you all,' she said, injecting the last bit of enthusiasm she could muster into her voice.

By the time she'd kissed the excited children, calmed the dog down, packed tins and dry food for him, with bottles of water and his bowls, she felt as if she was going to keel over.

As she fell into bed and Carl cuddled up to her she thought she was about to explode. She'd driven children around all day, cooked, cleaned, unpacked and repacked, finished the ironing, washed God knows how many piles of clothes, and now Carl wanted her to be a vixen between the sheets.

'Have you ever wanted to spend a couple of days in a cave by yourself?' she asked him, as she stared at the ceiling. She knew she sounded mildly unhinged but she needed to vent.

'Hmm?' Carl had only one thing on his mind.

'Or a tent at the top of a mountain would do,' she continued. 'In fact, I'd settle for a cardboard box in the middle of the woods.'

'I know …' He kissed her neck.

'Or I could snip my fingers off one by one with the pinking shears and feed them to the dog,' she said.

'Okay,' Carl said, pulling her closer, his face full of love.

Oh, sod it, Francine thought. I could be telling him I've had a visitation from the Archangel Gabriel with the weekend's winning lotto numbers and he wouldn't hear at this moment. She knew they were lucky to find one another attractive after all this time. But a massive part of Francine wanted to be alone.

After they'd made love, Carl fell asleep. She stared at his familiar features. He was a handsome man and had aged well. She was glad that he still loved her.

The holiday would do them all the world of good, she conceded. Carl was right. They needed a change of scene and a bit of quality time as a family.

At least she wouldn't have to cook and clean for the next couple of days. That would be a lovely treat. Carl would be there all day to help entertain the children. She didn't need to do the school run or go to the supermarket. She imagined the plush hotel towels and bathrobe.

Carl loved playing with the children in the pool. Maybe she could sit in the Jacuzzi or even squeeze in a manicure. She curled up against him, inhaling his familiar scent.

Cℬ

When he'd said they were making an early start, he hadn't been exaggerating.

At five thirty the next morning he flicked the upstairs lights on and ordered them all out of bed.

'Honey, do we seriously have to go now?' Francine asked, as she staggered around in a haze. 'Please let's leave a little later.'

'You'll thank me when we get there!' he boomed. 'No breakfast or any of that. We'll hit the road and stop for a snack on the way.' He whistled as he put the bags into the car. Francine had liked him being a morning person when the children were babies. He'd never complained about doing a five o'clock bottle. But right at that moment she could have stuffed a sock into his mouth to shut him up.

Mercifully, the children were too tired to argue much and sloped into the car, looking pale and shivery. Howie was delirious that they were all up and about so early. As he bounded from room to room, wagging his tail, Francine couldn't help but smile at him. He really was the most enthusiastic creature she'd ever met.

Carl's estate car was bursting at the seams as they set off just before six.

'Right, let's get this show on the road!' he exclaimed.

'Can you keep it down a bit, love?' Francine asked, trying not to sound as irritable as she felt.

'Crabby Annie's sitting in my wife's seat!' he joked. 'What have you done with my Francine?'

Howie curled up on the floor in the back and Cameron rested his feet on the puppy's back.

'I'm going back to sleep. It's the middle of the night still,' Cara said grumpily.

'I'm not,' Cameron chirped. As he and Craig turned on their

Nintendos and linked a game to play against one another, the first argument broke out.

'Turn them off,' Cara snapped.

'Cara!' Francine and Carl scolded in unison.

'It's so annoying. Pinging and making shooting noises. Why can't they play it on silent?'

'You could turn them down, boys,' Francine suggested.

'It's no fun if you can't hear the sounds!' Craig argued. 'Besides, it's two against one.'

'Either turn it down or I'll snatch it and throw it out of the window.' Cara glowered at them.

'Meanie,' Cameron yelled, and thumped her arm.

'Mum! He hit me,' she said, as if he'd just assaulted her with an iron bar.

'No hitting, Cameron!' Carl said. 'Apologise to your sister.'

'No! She's a pain and we all hate her.'

'Mum!' Cara said, and started to cry.

'Right, that's enough! No more hitting and no more saying nasty things,' Francine said firmly.

Cara grabbed her Puffa coat and pulled it over her head.

Conor turned on his Nintendo and joined in with his brothers' game.

'At least they're not arguing, even if our daughter is in danger of suffocation,' Francine whispered to Carl.

'It'll be worth it when we get there,' he assured his wife.

Four and a half hours later, Howie was trying to sit between the front seats. All the children were threatening to stab one another and Francine thought her head was going to split in half.

'You promised we'd stop on the way,' Cameron whined.

'I know, but we got such a good run at it there was no point in breaking the journey. Besides,' Carl said, glancing back and grinning, 'ta-da! We're here!'

Silence descended as they drank in their new surroundings.

The entrance was gated with an old-style swinging iron sign. It looked quite rusty and, in Francine's opinion, needed a lick of paint. Still, the tree-lined driveway was pretty, with breathtaking views of the sea to one side.

'Isn't this fantastic?' she said.

'It looks a bit old and skangy.' Cara pouted.

'It's rustic,' Carl corrected.

'That's code for old and skangy.' Cara raised her eyes to heaven.

The purpose-built hotel was like an elongated chalet. Painted a rather striking shade of mustard, it might have been the height of fashion at some point but now appeared dated and dishevelled.

'Well, there's no trouble with parking, which is a good thing,' Carl said, as he got out and stretched. 'Plenty of space close to the main door. That'll make it much easier to check in.'

Clambering out of the car stiffly, the family breathed in the fresh air. Howie rushed and piddled against a tree and shook himself from head to toe.

'Let's go inside and see if we can check in. Then we'll grab some food. I'm starving,' Carl said.

The reception area was on the dark side, with maroon striped wallpaper and stained wood throughout.

'Eau de cabbage,' Francine said, wrinkling her nose.

'Smells like the home my mother spent her last days in, Lord rest her,' Carl whispered. 'Still, it said on the website that they've just refurbished the rooms, so I expect they haven't got around to the communal areas yet.'

The receptionist, who looked about twelve, seemed irritated that they had appeared so early. 'Yes?' she said, folding her arms across her small chest defensively.

'Good morning!' Carl said cheerfully. When there was no response, he added, 'We're the Hennessy family. Party of six and one dog!'

Yawning, the girl poked at a computer and produced a form. 'Sign at the bottom. The dog can't go near the leisure centre or the main restaurant,' she recited.

'Here you go,' Carl said, smiling, as he returned the form.

'You're on the third floor,' the girl said in a sulky voice. 'Lunch is served until two.' She banged the room keys on the desk, stood up and sloped into a little back room, making it clear she wasn't open to any further chat.

'I can't imagine she's spent too much time in charm school, can you?' Carl whispered to Francine.

'She's utterly obnoxious,' Francine said, affronted on Carl's behalf. 'I've a good mind to ask to speak to the manager. That's not the type of welcome I'd expect from a four-star establishment.'

'Eh, I think it might be a three-star,' Carl said, coughing and looking away. 'Anyway, we're here now.' Clapping Conor on the back, he led the family outside to collect the luggage. 'All hands on deck. If we take a few things each we should manage to unload the car in jig time.'

There was a slight snag with Carl's plan. When they got to the lift it was the size of a coffin.

'I'm not going in that thing. Imagine if it stops,' Francine said, backing away in panic. 'I don't like lifts at the best of times, but that's dodgy.'

'You lot take the stairs, then,' Carl agreed. 'I'll come up in the lift with as much as I can get into it. When I get to the third floor, help me pull the stuff out, then I'll go down and load up the last of the bags.'

There was great excitement as they ran with Howie up the stairs.

'Let's see if we can beat the lift!' Cara called. Howie found the whole thing a bit overwhelming and began to bark.

'Shush, Howie!' Francine said, putting her finger to her lips.

'It stinks here,' Cameron complained.

Francine had to admit the place was kind of musty. She sincerely hoped the newly refurbished bedrooms were a damn sight fresher than the rest of the place.

The lift rattled to a halt just after they reached it.

'It sounds like it's going to fall apart,' Cara said.

'Don't be rude, please, Cara,' Francine scolded.

'Sorry, Mum.'

They lifted all the bags out and pressed the down button to send the lift back to Carl.

'We've no keys. Dad has them,' Craig said.

'He'll be along in just a minute,' Francine said. 'Meanwhile, let's have a look out of the window.'

'I can't see anything,' Cameron said. 'The glass is dirty. Daddy would be very pleased to have a go at it with his m'alectric power hose, wouldn't he?'

'We're on holidays, Cameron,' Conor said. 'It's not our job to clean the place.'

Carl arrived in the lift, looking a bit shaken. 'It mightn't be a good plan to use this fella too often,' he said. 'It shuddered to a halt for a minute. I jumped up and down and it got going again. But I wouldn't fancy being stuck in there for too long.'

'Have you got the keys?' Francine asked, feeling more stressed by the second.

'Certainly have. We've connecting doors so at least we can keep an eye on the children,' Carl said. 'Now, let's see what the rooms are like.'

The hotchpotch of clashing red-wine and moss-green patterns that greeted them was bad enough, but the musty smell of damp was vile. The connecting doors didn't quite fit the description in so far as they didn't exist. There was simply a space where two doors might have been once upon a time.

'Well, in fairness the hotel did mention connecting rooms rather than doors,' Carl said, with a good-natured grin. Francine went into the bathroom. The brown tiles, some of which were cracked, made the place look more like a cheap oven than the marble-encased luxury she'd been hoping for. Two sad-looking brown towels were the only nod towards the fluffy bathrobe and slippers she'd had in mind.

The queen-sized bed sagged and already Francine could imagine waking with Carl's elbow lodged in her neck.

'Ooh!' Cameron exclaimed, from the other bedroom. 'We've got bunk beds!'

Francine and Carl wandered into the adjoining room.

'I'm the eldest so I get a top bunk.' Cara threw her bag and iPod on to one.

'I'm next so this one's mine.' Conor tossed his Nintendo on to the other.

'I'm happy under here. It's like a little house,' Cameron said.

'I don't mind where I sleep,' Craig said, and claimed the last bed.

Francine found the children's room utterly depressing. The old metal bunks were made up with random covers and shapeless pillows. Their bathroom was similar to the other, except for its avocado décor.

Howie was having the best time. Sniffing like a demon, he cocked his leg against the double bed and prepared to pee.

'No, Howie!' Francine yelled.

'It might improve the smell in here,' Carl said, as a naughty grin crept across his face. 'It's kind of depressing, isn't it?'

'You can say that again,' Francine said. 'Still, the children don't seem to mind. Let's go and have a bit of brunch in the bar and investigate the swimming pool,' she suggested.

'You're right. Even if it's a bit shabby it won't stop us having a lovely time. The views are magnificent!' Carl joked.

When she parted the grey net curtains Francine had a perfect view of the hotel skip, along with a pile of rusting tractor parts. 'Ugh, bloody hell, Carl, look at that!'

'Well, the deal didn't actually state whether or not it included a sea view,' he said wryly.

'I don't think I can handle staying here,' Francine said. 'I'm beginning to break out in a sweat. It's really horrible.'

He put his arms around her and rocked her back and forth. 'It's a total dump. Hand on heart, it's all my fault. I might've known it was too good to be true, considering what we've paid for the break,' he said. 'But the kids are delighted. The dog is going to blow up, he's having so much fun sniffing, and we're away from the usual stresses and strains of life. Let's just try and make the best of it, yeah?' He tilted her chin up so that he could look into her eyes. 'This is one of those situations we'll laugh about in years to come.'

'I'm looking forward to that,' she said, 'because right now all I'm doing is dreading the thought of lying on those god-awful lumpy pillows and avoiding getting a verruca in the bathroom.'

'You're not getting into the spirit of this at all!' Carl laughed.

'Sure a verruca never killed anyone. And we'll appreciate Verbena Drive all the more when we get home.'

'Come on, Mum and Dad, let's go and explore,' Conor said enthusiastically.

'Who's hungry?' Carl asked, as he and Francine wandered into the children's room.

'Me,' Cara said. 'What'll we do with Howie while we eat, though?'

'Let's see where he's allowed to go and take it from there,' Francine answered.

'Can we bring our swimming gear now?' Craig asked, as he unzipped the suitcase and began to throw all the clean clothes on to the grubby carpet.

'Craig, don't!' Francine said. 'I have the swimming things in a separate bag. Don't leave your clothes on the carpet. It's not overly clean. Here's the swimming bag so let's get out of here,' she said.

They all chose to take the stairs, nervous of the small tin box the hotel called a lift.

Following the signs, they found the bar. It was hardly a hive of activity. In fact, the clientele was made up of an old geezer, accompanied by a grimy black and white Jack Russell tethered to the high stool with a piece of twine.

'Good morning!' Francine said. The man didn't respond.

The children were staring at him. He was well turned out in a three-piece tweed suit. He continued to stare ahead as if he was on another planet.

'Hi, there. I'm Carl Hennessy.' Carl held out his hand. Nothing.

'Perhaps he's deaf,' Francine whispered.

'Or he's given up talking unless he feels like it,' Carl said, out of the side of his mouth.

They all jumped as the man lunged forward and banged his empty pint glass on the counter.

A round woman, dressed in a nylon overall with far too much rouge on her cheeks, appeared, waving her little fat arms.

'Oh, hello!' she said, in pleased surprise. 'I'm Mrs Clear, proprietor, cook and housekeeper all rolled into one!'

'Hello, Mrs Clear. We're the Hennessy family and we've come for a mini break,' Francine said.

Mrs Clear waddled around from the back of the bar and shook hands with each of them, asking their names. 'All beginning with C, except for your good self, Francine,' she pointed out happily.

'Yes!' Francine was thrilled that she had picked up on their initials quirk.

'Can I get you people a bit of food or a drink?'

'Both, please,' Carl said.

Another loud bang from the old man's glass made them jump again.

'Good man yourself, Podge,' Mrs Clear said, patting him on the back. 'I'll sort you out with a fresh pint in two shakes of a lamb's tail.' Turning back to the family with a warm smile, she continued, 'What had you in mind? A cold snack, like a sandwich or a salad, or would you all eat a bit of a fry?' She looked at her watch.

'A fry would be a lovely treat, wouldn't it, children?' Francine asked.

They all nodded and took a seat. The ancient pleather-covered couches were sticky and not too clean. The chairs were fit for the skip and the chipped dark-wood tables were mismatched and bockety.

'I'll bring a bowl of water and a few kibbles for your dog too,' Mrs Clear said, as she waddled away. Howie seemed to find the presence of the Jack Russell calming. He lay on the floor facing the little dog and stared at him.

'We could all end up with *E. coli*,' Francine hissed to Carl.

'This is very awkward, all right. If we can't eat the food I think you'll have to stuff it in your handbag.'

'It's Miu Miu, Carl, and not the size of a shopping trolley! Where do you suggest I stuff six cooked brunches?' In spite of herself Francine began to giggle. Carl's shoulders shook as he tried to muffle his laughter.

As they were sizing up the kids' pockets, Mrs Clear returned with a massive tray.

'Now, I'll give the children and the bowler theirs first. Mammy and Daddy's are on the way.' She chuckled.

The full Irish breakfast looked stunning, with everything from scrambled eggs to fresh field mushrooms. When she returned with Francine and Carl's, she also brought freshly baked brown bread, country butter and home-made jam.

'Enjoy that and you can have a chat about what you might like for your dinner. I don't do menus,' she explained. 'I'd rather cook what's in season. I've a lovely rabbit if you're that way inclined but I can't recommend the goose enough.'

The children gasped.

'Is it a real goose?' Cameron asked.

'Certainly is.' Mrs Clear chuckled.

'And someone's pet bunny?' Craig asked, horrified.

'He was a wild fella that was out the back,' she said easily. 'Maybe you might like my home-made burgers with nice thick chips? I was thinking of a baked Alaska for your dessert,' she said, clasping her hands over her round tummy.

'That sounds wonderful,' Carl said. 'I'd say you'd be hitting the nail on the head with burgers and chips for this lot. Francine and I adore goose, don't we, love?'

'Mm.' Francine's mouth was full of brunch.

'That's settled, then. I'll do a lovely potato and apple stuffing with roasties and gravy – I can taste it already! Podge loves a bit of roast so he'll be happy too.' She nodded towards him. 'I call him the silent man! Sure he was never any different growing up. He's ten years older than me and Mammy always said I was sent to balance him out. I talk enough for the two of us!'

At that point she left them to finish their breakfast.

'I have to hand it to Mrs Clear, she mightn't be brilliant at cleaning but there was nothing wrong with that food,' Carl whispered.

'Certainly wasn't, and my handbag is still safe,' Francine said, as they began to giggle again.

The children were dying to go swimming so they shouted goodbye into the kitchen behind the bar. 'Cheerio, folks, see you later,' she called back.

'Bye, Podge,' Carl said. If the man heard he didn't acknowledge it. Howie had gobbled his breakfast and finished his bowl of water. As he passed the little dog at Podge's feet, he wagged his tail and yipped. The smaller dog sniffed him and yapped back.

'Howie's made a friend,' Cameron said. 'This is a great place.'

As they made their way gingerly along the corridor towards the pool, Francine had to admit she felt more relaxed than she had for a long time. The hotel might be a bit closer to Fawlty Towers than the Ritz, but it was certainly serving a purpose. The Hennessys were having fun together. This time yesterday she had felt as if she'd never smile again, let alone giggle into her breakfast like a teenager.

The pool was better than they'd imagined. It was certainly compact, but as they were the only ones using it that didn't matter.

After their swim, they decided to take Howie out for a walk. It was a crisp, clear November afternoon, and the sun shone for a spell. Howie was beside himself, bounding around happily as the children chased him up a field. Francine inhaled the fresh country air and held Carl's hand as they walked for miles. Out there, with nothing but green and an expanse of clear sky, she felt grounded once more.

'Doesn't nature bring the fragility of life to the fore?' she mused to Carl.

'Ah, it's always good to step outside our day-to-day bubble,' Carl agreed. 'We'll be all right, love,' he said, as he squeezed her hand.

Francine smiled. She hoped he was right.

Chapter 32

Jodi knew it wouldn't take long for the press to contact her once Mac decided to tell their story, but even she was surprised when the *World News* phoned the following afternoon. Less than twenty-four hours, she thought wryly. That was pretty impressive – even for Mac.

'I'll do a press release tomorrow. Of course you'll be on the list. Thank you for your interest,' Jodi said, as she hung up.

Noelle answered on the first ring. 'So he's finally done it,' she said.

'Yup.'

'How are you coping?'

'Do you know what? I'm ready. It's time for me to stop running from the past, Noelle.'

'Attagirl. Now, with regard to Darius ...'

'That's different. We'll leave it as it is.' Jodi was firm.

'As you wish. I've organised a press conference and you need to be in the Regal Crown Hotel in London tomorrow at eleven. I guessed you'd want to get straight back so I've booked day-return flights and a car. Lovely Kate will look after Saul,' Noelle said.

'Great. I don't like him missing school and I've more hope of avoiding the paparazzi if I come home.' Jodi sighed. 'They'll probably arrive in Bakers Valley but they'll get bored quicker here. Once you've seen one hedge you've seen them all.'

They chatted about what Jodi would say and Noelle wished her a pleasant journey.

On automatic pilot, Jodi pulled on her Hunter wellies, Puffa coat and a hat. The biting November breeze stung her cheeks as she marched determinedly up the avenue to Sebastian's kitchen door and knocked as loudly as her freezing knuckles would allow.

Sebastian opened the door and, without thinking, Jodi flung herself into his arms.

Wordlessly he led her to the sofa. 'Jodi … I … I don't know how to say this to you,' he stuttered, 'but all I can offer you is friendship. I'm too damaged and hurt to be anything more …' He looked grief-stricken.

'That's *all* you can offer? Sebastian, I've only ever yearned for people who care about me. Real people who have my back. If you can be one of those, you're offering me the biggest prize of all.'

'But I thought you might want more.' He blushed. 'Forgive my presumptuous arrogance. I thought for a moment that you were expecting us to …'

'Sex makes things messy. It's never helped me in life. If we can be there for one another without the mess, that's good enough for me.'

Pulling the Aran knit rug from the back of the sofa, he wrapped them in its warmth, cradling her in his arms protectively.

'My life is about to splash like an exploding tin of paint all over the press,' Jodi confessed.

'Why?'

Once Jodi began to talk it was as if a dam had breached inside her. She told him all about her relationship with Darius, that she adored him but that their marriage was a sham.

'But why would you do such a thing? A girl like you could have any man,' he said gently.

'Once upon a time Darius was my saviour. I couldn't face the bad press and I wasn't strong enough to shoulder the truth. But I'm older and wiser now. I've finished running away, Sebastian,' she said, as tears began to fall again. 'I'll never talk about Darius to the papers, though. We both owe it to Saul to keep that part secret. But some day soon we'll have to stage an amicable split. For both our sakes.'

'And now?' Sebastian wondered.

'Now it's time for me to face Mac.'

'Surely he can be silenced again.'

'No. I've paid in more ways than one. He won't be quiet for much longer, no matter what I say or do. So the time has come. Tomorrow will be awful but, as I know only too well, the press will feast on my pain. I'll be everywhere for a couple of weeks and then some other poor sod will take my place.'

It was time to collect Saul from school and pack for their brief trip to London.

'I could mind him for you tomorrow, if you like?' Sebastian asked shyly.

'Would you do that for me?' she asked, as she shrugged her coat on.

'It'd be my pleasure. What time do you need to leave for the airport?' he asked.

'There's the problem. I'll have to go at five in the morning.'

'No bother,' Sebastian said, a farmer once more. 'Sure I'll be up anyway. Tell the lad I'll be there when he wakes and I'll drop him to the school in my vintage car.' A sad smile spread to his eyes. 'Blake used to love it when I did that.'

Jodi hugged him again and thanked him for the offer.

As a few dainty flakes of snow flitted past, she pulled the zip on her Puffa coat as high as it could go. Oddly, she didn't feel cold any more.

ೞ

Moments later, Saul was jumping up and down in front of her. 'Sebastian's taking me to school in his olden-days car!'

'You bet!' Jodi said, grinning.

'That is going to be the best thing *ever*,' he said. Normally if Jodi told Saul she was leaving, even if only for a short time, he'd fret and make her feel guilty. But the promise of a trip in the vintage car and Sebastian's company changed all of that.

'We love Sebastian, don't we?' he said, holding her hand as they walked home.

'Yes,' Jodi affirmed. 'We do.'

Chapter 33

Francine squirmed as they crawled between the nylon sheets at the hotel. 'It's awful in here. The goose was delicious and Mrs Clear is a dear old lady but these sheets smell faintly of wee,' Francine said, shuddering.

'Don't move around too quickly there, love, or you might cause a spark with the friction,' Carl teased her.

Once again she found herself giggling at the awfulness of the room.

'Besides,' Carl continued. 'If we were in a five-star place with Egyptian-cotton sheets and snooty staff, they mightn't have appreciated Cameron's singing during dinner.'

'Or Howie joining in!'

The creaking of the bunk beds in the adjoining room ceased as the children fell asleep. The early start coupled with the fun-filled day had truly tired them out.

With no kitchen to escape to, Francine was forced to try to sleep. 'Carl?' she whispered, into the darkness.

'No!' he said, laughing. 'That stench was Howie, not me! I know I'm a man and you think all men are louts after drinking beer but, seriously, give me the benefit of the doubt.'

Francine giggled.

'I told Mrs Clear not to feed him sprouts.' Carl laughed.

'I never knew Golden Retrievers liked baked Alaska either.' Francine snorted.

The older woman had thought it perfectly normal to bring a proper dinner for Howie. Fair enough, she'd put it into a dog dish but he'd had the full works, including apple sauce.

Old Podge and his Jack Russell, Sniff, had been catered for too.

'Sniff loves other dogs coming to see her, so bring Howie in when you're having dinner and they can eat together,' Mrs Clear encouraged.

Although the couple of days away didn't feature fluffy bathrobes or pampering sessions, Francine felt more rejuvenated and relaxed with each passing moment of their break. 'Thanks for arranging this, Carl,' she said. 'You'll have to make sure you don't take any more time off work or you'll find yourself joining the growing unemployment queues.'

'I've been at the office day in day out over the last twelve years, barely missing an hour even when the babies were born,' Carl said. 'I know my partners don't begrudge me the time off and they've even said I should do it more often, within reason.'

The dull, thudding headache that Francine had been lugging around had shifted, as had the awful tight sensation in her chest. The change of scene had made her ready to take on whatever life threw at them next.

ଓଃ

Back at Bakers Valley school, Saul arrived in style aboard Sebastian's vintage car, feeling like the king of the castle. Children and mothers waved and called to him as they chugged into the car park.

386

'I bet Mr Matthews didn't think I'd arrive in this!' he shouted to Sebastian.

'I'd say you can guarantee he won't have seen such a thing too often,' he said, grinning. Hopping down and lifting the small boy to the ground, Sebastian grabbed his hand and strode towards the kindergarten room.

Even though several years had passed, the smell of books and children brought to him a flood of buried memories.

'Good morning, Saul. I see you've brought a new friend today.' Mr Matthews grinned.

'Sebastian brought me here in his old noisy!' Saul squeaked. 'I'm sure he'd take you for a ride if you like.'

'Do you do taxi services from the local on a Saturday night?' Mr Matthews said.

'Not yet, but that could be a good idea.' Sebastian smiled. 'See you later, Saul. Have a good time and I'll be here to pick you up.'

'Bye, Sebastian. Take care in the old car,' Saul said, wagging a finger at him. 'We mind each other,' he explained to Mr Matthews. 'Isn't that right, Sebastian?'

'Sure is. See you later.'

Either he chose not to notice or he was too caught up in bittersweet memories to see, but Jane, Andrea and most of the female population of the car park were either stubbing their toes or walking into door jambs as the gorgeous stranger strode by.

'He's divine,' Jane said in awe.

'He brought Jodi Ludlum's little fella in just now,' Jackie said, rushing to fill them in.

'But that's not Darius,' Jane pointed out.

'Well, no shit, Sherlock,' Andrea said, as her jaw dropped even further. 'Is he driving out of here in that vintage Rolls?'

'Looks like it,' Jackie said. 'Where's Francine? She'd know what's going on.'

'I haven't seen her for a few days, now that you mention it,' Jane mused.

'I know who he is,' Sarah interjected. 'That's Sebastian, Diane Corr's husband. I haven't seen him for a few years but his son Blake was in my daughter's class,' she said.

'He's Jodi's neighbour. God, he's gorgeous, isn't he?'

'Yeah.' The others sighed as they watched him rumble out of the gate in the Rolls.

❧

Meanwhile Jodi was taking her seat at a floodlit table where she was being blinded by flash bulbs. With no script or anyone else beside her, she waved her hand to command silence.

She was stunned by how many press people had turned up. Mac was nowhere to be seen, but then again, she mused, he didn't know she was doing this.

'It's been brought to my attention that an ex-boyfriend of mine has attempted to sell a story for a substantial-sum to the *World News*,' she began. 'I don't like blackmail. Neither do I think large amounts of cash should be handed out to low-life scumbags who reckon they can make a quick buck. In the current economic climate I felt strongly that a donation of a hundred thousand pounds to the underprivileged children's Santa appeal would be preferable.' There was a wave of muttering as the press jostled for a good view.

'So I have agreed to tell you the story today.'

'How do we know you'll tell us the truth?' a journalist shouted.

'Because what I'm about to say is so personal and so painful that I would be one sick puppy to make it up,' Jodi answered calmly.

More mumbling ensued as flash bulbs continued to go off.

'Eight years ago, just after I finished shooting a movie called *Into the Sunset* with that director ... Oh, what was his name?' Jodi tapped the table, playing with the crowd. 'That's it! Reggie Wilson.'

The journalists laughed.

'I had everything going for me and I felt like I was living the dream. On the night of the première, here in London, my acting skills were the only thing that got me through the post-viewing party.'

'What happened to you, Jodi?' a well-known journalist yelled. Everyone leaned forward.

'At the time I knew I was sixteen weeks pregnant with my boyfriend Mac's child. The anoraks among you will recall that I wore a billowing ball gown that evening.'

Indeed, Jodi had made the cover of every glossy that month in the distinctive Vivienne Westwood dress.

'There was a photo shoot with the leading actors, myself included, holding glasses of champagne.' Jodi took a deep breath. 'I don't drink alcohol, never have. My mother was an alcoholic and died of a drug overdose when I was a child. So that champagne, to toast the film's success, was purely for photographic purposes.' She sat up straight in the chair and willed herself to finish her story. 'As I attempted to leave via a back entrance to the venue the heel of my shoe caught in my dress. I tumbled down the steps, landing heavily on my stomach.'

Gasps filled the room as the women instinctively placed their hands on their bellies.

'I was rushed to hospital but the baby couldn't be saved.'

'But that was tragic, Jodi. How was Mac blackmailing you?' a journalist probed from the crowd.

'I was splashed across the cover of every magazine raising a glass without a care in the world. Mac said he'd tell the world that I was my mother's daughter – a drug addict and a drunk – and that the image you have of me is false.'

'Why didn't you tell people the truth before now?' a voice behind the flashing cameras asked.

'Because I blamed myself for hurting that baby. I grew up on a street and, indeed, in a world where drink and drugs were rife. No amount of money or fame could convince me that I was a good person.' Tears began to flow as Jodi drank in the shocked looks she was met with.

'I trusted Mac and thought he loved me. They say the first cut is the deepest and it scarred me.'

'What's made you speak out now?'

'Darius and Saul are the best things that ever happened to me. I know I'm blessed to have them in my life. But it's taken my return to my motherland and being integrated with families and other parents for me to realise that I can finally accept myself. I will always mourn my lost child and I will never forget the heartache and guilt that threatened to choke me at that time. But I've finished hiding. The story is yours to twist as you wish. You can tell it as I told you or you can embellish it at will.'

'Where is Mac now?'

'Do you still love Mac?'

'Did Darius know all this when you married him?'

The questions flew at her like bullets. Standing up, she leaned down towards the cluster of microphones and spoke: 'I'm leaving now. I have nothing further to say. I'm still the same person I've always been, except I can now hold my head a little higher. Thank you all for your continued support.'

As she moved swiftly out of the side door, Noelle ushered her into a waiting car. Jodi crumpled into a ball and buried her face in her lap.

'Well done, sweetheart,' Noelle said, and hugged her. 'The worst is over. He can't damage you now.'

'He'll probably give all sorts of interviews telling them what it was like to live with me, but good luck to him. I'm going home and I've perfect plans to hide away from the staring eyes of the village for the next while. Soon I'll be someone's chip-wrapping.'

Noelle left her, and the driver whisked her to the airport for her return flight.

കൃ

As she sat on the plane with an eye mask over her face, forcing herself to breathe evenly, all Jodi could think of was Bakers Valley and the true friends she had waiting for her.

By the time her driver greeted her in Dublin, a number of paps had gathered at the airport.

'We'll need to go out the side entrance,' he said. 'I've heard the story on the radio.'

'Thanks,' Jodi said gratefully.

'I'm sorry you went through such a trauma and, for what it's worth, I think the public will be on your side.' She'd met this man several times since her move to Ireland and he'd always been polite yet quiet.

'Thank you for saying that,' she said sincerely.

As soon as she turned her mobile phone back on a message beeped through from Darius. She didn't want to speak to him before an audience so she texted him.

Back in Ireland with driver will call u in a while

Laying her head against the leather seat back, Jodi felt as if a massive weight had been lifted from her chest. For so long she'd lived with the dreadful guilt that she'd killed her baby. She'd allowed Mac to convince her that the world would see her as a similar person to her own mother.

'Of all the things your ma did, she never killed either of you,' he'd blazed at her, during one of their frequent rows, before she'd finally walked away from him.

'I fell, Mac. It was an accident. Don't you think I blame myself enough without you adding to the guilt?'

'That was my baby too,' he said. 'Just because I'm a man, it doesn't mean I don't have any feelings.'

Hindsight was a great thing, Jodi mused. Now that she'd finally let go of the secret, she felt sorry for the poor, frightened girl Mac had suppressed for so long. What kind of a fool had she been to allow him to make her feel so guilty? She was fairly certain Mac couldn't really have given a toss about the baby.

Fair enough, it would've been his never-ending tie to her, which would've suited him nicely. But she could see so clearly that he'd never loved her the way she'd loved him.

Mac had known that and had always felt he had power over her. Maybe if she'd been less accommodating and forgiving, he would have behaved better. But either way he'd been genuinely astonished when she'd moved out of their apartment.

'I can't live with you any more. I love you so much but

you're not good for me, Mac,' she'd said, devastated.

Naturally he'd seen it all as a well-deserved kick in the nuts. But he'd assumed she'd be back once she'd calmed down and had a chance to get herself together.

The first shock had come when the bank had written to him saying he'd have to either take over the mortgage payments or leave. That the 'owner' had given him a month to make up his mind.

'Jodi, what the hell?' he'd asked, over the phone. 'Baby, this is silly. We both know we needed a bit of time apart, but come home now. I love you and I can't live without you. We belong together.'

'I can't, Mac. I want to believe you but you keep letting me down. Noelle says—'

'Ah, you don't want to listen to that old bag,' Mac interrupted. He and Noelle had never seen eye to eye.

'I do listen to her. She's my agent but she's also my friend. I trust her and she has rightly pointed out that you do not have my best interests at heart.'

'Baby. Nobody knows you like I do. We're from the same country, we understand each other. Don't let bitter old bags like Noelle turn our love sour.'

Jodi had hung up. Racked with sobs, she'd felt as if her heart was being ripped from her chest. She could see where Noelle was coming from and suspected she was probably right, but she loved Mac. She knew she shouldn't but she did.

If there was one thing Mac excelled in it was perseverance. He called Jodi constantly. He sent her cards with sweet nothings scribbled across them. He had flowers delivered to the set. He turned up as she was finishing a long day, threw his jacket around her shoulders and accompanied her home. 'I'm not even coming in. I just needed to see you and know you're all right.'

The first time she'd let him back into her life after the baby, he'd totally fooled her into believing he'd changed. She'd agreed to meet him for dinner and he wasn't his usual cocky self. 'I got myself a job. It doesn't pay much but I'm a props assistant on the gangster movie they're shooting down near the Docklands,' he'd said, looking at the floor.

'That's great, Mac,' she said.

'I feel like I'm finally taking responsibility. The drugs are finished with. I'm not dealing, even to friends, and I want out of that scene,' he said, fiddling with his napkin. 'I want us to be together again. That's all that matters, Jodi, you and me. I know I don't earn much but I'm trying ...'

'It's not about money, Mac,' she said, with tears in her eyes. 'Fair enough, when you grow up in a house where there's nothing, cash is vital. But I'm so lucky that I don't have to worry about that any longer. All I want is to be loved.'

'And I do love you, baby. You know I do. I've been an idiot and all I'm asking is that you give me another chance. I miss you and I need you in my life.'

Jodi had known Noelle would probably flip, but she honestly believed Mac was sorry. Underneath the confident party-boy exterior he was the most loving person she'd ever met.

It had taken him about a month to show his true colours once more. Jodi had returned at three in the morning from shooting to find him hosting a wild party in their apartment.

'Baby! You're here. Here she is, the star of the moment! Jodi, come and meet my friends,' he had slurred. She was engulfed in hugs from pissed and high strangers. Pulling the plug on the extortionately expensive Bang & Olufsen sound system, which Mac had ordered, she'd walked calmly to the door, held it open and waited. 'All of you leave, please. This is not my scene, and as it's my home, I would like you all to go. Thank you.'

She'd known everyone thought she was a boring stuck-up cow who wouldn't know how to have a good time if it bit her on the arse. But she didn't care.

'Don't think much of her, Mac. You'd think with all her fame she'd've learned how to enjoy herself,' one of the girls had said, as she winked at Mac. 'Call me again, won't you?'

'Cheers, see you all soon!' Mac had closed the door quickly. 'Baby, what's happening?' He'd tried to wrap himself around her as she'd made her way to their bedroom. 'I'm all fired up now and as you've sent the party away you'll have to help me out.'

'You're drunk and off your face on God knows what. Keep away from me, Mac.'

She'd slammed the bedroom door, removed her clothes and got into bed – alone.

Mac's absences had increased, as had his rolling home at all hours and fumbling around the place drunk. His job seemed to have fallen by the wayside.

Jodi happened to be shooting on location close to their apartment at the time, so he'd decided to drop in and have a coffee with her between takes. 'Wow, you look amazing. Tell Wardrobe you're bringing those tight trousers home tonight,' he schmoozed. 'Listen, I've been thinking, why don't I work for you full time? It would make sense. I'll be your manager. That way we'll get to see each other more and I can keep an eye on what's happening.'

'I don't need anyone, thanks, Mac. Noelle is great and the PR team she's been using lately are so professional that I'm getting great coverage. I've just been asked to do a shoot for L'Oréal's spring-summer makeup range.'

'I know, and you're amazing, I get that. But I think there's so much more potential for your brand.'

'I'm not a brand, I'm a person, and I've enough going on, Mac.'

'Sure it was only a thought. I'll take one of the job offers I have on the table then. The more interesting one doesn't start for another couple of months, though.' He looked at her to gauge her reaction.

'Then pick something else,' she said, and raised an eyebrow.

'I will. Listen, that awards thingy tomorrow night ...' He raked his fingers through his hair.

'It's the BAFTAs, sweetie.' She grinned.

'Yeah. I was down in Harrods and it seems most of the men are wearing custom-made suits and are really pushing the boat out. That tuxedo I have is a bit *passé* – could you stand me a new one?' Mac had had the right amount of humility and embarrassment on his face to convince her.

'Sure. Use the credit card. Besides, my dress has been sponsored by Dior. I'm getting an amazing necklace, too, from Tiffany's. I can't wait,' she'd said. 'I'll be like Cinderella going to the ball. You won't go out anywhere tomorrow, will you? I need you to be there with me.'

'I'll be there to hold your hand, don't you worry.'

'Miss Jodi, when you're ready!' Reggie boomed across.

'Hey, Reggie, how's it going?' Mac shouted.

Reggie turned away and walked back to the main camera man.

'God, he's a tricky bastard, isn't he?' Mac whispered to Jodi.

Giggling, she had kissed him, then gone straight to Makeup.

The following day, by the time she'd had her hair, makeup and dress fitting, Jodi knew she wouldn't have time to get back to the apartment. She'd phoned Mac four times and he hadn't answered.

As she sat in her limo on the way to the red carpet she tried his phone again. A text came through just as they pulled to a halt.

I'm here looking out 4 u x x

Screams and waving fans had surrounded her as she stepped out of the car. She had posed briefly for the photographers and, as was customary for her, had spent a good twenty minutes signing autographs and talking to the fans, who had turned out in droves to see her.

'We love you, Jodi,' they yelled.

Like a true lady, she'd worked the entire semicircle of railings, calling to people who were three or four rows back from her. 'I love you too, and thanks for coming to see me!' she'd said, smiling and waving.

Tugging at his jacket, Mac had appeared, looking mildly hassled. Her smile didn't waver as she whispered to him, 'Where the hell have you been?'

'Things to do, people to see, but I'm here now. Jesus, you look divine. Isn't my girlfriend the sexiest woman alive?' he shouted to the crowd. Wolf whistles and cheers gave him the response he needed. Holding his hand to his ear, he urged them to cheer louder.

Jodi waved and blew kisses, then hitched up the front of her dress and began to walk along the red carpet towards the entrance of the Royal Opera House.

Mac had linked her arm and posed like a pro as they halted at the main photographers' pool.

'Who's the gown by?'

'Dior – isn't it beautiful?' Jodi said.

'It's the hanger, not the dress,' one man shouted.

Moving inside, Jodi had wanted to hit Mac. He was as high as a kite and behaving as if he owned the place.

That pattern had continued for another year before she finally called a halt to their relationship.

Heartbroken and feeling as if she wasn't capable of earning anyone's love, she had been shocked when Noelle had sat her down saying Mac was threatening to sell their story. 'He's planning on spilling the whole shooting match. He even says he's spoken to some of the people from your old estate and they're willing to back him up,' Noelle explained. 'I know you're well able to deal with the backlash but, quite frankly, his timing isn't great. He's going to say you lost the baby because you drank yourself into a stupor. That he's never going to get over the loss of his child and he'll never forgive you. The low-life he's hooked up with from the Dayfield Estate remembers your mother. Mac has convinced him that you're your mother's daughter.' Noelle sighed heavily. 'I've nearly got this next deal in the bag. Reggie is at nine million pounds right now. So we don't need that little git messing this up.'

'What do you suggest?' Jodi was terrified.

So had begun the years of paying Mac to keep quiet. Her marriage to Darius had taken place soon after that.

None of them had anticipated how much Jodi and Darius would come to love one another.

Now, as Jodi dumped her handbag on the kitchen counter in her cottage, her mobile rang. 'Hi, Darius,' she said, instantly smiling.

'Don't keep me in suspense. I'm dying here for you. How was it? How was he? How are you, more to the point?'

'It wasn't that bad,' Jodi admitted. 'It's done now and I know the next couple of weeks are going to be a total pain, but I'll get through it.'

'You're so strong, honey.'

'Mostly down to you, Darius. You and Saul are my angels.'

'I'm so proud of you.'

'Thanks, sweetheart,' Jodi said. 'I'll keep you posted but I'm oddly calm about it all. I know I should be tearing my hair out right now and biting my nails to the quick about what's going to explode in the press. But I'm in a whole new zone.'

'I can hear it in your voice, darling.'

They chatted for a few minutes until Darius had to go.

'Call me any time, day or night. God only knows what's going to kick off with this story,' he said.

'Let them have their field day,' Jodi reiterated. 'The hiding is over, Darius.'

She hung up with a head full of mixed emotions. Relief, sadness, new-found happiness and, above all, excitement and hope for the future.

Chapter 34

Francine and Carl arrived home with a car full of their own hope. The children weren't fighting quite as much – Howie had spent the entire journey passing wind, uniting them in disgust.

'He's just done another ripper,' Cara had screamed at one point. 'All take cover!' Amid giggles, they held their noses and opened the windows.

'That was a good one, boy,' Cameron said, patting the puppy's head and grinning.

'He's going back on his proper food this evening,' Francine said firmly, as Carl and children dissolved into more giggles.

'Here we are, home, sweet home,' Carl announced. 'I for one am delighted to be free of the car and Stinker Howie.'

'It's not his fault really,' Craig said, defending him. 'Mrs Clear gave him scrambled eggs for breakfast. I don't think dogs are meant to eat that.'

'You're right,' Francine said. 'And I'm going to get Howie some charcoal biscuits.'

'When can we put up our Christmas tree?' Craig asked, as they all piled into the house.

'Well, I usually prefer to wait until the second weekend in December but I could make an exception, if you like,' Francine said. 'I'll tell you what, we'll decorate it on the first of December. Deal?'

'Deal.' Craig grinned.

'We'll have to do our Christmas lists too,' Cara said.

'For sure,' Francine agreed.

'Howie will have to get a stocking,' Cameron pointed out.

'He's already helped himself to so many, along with shoes and other things from the house, that I don't know if Santa will think he deserves another,' Francine said.

'Maybe he could get a present of a cork for his bottom to stop all that farting!' Conor laughed.

CB

Life in Verbena Drive went forward at a more even pace after the family trip. Cameron saw Nuala twice weekly, and although he was still prone to meltdowns, they were all learning how best to deal with them.

Mr Matthews had been brilliant too. He'd phoned and talked to Nuala so they could help Cameron together. 'It's best that we're all consistent. Once Cameron knows we're all on the same page, it'll make things smoother all around,' he had pointed out.

Francine was still baking, but most of her delights were now produced in daytime hours.

'Francine, will we be having our Christmas bazaar this year or would you rather leave it? Of course, Jane and I could take on the organisation if things are too fraught for you,' Andrea said, at drop-off time one morning.

That had been the prompt Francine had needed to get herself back into her previous routine.

She'd gone to the hairdresser's for the first time in months and relished having polished, properly coiffed hair once again. When she'd got home, she'd gone straight to her office and selected her Christmas trimmed-with-tinsel file. She'd call a parents' committee meeting that day and get on with delegating the jobs. Although it was an annual event, Francine was well aware that none of these things happened by themselves.

Glancing at her watch, she saw that she needed to speed back to the school and collect Cameron.

As she drove there, her mobile phone rang.

'Francine, this is Nurse Gillian at the Bakers Valley old folks' home.'

'Hello, what can I do for you?' Francine asked cheerily.

'We've had a bit of a catastrophe. Our oven has given up the ghost and I've been on to the health service and they've told me there isn't any funding to replace it,' she said, sounding devastated. 'I know you're fantastic at organising fundraisers and I was wondering if you could help.'

'You couldn't have phoned at a better time. I'm meeting the parents' committee either tomorrow or the next day to discuss this year's Christmas bazaar,' Francine explained. 'We haven't assigned a charity for our proceeds yet so I'm delighted to inform you that I've just taken an executive decision to appoint the home as the recipient.'

'Oh, Francine!' Nurse Gillian gasped. 'I don't know how to thank you.'

'No need. We'll be thrilled to help. Leave it with me and I'll keep you posted. I will, as usual, issue an invitation to all your residents to join the party on the day. There'll be tea and mince pies, of course, and the children's choir always brings a smile to their faces.'

By the time they'd hung up and she was making her way to

the classroom door Francine had a spring in her step. There was a sizeable gathering of mothers outside the classroom.

'Ladies, how are we all today? Now, I'll ring the others, but there's an emergency Christmas bazaar meeting in the hall here tomorrow morning at nine after drop-off. I've had a call from Nurse Gillian at the old folks' home. They're in dire straits and need our help.'

There was a bit of chatter and the women agreed they'd all be there the following day.

Francine knew she had a long and arduous battle ahead with Cameron. Nothing would be plain sailing with him, but she also knew her entire world didn't have to stop either. She felt more like her old self than she had for months.

Chapter 35

The dust settled amazingly quickly for Jodi. She'd made the front page of most of the papers and, other than a couple of expected nasty comments, that was it.

The only person she was still concerned about was Darius.

'I can't believe it'll be the first of December next week,' he said. 'I'm looking forward to getting back to London and coming to you guys for Christmas.'

'Saul is counting the days and so am I. We're going to have the most amazing Christmas,' she vowed. 'There might be an extra couple of people at the table – I like to look after my neighbours, you know!'

'It's a good job you live in the middle of nowhere with only one house nearby or you might end up being the topic of gossip.'

'Imagine people gossiping about me!' she said sarcastically.

Sebastian and Saul arrived back from a couple of hours on the farm as Jodi put the phone down. 'Hi, boys,' she said.

'Hi, Mum.' Saul pulled off his wellies and ran to hug her.

'That was Dad on the phone,' she told him. 'He's so excited about seeing you.'

'I can't wait to see him too. Maybe this time he can meet Sebastian properly.'

'Sure,' Sebastian agreed.

'Can he go up to your house and watch the mirror television?' Saul asked.

'Of course he can.'

Saul ran off to his bedroom to play with his Lego.

'I had such a sense of Blake at the school today when I collected Saul,' Sebastian said. 'Christmas always brings fresh sadness.'

'I wish I'd known him,' Jodi said.

'Thanks. I've come a long way this year, Jodi. It's made such a difference to me, having yourself and little Saul in my life.'

'Well, your friendship has given me the confidence to believe that all men aren't awful,' she said simply.

'Your faith would've been restored before long. I don't think I should get the credit for that.'

'It's taken me a long, long time to realise that I was in love with someone who never actually existed.'

'What do you mean?'

'Mac was there for me once upon a time,' she explained. 'He helped me make the transition from backstreet urchin to movie star. Full stop. All the rest was my yearning for love. When I lost that baby I felt it was God's way of showing me that I wasn't worthy of happiness.'

'Oh, Jodi ...'

'It took the move to the cottage for me to see myself from the outside. I know I'm successful and I'm bloody grateful for the opportunities I've had. But living a "real" life has made me see that I could dare to wish for real friendship too.'

'Of course you should,' Sebastian agreed. 'You deserve to find love again too, Jodi.'

The landline rang and Saul charged from his bedroom to

answer it as Jodi walked away from Sebastian, running her fingers through her hair.

'Hi, Uncle Tommy!' Saul said, bouncing up and down. 'Why aren't you on Skype?' Jodi was beside Saul now, a little concerned about her brother, but her son's huge smile and shouts of delight reassured her everything was all right.

'I have a baby boy cousin!' he said, hurling the phone at Jodi.

'Hey,' she said, as she caught the phone. 'Tell me everything!'

Tommy explained that Maisy had gone into labour a few weeks early and baby Liam had arrived an hour ago. 'He's tiny but so perfect, Jodi!' Tommy sounded exhausted but ecstatic.

'Oh, darling, I'm so delighted for you both. And you've gone with an Irish name!' she said, through happy tears.

'We thought he should fly the tricolour flag if he's going to grow up an Aussie!'

'That's fantastic,' Jodi said. 'Give Maisy our love, won't you? How is she doing?'

'She's brilliant, Jodi. I'm the luckiest man alive,' Tommy said.

By the time they'd hung up, Saul and Sebastian had gone off to make a tank out of Lego in the bedroom.

'That's great news,' Sebastian said, with a grin.

'I couldn't be happier for him,' Jodi agreed. 'Although I'd love Tommy to live right beside me, I'm glad he's going to have his own life down under. He's physically and mentally thousands of miles from the grim life he began.'

'You both are,' Sebastian said evenly.

Jodi sighed happily. For the first time ever, the pieces of the jigsaw puzzle that was her life were finally slotting into place.

Chapter 36

A couple of weeks later, as Francine helped Carl put on his beard and settle in the big armchair at the school's grotto (which was actually a four-man tent from Lidl with a large sheet of red felt draped over the top adorned with several yards of cotton wool), she had pep in her step once more.

'Where will I put the mistletoe?' Jane asked, as she wrestled with an enormous bunch.

'Glad you asked me that,' Francine said, with a twinkle in her eye. 'I've added a new feature this year! A kissing corner! I thought it would be a fun way of raising another few euro. It's fifty cents a kiss and people can stand under this ... Ta-da!' Francine produced a cardboard sign in the same shape as the top of a pagoda. She'd painstakingly decorated it with red and green fabric, cotton wool and glitter, and had even included a hook for the mistletoe to hang from. 'I've woven lights through it too, so once I hang it from the hooks on the ceiling above the stage and plug it in, it'll be amazing,' she said. 'I wanted it to go above the stage so that people can give each other a kiss in full view of us all so that we can clap and have a bit of a giggle.'

'That's a great idea,' Andrea said. 'I'm dragging John up there in a while. He'll probably want to box me afterwards but it'll be worth it.'

'Yeah, my Richard's going up, even if I have to drag him.' Jane laughed.

Once the PA system was hooked up, the Christmas music was pumping out and the fairy lights were switched on, the atmosphere was fantastic.

'There's nothing like the smell of mince pies to make you feel festive, is there?' Francine was buzzing around, putting the finishing touches to the cakes table.

'How much should I charge for second-hand CDs?' a woman asked Francine. 'Maybe two euro?'

'Whatever you can get,' Francine said practically.

There had been an overwhelming response to the call for gifts for the stalls that year. As well as donating money to the old folks' home's oven fund, Francine had asked for new toys to be placed in a special area for the St Vincent de Paul. As people filed through the doors, the pile of toys grew higher and higher.

'Isn't it wonderful to see what a generous community we have around us?' Francine clasped her hands in delight.

◌◌

Jodi and Saul were waiting impatiently in their car for Darius to emerge from the airport.

'I wish I could go in there and see him,' Saul said, his eyes pleading.

'Me too, but it's such a busy time that if Daddy and I are spotted it'll take us ages to get out of there. We'll miss the Christmas bazaar.'

A tap on the window sent Saul into excited screeches. 'Daddy!' He flung open the door and Darius jumped in, laughing.

'Hey, dude! Oh, my God, you've grown huge!' he said, genuinely startled. 'What's Mum been feeding you?'

'It's the country air,' Saul said, and Jodi did a double-take: he'd sounded exactly like Sebastian.

She hugged Darius and they clipped Saul into his booster seat between them. As they drove to the school the car was filled with excited chatter.

'Here's my school gate!' Saul shouted eventually, pointing wildly. Although Darius had passed by as he'd made his way to the cottage for the photo shoot a couple of months previously, he'd only seen a flashing glimpse of the place.

'We'll drop my bags at the cottage first. You and Mum stay in the car, and we'll be back here before you can blink,' Darius promised.

When the couple walked into the school hall a few minutes later, the villagers gasped. They were getting used to seeing Jodi, but they were unable to hide their awe at her and Darius turning up together.

Jodi had done her hair and makeup and was wearing a navy glittery dress with sky-high Louboutin shoes, topped off with an ink-coloured fur shrug tied in a large satin bow to one side. Darius was head to toe in Paul Smith and tanned to perfection after months of filming in the sun.

'Oh, sweet Jesus, I think I'm going to wet myself,' Jane said, grabbing Francine's arm.

'They look like something …' Francine hesitated.

'From a Hollywood movie?' Jane finished.

'Yeah!' Francine giggled.

Saul was thrilled to have his dad there and dragged him over to a group of little boys. 'Dad, these are my friends,' he said proudly.

'Hi!' they chorused.

'I saw you on a DVD. But you had a warrior costume on and a big dagger. Have you got it with you?' Max looked hopeful.

'Not today, I'm afraid,' Darius said. 'I just came on the plane and they're not too happy about daggers or guns in airports these days.'

Francine made her way towards the couple, with several adults creeping behind her. 'Look at us, we're like silly teenagers,' she said. 'They'll think we're hillbillies who've never seen the likes of them before.'

'Well, we haven't,' Jane said.

Jodi spun around and waved. 'Hi, ladies! Sorry we're so late. It looks like it's going really well,' she said. 'Come and meet my husband. Darius, these are my friends.'

After lots of hand shaking, with Jane holding on to Darius's hand that little bit too long, the focus was brought to the stage. Saul and Katie had decided to become the first couple to avail themselves of the kissing booth. As Saul held her hand and kissed her cheek, the whole place erupted into applause. 'What is he like?' Jodi giggled.

'Looks like he's going to gravitate towards the stage,' Darius said, with tears of laughter and pride in his eyes.

'Well, he didn't lick that off the stones,' Jane said. 'That's my daughter, by the way,' she explained to Darius.

'Will we start planning the wedding now or would you rather wait until after Christmas?'

'If we could have it in writing here and now before he hits the age of five and moves on, that would be great,' a man said, stepping into the conversation. 'I'm Richard, your son's future father-in-law.'

Jodi moved away to look at the stalls, happy that Darius was content to mill around and chat.

ᙅᔓ

As the bazaar drew to a close, the stalls beginning to look bare, the volunteers from St Vincent de Paul arrived.

'Ah, there you are,' Francine said, recognising them. 'You're here to collect the donated toys, aren't you?'

'Yes, please,' one of them said.

As they transferred the generous pile to their vehicle, with the help of the dads, Jodi approached them outside in the darkness. 'I just wanted to give you a personal donation. I'd rather you didn't make a song and dance of it, if it's all the same to you,' she said.

'Eh, sure, Ms Ludlum.'

'It's Jodi,' she said, smiling. 'Thanks a million, and keep up the amazing work.' Kissing both women on either cheek, she turned and strode back inside, mastering the pencil heels flawlessly.

One volunteer turned to the other and scratched her head. 'Did that really happen?'

'Either that or I'm sleep-walking, which isn't a great plan, considering the ice and the size of that van.'

Opening the brown padded envelope that Jodi had handed her, the woman looked stunned. 'There must be over ten grand in this,' she said quietly.

Turning it over she noticed Jodi had written something on it:

Please make sure Santa can get to all the children of Bakers Valley this year. <u>ANONYMOUS</u>

Epilogue

Christmas was magical in Francine's house. The impeccably decorated rooms were a little chewed at the edges. Howie had produced a couple of poos with bits of tinsel in them.

'Look, Mum,' Cameron said in awe. 'Howie's doing special Christmas poos for us. He's so clever.'

Instead of feeling faint, Francine caught Carl's eye and they laughed.

She was looking forward to ringing out the old and welcoming the New Year with the hope that it would bring happier times. While she and Carl were under no illusions about the hard work Cameron was going to generate for them, she felt certain of one thing. Life wasn't flawless and she no longer wished it to be. She still adored running her school committee and being involved in the community but she no longer felt the crippling pressure to be the perfect wife.

She appreciated all the good things she had in her life and realised that she was one of the lucky ones.

ᔆ

Jodi, Darius and Saul had the most relaxing and cosy Christmas morning ever. Saul nearly burst with excitement as he dragged his stocking into their bed to show them what Santa had left.

They managed to get dressed in time to knock on Sebastian's kitchen door at two o'clock for dinner.

'Merry Christmas!' Jodi said. 'This is Darius!'

'Hello, Darius. Merry Christmas,' Sebastian said, holding out his hand.

Darius shook it. 'Merry Christmas to you too,' he said warmly. 'Thank you for inviting me to dinner today.'

Saul shoved past his parents, hugged Sebastian and ran into the kitchen. 'Dad, look, it's the mirror television I told you about!' he shouted.

Sebastian had cooked a traditional turkey dinner with all the trimmings.

'Can I set the table?' Darius asked, as he accepted a glass of champagne.

'Sure. Décor isn't really my forte, I'm afraid,' Sebastian admitted.

'That,' Darius said, 'is where I come in.'

Unabashedly rooting around in the kitchen cupboards, Darius transformed the table into a scene straight from *Alice in Wonderland*.

'How did you do that?' Sebastian asked, impressed.

'Effortlessly,' Darius said, with a very serious expression. Jodi burst out laughing and Sebastian grinned.

By the time they'd finished the delicious meal, all four were wearing silly hats and smiles to match.

Sebastian and Darius hit it off brilliantly, chatting about everything from planets and stars to politics and fashion. Sebastian could already see why Darius and Jodi had stayed married for so long. Darius was a great guy and clearly adored Jodi and Saul.

Darius's phone rang. 'I'm just nipping outside for a moment,' he said, with a grin. Through the window, they could see him chatting, waving his arms and gesturing.

'Bloody mobiles,' Jodi said good-naturedly. As if on cue, her own phone pinged.

'Who's that, then?' Sebastian asked, as he stretched lazily.

'Nobody,' Jodi said, but there was an undeniable flush of colour in her cheeks.

'Tell me!' Sebastian pushed.

'Ah, it's just Harry,' she said mysteriously.

'Who?'

'Better known as Mr Matthews,' she whispered, so Saul wouldn't hear.

'Ooh, right,' Sebastian said, with a nod and a wink.

Jodi responded with her own nod and wink, then added a wide grin.

'Jesus, it's cold out there,' Darius exclaimed, as he dashed back inside and threw himself on to the Aga.

'Who were you talking to all that time, sweetie?' Jodi said, in a teasing voice.

'Ah, it was just Mike,' Darius said. 'I was telling him where we are and how much fun we're all having today.'

'Oh, I didn't realise you'd told him anything,' Jodi said, raising her eyebrows and looking a little cross.

'No, I didn't,' he said, faltering. 'Well, I did, but not for publicity reasons.'

'But, Darius, I thought we agreed we'd only announce a change in circumstances,' Jodi looked down at Saul, 'when we'd decided the time was right and it could be done with minimal damage.'

'Don't get excited, honey,' Darius said gently. 'I told him as a friend.'

'Fair enough,' Jodi said, throwing her hands up. 'I guess you have to talk to someone and it's easy for me to get annoyed. I'm just worried in case this affects Saul, that's all. I can cope with stuff about you or me but once it runs even close to involving him,' she gestured sideways with her head, 'it scares me.'

'I understand, but he's my friend,' Darius said again.

'I know and, believe me, Noelle is my friend too,' Jodi said apologetically.

'No, Jodi.' There was a slight pause. 'Mike and I are *friends*.'

'*Whaaat?*' Jodi had just taken a swig of Fanta and nearly choked. Sebastian banged her on the back. 'Take it easy there,' he said.

'Sorry,' she said, as her eyes watered. She smiled, then hugged Darius and whispered in his ear, 'I'm really pleased for you.'

'Thanks,' he said. 'It's only recent and I'm treading carefully but he knows me, warts and all, so for the first time I feel confident about a relationship.'

'You couldn't make this up,' Jodi said, giggling. 'If people even knew the half of it …'

'Yes,' Sebastian said solemnly. 'What *would* the neighbours say?' He put his hand on his hip and shook his head in mock disgust.

As Saul joined them, peering up to see what all the laughing was about, Darius sat him on the Aga beside him.

'This is the bestest ever.' Saul beamed. 'All my favourite people in one place!'

Jodi smiled delightedly. On paper, Saul had the most dysfunctional family imaginable. But to look at his happy face anybody would be forgiven for picking him out of a line-up as one of the most contented children they'd ever met.

It was amazing, Jodi mused, how being true to herself had led her to a better place than she'd ever imagined. Many roles in her life required talented acting but she had grasped that life wasn't a dress rehearsal. Unless she was being paid an exorbitant fee, with a camera pointing at her, Jodi was finally ready to be herself.

Read on for an exclusive extract of Emma's heartwarming new novel *The Summer Guest*

Chapter 1

Lexie glanced at her watch, making sure she had enough time for another cup of coffee. The remnants of breakfast festooned the table. She smiled to herself. Her husband, Sam, was such a creature of habit. As regular as clockwork, he stacked his coffee mug on top of his toast plate, with the knife neatly tucked alongside, but it never occurred to him to transport the pile across the kitchen to the dishwasher.

This was Lexie's favourite moment of the day. She flicked off the radio, posted a capsule into the Nespresso machine, placed her already used cup under the spout and pressed the brew button. She and Sam liked to hear the news headlines followed by the round-up of that day's newspapers, and after that, Lexie relished a few minutes of silence. She felt it set her up for the day ahead.

As she crossed the kitchen to the bay window seat, her leather-soled ballerina pumps made a satisfying sound as they connected with the waxed wooden floorboards. She perched on the long, spongy cushion and gazed out into the oval railed-in park opposite. The late May sunshine flooded the neatly kept communal space. Although each of the houses in Cashel Square had fine-sized gardens, the residents all made use of the wooden benches in the park. They took turns to tend the flowerbeds and keep the place clean. It was too small to appeal to gangs of youths and the absence of swings or play equipment meant it rarely attracted nonresident families.

Lexie sipped her coffee and closed her eyes to savour it. It was just the right temperature, black and strong with no sugar and a delectable covering of creme.

'I hope you don't liken your coffee to your taste in men,' Sam had joked when they first met, flexing a long arm and pulling his fingers through his auburn hair.

Luckily for both of them, Lexie's taste in men and coffee differed hugely. Soon after meeting they both realised they'd found their soul-mate. They had a no-fuss registry-office wedding, with her friend Maia as chief bridesmaid, flower girl and best man all rolled into one, followed by a lunch with immediate family as the only additional guests.

Property prices were beginning to rise, so they decided to take the plunge and look for a house to buy. One Sunday afternoon, out for a walk along the promenade in the seaside Dublin suburb of Caracove, they'd happened upon Cashel Square. It comprised eight detached two-storeyover-basement dwellings set in a horseshoe, with the park in the centre, and they'd guessed it was well out of their league. The door to number three had been open and a sandwich board told them there was open viewing. They were the sole viewers and the estate agent seemed thrilled with their arrival.

'It's a wonderful property but requires a small amount of imagination,' he said.

Lexie and Sam had looked at one another and grinned. They knew that meant the place was in dire need of renovation.

'It certainly needs a lot of loving,' Lexie said, as they wandered from room to room.

'It has massive potential,' the estate agent said, injecting as much positivity into his voice as he could.

'Yes, massive potential for us to pour an endless bag of cash into it,' Sam scoffed.

'Can we have a quiet word in private?' Lexie asked, as they finished their tour.

'Be my guests,' the estate agent said, yawning.

Lexie took Sam's hand and led him back into the kitchen. 'Sam, I can see us living here,' she whispered. 'I've totally fallen in love with it.'

'It could be amazing, but it's not what we're looking for, is it?' Sam said, as he rubbed a hand across the peeling plaster on the main wall.

'I love it,' she repeated. A giggle escaped her as she noticed the colour draining from her husband-of-three-weeks' face.

'I don't like that dancing in your eyes, Lexie,' he said, with a slow smile.

'Let's make an offer,' she begged. 'One well below the asking price and verging on insulting and see where we go.'

'We're only starting out, hon,' he reasoned. 'This is a massive undertaking. It'd be years before it's back to its former glory. And even longer before we'd manage to pay back everything it'll siphon from our bank accounts. Old places like this are bottomless pits when it comes to money.'

'Perfect!' she said. 'We have all the time in the world. We're at the beginning of our journey. Let's do it together. You, me and number three Cashel Square!'

Lexie knew Sam found it hard to say no to her. Especially when she talked incessantly about the house. Several weeks passed after the initial viewing. Instead of giving up on the idea, Lexie was verging on obsessive.

'You're annoying me and I don't even live with you,' Maia said. 'Poor Sam now knows he married a lunatic. I reckon you should rein it in a bit. He'll go running for the hills if you don't stop with the crazy house talk.' Maia was a divorce lawyer and, although she had a very happy marriage with steadfast, calm Josh, she had a habit of seeing the worst in every union.

'I've seen it a million times – couples torn apart when one or other of them becomes fanatical about something. I told you about the pair who'd been married twenty-four years when it all went belly-up,' she warned.

'You said he was a sex addict and she was a raving alco. That's hardly comparable to wanting to build a home with the man I love,' Lexie said. She had a feeling deep down that Sam was just as keen as she, but he was attempting to be the voice of reason. She chipped away for the next few days until he uttered the words she'd been dying to hear.

'All right! We'll put in a measly offer. Will that stop your nagging?' he asked good-naturedly.

To their astonishment, the offer was accepted.

'It's an executors' sale and the family have instructed us to move quickly,' the estate agent explained.

Family and friends were marvellous, donating furniture and turning up in droves to the many painting parties the couple held. 'We'll provide the materials and pay you in beer and pizza,' Lexie promised.

By the end of that first summer of 1998, Lexie and Sam had a kitchen-living room, bathroom and bedroom in liveable order. The replastering wouldn't have won any DIY awards, but it was good enough to keep the damp out and the heat in.

'It looks like an enormous monster arrived in and vomited Ready Brek all over the place,' Maia teased. 'And as for tramping about on mangy old floorboards, nah. I'm happy in my apartment.' She shuddered.

'That, my dear,' Lexie said, linking her arm, 'is where you and I differ. I would go clinically insane in that dog-box you call home. Give me vaguely lumpy plasterwork done by caring but not the most professional of friends and vast open spaces any day.'

Penelope, Lexie's mother, was probably more in Maia's camp when it came to the house. She didn't do mess or dust or, God forbid, mismatched furnishings. 'You can do the rest as you go along, I suppose,' she said uncertainly, as she perched on the edge of a rather saggy sofa, clutching her handbag.

'Mum, you don't have to hold your bag like a life-raft. You're not going to drown on old goose-down cushions. Sam and I are delighted to have this place and we're not in a hurry to have it looking like something from that glossy interiors magazine, The White Book.'

'So I've noticed,' she said. 'Still,' she brightened, 'as the children start to come along, so too will the decorating.'

'Don't hold your breath, Mum,' Lexie said. 'Children aren't even a topic for discussion between Sam and me right now.'

'Well, that's a bit of a silly thing to say, don't you think? All married couples turn their attention to having a family at some point. Anyway, we don't need to worry about it this second,' Penelope assured them. 'Needless to say your father and I are longing to be grandparents, but your brother just scratched that itch for us with the birth of gorgeous baby Amélie! I'm just saying, that's all.'

For the most part, Lexie and Sam kept to themselves. The neighbours in the remaining seven houses were friendly but never intrusive. They'd exchange pleasantries in passing and bid one another good day at the park. Ernie and Mary in number two fed Tiddles, the cat, if Lexie and Sam were on holiday.

Now, fifteen years later, there were still many nooks and

crannies of number three Cashel Square waiting to be lovingly restored to their former glory. Lexie and Sam had made some headway, of course. They'd replaced the saggy old sofas with gorgeous cream leather ones. All the original fireplaces, ceiling cornices and floorboards had been carefully brought back to their prime. Sam had found a craftsman who'd moved into the basement for six months so he could rethread the sash windows and repair the hinges and panels of the shutters.

But the new kitchen they'd put in last year had cleared their rainy-day account. Many other rooms were still filled with junk or waiting to have the right furniture added.

Their long-term plans had changed since 1998 too. After an accident, Lexie had been forced to change tack with her career, but things were finally beginning to look up for them, despite the global recession.

Sam was now a shareholder in the computer-programming firm where he worked. But Lexie's promising job in graphic design had come tumbling down, literally. She'd been up an extendable ladder doing some careful ceiling-cornice painting when it had collapsed. She'd known by the cracking sound that her arm was broken. She'd landed on it awkwardly and it was twisted in a direction she knew wasn't natural. Crawling to the phone, she'd called Sam, then Maia.

True to form, Sam was calm and said he'd phone the ambulance. 'Stay where you are and I'll be with you in a jiffy. I love you.'

Maia was OTT as usual. 'You what? Jesus H. Christ, Lex. Is your arm hanging off or what?'

'No,' she sobbed, 'but it's really bad. Sam's on the way and so's the ambulance.'

'Well, don't go to St Mary's Hospital – they use knives and forks to sew people up. I had a client who went there to have a baby. Emergency section, baby was coming too soon, blah, blah. She had pains in her side for two months after the operation so she ended up in another hospital where they removed a fecking needle the other clowns had left there!'

'Okay.' Lexie had winced. 'I'm going now. I'm in so much pain I think I'm going to die.' She'd dropped the phone and promptly passed out. By the time she woke she was in recovery. Sam and Maia were on either side of her bed gazing anxiously at her. 'Hey,' she said weakly. 'What's happened with my arm?'

'You've had some pins put into your wrist,' Sam said gently. 'The surgical team said it was a bad break, honey.'

Maia was chewing the inside of her lip, looking agitated. Sam was smiling kindly.

'What?' she asked, turning to Maia.

'You're gonzoed,' she said. 'You're lucky they didn't saw your hand off and leave you with an unsightly stump.'

'Maia!' Sam said, growing irritated. 'Don't be so dramatic. Lexie had a horrible fall. She's going to be fine, though.'

Lexie adored Sam, but Maia was one of the only people in the world who'd tell her the truth. They'd been friends since school and, no matter what happened, they had each other's backs.

As it turned out, Lexie's injuries were closer to Maia's assumption than Sam's. 'Why did I have to break my left wrist?' Lexie wailed two days later. 'The doctors were so jubilant about the fact it wasn't the right.'

'They weren't to know you're left-handed,' Sam said, wiping away a tear. 'We'll get you the best darn physiotherapist in Dublin, and before long you'll be back in work and, most importantly, back painting your beloved portraits.'

Lexie really wanted to believe Sam. Her job was sacred to her and she was bringing so much extra business on board that her bosses had already offered her a rise. She knew it was only a matter of time before they suggested she become a partner. But all that paled into insignificance when it came to the way her painting made her feel. If a day was stressful or a week took its toll, she'd burrow away in the back room and paint.

Any time Sam suggested making the room more organised or even putting in some proper work surfaces, she balked. 'I love it this way. I know where things are and it allows me to be creative. I have to be regimented in work. This is my zone.'

Seven months later, despite her best efforts and many hours of painful physio, Lexie had to admit defeat.

'If things change, let us know,' Herman, her boss, said. 'The door is open whenever you get the control back in your hand.'

Lexie hugged him, accepted the farewell voucher for a massage treatment, and knew in her heart of hearts that she'd never be back at the graphic design company.

The cloud that shrouded her life could possibly have ruined everything, had Reggie, her father, not come to the rescue. She was wallowing in the house, day after day, slipping slowly into a depression when he singlehandedly changed her destiny.

'I'm downsizing the company. I can't keep going with all the printing shops. Besides, lots of our customers are using cheaper on-line companies nowadays.'

'I'm sorry to hear that, Dad,' Lexie said. 'I know what it feels like when you're no longer in a position to fulfil your potential.'

Reggie patted her hand, telling her she was going to do that and more. He handed her a set of keys and told her the premises, which were strategically situated on the sea road a mere mile from Cashel Square, were hers, rent free, until she established a decent income.

'But what on earth can I do with your old printing shop?' she asked.

'How about setting up a gallery?' Reggie said.

Lexie sat back and allowed the idea wash over her. Astonishingly, she didn't feel averse to the idea. In fact, the more she thought about it, the better it sounded. 'If I'm starting my career from scratch I may as well do so within walking distance of here,' she reasoned. 'The doctors say I'll be able to drive again in a few months, but for the moment it would more than suit me to be able to walk to work.'

'Of course,' Reggie said. 'It's the perfect area for a gallery, what with the promenade, the park and the pedestrian shopping area.' He had occupied the building for more than twenty years and knew the footfall was there. 'I'll help you decorate and I'm sure your friends will too. I ran the idea past Sam and he thinks it sounds wonderful.'

'So you've pretty much set me up. All I need to do is arrive, eh?' Lexie said, grinning. Throwing her good arm around her father's neck, she let him hold her like he did when she was little. She thanked God she had such amazing men in her life.

'You're such a jammy cow,' Maia said, when they met for coffee that afternoon. 'I wish my father was like yours.' She sighed. 'But I guess I'd need to have a relationship with him and actually know him in the first place!' They giggled. Maia was blunt to a fault. Especially when it came to awkward or emotive subjects. When they'd first met, some of the girls in their class at school didn't get her sense of humour but it was the thing Lexie loved most about her. They'd been drawn to one another since the age of ten and Lexie couldn't imagine her life without Maia.

After her father had walked out on them, Maia's mother had worked a lot, leaving Maia and her brother John to their own devices. As a result, Maia had decided the only way was out. Out of the house and into a job that would pay.

'I want to earn shedloads of cash and go on foreign holidays wearing designer gear while quaffing champagne.' Nothing got in Maia's way once she set her mind to something. Although Lexie had a lump in her throat and pride in her heart the day Maia graduated from law school, she wasn't surprised. 'You did good, kiddo,' she said, hugging her.

'I'm only getting started,' Maia said, with a shrug of her shoulder and a subtle nod to the right. Lexie glanced sideways and made eye contact with a gorgeous guy.

'Let me introduce you to Josh,' Maia said. She pulled Lexie close and whispered, ever so quietly, 'Great in bed, brains to burn, and I'm going to marry him some day.'

❀

In the early days Lexie was at the gallery morning, noon and night.

'Sometimes I wonder whether you love the art more than me,' Sam said, with an exaggerated pout. 'I know you're struggling to work with one hand a lot of the time, but I can't help feeling left out.'

'Don't be ridiculous.' She giggled. 'There are one or two pieces I like less than you.'

All jokes aside, Lexie knew she needed to push hard to make her business a success. She was determined to look after her clients and form good relationships. If the gallery were to survive and thrive, she needed to breathe life into it. She buried all her bitterness and disappointment by focusing on the job in hand. At the time she'd thought anything other than being an active artist was a come down, such was her love for painting. Owning a gallery was the next best thing and she knew it was an opportunity and the perfect way to avoid plunging into a pool of dark depression.

'The paintings and sculptures are the blood and I need to be the heartbeat,' she explained to Sam.

Luckily for both of them, Sam got it. More than that, he got Lexie. Now, nine years later, the gallery was thriving and had survived the testing recession.

Draining her coffee cup, Lexie placed it in the dishwasher with the rest of the breakfast things and turned the machine on. She adored her new kitchen and still got a kick out of closing the integrated dishwasher door. It had been a long time coming, but the gorgeous refurbishment even met with Penelope's approval. 'It's wonderful, darling,' she said. 'I'd say you're able to relax in here far more now, and it's better for poor Sam to have a proper place for his dinner. That old falling-apart kitchen you had before must've made him feel quite depressed after a hard day at the office.'

'Sam never complained,' Lexie said, trying not to get irritated with her mother. 'In fact, I pushed for the new units more than he did.'

Taking the stairs two at a time, she grabbed a cardigan to pop in her bag in case there was a cool breeze coming in from the sea. She brushed her teeth, then checked her face in the mirror for flakes of mascara or stray spatters of eye-shadow on her cheek. Pulling her long dark hair into a clip, she decided she'd do. She hoped the short walk between the house and the gallery would kick-start her tan. She thought of poor Sam, who went the colour of a beetroot almost instantly in the sun. Even if they were sitting in the garden for a drink he had to lather himself in high-factor cream. Yesterday evening she'd brought them a glass of chilled white wine each, and tossed the tube of sun screen to him. 'From blue to burn in sixty seconds! That's my man!' she said.

They teased one another endlessly, that was their way, but underneath it, they were inseparable. The only time she knew Sam got slightly peeved was when she and Maia went too far with the sisterhood gibes. 'When God created man she was only joking,' Maia had slurred last Sunday, at their barbecue.

'Lex,' Sam whispered, 'don't get into the whole men-are-worms vibe. It's embarrassing for Josh and me.'

❀

As she ran down the stairs, plucking her handbag from the hall table, the photographic portrait, taken around the time of their engagement, stared back at her. She was incredibly fortunate that their relationship had stood the test of time, she thought. So many of their friends were now either single or in second partnerships. Maia was making a very nice living on other people's failed marriages.

The second she banged the front door shut, her mobile rang. Stuffing the cardigan into her bag, she retrieved her phone just in time. 'Hi, Mum,' she said.

'Hello, love. Isn't it a lovely bright day?' Penelope said.

'Hm, gorgeous,' Lexie said, shouldering the phone to her ear as she turned the Chubb lock in the door. 'I'm just on the way to the gallery. Any news?'

'I could ask you the same,' Penelope responded.

'Not a dicky-bird,' Lexie said. 'I'll be in work until lunchtime. Kate is covering the afternoon shift and I might head out for a run on the pier later. What are you up to today?'

'I was going to see if you'd meet me for lunch,' Penelope said. 'Dad and I have been chatting. Your fortieth birthday is around the corner. Have you any plans at all?'

'It's not until September, Mum. It's May now, for crying out loud!'

'It'll be June tomorrow,' Penelope corrected. 'Poor Amélie starts her fifth-year exams in the morning. Billy and Dee are tearing their hair out with her. She hasn't opened a book, you know.'

'I'm sure she'll be fine. My niece is a clever girl. She's probably done more work than they think.'

'Well, unless they've added a study hall to the shopping centre, I sincerely doubt it. She's turned into a bit of a madam lately. Dee is at her wits' end. She'll be leaving school next year. The time to cop on is running out.'

'Lighten up, Mum, for Pete's sake! Amélie's seventeen. She's supposed to rebel against everything. I'd be more worried if she didn't,' Lexie said.

'Now, that's just ridiculous, Lexie. Amélie is in danger of becoming a problem. Billy is too soft with her and leaves all the disciplining to Dee. It's not right.'

'Mum, it's none of our business what Amélie, Dee or Billy does in the comfort of their own home. I doubt Amélie is the first teenager to find study a bore and she certainly won't be the last.'

'You treat her like one of your friends, Lexie. I'm not sure that's appropriate, considering her current behaviour. Maybe if you took a more removed approach to her it might help Dee and Billy,' Penelope suggested.

'I can't help it if Amélie thinks I'm cool,' Lexie quipped. 'Besides, she needs to feel there's at least one person batting on her team. I remember what it's like when you think the whole world is against you. I wouldn't go back to being a teenager for any money.'

'Well, that's neither here nor there,' Penelope said. 'So, can you meet me for lunch later? Why don't we go to the noodle bar on the promenade? Say, one thirty? Will that give you enough time? We can have a better chat face to face.'

Knowing her mother would probably turn up at the gallery if she didn't meet her, Lexie agreed. At least this way they'd be in a neutral venue and she could leave if necessary.

Chapter 2

As she walked into the arrivals area of dublin airport, Kathleen felt more at ease than she had for weeks. The luggage trolley had a mind of its own and kept veering to the right. Stopping to scan the crowd, she waved tentatively at the man holding a sign with her name on.

'Kathleen Williams?' he asked.

'That's me,' she confirmed happily.

'Let me take that yoke for you,' the man said, commandeering the trolley. 'You'll do yourself an injury. It's easier to control a box of frogs than one of these things.'

Kathleen thanked him and grinned from ear to ear. It'd been such a long time since she'd heard the Irish wit first hand. Her parents had immigrated to America to find work when she was a child. Now a silvery-blonde woman of seventy-four, she'd forgotten how much she loved this type of banter.

'So let me guess,' the taxi driver said, as they sat into his car. 'You're here to find your roots?'

'Got it in one!' Kathleen said. 'I'm not totally bats, though. In my defence I was born in Dublin and lived in Caracove until I was eight. So I've got fairly fresh roots here – for an American,' she added.

'Fair enough.' He nodded. 'So what brings you home after all this time?'

'My husband, Jackson, bought me a ticket and it would've been rude not to use it,' she said.

'Didn't he want to come with you?'

'He couldn't make it this time.'

'Probably better off that way.' The man chuckled. 'Visiting old haunts with someone else is almost as bad as going shopping, if you ask me.'

Kathleen laughed.

'So where are we going?' the driver asked.

'Caracove Bay, please.'

'Ah, Caracove Bay by the sea!' he said. 'Lovely spot, isn't it? You'll see a big change, I reckon. For the better, mind you. They've done up the promenade area – paved it and built lovely glass-fronted restaurants. The big park is a hive of activity now too. The old swings were repaired and a whole host of kiddie rides and slides have been added.'

'How wonderful!' Kathleen said. 'Is the bandstand still there?'

'Indeed it is. There's music of all sorts at the weekends and during the summer.'

'That sounds gorgeous,' Kathleen said. 'What about the town? Is it still buzzy?'

'Some of the shops have closed down due to the recession, but the main street is still as alive as ever, I think you'll find. It's pedestrianised now and it works well. There was some talk of a modern shopping centre being added a couple of years back but so many of the locals objected the idea was scrapped. I think they were right, too. Caracove Bay has managed to hold on to her old-world charm without remaining in the dark ages.'

Kathleen marvelled at the changes as they made their way

down the impressive motorway. 'None of this existed when I left. It's unrecognisable, actually,' she said, a little deflated.

'Ah, it's all built up along here, but once we turn off and veer towards the coast you'll see some familiar sights.'

The driver was right. Less than an hour later, as they went along the sea road, Kathleen was like a child in a sweet shop as she pinned her gaze on the sights. 'The old swimming baths! There used to be an ice-cream shop there.'

'Indeed there was,' the driver said. 'That must be gone twenty years by now. Are you staying at the Caracove Arms Hotel, love?'

'Oh,' Kathleen said, suddenly flustered. 'Would you believe I haven't made a reservation? I've had a bit of a gruelling time of it lately. I thought I was doing brilliantly just getting here. I hadn't thought ahead.'

'I'm sure they'll have plenty of room. I know a couple of the staff there. I'll see they look after you.'

'Would you mind if we pop by my old house first?' Kathleen asked. 'I've written to the owners asking if I might call some day. Do you think they'd allow me?'

'I'm sure they would. A lovely lady like yourself. Why not, eh?' he said cheerfully. 'There's no harm in asking, I'd say.'

'Yes, indeed. The address is number three Cashel Square, Caracove,' she instructed.

'No bother, love,' said the driver. 'It's literally five minutes away.'

Suddenly Kathleen was quite overcome with emotion. She wasn't sure if she wanted to laugh or cry. After all this time she was going to see her childhood home again. She wished Jackson were there to share the moment.

'Here we are, Cashel Square.'

As the driver turned the cab into the left, the park, with its white-painted iron railings, came into view. Kathleen gasped as they pulled up outside number three. 'Wow! It looks better than I remember,' she managed, her voice quite choked.

'The owners have spent a few bob on it, I'd say.'

'It certainly looks well loved,' she agreed. 'Could you give me a moment?'

'Take all the time you want, love,' the driver said, turning off the engine.

Kathleen released her seatbelt and eased herself out of the car. She was stiff from all the travelling. Inhaling deeply, she was holding back tears.

The once black door was now a cheerful shade of cornflower blue. The brass fixings were polished to a gleaming shine, and the woodwork around the window frames was flawless.

Wooden boxes were filled to spilling point with delicate blooms in varied shades of pink. The railings were expertly painted without a sign of rust. The granite steps were scrubbed, showing none of the dirt she remembered from her childhood. Memories of days at the beach, trips to the town and cold winter winds echoed through the corridors of her mind.

Afraid she'd get caught snooping and ruin her chance of being allowed inside, Kathleen pulled the letter she'd written on the plane from her handbag. Under her signature, she added the name of the hotel she was planning to stay at and popped it into the iron post-box attached to the gate. Saying a quick prayer, she hoped with all her heart that the owners would be welcoming.

'Is that it?' the driver asked, looking surprised. 'I thought I'd have time for a quick nod-off.'

'I don't want to appear too pushy,' she said. 'I'm terrified of being told to go away.'

'If they're any way decent, the owners will invite you in,' he assured her.

Kathleen stared at the square as they drove around the park and out the other side. She rattled her brain to remember the neighbours' names. 'Mrs Caddy lived in number eight,' she recalled. 'She hated children and we called her Mrs Crabby behind her back.'

'We all knew someone like that as children!' The driver laughed. 'You'd wonder why they were so cranky. I'd never bark at a small child now that I'm an adult, would you?'

'I certainly wouldn't,' she agreed. Although she was reluctant to leave Cashel Square, Kathleen was truly worn out. Jet lag and exhaustion crept over her, making her eyes burn and her limbs long to stretch out.

Mercifully the Caracove Arms had a room available. True to his word, the driver spoke to his friend and made sure she was welcomed with open arms.

'Thank you for being so lovely,' Kathleen said, handing him the fare with a generous tip.

'The pleasure is all mine. Great to meet you and I hope you have a fantastic stay.'

❖

Not up to facing a table for one, Kathleen ordered a portion of Irish stew and a glass of cold milk to be served in her room. She managed to stay awake long enough for the meal to be delivered. The lamb was cooked to perfection. Knowing she shouldn't give in to sleep until that evening if she were to overcome the jet lag, she perched in an armchair and tried to watch the television. She toyed with the idea of turning her cell phone off and decided against it on the off-chance that her letter might prompt a response. Before long her head slumped forward as sleep enveloped her.